W9-DFI-191

SASS & Serendipity

JENNIFER ZIEGLER

Text copyright © 2011 by Jennifer Ziegler
Cover art copyright © 2011 by Le Avison/Trevillion Images

All rights reserved. Published in the United States by Ember,
an imprint of Random House Children's Books, a division of Random House, Inc., New York.
Originally published in hardcover in the United States by Delacorte Press,
an imprint of Random House Children's Books, New York, in 2011.

Ember and the E colophon are registered trademarks of Random House, Inc.

Visit us on the Web! randomhouse.com/teens

Educators and librarians, for a variety of teaching tools, visit us at
randomhouse.com/teachers

The Library of Congress has cataloged the hardcover edition of this work as follows:
Ziegler, Jennifer.
Sass and serendipity / Jennifer Ziegler. — 1st ed.
p. cm.
Summary: Unlike her romantic sister, Gabby is down-to-earth and does not put her trust
in relationships, but when the richest boy in school befriends her, she discovers that
emotional barriers might actually be getting in the way of her happiness.
ISBN 978-0-385-73898-9 (hc) — ISBN 978-0-385-90762-0 (lib. bdg.) —
ISBN 978-0-375-89681-1 (ebook)
[1. Sisters—Fiction. 2. Interpersonal relations—Fiction. 3. High schools—Fiction.
4. Schools—Fiction.] I. Title.
PZ7.Z4945Sas 2011
[Fic]—dc22
2010032349

ISBN 978-0-375-85964-9 (trade pbk.)

RL: 5.0

Printed in the United States of America

10 9 8 7 6 5 4 3 2 1

First Ember Edition 2012

Random House Children's Books supports the First Amendment and celebrates the right to read.

For my sister, Amanda

Acknowledgments

As it is with all my novels, I had many "birthing" coaches while I labored on this book. Yes, it is my baby, but it would not have been delivered as speedily or safely or in as good a shape if it weren't for the following people: Stephanie Lane Elliott, who makes me a better writer; my mother and father and my husband, Carl, and our lovely children, who all make me a better person; and Erin Murphy, who so serendipitously came into my life.

Big thanks and hugs also go to Krista Vitola, Stephanie Moss, Julie Carolan, Lisa Holden, Joe and Louise McDermott, Lisa Clayton, Kate Slaten, Gillian Redfearn, Brian Anderson, Chris Barton, Gene Brenek, Tim Crow, Debbie Gonzales, Cynthia and Greg Leitich Smith, Shana Burg, Bethany Hegedus, Varian Johnson, April Lurie, Margo Rabb, Dorothy Love, and all the members of the Austin SCBWI.

I do not want people to be very agreeable,
as it saves me that trouble of liking them a great deal.
—Jane Austen in a letter to her sister Cassandra,
December 24, 1798

o   o   o

A lady's imagination is very rapid; it jumps from
admiration to love, from love to matrimony in a moment.
—Jane Austen, *Pride and Prejudice*

CHAPTER ONE
Gene(sis)

The dress in the window of Shelly's Boutique was not a taste-ful pink. It was an unnatural, overly shiny, shout-in-your-face pink. Barbie-aisle pink. Putrid-antidiarrhea-medicine pink. Slutty-disco-queen-on-LSD pink.

Or, as the residents of Barton, Texas (population 5,853), would probably refer to it: *hawt pank.*

Gabriella Rivera automatically curled her upper lip—making her tilde mouth, as her mother liked to call the expression—and muttered, "God, look at that. When did hooker fashions become formal wear?"

Mule quit slurping down his sixty-four-ounce Dr Pepper and shrugged. "What do you expect? It's prom season."

"It is *not* prom season," Gabby replied. "It is the middle of March. I barely survived the big Valentine's freak-out with-out throwing myself off a cliff. Now I have to see this crap everywhere for two months?" She gestured toward the display window.

Mule considered the dresses while continuing to sip from

his near-empty soda cup, making loud squelching noises through the straw.

"Besides, prom shouldn't even be a season," Gabby went on. "Not like a holiday season or flu season. It's just a dumb party."

"So? It's not like you're going anyway," Mule pointed out. He stuck the straw back into his mouth and sucked noisily. Gabby resisted the urge to grab the monster-sized drink out of his hand and chuck it at his head. She imagined the crushed ice scattered about his brown curls, glistening like jewels, and the weak soda residue spattering his white T-shirt with the faded Captain America image on the front.

She didn't know why she was so annoyed with him today. His know-it-all tone was getting on her nerves even more than usual. Maybe it was because school had been extra-infuriating that day, with everyone shrieking about prom. Or maybe it was the fact that she had to go to her lame job at the lame movie theater in half an hour.

Or maybe it was because her dad was coming for a visit at the end of the week, just like he did every third Saturday of the month. A stale routine of dinner and some sort of god-awful bonding ritual in the form of cheap entertainment—like bowling or minigolf.

Or maybe it was because she knew her younger sister would be an off-the-charts lunatic this weekend. Daphne was usually late and unprepared. But when Dad came she'd spend hours trying on different outfits (tossing her rejects on the floor between their beds) and then sit on the porch waiting for him a half hour early—completely insensitive to their mom's feelings. It had to sting seeing your daughter make a big gushy deal over your deadbeat ex, but did Daphne care? No. Watching her squeal and bounce over his arrival, you'd think he was rescuing her from the clutches of an ogre.

Basically everything in Gabby's life sucked right now. So she really didn't want to hear Mule's actual sucking sounds.

"But don't you hate all this romantic bull?" she went on, hoping to drown out the noise with her own voice. "It's even worse than Valentine's Day. Instead of cheap, five-dollar crap everywhere, there's like chintzy, three-hundred-dollar crap everywhere."

"I don't know," Mule said, making a neutral half smile, half grimace. "It doesn't bother me too much. I figure, as long as they don't *make* me go, I'm okay with it."

Gabby sighed. Of course he would just accept it. Mule accepted everything stupid and horrible in life. Including his rotten nickname.

Seventeen years ago, for some strange reason, every woman who gave birth to a boy in Fayette Memorial Hospital had named her son Samuel. Four boys—all in the same grade. By the end of elementary school it was all sorted out, though. Samuel Milburn got to be Sam, since he was the biggest and coolest—and he basically claimed it first. Samuel Farnsworth, the next coolest (and most spastic), got to be Sammy. And Samuel Moore got to stay Samuel. That left a skinny, half-Jewish wiseass named Samuel Randolph with nothing but the second syllable to set him apart from the others. Thus the moniker Mule was bestowed upon him, and since none of the other Samuels had had the decency to move away, die, or get a sex change, he'd had to keep it throughout his school career.

"What's the theme again?" Mule asked.

"What?"

"This year's prom theme. What is it?"

Gabby made her eyes big and dumb-looking. "A Walk in the Clouds," she said breathily.

Mule snorted. "Sounds impractical. Why not call it Bird Crap on My Tuxedo? Or Bugs in My Teeth?"

"A 747 Ruined My Hair!" Gabby mock screeched, grabbing her long, dark waves.

The two of them laughed and pantomimed some more, hooking elbows and flapping their free arms. It was supersilly and totally juvenile, but Gabby didn't care. At least she got a good laugh in before work.

Mule was always good for that—when he wasn't being annoying.

Ms. Manbeck was going to lose it.

Daphne Rivera raced down the corridor from the gymnasium, through a pair of squeaky metal doors, and up the stairs to the 200 wing. The skirt of her JV cheerleading uniform swished rhythmically about her legs and her ponytail swung in an almost complete circle.

She was *dead*. Ms. Manbeck would surely kill her in some slow, torturous way. This would be Daphne's third tardy this grading period, and her teacher was going to shriek nonstop. She'd probably do that weird twitchy thing, the one that made it look as if her face were being sucked backward into her left eye socket. She might even call Daphne's mom.

That was all Daphne needed. Her mom had been so stressed lately about the bills and her job. If she got a screechy phone call from Ms. Manbeck, she'd start handing out punishments as if they were Halloween candy—a you-should-know-better-young-lady lecture . . . grounding . . . cell phone confiscation . . . and . . . *Oh, god!* She might change her mind about letting Daphne go to prom this year! Just the thought made Daphne tuck her head for better aerodynamics and put on a burst of speed on the next flight of steps.

It wasn't her fault. She hadn't meant to take so long in the bathroom. It was just that cheerleading practice had been extrahard that morning, what with the JV finals coming up. And then Sheri Purnell had told everyone that a new guy was starting school that very day—an amazing-looking new guy. So Daphne had figured she should wash her sweaty face and redo all her makeup. She had to make a good first impression, right? Some things were more important than calculating the volume of a cylinder.

Only, what did it matter, if she ended up dead and buried with old Ms. Manbeck cackling over her grave?

Almost there. Just a few more steps to the landing, a hard right, and a quick sprint down the hall. Daphne stared down at her tennis shoes, concentrating on propelling them as fast as they would go.

She hit the top step and swerved right. But just as she was making the turn she collided with something big and solid and instantly bounced back. Her arms flew out to brace herself—only, there was nothing to grab. Just air. Meanwhile, all the stuff she'd been carrying scattered. Her purse plummeted out of sight, pens and papers shot everywhere, and her Cherries Jubilee lipstick soared over her head.

It occurred to her, in a vague, oddly detached way, that she was plunging backward into the stairwell. And that she would very likely get hurt.

Maybe Ms. Manbeck won't be so hard on me now was her next thought.

Then, all of a sudden, she was being yanked forward. Someone had grabbed her right arm and was pulling her with both hands. She felt herself reverse direction, her head whiplashing slightly . . . until the someone lost balance. Then, just as suddenly, she was falling forward, watching helplessly as the scuffed vinyl floor came zooming into view.

She didn't hit the floor. Instead, she landed on a pair of khaki trousers. With legs in them.

She glanced up at the someone. It was a *male* someone—a *cute male* someone—sitting half stunned in the empty hallway with Daphne sprawled across his thighs. His backpack and all its belongings were strewn for a couple of yards behind him.

Daphne couldn't talk or move. For one thing, all her breath had been pushed out of her—possibly by his knees. For another thing, her mind was having a tough time catching up with what had just happened. One moment she was tumbling toward certain bone-breaking injury, and the next moment she was lying on top of a gorgeous guy.

This is the new kid, she realized. Sheri was right about how yummy he was. Tardy or not, Daphne was grateful she'd taken the time to get fixed up.

The cute guy gave a somewhat cartoonish shake of his head. He blinked hard a few times and focused on her. "Whoa. Are you okay?"

"I'm . . ." was all Daphne managed to say. After that her lips moved soundlessly. It was all the air and all the thought she had in her. *Was* she okay? She had no idea.

"Let me help you up," he said. He wriggled slightly and broke into a sideways grin. "Uh . . . then again, I guess you need to get up before I can get up."

"Right." She wanted to laugh, but all that came out was some shallow panting. By now she'd regained feeling in her limbs, and she made herself crawl backward off him, carefully minding where she placed her hands.

"Watch the stairs," he said, grasping her forearm.

Sure enough, her right foot was already dangling off the top step.

"Don't move." He let go of her, slid his left leg out from beneath her hands, and scrambled to his feet. "I've got you," he said, reaching down for her.

Daphne, still a little dazed, slowly grabbed hold of his hands. Soon she felt that familiar yanking strength and she rose from the floor.

"There," he said, as he grasped her shoulders and steadied her. "All safe." He gave her a final pat and took a step back. His mouth crooked into an awkward smile and he glanced up and down the empty hallway, as if suddenly embarrassed.

Daphne felt as though she should say something, but she

was too woozy from all the yanking and falling and hand-holding, and from finding herself abruptly in the arms of someone so good-looking. She studied him closely as she wavered on her feet, trying to regain her senses. Nutmeg-colored hair that swirled around his forehead and ears. Light teal eyes. Matching clefts, like tiny cleave marks, on the tip of his chin and between his nostrils. And not only was he handsome, he seemed nice, too.

"I'm really sorry," he said. "You just came around the corner and *bam!* It all happened so fast."

She shook her head. "No, it's my fault. I was hurrying because I was late. I wasn't paying attention." She glanced back at the very deep, very solid-looking stairwell. "I can't believe I almost fell down that."

A new thought occurred to her, one that slammed her almost as hard as their collision: he'd *rescued* her. He'd practically saved her life! It was so . . . romantic. Just like in the fairy tales. Just like Westley saved Buttercup in *The Princess Bride*. Like Superman saved Lois Lane. Like James Bond saved . . . well . . . everyone.

She stared up at him with newfound awe. "You got me just in time."

"I just . . . you know. Reflexes. I play tennis." A peachy-pink shade spread across the tops of his cheeks, and his eyes broke from her gaze.

He was even kind of shy. How adorable.

"I'm Luke, by the way. Luke Pascal. I just started here today," he said, offering his right hand.

Daphne stifled the urge to giggle. It seemed so formal—

silly, even—considering they'd just been tangled up together on the floor. "I'm Daphne Rivera."

"Nice to meet you, Daphne. Again, sorry about the bruises. Can I help you pick up your stuff?"

Before she could protest, Luke started scurrying about, snatching up her purse, her book, her notebook, and a few errant papers. Daphne managed to retrieve her lipstick and her purple gel pen, but mostly she watched him as he kept bending over, fetching her things. She marveled at his broad shoulders inside his pale blue polo shirt, and she tried to recall the feel of his legs underneath her. He said he played tennis, so she imagined they were probably quite muscular. And tanned.

"Here you are," he said, holding out her things.

"Thanks." Daphne felt a little sad and panicked as she took the items. She didn't want this encounter to be over yet. "Let me help you with your stuff," she said, setting hers down. Death by Ms. Manbeck could wait.

"No, no. I can—"

She held up a hand to silence him. "I insist. It's the least I can do since you saved my life."

He flashed her a shy grin. "All right."

They moved about the hallway, silently retrieving his scattered belongings. Daphne tried to prolong the moment as much as possible, allowing pencils to roll away from her and papers to slip from her fingers. Eventually she came to the last stray object: a thick, battered paperback.

She picked it up, wiped some grime off the cover with the hem of her sweater, and stared down at the title. Sudden and severe prickles spread up her arms and over her face, concentrating in her scalp, as if each thick black hair stood wriggling in its follicle.

"You . . . you're reading *Jane Eyre?*" she stammered. It was a sign. It had to be. Why else would Fate drop her on top of a beautiful boy who just happened to have her hands-down all-time favorite book in the world in his possession?

"Huh? Oh. Yeah. I am. Or . . . I was. It was required reading at the last school I went to."

"Oh my gosh. Don't you just love it? It's so . . ."

"Romantic, right?" He smiled wide, and his dimples looked just like single quote marks around his mouth. "That's what my mom always says about it. She's crazy about that book."

"Me too!"

"Yeah. I guess they really don't write stuff like that anymore."

"I know!"

"Actually I got a copy of some BBC production of it for Mom last Christmas. I couldn't believe it was on the clearance rack."

"No way!"

Daphne suddenly became conscious of her bouncing feet and blaring two-word replies. She must seem like the literature cheerleader.

"I mean . . . Figures, you know?" she said, steadying herself. "People today, they're all about car chases and aliens and stuff."

Luke cocked his head and scrunched up his eyes, until the barest blue-green twinkle was visible. "You know . . . my mom would really like you. Maybe you should come over and watch our *Jane Eyre* sometime."

Daphne couldn't speak. He wanted to watch *Jane Eyre* with her . . . *with his mother!* How sweet! How old-fashioned! How . . . meaningful.

It was Fate. It had to be. The moment she'd been expecting ever since she had learned about True Love. She'd been attracted to Luke before this conversation, but now she was certain he was the One. The signs were just too obvious to ignore: He'd saved her life. He loved *Jane Eyre*. He was perfect.

"Well," he said, shouldering his backpack. "I hope we *run into* each other again soon."

Daphne laughed and bounced the toe of her sneaker on the floor.

"Only not so hard next time, okay?"

"I promise," she said.

They stood there, grinning at each other. Neither of them seemed able to walk away.

"So . . . bye," he said, turning toward the stairs.

"Bye," she echoed.

She watched as he slowly sank out of sight. Then she leaned against a row of lockers and shut her eyes. The swoopy feeling returned, same as before. Only now she understood it for what it truly was. It wasn't the fallout from a collision, it was an honest-to-goodness run-in with destiny.

How could Daphne go to class after this? Forget the relationship between points and angles—this was a *real-life* relationship, not just numbers on a page. This was a day she would tell her kids about until she was gray and arthritic and wearing support hose on her unusually shapely-for-her-age legs.

The Day I Tripped Your Father and We Fell in Love.

CHAPTER TWO
Antithe(sis)

"I'm in love!" Daphne sang out as she twirled into the bedroom she shared with Gabby, her arms raised like those of a ballerina in perfect fifth position.

"Again?" Gabby didn't even bother to glance up from her desk. Daphne noted the buzzy sarcasm in her older sister's voice—not that it was all that different from her usual tone. Gabby had no music to her. No spark. No glow. It was as if she went out of her way to be dull.

"But this is it! I mean it. This is for real!" Daphne went on. "He's so perfect." She lay back on her daisy-patterned bedspread and gazed at the nothingness above her. Soon the memory of a face superimposed itself on the dingy spray-acoustic ceiling.

Floppy brown hair . . . Blue-green eyes with incredibly long, dark lashes . . . That cute little groove in the center of his chin . . .

Luke Pascal. *Luke.* She even loved the name. It reminded her of such encouraging words as "like" and "luck." Or even "lick." She stared at the imaginary image and mouthed the name, exaggerating the feel of her tongue against her teeth when she made the "L." A tingling sensation surged through her, just like the time she plugged in the old waffle iron with the frayed cord—only better.

It was love at first sight. It had to be.

She loved the way Luke kept his head down and only looked up with his eyes, making his forehead crease like a puppy's. She loved how he laughed without making any noise—just a big smile and shaky shoulders. She loved how he wore khakis instead of jeans.

And she loved the way he had saved her life, like a prince in a fairy tale. . . .

Gabby suddenly spun around in the creaky antique chair. Luke's adorable image disappeared, and Daphne found herself gazing at her sister's scowling face.

"Do you *mind?*" Gabby snapped. "I'm trying to study for a test."

Daphne frowned. "What? I'm not doing anything."

"You are. You keep sighing."

"I am not sighing."

"You are so! You're sighing and making little humming sounds. It's annoying."

"Come on." Daphne sat up and crossed her legs, bouncing her knees to make the mattress shimmy. "Don't you want to hear about it?"

"About some guy? No freaking way."

"Why?"

"Because it's stupid. You fall in love every week." Gabby

whirled back around and glared down at her homework. Calculus, Daphne guessed, judging by all the numbers and lines.

"Aw, come on. Talking about stuff makes it all seem more real. Besides, it was so amazing what happened. Much more exciting than that boring homework."

"This boring homework is going to help me pass a major exam tomorrow, which will help me get the Waterhouse Scholarship, which will let me go to UT and get away from you and this boring little town. Which reminds me . . ." Gabby glanced at the clock on the nearby dresser. "Mule is coming over later to help me study. Promise me you won't bug us like you usually do."

"I don't bug you."

"Maybe not on purpose—and I stress 'maybe'—but you do. And my math grade has to come up five points if I ever want to win a full scholarship. So please, I'm begging you, don't be so . . . *you* tonight." Gabby gave her one last glower and stared back down at her lines and numbers.

Daphne stopped shaking the bed. Her posture bowed and the little electrical sparks quit rushing around inside her, until she felt like her plain old boring self. It was so unfair. Just because Gabby was older and smarter didn't mean she had to treat Daphne like a toddler. And why did she have to put everyone in a sour mood just because she was always in one?

Daphne hopped off the bed and stared out the window, wondering in which direction she'd find Luke. "He's so perfect—much better than any of the guys from here," she went on, trying to get back that fizzy feeling. "You probably heard about him. He just started today. He's only a grade behind you. Sheri said he's a junior."

Gabby glanced up long enough to make a face. "*Him?* Come on. He's not even that great."

"What are you talking about? He's amazing."

"This town is so small that any new guy, no matter how weird, seems *amazing* to all the boy-crazy girls. Get some perspective. He's okay. But Prince Charming he's not."

"What do you know?" Daphne grumbled. She was mad that Gabby was determined to ruin her good mood, but she also felt pity for her sister. It was sad that she couldn't share this thrill with Daphne. That she'd rather do *math.*

Daphne remembered when her sister used to be fun. Back when they'd shared the old canopy bed—the one that matched the desk they still had. They used to giggle and whisper and warm their cold feet on each other. Gabby would make up stories. Like the one about the baby that formed a rock band. And the one about the cat that became a spy.

Back then they used to talk about everything. Even boys. Gabby was going to marry Harry Potter and Daphne was going to marry Prince Phillip—the one from the *Sleeping Beauty* movie. Who cared that he was a cartoon? He was hot. They were all going to live in the same castle and have a ball every night. A literal one. With beautiful, glittery dresses and crowns on their heads. Gabby was going to talk to animals and ride around on a dragon. Daphne was going to learn to fly from the fairies and take swimming lessons from the mermaids.

Why did the stories stop? Why couldn't they talk and laugh like that anymore?

Daphne flopped back on her bed. "Dad's coming this weekend," she said, just to change the subject. But as soon as she heard herself mention it, she realized she was being dumb.

Gabby blew out her breath so hard, it rustled the papers on the desk. "Yeah, great," she said. "That's all I need."

Daphne knew it was stupid of her to mention Dad. Just because Gabby was Mom's favorite, she felt she had to take their mom's side against him. But it still made Daphne mad to hear Gabby talk about him that way. It wasn't his fault that his job as a construction foreman paid him so sporadically. Even if his payments were sometimes late, he never was. Daphne practically lived for their Dad weekends—in fact, she wished they could see him more.

Again Gabby swung about. "Do you *mind?*" she snapped.

Daphne frowned. She started to say she wasn't doing anything, but before she could open her mouth, Gabby pointed to the index finger poked between Daphne's lips.

"Please quit with the nail biting!"

Oh. That.

Daphne hadn't realized she was doing it. It was a bad habit she'd started recently. Whenever she was thinking hard she would stick her fingernail between her teeth, bite down, and then yank it out again, making a popping sound. The result wasn't so much that her nails got chewed off as that they got scraped down, little by little. She did it so much in biology class, apparently, that Mr. Hathaway had offered to buy her some gloves.

She stared at her sister. It was so unfair. Not only was Gabby smarter, she was prettier, too. Long wavy hair. Everything just the right size and evenly spaced out. A perfect face, even when it was scrunched up in frustration. If Daphne had turned out more like Gabby, all straight As and neat-freak genes, maybe things would be easier at home. Maybe she and Gabby wouldn't fight so much. Maybe then her parents would still be together.

Mom had said it would get easier when she and Dad had announced the divorce two years ago. But it hadn't. If anything it was tougher. Since Dad was gone and Gabby was basically perfect, Mom focused all her nagging on Daphne. And Gabby had promoted herself to second-in-command and started bossing her more than ever.

With everyone constantly on her back, Daphne was starting to understand why Dad had left. She seemed to remember that it had been different when she was little. There was more laughter, less talk about stuff like utility bills. But like Gabby, Mom at some point had just . . . stopped being fun. Daphne would have gone to her right now to tell her all about Luke's saving her life if she didn't know it would bring on a lecture about the importance of schoolwork.

"Everyone in this house is so boring," Daphne grumbled. "All you guys care about is work."

"Speaking of . . ." Gabby turned around again. Her eyes were superfocused and she leaned forward ever so slowly, like a lioness ready to pounce. "Please tell me," she said, "that you went by and applied for that job today."

Dang! Once again, her sister was spoiling any chance of a

good mood. Daphne couldn't decide which she was angrier about: the fact that she'd forgotten to go by the Lucky Wishbone and apply for that hostess job, or the fact that Gabby had already guessed that she'd forgotten and was laying a trap for her.

"No, I . . . didn't have time," Daphne lied.

Gabby tossed down her pencil. "Damn it, Daph! This is, what? The *third* time you forgot?"

"I told you. I got busy."

"Right. So swooning over some random guy is more important than helping out your family?"

"No."

"Well, which is it? You either forgot or you didn't think it was important enough."

"Shut up!" Daphne yelled, jumping up from the bed. God, she hated her sister! It was as if she enjoyed making Daphne look bad—making her feel bad. "You're just jealous that I can get real boyfriends."

"Boyfriends?" Gabby rolled her eyes. "Those genetically challenged hicks? I wouldn't even want any of those lame-asses to wash my car."

"You don't have a car! And they aren't lame!" Daphne winced at how whiny she sounded. Okay, fine. Those guys she'd dated might have been lame, but Luke was different. Todd Carothers said Luke had actually lived in Belgium for a little while. He read Brontë. He'd saved her life! "What do you know, anyway?" she spat. "At least *I* have a social life. What do you have? A pet nerd?"

It was dumb to hold that over her sister, she knew. But it

was the only thing she had. Daphne was the popular one. Gabby was both the smart one *and* the pretty one.

"Girls! What's going on in here?"

Daphne glanced back and saw her mother looming in the doorway. Great. Now Mom would fuss at her. It would be two against one.

She wanted to keep holding on to her anger, but why did her mom have to look so bad? Her dyed red hair had inch-long brown roots, and her makeup was all stale and cakey-looking, smearing a little around the eyes. Her mom could be so pretty, yet lately she always looked as if she'd walked out of a hurricane. It made Daphne feel guilty.

She didn't want to feel guilty. It wasn't her fault things had been tough for her mom since Dad took off. Maybe if she'd been nicer to Dad he wouldn't have left her. Maybe she should have fixed her hair and face more instead of worrying about the kitchen floor.

Gabby turned around in her chair and smiled sarcastically. "Didn't you hear, Mom? Apparently Daffy doesn't have to get a job because she's in lo-ove. *Again*."

"Shut up! At least I have a life! You always use work and school as an excuse not to have one. *I'm* the normal kid."

"How normal are you going to feel when we're living on the street? Or maybe you don't even care. Maybe you *want* to walk the streets since all you care about is guys."

"Gabriella!" Mom shouted. "That's an awful thing to say!"

Daphne sensed an opportunity. She looked over at Gabby with a stricken expression and started heaving as if she were close to tears. "You're so mean!" she cried.

It worked.

"Apologize to your sister right now!" her mom said, folding her arms across her chest.

Gabby's smug look fell away. "What? Why? She's the one who—"

"*Now*, Gabriella!"

"It's not fair! *She* doesn't have to work. *She* doesn't have to get good grades. She gets to be a screwup just because she's younger!"

"Say you're sorry or you're grounded!" Mom's voice was getting shrill.

Daphne could see her sister mulling it over. Grounding wasn't a good threat, since Gabby had to go to work. Plus, her mom would never send Mule away if he came around to visit. And it wasn't as though Gabby had any other friends.

Just then her mom shut her eyes and pressed her fingertips to her temples. "Please, Gabby. Do the right thing. I'm tired. I don't need this right now."

That did it.

Gabby let out the world's longest sigh and turned toward Daphne. "I'm sorry," her mouth said, even as her eyes lobbed hateful curse words her sister's way.

Daphne made sure her back was to her mom before shooting Gabby a big, triumphant smile.

As soon as their mother walked away Gabby whispered, "Oh, grow up," and bent back over her math homework.

Who cares what she thinks, Daphne thought as she sat back down on her bed, her chin raised victoriously. For years she had been hoping something big would happen to her. Something magical. Something amazing. Something that would save her from this sad little house with its sad little in-habitants. Now the something—the Someone—had finally arrived.

And nothing and no one was going to ruin it for her.

"Uh-oh," Mule said as soon as Gabby opened the front door. "Another fight?"

Gabby absently touched her face. "Is it that obvious?"

"Let's just say . . . I hope it isn't me you're mad at." He carefully sidestepped past her into the living room.

"It's just . . . you know. Family stuff."

Mule nodded. "Dad or sis?"

She glanced around. Daphne was in their room and Mom was in the shower, but she still didn't feel like discussing things with them nearby. "Come on," she said, picking up her notebook. "Let's go on the back deck."

They stopped in the kitchen on the way, to grab some sodas from the fridge. Mule was a huge Dr Pepper nut, but their mom had started trying to save money lately by buying the store version: Mr. Brown. It wasn't as bad as the name made it sound, but it wasn't as good as the real thing, either. Still, Mule never complained. Once supplied, they headed out the back door onto what Mrs. Rivera referred to as "the deck" but was actually a sagging back porch crammed with metal patio furniture that used to be white but was now flecked with orange spots where it had rusted.

Mule unzipped his backpack and pulled out a notebook, his calculus textbook, two pencils, and a family-sized bag of Doritos. Then he sat back in his chair and stared right at Gabby. "So tell me what happened."

Gabby tapped her own pencil against the side of the iron table. "Nothing. Just . . . stupid Daffy. She's such a child! She refuses to be responsible. All she wants is for her life to be like some old-fashioned romance, like *Gone with the Wind* or *Casablanca*."

"I kinda like *Casablanca*."

"You would. You and your Nazi-fighting fetish. You probably still play with little green army men, don't you?"

Mule didn't reply. He just took a long drink from his can and stared out at the yard. Gabby's words seemed to hang above them like storm clouds. She realized how snide she sounded. "Mule? Do you think I'm mean?"

"Is this a trick question?"

"No, I want you to tell me the truth."

He shook his head. "Uh-uh. I ain't going there."

"Come on, just answer. And don't say 'ain't.'"

Mule's head picked up speed. "Forget it."

"Then you *do* think I'm mean, don't you? You just don't want to say anything. Probably afraid I'll do something mean."

"Look . . ." Mule blew out his breath and scratched his floppy curls. "You're not exactly the tender type. You're not all sunshine and rainbows and kitties with ribbons around their necks. But so what? I mean, I like being around you. Obviously."

Gabby knew Mule was being straight with her, but somehow she wasn't comforted. She liked him. She tolerated his flaws better than almost anyone else's—except maybe her mother's. She genuinely considered him intelligent about most things. And she probably depended on his presence more than she would care to admit.

Yet that was just it. His endorsement didn't count for much. For one thing, it was rather backhanded. He might as well have said "So you're a hag. So what? I'm still here." But also, it was silly that he used his spending time with her as evidence, since it wasn't as if he had a lot of other choices. Neither of them had a social life beyond each other.

Mule gestured toward her. "See? Now you're pissed."

"I'm not. I'm just . . . Crap. I don't even know why I asked you." She clutched her can with both hands and crinkled the aluminum slightly.

"Why does it matter, anyway?"

"It doesn't. I just let my stupid sister get to me. That's all. She's doing it on purpose, too—pulling all this stuff right before Dad comes to visit. As if things weren't stressful enough. The scholarship application is due in a few weeks and I still only have Bs in calc and physics. And if I don't get full tuition I'm screwed. Even the maximum amount of loans will cover only so much. I could end up working full-time *and* going to school. Then I'll totally lose my mind, like Jack Nicholson in *The Shining*. Only instead of an ax, I'll crack skulls with this textbook." She lifted her encyclopedia-sized *Calculus and Applied Concepts* in both hands and shook it for effect. "Then I'll go to prison and Daphne will become the good, responsible daughter. Then the world will stop turning."

Again Mule remained silent, and again Gabby replayed her words. Here she was, going on and on as if she were the only person in the world with problems. And she complained that Daphne was selfish.

"Anyway. Enough about me," she said, lowering the book. "How's your dad doing?"

Last year Mr. Randolph had injured his back at the processing plant where he worked, leaving him bedridden. Two operations hadn't improved things much, and Mule had been required to help take care of him, especially at night and on occasional weekends when his mother worked her nursing shifts at the county hospital. That was another reason he didn't have much of a social life. Or a job.

"He's okay. He's gotten hooked on a couple of talk shows, which is no big deal except he's starting to take more of an interest in my life. Asking me how much gluten I eat, suggesting I try breathing exercises. This afternoon he saw something on prom fashions and asked who I was going to take."

Gabby snorted. "Did you say no one? That the whole thing is a big waste of money?"

"I told him I hadn't decided. I didn't want to, you know, crush his spirit or whatever." He let out a nervous-sounding chuckle. "Do you know what he said then?"

"What?"

"He said, 'I heard that kids today go with their friends. Maybe you and Gabby should go together.'"

"Man, he really has been watching too much crap TV. Why would we waste hundreds of dollars to have a lousy time among people we can't stand? We could spend a fraction of that staying home with a movie. That would be infinitely more fun."

Mule nodded. He didn't seem to be agreeing with her as much as marking the beat of an unheard song. His eyes fixed on the moths fluttering around the nearby lamp.

"Hey, did I tell you Daphne begged and pleaded and cried until Mom said she was allowed to go this year?" Gabby leaned sideways to recapture Mule's attention. "So typical. Mom and Dad said I couldn't go till I was a junior, so of course she gets to go when she's a sophomore."

"So? I mean, you hate prom anyway. Why do you care?"

Gabby felt a little stung. Mule should be upset at the injustice of it all instead of pointing out any mild hypocrisy on her part. "It's just the principle of the thing," she explained. "Daphne always gets her way and I always have to do what they say. I'm the do-gooder and she's the big baby and that's how it will always be. Forever and ever. I could win the Nobel Prize and they'd probably try to make me share it with her."

As Gabby paused to take a breath, she felt the heat in her throat and realized she'd once again commandeered the conversation. What kind of friend was she? She was supposed to be asking Mule about his problems.

"Sorry. I didn't mean to make it all about me again," she said. "I guess I am mean."

"Hey." Mule reached over and jabbed her shoulder. "You aren't mean. You're just . . . venting. It's what you do. You bitch and moan and call people names, and then you're better. At least, for a while."

She rolled her eyes. "Sounds like loads of fun for you."

"I don't mind."

Gabby stared at him. Mule was smiling that sideways

smile he reserved just for her. Half amusement, half annoyance, with just a touch of a smirk. It never failed to make her feel better. Yet something about that grin seemed different today. Looking more closely, she realized that it wasn't the smile that had changed, but the face it sat on.

After years of waiting, Mule had been so proud when he finally got facial hair that he refused to groom it. Unfortunately, it grew in sparse little patches on the sides of his mouth and tip of his chin, giving him a sleazy, Fu Manchu sort of look. Today, though, Gabby noticed he was clean shaven, and his cheeks and jaw were more angular than she remembered. She also saw that his skin had almost completely cleared up, and his shoulders even looked a bit broader. When had all that happened?

Probably months ago, but she was only now getting around to noticing. Because she was mean.

"Mule . . ." She took a deep breath. "I know this sounds cornball, but thanks for . . . for being you."

Mule's head jutted forward, as if her words somehow upset the balance of his skull upon his neck. "Uh . . . sure," he said with a chuckle. "It's what I'm good at. I'm good at being me."

Gabby winced. She was not expressing herself clearly—more proof that she wasn't all that skilled at being nice. "I mean . . . thanks for being the only sane person around. The whole town is going nuts about prom. Daphne's all gaga over some new guy. Thank god you're smart enough not to buy into that true-love crap."

"Yeah, well, I don't know . . ." Mule scrunched up his eyes. "Are you saying there's no such thing as love? At all? Ever?"

Gabby squirmed in the metal chair. Once again she

seemed to have said the wrong thing. "No. I mean, I think people love their families and their best friends and their dogs. And I do think there's such a thing as, you know, *attraction*. But the idea that there's someone out there who completes your soul, blah, blah, blah, that's just a big illusion people buy into. Like believing in the Easter Bunny."

Mule kept looking at her, chin in hand, forefinger tapping his mouth—the same expression he wore while figuring out superhard math problems. "Okay, just playing devil's advocate here, but . . . why is it so wrong to believe in true love?"

"Because," Gabby began. Then she paused. The word dangled lamely in the air between them. Why had she even brought up the topic? She'd wanted to be nice, but somehow it had backfired. "Because it's stupid. And dangerous."

"Dangerous?" Mule repeated, his eyebrows flying high on his forehead.

"Look, just forget it. We've got work to do." Gabby quickly opened her book, the heavy cover making a gonglike sound against the iron tabletop.

She kept her focus on page 274, trying to block everything else out. But she could tell Mule was still peering at her as if she were a particularly baffling lab specimen. It made her feel fidgety.

It was sad, really, when calculus was easier than conversation.

"Wha-a-a-at?"

Gabby lay in bed, sleepless and frustrated, tormented by her racing brain and the call of a nearby frog. It seemed to be chiding her, doubting her every thought.

"*Wha-a-a-a-at?*"

Meanwhile, her sister lay in deep slumber, her thick lashes faintly fluttering, round cheek smushed against the pillow, mouth slightly open. Once in a while she'd make a cooing sound and shift positions, but otherwise she seemed completely at peace. Daphne looked so young when she slept— not much older than the days when she'd sucked her thumb. It made it hard to be mad at her. Although Gabby still was, kind of.

The study session had been going along fine until Daphne had started playing the sound track to *Wicked* at a ridiculous volume. Gabby had gone inside to complain and they'd ended up in a squabble that led to Mule's excusing himself to go home. And Gabby had still needed his help on two sets of problems.

Now she couldn't clear her mind and fall asleep. It wasn't just the math or the bickering or the loud, melodramatic music that troubled her. She also kept replaying her earlier conversation with Mule, and each time she did she found something else to kick herself about.

She'd sounded mean. She'd sounded stupid. She'd hogged the conversation way too much.

It was true what he said about her need to vent around him. There was something about Mule's safe, loyal omnipresence that allowed her to lower her defenses. All he had to do was ask how her day went and suddenly all her pent-up stress would come spewing out like the contents of a punctured aerosol can.

Of course, no matter how blabby she got around Mule,

there were a few things she could never tell him about—which meant she couldn't tell anyone.

For example, no one knew about the time when she was five and gave herself a pet. Her parents wouldn't let her have a dog (no fenced-in yard) or a cat (allergies), so one day she caught a small brown toad behind their house and decided to adopt him. She named him Hoppy and placed him in an old mop bucket too high for him to escape from, along with a dish of water and some pulled-up grass. Only she'd forgotten to keep him out of the sun. The next day she'd found his withered, half-baked carcass next to the empty water dish, with black ants crawling all over him. She still felt too guilty to tell anyone about that.

Also, no one knew that she occasionally had the same dream. In it she's trapped at the bottom of a deep hole, and a nameless, faceless guy pulls her out and kisses her—a tender, soft, slow kiss that makes it seem as if she's melting into an oozy puddle. She'd be too embarrassed to tell anyone about that. Not just because it was cheesy, the type of fantasy Daphne probably entertained all day every day, but because she was pretty sure she knew who her nameless, faceless rescuer was.

And that was the third thing she could never tell Mule or any other living being in the universe about: her secret time with Sonny Hutchins.

Gabby felt a chill and snuggled down into her covers, making the old mattress groan. At night everything seemed harsher. Noises. Shadows. Memories. A pain welled up in the center of her body, dull but familiar, like an old injury re-asserting itself.

It had happened when she was thirteen. Her mom and dad had talked her into joining a kickball league, convinced that all that team spirit would make her more social, less serious and uptight. Only it had ended up being a disaster.

Her offensive game was fine. She could run well, and her kicks were fairly decent. But no matter what her position in the outfield, she couldn't manage to catch the ball. Every time it flew toward her, she would close her eyes and shield her head with her arms, and no amount of training could break her of this reflex. The more athletically gifted girls seemed to take her shortcomings personally and froze her out of all conversation. So instead of finding new friends, Gabby had ended up more alienated than ever.

Eventually she just stopped going. But rather than argue with her parents about it, she made sure she went somewhere else during that hour and a half she was supposedly at team practice, to prevent them from growing suspicious. She would wander out of sight behind buildings, looking for loose change scattered on the pavement. Or she'd climb the big live oak in Monroe Park and read.

One day Gabby had been following Chandler Creek, searching for fossils and keeping an eye out for water moccasins, and she'd ended up roaming farther than ever before. The noises of town gradually faded and the brush grew higher around her, forcing her onto the bank. After a while she came upon a clearing she'd never seen. A gently sloping grassy bluff that provided a scenic view of the nearby hills. She wandered into the field and, for some bizarre reason, lifted her arms and started twirling about like Julie Andrews in *The Sound of*

Music. Even now, she shuddered a bit at the memory. How unlike her. She must have gotten stoned off the stagnant creek-water vapors.

She'd continued spinning and staring up at the sky until a voice called out, "You aren't going to dance off the edge, are you?"

Gabby stopped midwhirl and began scanning the vicinity for her onlooker. She felt as if she'd been intruded upon, but in essence, she was the interloper. She had been the one who showed up second.

"Let me guess . . . Julie Andrews?" came the voice again.

This time she spotted him. It was Sonny Hutchins. He'd been leaning up against a tree, watching her, partially obscured by shadows and branches. Sonny was two years older and went to a private school, but she'd known who he was. For one thing, he was kind of famous. He came from one of the oldest and most well-connected families in town, and his relatives were always leading parades and running for office. But also, every summer their fathers were tapped to judge the annual chili cook-off.

What was he doing there, sitting under a cypress in the middle of nowhere, away from all his friends and fancy relatives?

She must have stood gaping at him longer than most sentient beings would have, because he asked again, "So was I right? Channeling your inner Julie?"

Gabby had nodded and then he'd smiled. She could still see it in her mind—the way leafy shadows played across his face; the way a tiny gust of wind lifted a few strands of hair on the top of his head and they danced about, waving in all directions like insect feelers.

That was another thing Sonny was famous for: his looks. Delicate, almost pretty features. A lopsided grin. Blond hair that he somehow managed to keep fairly long, in spite of his superpowerful, superconservative parents. A guy so attractive, it was intimidating—even though he seemed friendly enough. Every festival he would chat with Gabby a bit and make witty observations about the various entries. Meanwhile, she would barely manage to squeak hello and probably turned redder than Eddie Hardee's celebrated batch of Crying Marine Chili con Carnage.

She assumed Sonny didn't recognize her, so she nearly lost her balance when he cocked his head and said, "Gabby, right?"

Once again, all she could do was nod.

"Thought so," he said. "Come over here and look at this." He held something in his right fist.

She'd gone right over to him. It still made Gabby shake her head. Older guy she barely knew. The seclusion of trees. Too far away for anyone else to hear or see her. But she trusted him. She hadn't even stopped to think—she'd just walked straight to him as if pulled by an invisible tractor beam. Then she sat down beside him and peered into his cupped hands.

He'd been holding a caterpillar. Soft and plump, about the length of his pinkie finger, with thin yellow, black, and white stripes along the width of its body. The larva of a monarch butterfly.

"I found it on one of those leaves," he said, nodding

toward a clump of lush green plants. Gabby thought it was sweet the way he stroked the creature's back with the tip of his forefinger as it slowly inched up his palm.

"That's milkweed. It's their food. This area is part of their breeding ground," she'd said, ever the good student.

"I always knew you were smart," he said.

Gabby felt her face flush. "What do you mean 'always knew'?"

He shrugged. "I noticed how your dad has you tally the score sheets while he does the tasting at the cook-offs. Plus, I've seen you around. You're always reading and coming in and out of the library."

Her breath seemed to run out. Sonny had noticed her? He'd wondered about her?

"Of course, I always thought you were pretty, too," he went on, smiling crookedly into his lap. He seemed almost bashful. "I was planning to ask you out when I got my license."

She made a gasping noise—partly from shock and partly because she hadn't inhaled in several seconds. Sonny noticed and glanced up. He didn't look shy anymore.

"I remember you telling your dad you preferred seafood," he said. "So I thought we'd go have scampi. Then maybe come up here."

"Up here?" she repeated, finding her voice.

"You know what this place is, don't you?" he asked.

Gabby shook her head.

"It's Make-Out Ridge."

As an unpopular eighth grader with only one friend to speak of (Mule, skinnier and shaggier, and scarily obsessed with *Dr. Who* at the time), Gabby had only heard of the spot where high schoolers met to hook up. Looking around, she could see, logically, why it had been chosen. Even though it was just a few blocks from the town by foot, it was still rather remote by car, lying at the end of a winding dirt road. Cedar and mesquite trees bordered the field, obscuring the nearby homes and gas stations.

She watched as Sonny gently set the caterpillar onto a stalk of milkweed. "So," he said, grinning at her. "Would you like to make out?"

She probably should have said no. A reasonable girl would have been shocked and offended. Coming from any other guy, such a question would have been laughable or even disgusting. But Sonny made it sound sweet.

For the first time ever, she wasn't stupefied by him. Gabby found herself smiling and nodding, and then scooting near enough for Sonny to wrap his long arms around her. To this day she wasn't sure why she did that. There was just some quality about Sonny that made her trust him—and want to get closer.

Hormones, Gabby told herself, changing positions on her lumpy mattress so that she faced the window. She'd fallen victim to biochemistry, that was all. It was astounding how primitive urges could have such a hold on a person. The passion she'd felt as a thirteen-year-old was understandable. Just intense curiosity and an excess of glandular activity. But sometimes even today, four and a half years later, the memories of his mouth against hers created little warm spots all over.

For almost an hour they'd sat on the grass, kissing and leaning up against each other. They didn't talk at all, except for one time when he pointed out a kingfisher that had stopped off at the creek. Mainly they just smiled sheepishly between smooches, until Gabby caught sight of the time on her watch and realized she had only ten minutes to get back to her house. The fear of getting caught snapped her out of her hormonal trance and made her leap to her feet.

"What's wrong?" Sonny asked.

She suddenly felt woozy and confused—and more than a little embarrassed. "I gotta go," she blurted.

"Wait!" he'd called out. But Gabby was already scrambling down the nearby bank, heading for home. She didn't even say goodbye or thanks, just pointed herself toward town and sprinted away. Her panic had somehow given her superhuman speed, too. She arrived home only two minutes late and covered in sweat, which her parents attributed to a vigorous kickball practice.

She didn't tell anyone about her encounter. There were even times over the next couple of days when she couldn't be sure it had really happened. It was just too exhilarating and confusing, too outside her usual sphere of experiences. She had no idea how to file it away in her mind.

Gradually logic reasserted itself. It scolded her for being so rash, and it demanded some sort of definition for what transpired in the clearing. Was she now in a relationship with Sonny? Would he call her? Or would she turn an even deeper shade of scarlet at the next cook-off?

She wanted to trust her instincts. She wanted the

encounter to mean something—something big. It certainly felt powerful, and he'd said he liked her, but . . . what if it was all bull? What if he did that sort of thing all the time, lay in wait for some silly girl to come dancing along? He seemed to not just know her, but *know* her—and yet maybe he said stuff like that to every female whose name he could recall.

Only she couldn't forget the image of him holding the caterpillar, how gentle he'd been. It made her want to believe that he'd been honest with her. And in a way, it made her want to be that caterpillar, on the verge of a striking meta-morphosis that would transform her from a lonely outsider into someone who was happy, well-liked, and maybe even loved.

Gabby knew she'd have her answer when she saw him again, even though the thought terrified her. She had to know what he was thinking.

Only . . . she never did see him again.

The next Monday at school she vaguely noticed that something was different. Instead of the usual lazy sprawl of students resisting the start of a new week, everyone stood buzzing about in neat little clusters all over the front lawn. She assumed it was football-related fervor, the usual reason for any irrational enthusiasm among her classmates. And then Jana Pennington bounced right into her path. Her face looked grave, but her eyes seemed to flicker with excitement.

"Did you hear about Sonny Hutchins?" she asked Gabby.

"What? What are you talking about?" Gabby seemed to recall that she halfway snapped at the girl. She was sure

Jana had found out about the secret kissing session and was teasing her.

"You mean you don't know?" Jana seemed inordinately thrilled to discover this fact. "You didn't hear about Sonny Hutchins and Prentiss Applewhite?"

Prentiss was Sonny's older cousin, and the two of them were inseparable. Gabby always kept an eye out for Prentiss's flashy convertible since Sonny was typically in the passenger seat. Prentiss was just as rich and was considered equally handsome, but he was stupid. The winter before, he'd gotten drunk and fallen out of a pecan tree, breaking his arm. A couple of months later he got drunk and drove into the duck pond in Monroe Park.

"What about them?" Gabby asked, already feeling uneasy. It was as if, somehow, a part of her already knew.

"They were in an accident out by the reservoir. They say Prentiss is okay, but Sonny died."

Gabby's next reaction had no classification. She simply . . . stopped. Her eyes couldn't focus. Sound grew tinny and distant. Her lungs felt like two flimsy, twisted sacks. Yet even as her body reacted, her mind was unable to grasp the news. Sonny *died*? Sonny was *dead*? His body would no longer move? It was unfeasible, even silly, to imagine his lips cold and his eyes glassy. That he would never again smile or laugh. Or pick up caterpillars. Or kiss.

Gabby glanced hazily at Jana and the little knots of people around them. They were all wide-eyed and extra-animated, as if the whole horrible ordeal were a drama written expressly for their entertainment. Maggots. She hated them all.

It disgusted her how everyone seemed to feed on the news. Conflicting rumors spread for weeks, each one more ridiculous than the last. As she walked the school corridors, she couldn't help picking up snatches of conversations, as if she were slowly turning a radio dial. "The speedometer was frozen at a hundred and twenty. . . ." "Prentiss was drag racing. . . ." "Sonny was the one driving, not Prentiss. . . ." "They were trying to outrun the cops. . . ." People simply refused to believe the truth: that some stupid teen with a drinking problem crashed his car and killed his sweet, innocent cousin in the process. No. They'd rather twist the details and make up scenarios, just for added shock value. It was revolting. And selfish.

But then, Gabby was just as bad. As she went through the rest of the day and that week, stumbling from class to class, crying in the safety of a restroom stall or in the shower at home, she couldn't help thinking what his death had cost *her*. She would never again kiss Sonny. She would never know how he'd really felt about her. And her potential new existence, her new specialness, would never, ever happen.

She didn't tell anyone what was wrong with her. There was no way she could explain it without its seeming foolish. Besides, her few stolen moments with Sonny were all she had of him. She wouldn't share them.

Although she'd always been somewhat aloof, Gabby quickly became even more of a loner, avoiding crowds and meetings and chatty gossips like Jana. She even pulled away from Mule for a while, certain he'd be able to divine that something was horribly amiss. Instead of morphing into a butterfly, as she'd hoped, she withdrew further into a protective cocoon.

Gradually she came to live with her secret. The trick was to ignore it, to let it fall into her hidden depths like a stray coin or a discarded scrap of paper. Most days she didn't even think about Sonny. But every now and then, the memories crept up on her without warning. Usually nights when she couldn't power down her brain. Or times when the world around her seemed so fixated on love.

"Wha-a-a-a-at?"

The frogs again. It was as if they were doubting her, teasing her about holding on to some residual lovesickness. That, or they were still upset about the demise of Hoppy, their fellow amphibian.

Enough thought. What she really needed was sleep. No math, no stress, no memories, no haunting by a faceless dream guy. Just rest. Then tomorrow she could start being a nicer person, an understanding sister, and a more attentive friend.

"Wha-a-a-a-at?"

CHAPTER THREE
Cri(sis)

"Daddy Daddy Daddy Daddy!"

Daphne raced across the living room and threw her arms around her father's neck, squeezing hard to let him know how much she had missed him and breathing in his familiar spicy aftershave.

"There's my baby girl." He clutched her tightly and lifted her off the floor a couple of inches, swinging her back and forth. Then he set her down and put his rough hands on either side of her face. "*Que tan guapa*," he said. "I'm going to put some guards around this house to keep the boys away."

"Don't you dare!" Daphne laughed, feeling that familiar lifting sensation she got in her chest whenever he arrived, as if her heart was getting pumped up like a balloon.

She was proud of her dad. Ernesto Rivera was probably the handsomest man in Central Texas. Tall and strong-looking. As a tiny girl she'd always felt so safe around him and made him tell her bedtime stories about rescuing her from monsters or aliens or costumed supervillains. He even looked a little like Superman, with his thick, dark hair and wavy forelock. But he laughed and joked a lot more, and Daphne was very proud of the fact that she'd inherited his wide smile.

She wished her mom had done more to deserve him. They had never really told the girls why they broke up, but Daphne could guess. She wasn't stupid. Her mother was just too cold, too . . . dull. She only cared about things like bills and college and using the carpet rake twice a week to keep their plush pile from looking like a grimy doormat. Meanwhile, her dad was into *real* life. He loved all the things Daphne loved. Like movies and music and exciting stories.

Daphne's last birthday truly demonstrated for her the differences between her parents. Her mom had given her a thick envelope. Inside was a hokey card with lots of flowers and cursive writing talking about how a daughter is a daughter forever, blahbitty blah, and behind it she'd tucked a one-hundred-dollar savings bond. At first Daphne had thought it was like a check or a gift card and that she could use the money whenever and wherever she wanted. Then her mom explained that she couldn't cash it in until she was grown and that she was supposed to use the money for tuition and books. Then—and this was the worst part of all—*she took it back!* Said she'd wanted to show it to Daphne, but that she would be keeping it in their safe-deposit box at the bank.

It was the lamest present Daphne had ever gotten.

Thank god her dad had shown up just a few minutes afterward and given her his present. His was also a fat envelope—a silly Snoopy card and a booklet full of free bowling passes. She'd been so moved she actually cried, and she couldn't help remembering all those times he'd taken her and Gabby to Thunder Alley; how they would bowl and eat chili dogs and hang out with guys who had their own balls and bags and drab, untucked shirts with names like Hank or Chuy stitched above the breast pockets. Gabby, of course, had hated those trips and spent most of the time reading some mystery novel. And their mom had always complained that their dad kept them out too late and among the wrong kinds of people. But Daphne had always loved it.

Why couldn't her mom give her meaningful gifts like that?

"Are we going bowling today?" Daphne asked. Lately they'd been using the passes during his visits.

"Sorry, *mija*. I don't have enough time today. But let's start with lunch, anyplace you want to go, and then we'll see what we can do after."

Daphne felt a tiny thud of disappointment. "Just one game?"

"We'll see."

"I don't want to. We went bowling last time," Gabby said, stepping forward. She usually stood next to Mom whenever their dad showed, as if she thought the woman might faint at the sight of him and needed someone there to catch her. Or maybe it was just a way to remind Dad whose side she was on. Either way, Daphne thought it was mean. She wondered if Gabby had even bothered to hug him hello.

"No one asked you," Daphne snapped.

"Hey, I get a say, too. This isn't just about you."

"Girls," Mom said in her warning voice. "No fussing. You agreed, remember?"

The sisters held their tongues and resorted to glaring at each other.

"How are things, Lizzie?" their dad asked their mom.

Mom raised her eyebrows as if she thought it was a stupid question. "They could be better. My account and I have been waiting for . . . things."

Daphne stared down at their unraked brown carpet, embarrassed by her mom and unable to bear the shame on her dad's face. Why did Mom always have to bring up money?

"But I already told you," he said. "On Tuesday we—"

"Stop," Gabby interrupted. "Daffy and I agreed not to fuss. So you guys shouldn't, either."

Everyone fell silent. Daphne let go of her annoyance long enough to shoot her sister a grin.

Sometimes Gabby's grumpy nature came in handy.

"Wednesday is his plaid button-down, which makes him look like an old, skinny lumberjack. Thursday is blue oxford that's getting too small and starting to show his undershirt between buttons. And Friday is white shirt day. Well, it used to be white. Now it's the color of . . . coffee-stained teeth. Especially around the armpits." Daphne shuddered.

Her dad reached out and put a hand on her arm. "That's enough for now, *mija*. Take a break and eat some fries."

"Yes, *please*," Gabby muttered.

Daphne knew she was talking too much. She couldn't help it. She tended to do that whenever she got nervous or excited, and right now she was superly both.

Because Luke was there.

She'd noticed him walk in right after her father had asked,

"How's school?" and it made her usual reply—"Fine"—morph into a fifteen-minute ad-libbed speech on Mr. Hathaway's wardrobe. But apparently the rest of the table wasn't all that interested in her fashion-doomed biology teacher.

"I'm going to grab some more iced tea, and maybe some jalapeños," Mr. Rivera said, pushing his chair away from the table. "Do you girls need anything?"

Gabby shook her head.

"No, thank you," Daphne said.

"Okay. Don't eat my fries," he teased.

As he turned toward the front counter, Daphne let her eyes hop from him to Luke, slumped forward in his booth. He still hadn't seen her, but surely he would soon.

She should play it cool. Only . . . it was hard watching him without obviously watching him. So instead, she stared at the neon beer sign over his head, the thirsty-looking leaves in the planter outside the window, and the wooden cowboy and cowgirl on the restroom doors at the end of his row.

"Will you please eat?" Gabby said.

Daphne narrowed her eyes. "What are you, my mom?"

"Dad paid money for this. He's not giving us much else these days, so you should at least take advantage of the free meal."

"Shut up." Daphne hated the way Gabby always complained about Dad. Even when he was just a few yards away. "I'm just not that hungry. That's all."

It was a lie. Even as she spoke her stomach rumbled and popped like a thunderstorm. But she never could eat in front of guys she liked.

Of course, it wasn't as if Luke were looking at her right now. But when he did, she was *not* going to have barbecue sauce all over her chin.

Daphne twirled her plastic fork in her coleslaw and tried to strike a dazzling pose in her chair, just in case Luke should glance her way. Unfortunately, he was still frowning down at the laminated menu as if it were a bomb he needed to defuse.

Gabby made a huffing sound. "For god's sake, just go talk to the guy."

"What?" Daphne's face grew prickly. How had she known? Gabby's back was to the door *and* the booth he'd sat down in. No way could she have seen him.

"Come on. It's so obvious. You went all spaz a little while ago and you keep looking at something over my shoulder. Plus you're doing that nail-biting thing again."

Daphne was surprised to find her left thumbnail between her two front teeth.

"Is it one of your regular boy obsessions? Or is it that new guy?"

Daphne ignored Gabby's snide tone. "New guy."

"Please, just go say hi so we can all act normal again. Normal for us, I mean."

"But that's so . . . forward," Daphne whispered. "Besides, I probably look gross close-up. I didn't do my hair and I'm barely wearing any makeup." She wished she had dressed up more, worn something more feminine. Like her old-fashioned peasant blouse or one of her too-short-for-school skirts. And she really wished she could sneak on some more makeup. But glossy lip tint and a light dusting of blush were all she could get away with when her dad came over.

"You look great. I think you look better this way. All that gunk on your face just makes you look cheap."

"Gee, thanks," Daphne muttered. But secretly she felt better. Gabby wouldn't say she looked good unless she really meant it.

She could do this. She could quickstep past Luke's table to the bathroom, primp a little, and then act surprised to see him as she walked back.

Gabby shot her an impatient look. "Now. Before Dad gets back."

"Okay, okay."

Daphne got to her feet, swished her hair out of her face, and began to stride to the ladies' room. Suddenly it was as if walking were brand-new to her. She was acutely aware of every tiny movement and kept modifying things as she went along. She tilted her head a bit to try to look casual. She threw back her shoulders. She swung her arms less, and she swung her hips more. She even hummed some made-up tune. She hoped she was managing to look elegant yet relaxed, and not like some weirdo with a hundred different nervous tics.

As she passed Luke's table, she held her breath and forced herself not to look at him. Easy-breezy. Just a girl bopping over to the restroom. Lah-di-dah.

Eventually she reached the door to the ladies' room. But right as she was lifting her hand to push against the cowgirl cutout, she heard Luke shout, "Hey, Daphne!"

So much for primping. She turned and saw him leaning sideways out of his booth, craning his head around to look at her.

"Oh, my gosh. Hi!" she exclaimed. She smiled wide and did another awkward walk to his table. "Luke, right? Wow. Crazy seeing you again. What a coincidence. Hi there."

Ugh. Her mouth was moving like some brainless, uncontrollable thing. Like a beheaded chicken flapping around a farmyard.

"What are you doing here?" he asked.

"I'm with my dad and sister," she said, pointing toward their table. Her father had already sat back down with Gabby and was watching her closely.

Suddenly she regretted telling him that. Did being out with her father make her seem like a baby? And what if Luke looked at Gabby and noticed how much prettier she was? Even her back, with all her cascading dark waves, was a lovely sight.

"And what about you? What are you doing here?" Daphne asked him, leaning sideways to block the view of her gorgeous sister.

"I'm supposed to meet these guys Walter Lively and Todd Carothers. Know them?"

"Of course," she said, a little too loud and cheerleadery. "I mean . . . you know. Everyone kind of knows everyone in this town."

"Right. Well, I guess no one knows me yet. But those guys were cool to invite me along." He glanced at the expensive-looking silver-toned watch on his wrist. "Sure hope they show up," he added with a low laugh. "We're supposed to grab some food and then go bowling."

Daphne's eyes popped wide. "Oh, my gosh! I love bowling!" It was another sign. It had to be. "I go all the time with . . . with people."

"I'm really not that good. But, hey. It's fun."

"I could teach you."

Luke smiled. "Oh yeah?"

"Sure."

A familiar figure walked past the window. Only Walt Lively made that lurching movement, as if his upper body were dragging his lower half along. Daphne had grown familiar with it during three months of intense scrutiny when they'd kinda-sorta dated—or, more precisely, accompanied each other to three baseball games that had ended in three similar arguments when she wouldn't let him feel her up. But that was last school year, and now she couldn't even remember why she'd liked him in the first place. He was all-right-looking. Tall and rangy. Freckled. Close-set eyes and thick brows that stood straight up and blended into his bangs. Boring-cute. Could even be more attractive if he smiled now and then and didn't spit on the ground every few seconds.

She didn't dislike him now; she just didn't feel much of anything—except annoyance that he'd shown up just as the conversation was getting good.

The door chimes jangled and Walt shuffled toward them, wad of snuff making his left cheek bulge, cowboy boots scuffing the flecked vinyl floor.

"Hey," he said, nodding at them. "Carothers is going to be

late. He wants to meet us at the alley. We can just buy hot dogs there."

"Oh. Okay. That's cool." Luke grabbed his drink and slid out of the booth.

"So . . . ," Daphne said suddenly, not wanting him to leave until she'd made some sort of progress. "Maybe you should give me your cell number and we could bowl a game sometime? I'll give you those pointers."

"Sure, yeah." He patted his pockets as if looking for a pen.

"Here." Daphne pulled her cell phone out of the back pocket of her jeans, clicked on New Contact, and handed it to him. "Just enter it and hit Save."

As he punched in his number, Daphne rocked on her sneakers and tried to ignore Walt's smirking face.

"There you go," Luke said finally, giving her back her phone.

"Great," she said. "I'll text you and we'll go bowl or something."

"Yeah. Or something. I don't really know what else there is to do around here. Maybe . . . go for a walk? Take in the air?"

Walt snickered.

"We could take in some *Jane Eyre*." Daphne was so pleased with herself for coming up with that. Normally it was Gabby who said the clever stuff. Or Daphne would think of something hours after a conversation had ended. But this was brilliant. A perfectly timed reminder of their shared love of Brontë.

Only Luke didn't say anything. He didn't even react. She

was probably so breathless from being near him that she hadn't said it loud enough. *Dang!*

"Well . . . see you later," Luke said, touching the small of her back as he went by. He shot her one of his adorable, head-ducking grins and then headed for the door, Walt ambling along beside him.

Daphne remained in place. The six square inches where his hand had pressed against her felt different from the rest of her skin. Like a burn or a swelling—but in a good way. Sure, he'd only been squeezing past her, but the contact had seemed significant.

"Man, you don't waste time, do you?" she heard Walt mutter as he and Luke loped off.

Luke said something in reply, but Daphne was too far away to hear it. She watched as he paused at the exit to drop his Styrofoam cup into the nearby trash can (yet another sign of his gentlemanliness) and stepped outside, disappearing with Walt among the trucks and cars of the parking lot.

Walking back to the table, Daphne could see Gabby and her dad blatantly *not* watching her. Instead, they sat hunched over their fries as if in prayer and didn't look up until she reached her seat. Were they trying to give her privacy, or were they embarrassed by her? Most likely one of each.

But not even her awkward family life could ruin this moment. This knowing. This stirred-up feeling. As if her inner organs were frolicking about inside her. Stomach leaping over lungs. Pancreas strumming her intestines. Heart twirling round and round. How could she ignore it? How could she pretend her future hadn't just plunked down in front of her?

I'll see you later, he'd said, patting her back—practically embracing her. *He*, Luke, would see *her*, Daphne, later. As in soon. As in he was looking forward to it.

Her life was finally in motion.

"Oh, give me a break," Gabby muttered.

"What?" Daphne said, annoyed that the remark had pulled her out of her reverie. "You were the one who told me to say hi."

"Yeah, but I wouldn't have if I'd known it would make you even moonier. We can't sit here all day, you know."

"Gabriella. Let your sister have fun," their dad cut in, his voice softly chiding. "She's young. She's doing what she should be doing."

"Yeah," Daphne said.

Gabby's eyebrows scrunched together. "What's that supposed to mean? That *I'm* not doing what I should? That if I don't throw myself at every pimply guy in town, then there's something wrong with me?"

"Luke is *not* pimply."

"I'm just saying she should have fun and you should have fun. No matter what you think that is," Mr. Rivera replied. "Daphne likes people. And you like . . . other things."

"She sure doesn't like people," Daphne muttered.

Gabby threw her napkin onto the table and pushed back her chair with a loud screeching sound.

"*Mija*, relax. We're having a nice lunch."

"I'll be outside waiting. I need some air."

"Or some *Jane Eyre*," Daphne said, smiling secretly to herself.

Gabby looked at her as if she saw spareribs sticking out of Daphne's nostrils. A second later she was charging out the restaurant's glass door into the sunny glare beyond.

Her father sighed and gently set his own napkin on the table. "I wish Gabriella weren't so angry."

Daphne tried to appear sympathetic; she was still feeling floaty after her talk with Luke, and it was tough to not smile But even though she would try to look serious on the outside—for her dad's sake—she refused to let Crabby Gabby ruin her good mood.

"She's just full of herself," she replied, picking up a piece of corn bread. "Gabby's mad at the whole world."

Mr. Rivera shook his head. "No. I think she's mad at just me." His eyes looked sad as he stared out toward the parking lot. But just as Daphne was starting to feel worried, he smiled at her. "But you're my happy girl, right? *¿Mi pájarita?* I hope you always stay that way."

"Don't worry, Daddy," Daphne said, remembering Luke's sea-green eyes. "I'm going to."

"I hate barbecue," Gabby muttered. She licked a Kleenex and swiped at a drop of sauce on her shorts, but all she managed to do was spread the stain. Stupid caveman food. Dead animals smothered in messy sauce.

"Well, I love it." Daphne grinned at her from the front passenger seat—a smug "so there" kind of smile. Gabby was thrilled to see a small string of beef wedged between her sister's two front teeth.

Good. Hopefully it had been there when she was talking to that nervous-looking guy she was so hung up on.

"We can go there again next time, if you want, Daddy," Daphne said, turning toward their father with big brown bunny eyes.

Gabby thought she should probably hate the way her sister always curried favor with their father, but it was just so pathetic. Then again, it always seemed to work.

"If you want, *mijita*," Dad said.

Her dad had been outrageously nice to Gabby since she'd rejoined them in the parking lot. He'd tried his usual stuff— cracking lame jokes and giving her compliments on her good grades—but none of it worked. She was just too old and experienced to fall for his I'm-such-a-great-guy act.

It had been made clear at lunch that he thought she was a freak, which was so unfair. Just because she wasn't some perky, squealy thing like Daphne, he was somehow disappointed in her. Gabby had always assumed this was the case, but now he'd practically admitted it. So no way was she letting him off the hook.

What made it worse was that the whole world judged her the same way. "Your sister is so *sweet*." "Your dad is so much *fun*." Meaning they were shocked, since Gabby possessed neither of those traits.

Gabby used to think her dad was nice and fun and heroic, too. Then she wised up—or simply grew up. Anytime she or Daphne asked why their parents' marriage had ended, they always got the same answer: "It's complicated," followed by standard consolations that it had nothing to do with them. But it was just so obvious it had been their dad's fault. All the bickering about money. His refusal to work longer hours or search for a better job. The way he always wanted to bowl or play poker with his sleazebag friends. She had been able to tell things were strained between her parents, despite the fact that they had tried to shield her and Daphne, fighting mostly after the sisters had gone to bed. By day they had persisted in the world's worst charade of a functional married couple.

One evening when she'd been ambushed by memories of Sonny and couldn't sleep, Gabby had gotten up to get a drink of water and overheard them talking in the living room. ". . . can't take much more," her mom was saying. "Even the girls have noticed something's wrong. We have a problem, Ernesto. What is it?"

Gabby knew she couldn't venture out there and interrupt them, but she couldn't go back to bed, either, not after what she'd heard. So she leaned into the shadows and listened for her father's reply. "I just . . . I don't think I love you anymore," came her dad's hushed voice. "I'm sorry." Her mom had uttered something, but Gabby couldn't make it out. Then her dad said, "No! There's no one else. I'm just not happy. You aren't, either. How can the girls be happy if we aren't? We tried, but it's over, Lizzie. We have to face the truth."

Three days later her dad had loaded up his car and headed for San Antonio, leaving them behind like a half-finished game of Monopoly.

"Nice." "Sweet." "Pleasant." "Fun." They were all nonsense words as far as Gabby was concerned. Just because someone talked a good talk, it didn't mean they were a better person than their quieter neighbor. Just because they could crack a few jokes didn't mean they should be voted president.

And even if someone was likeable, it certainly didn't mean they'd make a great husband or parent.

There were much better traits than friendliness and good humor. Like loyalty, for instance. The ability to stick around.

"What are we going to do with all this leftover food, huh?" her dad asked, glancing from Daphne to Gabby's reflection in the rearview mirror. "Think your mom is hungry?"

Gabby clenched her teeth. He was probably trying to come off as noble. *Can't pay his ex-wife his child support on time, but no matter. Here are some free ribs!* "She won't be interested," she replied, staring back at his eyes in the mirror. "She's trying to cut down on red meat." She didn't tell him this was mainly because beef was expensive, not because of any health reasons. Her mom wouldn't want his uneaten lunch anyway.

"What about you, *mija?*" He gently tugged a lock of Daphne's hair, the way he used to tug on her pigtails. "You still hungry?"

"No," Daphne said in a sullen voice. "You take it." She slumped against the doorframe and stared out the window, chomping down on her right index fingernail.

Here we go, Gabby grumbled inwardly. It happened after every visit, during their drive back home. As soon as Dad turned off the smooth pavement of the town's main avenues onto the scarred, neglected asphalt of the residential roads, Daphne would start pouting. And it only got worse after that. She'd be tearstained and sniffly as he said goodbye, and as soon as the Honda disappeared into the distance, she'd be on her bed wailing.

"Well, okay then. I guess I'll take it." Her dad patted the

Styrofoam box wedged between him and Daphne. "Hate to see good food go to waste."

Soon they were pulling into the driveway. Thank god it was over! Almost two hours of her weekend wasted on Dad's small talk, Daffy's histrionics, and high-calorie, colon-busting food. Maybe Mule would be up for a walking vent session. That way she'd be out of the house for most of Daffy's bawlfest.

The second Dad threw the car into park, Gabby was out the door. "Okay, bye," she said, and bounded onto the porch before he could ask for a hug or look at her in that droopy, disappointed way, as if to show how much she was making him suffer. She knew he wouldn't follow her. He rarely stepped inside at drop-off time—probably too much like returning to the scene of a crime. Meanwhile, she could hear Daphne behind her, whimpering and pleading for Dad to stay longer. The usual drama.

As Gabby reached for the door handle, she was surprised to see it turn before her eyes. A second later Mom was standing on the threshold, frowning.

"We've got a problem," she said to Gabby.

One, two, three . . . Gabby counted the worry lines on her mother's forehead. Three? This must be something serious. "What's wrong?" she asked, following her into the living room.

"I just heard—" Her mom paused as Daphne came trudging up the steps behind Gabby, whining the whole way.

"I don't see why he can't stay a couple more hours," she bawled at them. "Why can't he just come in for a while? Why do we have to treat him like some stranger and—"

"Shut up!" Gabby snapped. Daphne flashed her a hurt expression. "Something's happened and Mom's trying to explain."

Her mom glanced at each of their faces, as if she couldn't decide who to focus on. Gabby forced the worry out of her expression and sure enough, her mother's gaze landed on her. "I don't want anyone to panic," Mrs. Rivera began, "but I just found out we have to move."

"What?" Gabby exclaimed.

Daphne let out a gasp. "Why? What did we do?"

"Nothing. Our lease is up, and apparently Mr. Tibbets is raising the rent. A lot. He's very apologetic about it. For years he's kept it the same rate. But he has to keep up with expenses and taxes, and there's no way we can pay the new amount. So . . . we go."

"Go? Go where?" Daffy asked, her whine now at a higher pitch.

"I don't know. But we have less than two weeks to find a place." Her eyes sagged guiltily. "He sent a letter with our last bill, but I only opened it now. It was stupid of me. I've just been so busy . . . I should have been more on top of things. . . ."

"It's not your fault." Gabby threw a protective arm around her mother's shoulders. "Dad just needs to get us the support money. Then we can pay the rent."

Mrs. Rivera shook her head. "No, you don't understand. Even with your father's support we can't afford the new rate. We have to leave."

Gabby studied her mom. Her face looked pale and worn, hastily assembled, slack with sadness in some places, stretched with tension in others. It was further proof that her mother had suffered more from the divorce than her dad.

Gabby could hear the Honda's grumbly motor fading into the distance. She'd been so relieved that the visit was over, but now she was suddenly angry that her dad wasn't there with them, helping them face all this. *Go ahead. Run away,* she thought. *That's your answer to everything.*

"It's not fair!" Daphne said. Her bottom lip quivered and tears streamed down her cheeks. "If Dad moved in, I bet we could afford it. We wouldn't have to leave if he came back."

"That is *not* an option," Mrs. Rivera said.

"But why?" Daphne wailed.

Mrs. Rivera shut her eyes and sighed heavily. "Sweetie, we have a pressing issue we need to deal with. Please don't turn this into something else entirely."

"But—"

"Be quiet!" Gabby snapped at her sister. "This is about us, not Dad."

Daphne made a face and crossed her arms over her chest, but at least she went silent.

"It'll be okay, Mom," Gabby said. "We'll start looking for someplace right now."

"Thanks, honey," her mom said, embracing her. "I appreciate your help."

Over her mother's shoulder, Gabby could see Daphne hurrying down the hall toward their room.

"Hey! Where are you going? We have a problem here!"

Daphne spun around. Strands of her hair clung to her wet face. "What am I supposed to do?" she wailed.

Gabby thought for a moment. "Fine. Go," she said. "You're useless anyway."

As always, it was up to her.

An hour and a half later Gabby found Daphne squatting inside their closet, still crying.

"God, not this again," she said.

Daphne didn't reply. A stack of photo scrapbooks sat in front of her. The one on top was open to shots of the two of them playing outside the time it had snowed in Barton. When was that? Gabby couldn't remember exactly. Probably eight years ago. That was when they'd lived on Tonkawa Lane, when Dad had had that awful mustache. And Mom had looked so much . . . softer.

Gabby pulled her eyes off of the image, focusing instead on the part in Daphne's hair, which ended in a tiny cowlick in the back. Daphne hated it since it always went in the exact opposite direction she wanted it to go, and no gels or sprays or styling utensils could make it behave. But Gabby had always liked that rebellious little lock. Daphne had had it since she was a toddler, and Gabby used to twirl it in her fingers when they snuggled up together. Maybe all those years of her fiddling with it had made it so mutinous.

"So we came up with a plan," Gabby said, resisting the urge to toy with the cowlick. "Mom and I will find us a new place. You'll get a job and contribute a small amount with each paycheck. Plus, Mom and I are going to ask for more money at our work. If Mom gets her hours extended, you'll have to help out more around the house. All right?"

"Okay," Daphne said, without looking up. She sniffed a few times and turned the page, revealing more shots of their snow-day revelry.

Gabby sighed. "I don't get it," she said. "Why do you always do this to yourself?"

"Do what?"

"This." Gabby waved toward the photo albums. "Wallow in the past. It's not like it can magically change the present, you know."

Daphne glanced up at her with watery, red-rimmed eyes. "I know. And I don't always do this to myself. Just now and then. When I feel like it."

"But why do it at all? It only makes you depressed."

"No, it doesn't."

"What are you talking about? You're bawling your eyes out."

"Of course it makes me cry. But then I feel better."

"What? You're making no sense. If reliving the past upsets you, stop doing it."

"I like remembering that there were nice times. That things weren't always so crazy."

"Whatever." Gabby shook her head. *God.* It was like the girl wanted to be miserable.

That was the thing about memories. It was impossible to recall only the good ones. Instead, you had to take good, bad, sad, and embarrassing all in the same bundle, like a cable TV plan.

Gabby would give anything to eradicate all the awful moments of her life, to take a magic squeegee and wipe away her parents' fights, her grandmother moaning in a hospital bed, excruciating situations at school, and all traces of Sonny. . . . Not that her time with Sonny had been bad; remembering it just brought on bad feelings. And yet here was Daphne deliberately seeking out such emotions, purposely reviving them. It seemed so pointless and reckless.

Daphne flipped another page to reveal an eight-by-ten glossy of Gabby in the midst of a hellish puberty, all braces and pimples and crookedly cut bangs.

"Oh, please!" Gabby exclaimed. "At least turn the damn page. I really hate that picture."

"I like it," Daphne said in a completely serious tone. "You look so . . . happy. You never smile that way anymore."

Gabby gazed down at her younger, metal-enhanced grin. It was true. She did look happy, in a goofy and completely oblivious way. That girl's biggest worry was that she'd never learn how to do a perfect cartwheel; she couldn't even fathom how much suckage was just waiting to happen to her.

Growing up, it seemed, was just a series of disenchantments. First you find out there's no Santa Claus; then you find out there's no such thing as a happily-ever-after. Then you end up working some soul-sapping job where you have to wear red knit polyester and get bossed around by an evil ghoul.

So of course Gabby didn't smile that way anymore. She knew things now that that girl didn't.

CHAPTER FOUR
Per(sis)tence

"Are you sure you won't have any other units available in the next few weeks? . . . I see. . . . Yes, I understand. . . . Please hold on to my number and call me if anything should open up. . . . Thank you." Mrs. Rivera turned off her phone and stood staring out her bedroom window.

Gabby waited a few beats before saying "So . . . no luck, huh?"

"No."

Just one tiny word, and it sounded distant, feeble. Gabby wanted to spring forward and throw her arms around her mom. Instead, she forced herself to stay in the squeaky vinyl office chair in front of her mom's desk. The last thing Mom needed was for Gabby to behave like a scared little girl. She should act strong—even if she didn't feel it. That would calm her mother better than any hug.

She glanced back at the screen, searching for the most uplifting detail she could find. "There's a duplex on Briar Street. It's only one bedroom, but we've got that sleeper sofa."

Her mother turned just enough to shoot her a pained expression. "Please don't tell me it's come to that."

"No, no. There are other postings. I mean . . . not right now. But people put up new posts every day."

"I just can't do a sleeper sofa every night. Not at my age." Her mom shook her head over and over and over.

"I could sleep on it," Gabby suggested.

"And I sleep with Daphne?"

"Or maybe we could set up your bed in the living room and get rid of the couch?"

"God, that sounds so pathetic," her mom said, massaging her forehead with her fingertips. She slumped onto the stool in front of her vanity and faced herself in the mirror.

"It's just for a little while," Gabby said, rising to her feet. She walked over and stood behind her mom. "I'm sure we could do it."

Her mom's reflection shot her a wry smile. "By 'we' you mean me and you, right? My god, can you imagine your sister's reaction?" she asked, chuckling. "She'd disown us."

"Hey. Another plus."

"Be nice, now."

Gabby shrugged. "I'm just saying, more room for us. That's all."

"Where is Daphne, anyway?"

"Not here helping, that's for sure. Probably off somewhere moping. Or daydreaming over her latest guy obsession."

"What am I going to do with that girl?" her mom muttered. "I have this horrible feeling she's going to end up making the same mistakes I made."

"Like what?" Gabby asked, knowing she needed to let her mom vent the way Mule did for her. Meanwhile, she moved to the dresser, picking up and putting down displayed keepsakes as if she were browsing in a gift shop. Framed school portraits of her and her sister. A green ceramic box where her mom stored her earrings. A sculpture Gabby had made in second grade of what was supposed to be a peacock but instead resembled an emaciated turkey.

It was a lame attempt to appear calm when, in fact, her insides felt heavy and twisted, just like the grade-school art in her hand. She knew exactly what her mother was going to say.

"Making a man my whole life."

Gabby had listened to this lament many times, and it never failed to brew up a frothy mix of emotions. On the one hand, she was proud that her mom thought her mature enough to confide in, treating Gabby as if she were an equal. But it also made her feel a little insecure. She wished her mother would stop blaming herself for putting too much faith in her marriage, especially since she wasn't the one who had given up on it.

Plus, there was still a side of Gabby that hated hearing it. The marriage couldn't have been *all* bad. After all, Gabby and Daphne had come out of it. So did their mother regret having them, too?

Gabby set down the deformed peacock and walked up behind her mother, resting her hands on her shoulders. "It'll be okay," she said, staring at her mom's image in the mirror. Her face looked as if it had cracked from too much pressure, creating stern fissures on her brow and around her mouth. Her mom seemed literally broken. Gabby had to protect her.

"And don't waste time worrying about Daphne," Gabby added. "You know she'll be fine. The girl can bounce back from anything."

"I hope you're right."

"We'll find a place to move into. You'll see. Tomorrow they'll have new ads online, I'll be able to ask Pinkwater for a raise, and Daphne will get that hostess job. It'll all work out."

Gabby's mom reached up and patted her left hand. "Thanks, sweetie. I'm so glad you're sensible. Promise me you'll always keep both feet on the ground, okay? Promise me you won't go crazy over a handsome face and mess up your life."

"Not much chance of that in this rat hole of a town," Gabby said, smiling crookedly. Her mom looked relieved.

Gabby didn't want to tell her that her warnings were unnecessary. She'd made up her mind soon after the divorce to never end up in her mom's situation: alone, panicked over bills, with a child or two to look after. She would always have money, independence, job skills, and a backup plan—or five. Plus, she'd already gone crazy over a handsome face. Losing Sonny and that silly alternate universe she'd hoped for with him had messed her up enough as it was; she couldn't imagine how badly it would have hurt if there'd been an actual relationship.

So no. Gabby had learned her lesson: you can only rely on yourself in life. She knew that fairy-tale endings only happened in books.

Daphne, on the other hand, was a lost cause.

Daphne lay sprawled on the green and beige striped couch they'd gotten from Grandma's house—the one that still smelled like a mixture of White Linen perfume and Aqua Net. Her eyes were raw and crusted from her big cryfest the day before, which had lasted late into the evening. She felt as she usually did after those bouts of sobbing: purged, weary, and noble in her sadness. She imagined herself as a tragic character in an epic miniseries, the kind who wore beautiful dresses while staring pensively out rain-streaked windows. Lonely and misunderstood, but not too far gone to forget to brush her hair and apply a light coating of Tawny Mountain lipstick. In those films the heroine was always rescued from her predicament by a handsome and very well-off guy who could somehow look manly in leggings. And that was exactly how Daphne wanted her story to end. (Only without the form-fitting man pants.)

Normally on Sundays she stayed in bed until noon, but today, she was up by nine-forty-five. At ten-thirty she figured it was late enough to text Luke, so she sent him a quick message—**HOW WUZ BOWLING AND HOT DOGS?**—and then sat cradling her cell phone as if it were a baby bird, eagerly awaiting his reply.

She could hear her mom and sister in the next room. The door was shut, so she couldn't make out any words, only the rising and falling of their voices like droning bumblebees. But she could tell by their tones that they were still in ultraserious mode about having to move.

She supposed she should go help them, but why? They'd only tell her she was doing everything wrong. Besides, the more she thought about it, the more she was kind of glad they had to leave. They'd moved into this slummy little house right after the divorce two years ago, and Daphne had always hated it. It reeked of sadness. And also—because the previous tenant had had a lot of cats—it reeked of cat pee and tuna fish. The windows were too few, the closets too small, and the rooms impossible to brighten. Even when they opened all the curtains and switched on all the lights and lamps, it still seemed as if they lived at the bottom of a well.

Daphne set her phone on the coffee table. Then she stood and stretched her arms, glancing around the living room to see if there was anything, any corner or nook or view, that she would miss about the house. But she couldn't find a thing. The main problem was that there were no good memories here. Since they'd arrived it had been an endless blur of crying, arguing, and freak-outs about money. All that negativity seemed to have seeped into the fake wooden paneling and gathered like moss on the bumpy spray-acoustic ceilings.

It had never been a home. Instead, it had always felt like one of those cheap motel rooms they used to stay at on their way to some vacation destination. A place to shower and crash in but not truly live in.

All of a sudden Daphne's cell phone let out an irritable buzz and scooted three inches across the coffee table. She quickly snatched it up. She was so startled and excited that her fingers trembled, and it took a couple of fumbling tries before she managed to call up her message on the screen.

HAD FUN THX. THIS IS DAFNE RIGHT?

It felt as if a mini-explosion went off in her chest. Yes! He'd written back!

Daphne ran her fingertip across the line of text. Somehow the words looked sweet coming from him. The font seemed pretty, and the sentences brimmed with meaning. He'd thanked her for her message, which meant he was happy to hear from her. And he'd used her name! He couldn't spell it, but so what? Just knowing that his fingers had typed it out made her shudder with excitement.

YEP ITS DA

She paused. She really didn't want to point out his misspelling, so she backed up and tried again.

YEP ITS ME. GLAD U HAD FUN.

She hit Send and perched on the edge of the couch, rocking back and forth with anticipation. And she waited. Her hands were so sweaty, she had to wipe them on her lap a couple of times so she didn't lose her grip on the phone. And she waited, and rocked, and waited some more.

Finally the phone vibrated. Even though she'd been expecting it, she gave a little yelp of surprise.

NEED HANDS. CALL ME INSTEAD?

Yes! Of course she would call him!

She chose him off her contacts list and pressed the button to connect. Two rings later she heard his voice in her right ear. "Hello?"

"Luke, it's Daphne."

"I figured," he said with a chuckle. "This is better. I'm trying to make something to eat and I can't really do that and text too."

"Wow. You're cooking?"

"Well . . . it's just a sandwich. It's going to be a really good one, though."

She laughed. "Hey, that counts."

"Besides, I'm not much into texting. All that typing and writing—it feels too much like school."

Daphne wasn't sure what to say, so she just giggled again. How come she hadn't noticed how sexy his voice was before?

"Maybe I'm just old-fashioned."

"Me too!" she said. "I'm so old-fashioned, sometimes I feel like a freak."

"Ha! I know what you mean. My friends at my old school kept teasing me about moving to the backwoods. They think it must be so boring here. But you know, I like small towns. You guys actually have a Main Street. And that's its actual name."

"Yep," she said. "We're very Norman Rockwell around here. We even have swimming holes." She congratulated herself on remembering the name of the artist known for his wholesome and funny pictures of small-town life. Of course, she only knew about him because Gabby referred to him all the time when talking about Barton—usually in a snide tone. But still, Daphne was impressed with herself and hoped he would think she sounded smart.

"I love that the guy at the nearby gas station already knows my name," Luke said.

"Gus?"

"Yeah! Gus! I love that his name is Gus, too."

"We used to have a drive-in theater, but that closed when they built the new cineplex. And there was this general-store-type place, but that closed when the Walmart came."

"Aw, too bad."

"But Quick's Pharmacy still has a real old-fashioned soda fountain."

"Really? Cool! You know, we should go there and, like, get a sundae with two spoons."

Daphne felt like squealing, only she wouldn't let herself. Instead, the squeals built up inside her until it seemed her upper body might burst open. "That would be so great," she said. "I wish I had something old-fashioned to wear. Like . . . a poodle skirt."

"You'd look nice in a poodle skirt," he said, his voice a low murmur.

Daphne fell sideways on the couch and hugged herself with her free arm. This was by far the sweetest conversation she'd ever had in her life.

"So . . . when do you want to go there?" she asked, barely able to take in enough breath to speak.

"I don't know. Do you have plans tomorrow after school?"

Daphne thought about her promise to stop by the restaurant and apply for the hostessing job. But there would still be plenty of time to do that after hanging with Luke, right? There was no reason she couldn't do both.

"No. No plans. Let's go."

CHAPTER FIVE
Irre(sis)tible

"Sam Milburn has the most amazing tongue!" Lynette Harkrider exclaimed, gazing upward as if she could see a little thought bubble with his image in it.

Eight other girls, including Daphne, leaned toward her as if she were magnetized.

"He's so cute!" Sheri Purnell said, emphasizing every word in her sentence.

Daphne thought Sam resembled a lizard too much to ever be considered good-looking. His eyes were so far apart, they were practically on the sides of his head, and he seemed almost hairless with his crew cut and sparse brows. Plus, like his reptilian brethren, he apparently had mad tongue skills. But she kept quiet. As a junior varsity cheerleader, Daphne had to defer to the varsity cheerleaders' superiority. And Lynette was the most alpha one of them all.

She wasn't even head cheerleader—that was Tricia Albright. But Lynette was the mouthiest and, according to public opinion, the prettiest. She had expertly styled honey-colored hair and skin that was a matching honey hue, and her daily makeup job was as elaborate as a Monet painting. Daphne didn't think Lynette was anywhere near as beautiful as Gabby; in fact, underneath all those dabs of color, Lynette was rather freckled and ordinary. But she did have the best legs of all the cheerleaders, and her painstaking morning routine probably should count for something. Thus, Lynette reigned as Queen Supreme at Barton High. And, of course, Gabby was too much of a sourpuss to seriously compete for the title.

"And he's got these killer abs," Lynette went on. "I mean, like, *underwear model* abs."

"Is he taking you to prom?" Tricia asked.

Lynette made a face as if it was the most absurd thing she'd ever heard. "No way. It's not serious or anything. We're just having sex."

Daphne stared at Lynette, with all her sultry confidence, and then studied the rest of the girls in her pre- and post-school hangout crowd. Being a cheerleader with a perky personality, she was part of the group by default, yet she often didn't feel like one of them. She tried to emulate their style, painting her nails the color of the month, wearing slinky tops from the accepted stores (which she often had to hide under sweaters around her mom and dad), flirting with the jocks, and subscribing to similar views on boys, fashion, and which celebrities were considered awesome and should be copied. She didn't have the years of gossip experience or the income bracket to be pitch-perfect, but she had managed to fake it so far. However, the one thing she never succeeded in adopting, or even credibly imitating, was their laid-back attitude toward sex.

Just sex, Lynette had said. *Not serious.*

But how could sex not be serious? How could taking off your clothes in front of a guy and letting him touch you all over *not* be serious? Lynette and the others made it sound like a game of checkers.

It wasn't as though Daphne were antisex. She loved it— or at least, she was pretty sure she would when she tried it. But to her it was something epic. Something that should be done on a deserted tropical beach or in a bedroom strewn with rose petals and lit by candles. Not in the dirt-strewn bed of a Dodge Ram or the auditorium's fusty-smelling costume loft, in full view of any cockroaches or theater tech geeks. She didn't want a cheap-sex kind of relationship. She wanted a guy who would look at her as if she was the most beautiful and amazing creature on the planet, who would pick her wildflowers and call her by a cute nickname and write her sweet little notes that he would tuck in secret places for her to find later. She wanted love—without all the smirks and cynicism. Real, unapologetic, romantic love.

Daphne's anxiety must have shown in her expression, because suddenly Lynette was looking straight at her, her eyebrows raised into two perfectly plucked semicircles.

"What about you, Daff? Who have you been messing around with?" she asked. Or rather, demanded.

"Um . . . no one right now," Daphne replied. Then she laughed. Not because it was funny—just to keep things light and make some extra noise.

"But isn't there someone you like?" Lynette went on, one eyebrow now higher than the other.

"Well, yeah . . ." Daphne hunched slightly.

"I bet it's the new guy," Rachelle Waverly said. "I saw her waving at him in the hall today."

"And Walt said they were totally flirting at Hawthorne's Barbecue," Sheri added.

Daphne just stood there, grinning stupidly, hoping that steam wasn't rising from her face. She hated that they were talking about her as if she weren't there. And she hated that they knew about her feelings for Luke. Not that it was a secret, necessarily, but there was no way they could understand how special her relationship with him was—or would be. She didn't want them to twist it and spoil it with their small talk.

"You mean Luke?" Lynette seemed completely reinvigorated with this news. "Oh, my god! He's, like, so preppy. I thought he was gay."

"He came from a prep school!" Daphne said, a little too quickly and loudly.

Lynette held out her hands in mock surrender. "My bad. Obviously you would know whether he was gay or not." She cracked up. The rest of the group started laughing hysterically.

Daphne giggled for the sake of solidarity, even though she didn't think it was funny. And frankly, she didn't really understand the comment.

"Look, there he is." Megan Denson pointed across the courtyard. Daphne's and seven other pairs of eyes followed her finger. Sure enough, there was Luke, standing next to the flagpole. He was rummaging through his backpack, pausing every now and then to glance around at the people scurrying past.

He's looking for me, Daphne suddenly realized. *He's pretending to be busy while looking for me.*

It was the sweetest thing ever.

"Mmm. He really is cute," Lynette said, making her voice low and provocative. "*So* glad to hear he likes women. If you're worried, Daff, I'd be happy to make sure."

Again the group of girls burst out laughing.

"Ha, ha. No, that's okay," Daphne said with a lame chuckle. "Ha, ha, ha."

"You should go talk to him, Daff," Rachelle said tauntingly.

Daphne couldn't help grinning. "Actually, we sort of have plans. So . . . bye, I guess! See y'all tomorrow!" She shouldered her book bag and walked away.

She knew they would continue to talk about her after she left, distorting her and Luke's special connection and making it into something crude. But she couldn't worry about that right now. Right now she was just dizzy with joy at the sight of him.

It was almost scary how Luke had become so important so quickly. To think that only a week earlier she'd been walking these school corridors, totally clueless about his existence. She'd eaten her meals without composing cute text messages in her head. And she'd lain in bed without wondering what he was doing and whether he was thinking of her, too.

This had to be true love. No other guy had ever made Daphne feel this way. All her other crushes had been stupid and babyish. But this felt real. Important, even—as if she were fated to be with Luke. She wouldn't be surprised if it was inscribed on an ancient scroll somewhere.

She crossed the courtyard in a few bounces and landed at his side. "Hi!" she said.

Luke looked up at her and smiled. "Hi."

"Whatcha looking for?" She pointed to his backpack.

"My cell phone." His forehead creased into a helpless expression. "It always ends up at the bottom."

She giggled. "You expecting a call?"

"Maybe. I don't know. It's not like I've met a lot of people so far." He grinned a rather sad, lopsided grin and Daphne instantly felt foolish. Why did she have to ask him such a stupid question?

"But I did have a nice call yesterday," he added, looking right at her and widening his smile.

Daphne's heart seemed to swell inside her like one of those sponge toys that pop into animal shapes when you add water. One adorable grin from Luke and *sproinggg!* Instant giraffe.

"Ah! Found it." He pulled a sleek smartphone out of his bag and held it up.

"Wow, that's a nice one!" Daphne exclaimed. She was suddenly aware of her own phone—a three-year-old hand-me-down from her dad in the front pocket of her messenger bag. It was practically two cans attached with a string. Everybody seemed to have nicer phones—nicer everything—than she did.

Luke's phone let out an electronic hip-hop tune as it powered up. "So let's go," he said, slipping it back into his pack. "Where is this place anyway?"

"Just follow me." She ambled in the direction of downtown, pulling him with her smile. Luke returned the grin and fell into step beside her.

"So does this place have root beer floats?" Luke asked as they crossed Jefferson Street toward the center of town. The chatter and traffic sounds of school dismissal had faded to a low drone.

"Yeah." Daphne's eyes swiveled up to the cloudy sky. "I mean . . . I think so. It's been a while since I've been there. But I'm pretty sure I've had one before. I think I've had one of everything. My dad used to take us all the time when he . . ." She paused. She had been about to say *when he lived with us* but decided not to. It sounded so pitiful. Plus, it still hurt to admit out loud that he'd left. ". . . when we were little," she concluded. That was better. She'd tell Luke the truth eventually, but not today. Today was going to be all about fun.

As they crossed the small footbridge over Chandler Creek, she caught sight of their dim reflection in the water below. There they were. The two of them. Side by side. Her big mass of dark tresses and red T-shirt, and his russet-colored hair and green button-down. The images were all wavy, almost dreamlike. Daphne hadn't even realized she was smiling until she saw her white teeth shining back at her on the rippling surface.

Luke stopped, rested his forearms on the wooden rail of the bridge, and gazed upstream. "Wow. This place is so cool," he said, gesturing toward the water, the live oaks on the shore, and the cluster of nineteenth-century storefronts on the street beyond. "Small but nice. Like Mayberry or something."

"It is," Daphne agreed. She'd never fully appreciated how

special her town was, but Luke was right. For some reason, it seemed extrapretty right now. She loved the way patches of light danced on the ripples below and the way the live oaks bowed reverently toward the water. Beyond the trees she could see the very tops of Main Street's buildings, with their dates of completion etched below their curvy rooflines: 1898. 1901. 1903. The smell of brisket from Hawthorne's Barbecue comingled with the scents of caliche and pecan buds and fresh grackle poop. There was even a sound track of local noise to go with the postcard-pretty scene: the trickling of the creek in its limestone bed, the whir of unseen cicadas, and the creaking of the weather vane atop the old, restored Grayson house, now used for the chamber of commerce.

"Hey, lookee here."

She looked at Luke and found him completely bent over. He picked something up off the worn planks and held it up between his thumb and forefinger. A tarnished penny.

"That's lucky," she remarked.

"For you," he said, holding it out to her.

Daphne glanced from Luke's aqua eyes to Lincoln's somber profile cushioned within his open hand. It was so sweet! Maybe even symbolic. Today a penny . . . Soon, a bouquet of flowers . . . And after that, on some beautiful day, perhaps in this very same spot, a promise ring . . .

"Thanks," she said. Her fingertips brushed against his palm as she took the coin, and a warm sensation skittered up her arm.

None of the other guys would do this. They never stopped to pick up pennies or take in the wonder of their surroundings. All they cared about were their trucks and the score of the latest football game. Once again Daphne had an overwhelming sense that this was significant—part of her personal history in the making. Someday she and Luke would be sitting on a porch, holding hands and watching the sunset, and Luke would say, "Remember the first time we went to Quick's Pharmacy?"

And the penny would be in a little frame hanging on their wall.

They started walking again, past the post office and the new white brick library that had been completed the summer before. Eventually they reached the limestone facade of Quick's Pharmacy.

"So this is it," she said, gesturing toward the large, curved display window. Inside, on a shelf covered in red felt, lay an assortment of products. Shaving cream, toothpaste, baby lotion, aspirin, shoe polish, cotton swabs, Wrigley's spearmint gum, and a Day-Glo green water pistol. Propped in the corner was the soda fountain menu. *Shake or malt (chocolate, vanilla, or strawberry) . . . $4.00! Brown cow . . . $3.00! Soda . . . $2.00! Alma's pimiento cheese sandwich . . . $4.50! Pie of the day . . . $3.50/slice!*

The door chimes tinkled as Daphne and Luke stepped from the sidewalk into the air-conditioned interior. They paused just inside the entrance, letting their eyes adjust to the dim light.

"This is awesome," Luke said.

"Yeah." Daphne took a deep breath of cold, stale-smelling air. She felt as if she were seeing the place for the first time, and she found herself gazing in wonder at the pressed-tin ceiling and the curvy chrome barstools at the nearby counter.

How was it that she'd never noticed how wonderful this place was before? So quaint and charming. The perfect backdrop for a classic romance.

They passed shelves stacked with hair products and headache remedies and sat down on two stools.

"Well, hello there, darlin'!" Mr. Mason emerged from behind a display of sewing notions and stepped through a wooden gate to the area behind the counter.

Daphne smiled. Gabby always hated when men called them darling or sweetheart or doll. She said it was sexist and demeaning. But Daphne liked it. She even thought it was polite, in an old-Southern-gentleman sort of way.

"Haven't seen you for a while now," Mr. Mason went on. "You sure are growing up fast. I hardly recognized you."

Daphne grinned and laughed. Ironically, she thought Mr. Mason hadn't changed at all. Perhaps his hair and trim beard were a little whiter, and his belly seemed to strain against the buttons of his checkered shirt a bit more, but otherwise he looked the same as he always had.

"What can I get y'all?" he asked.

"Um . . ." Daphne looked quizzically at Luke.

He shrugged. "How about some floats?"

"Maybe we could share one?" she suggested. "I'm not all that hungry."

It was a total lie. She was so hungry she could probably drink a whole one by herself. But she wanted to complete that traditional portrait: the two of them sitting together with the soda glass between them, their bodies making the shape of a heart as they bent forward to sip from their straws.

"Okay. Uh . . . one root beer float, please," Luke said.

"With two straws," Daphne added, swiveling back and forth on her stool.

"Coming right up." Mr. Mason gave a quick nod and then headed for the soda machine at the opposite end of the counter.

Daphne looked over at Luke and smiled. He smiled back—not a stiff, awkward one or a cocky smirk, but a warm, gentle one. A *real* smile. Her left tennis shoe tapped against the railing at the base of the bar. It was tough to keep still while her insides seemed to be doing one of her cheer routines, the hard one with all the flips and the pyramid building. She wondered if Luke was feeling it too—this sense that Fate was in play, that powerful forces were nudging them together. Of course he felt it. How could he not?

All of a sudden the sound of muffled hip-hop music welled up close by. It seemed inappropriate for the setting, wrecking the illusion that they'd tiptoed back in time.

Luke rummaged in his backpack and pulled out his phone, silencing it with a finger tap. "Hello?" he said, pressing it to his ear. He turned on his stool so that he faced the back of the store. "No. Just grabbing a snack . . . Oh, yeah. Sure . . . Okay. See you in a sec." He lowered his hand and tossed the phone back into his bag. "I've got to go," he said, swiveling back toward Daphne.

"What? Why?" Daphne winced at the whine in her voice, but she couldn't help it. Things had been so perfect, and now this.

"I'm stupid. I just totally forgot I was supposed to do something with the guys. Could we . . . try this again sometime?"

His eyes were so droopy and sorrowful, she couldn't help

feeling a little better. Besides, he wanted to meet up with her again. That couldn't be bad.

"Sure," she said, making herself grin.

"Here." He fished a wad of bills out of his front pocket and placed a ten on the countertop.

"But that's too much," she protested.

Luke waved his hand as if erasing her words. "Don't worry about it. Just take it."

"All right."

"Okay then . . ." Luke slid off his stool and draped his pack over his right shoulder. He paused, awkwardly shifting his weight from foot to foot. Was he going to kiss her?

She leaned forward slightly and lifted her chin, correcting the flight path between his lips and hers. But to her disappointment, he extended his right hand. A handshake?

Of course. She supposed it was proper for a first date at a soda fountain.

She managed a flimsy smile and slipped her palm into his grasp. Only instead of pumping it up and down, he simply held it. Then he slowly pulled her toward him and pressed his mouth to her forehead. At first Daphne was disappointed. It seemed odd—like a kiss her dad would give her. But as his lips lingered against her skin, she shut her eyes and enjoyed the feel of it. It was romantic, even, in an old-fashioned way. Conservative, but full of the promise of something bigger later.

After a while his hand and lips let go. Daphne opened her eyes, hoping to catch a smile on his face, but he was already heading out the door. She watched him stride down the sidewalk. The spot where he'd kissed her tickled a bit, as if it were giving off sparks, and she wondered if it could have left a mark, like Harry Potter's scar or the glittery bubble shape made when Glinda kissed Dorothy.

"Here you go!"

A frosty glass suddenly appeared in front of her. Mr. Mason plopped a straw into either side of the float, said, "Y'all enjoy it now," and ambled off toward the back.

Daphne pulled out one of the straws and licked off the ice cream before setting it down on the counter. Then she twirled around on the stool, sipping from the remaining straw.

She had too many emotions inside her, all scampering about and wrestling each other. The excitement over the kiss . . . The regret that he had to go . . . The joy that came with things like root beer floats and lucky pennies . . . But mainly she just felt restless. She was ready to officially start her happily-ever-after with Luke.

She could already see it. He would walk her to and from her classes, carrying her books the whole way, and all the girls in school would envy her. He'd invite her over to meet his mother and watch *Jane Eyre* on TV. He'd meet her dad and the two of them would become like father and son. Then her dad would come visit more often and maybe even move back to town.

He was her handsome prince who had come to rescue her from her dreary, ordinary life. The only one who saw how special she really was. Just like Cinderella, but without the magical ball.

She whirled around on the stool and sat leaning against

the bar, kicking her feet out in front of her. Through the window she could see Mrs. Plata sweeping the sidewalk in front of the gift shop. Next door was Shelly's Boutique, with its strangely posed mannequins and tinted lighting. In the corner of the display window stood a piece of posterboard with the word PROM! in iridescent orange letters. . . . And next to that stood a mannequin wearing the most beautiful dress Daphne had ever seen. Bright pink—the same shade as cotton candy and teacup roses and kissable lips. The color of romance and all things feminine. *Her* color.

Daphne's mouth let go of the straw and curled into a wide grin.

Maybe there *would* be a magical ball after all.

"Yes, hi. Do you still have the apartment available? The one advertised online last Sunday? No? Well, do you have anything else? I see. Thanks anyway."

Gabby hung up her cell phone and glanced back down at the page of For Rent ads she'd printed that morning, neatly folded and dotted here and there with circles she'd drawn in red Sharpie. Picking up her pen, she drew an X through the two-bedroom, two-bath condo off 290. That made four noes—if you didn't count the guy who'd seemed drunk and kept asking what kind of shoes she had on; she'd no'd that one, too. Now her only hope was to wrangle a raise out of Mr. Pinkwater when he got back from his dinner break. And "hope" and "Pinkwater" rarely belonged in the same sentence.

Gabby's face stretched in an enormous yawn. All these

late nights trying to improve her calculus and physics grades were starting to add up, making her feel weary and headachy. She let out a long, defeated sigh and fell forward, resting her head on the counter. This was one reason she preferred manning the ticket window to selling concessions. Because of the set movie times, all the work came in waves, allowing her a break between features. Plus, it gave her a clear view of the parking lot so she could see when Pinkwater returned. Which shouldn't be for another fifteen minutes. Giving her an opportunity to rest her eyes . . .

A sharp rapping sound jolted her upright. Gabby blinked rapidly, trying to refocus on her surroundings. Gradually, a figure came into view. Someone was standing just outside the glass partition. Tall. Broad-shouldered. Eyes the same color as the bottle of glass cleaner in the corner of the booth. Prentiss Applewhite. The town's iconic rich boy . . . and the reason Sonny Hutchins was dead.

Again Gabby felt that ache in the exact center of her body, like the ghost pain of a missing vital organ. Prentiss freaking Applewhite was standing just a few inches away, looking at her. No, *grinning* at her. As if he didn't have a care in the world. As if his presence, in and of itself, was a reason to rejoice.

But of course he'd feel that way. He had never had to pay for driving drunk and killing his cousin. His powerful family had stepped in to rescue him, as usual. They actually had the gall to go along with rumors that Sonny was the one driving when everyone knew it had to have been Prentiss on one of his drunken sprees. The Applewhites' fairy-tale version even made it into the newspaper, such was their power. Some said they had paid people off. Whatever they'd done, it worked. As far as Gabby knew, Prentiss was never jailed or sentenced to pick up trash or even issued a ticket. Apparently laws didn't apply to rich people. So in Prentiss's mind he was perfect, and he probably assumed she thought the same.

"Hi there," he said. He grinned at her, showing off flawlessly straight white—and no doubt expensive—teeth. The guy was incredibly handsome in that standard sort of way. Dazzling smile. Big, dopey-looking blue eyes. Short blond hair in some sort of hip, messy-on-purpose style, with bangs that stuck up like a fish fin. And the most ridiculously chiseled jaw. He was like a cartoon hunk come to life.

Even before the accident the town's residents loved to talk about him. He and his family lived in a gigantic Victorian at the end of Elmhurst Drive, one of the nicest homes in the town, if not the whole county. Because the Applewhites deemed Barton schools not good enough for their precious son and sent him to some Episcopal academy in Austin, Prentiss sightings had always been limited to holidays, summertime, and occasional weekends. Gabby had only seen him a few times herself after the accident, driving around in his candy-apple-red Mustang (which was, surprisingly, still intact). But he'd hardly been spotted at all since he'd started at the University of Texas last fall.

So what was he doing there on a weekday? Didn't he have classes?

Most likely he was skipping. Since being in one of the town's wealthiest families gave him something like diplomatic immunity, Prentiss probably assumed a college degree was automatic, whether he went to class or not.

"Can I help you?" she asked through a tightly clenched smile.

"I don't know . . . ," he said, his voice trailing off as he turned to peruse the Now Showing! movie ads along the brick wall of the cinema.

He didn't know? Then why the hell had he bothered to knock?

Gabby impatiently tapped her pen against the counter, fighting the urge to spray him with glass cleaner through the tiny cutout hole. Meanwhile, Prentiss rocked on the heels of his Tony Lamas as he scanned the posters, completely disregarding the fact that he was wasting her time.

Oh, come on. It wasn't as though they were great art. One, for a romantic schmaltzfest that Daphne had already seen twice called *Love, Lorna*, featured a tearstained letter in soft-focus. The next, which basically showed a pile of bloody body parts, was for a horror flick called *Writhe*. But the one Gabby hated the most was for the new movie that had just opened a couple of days ago. It depicted a stoic muscleman holding a machine gun while a leggy redhead sidled up against him. Snippets of reviews stood out in all-caps lettering across the top, with phrases like "HIGH-OCTANE!"—as if a film could fuel a pickup truck.

"So what's good?" Prentiss said suddenly, turning to face her.

Gabby frowned. "You're asking me what you should see?"

"I feel like a movie, but I'm bumfuzzled as to which one. You work here, right?"

"Obviously."

"Well then, I figure you can recommend a good flick."

"*The Godfather* is very good. You can even watch it from your home entertainment system. At home."

Prentiss laughed. "I guess. But I kind of want the live theater experience. Surround sound. Popcorn. Surely you're at least a little familiar with these here options." He smiled wide, revealing his pearly teeth. "So what do you like?"

Gabby folded her arms over her chest. "Giving recommendations is not part of my job."

"I suppose. But you could try to sell me on something. It probably wouldn't hurt." He continued to grin at her, as if she were some sassy court jester sent to amuse His Highness. "I mean, you do want my business, don't you?"

"Frankly, it doesn't matter to me whether you come in here or not. And anyway, they all suck. . . ." At that moment, Gabby noticed movement just past Prentiss's left shoulder. Mr. Pinkwater's gold Buick was pulling into its spot in the front row. "But . . . I guess if you really want a suggestion, you might like *Rules of War*. It's supposed to be very"—she swallowed—"high-octane."

"Cool. Give me one ticket, please."

"Just one?"

He flashed another gleaming grin. "That depends. Would they let you come see it with me?"

Gabby could feel the blood percolating in her cheeks. She'd been surprised, that was all. She'd assumed he'd be meeting some giggly, jiggly thing with too much makeup. Only now he probably thought she wanted to check out the backseat of his Mustang.

"No. No . . . ," she stammered, wondering if she should try to explain.

"Aw, too bad. Then just one." He slid a twenty-dollar bill into the tray at the bottom of the partition.

Her face still steaming, Gabby made his change and pressed the button for the ticket. "Thankyouverymuch. Theater'sonyourleft," she said without making further eye contact. She was having a bad enough day without some tanned sociopath thinking she was melting under his smile. How could someone like him even be related to Sonny?

"Thanks for your help," Prentiss said.

"Uh-huh," she replied, still not glancing up. Instead, she concentrated on reorganizing the cash drawer.

"Hope you have a nice day," he went on.

"Mmm," she grunted as she straightened the stack of credit card receipts.

For several seconds he remained standing in front of her, either waiting for the usual squealing and panty throwing he got from local girls or to double-check that she'd handed him the right amount of money—she wasn't sure since she wouldn't look up. Eventually his shadow moved off, reexposing the setting sun behind him, and she could hear his cowboy boots clomping toward the entrance.

She had a minute and a half to feel relieved, and then Mr. Pinkwater's stooped form shuffled into view, heading for the doors of the cinema.

"Mr. Pinkwater?" she called out. Unfortunately, he didn't hear her and stepped through the entrance, the sparse fluff on his bald head flying upward as he passed under the AC vent.

Gabby groaned. Just her luck. Now she had to leave her post if she wanted to speak to him. For an old guy, he sure moved fast.

She could remember first meeting Mr. Pinkwater when she was little and her dad had brought her and Daphne to the movies. She'd thought he was ancient then, and that had been over a decade ago. She had no clue what his actual age was, but she wouldn't have been shocked to discover it was in the triple digits.

Mule's hypothesis was that Pinkwater had actually died sometime near the turn of the millennium but just kept on working as a zombie. Not a bad theory, since he did have snaggly teeth and crepey, mildewy-looking skin that hung over his eyes and gathered in loose folds around his neck— and he did like to show the horror flicks. But Gabby doubted there were enough people with actual brains in Barton to sustain a real zombie.

She leaned the BE BACK SOON! sign against the window, stepped out the rear door of the ticket booth, and fell into step behind Mr. Pinkwater as he lurched across the lobby.

Lila, her loud, twentysomething coworker, was stretched across the candy counter in a cleavage-baring pose talking to Prentiss. As soon as she saw her boss, she quickly stood up straight and smoothed the front of her red polyester uniform.

Gabby caught up with Pinkwater at the door to his office. "Mr. Pinkwater? Could I speak with you for a second?"

His bleary eyes found hers. He looked inordinately shocked, as if he couldn't understand what language she was speaking or even fathom what type of creature she was. "I suppose," he said eventually, starting the sentence with a sigh. "Come inside."

It took a couple of minutes for him to unlock his office, set down his briefcase, and settle into the leather chair that looked as cracked and ancient as he did. Meanwhile, Gabby stood patiently in front of his desk. She stared down into a cut-glass candy dish piled high with petrified peppermints and butterscotches, no doubt the very same mass of sweets that had been sitting in that bowl on the day he'd hired her— three years ago. It was a bad sign. Proof that Pinkwater had rarely asked people into his office for happy reasons, like raises and promotions.

Mr. Pinkwater looked over at her and frowned. "Have a seat," he said, gesturing toward a square metal and vinyl chair that had been shoved carelessly into the corner. As Gabby pulled it over to face his desk, she noted that the seat and armrests were covered with a fine layer of dust. Even more proof of Pinkwater's bah-humbug, don't-bother-me nature. While he busied himself with some papers, she snatched a Kleenex from a box on the desk and wiped off the cushion before settling onto it.

Gabby glanced at the clock on the wall above Mr. Pinkwater's shiny head and realized that her sister was probably applying for the hostess job that very moment. Hopefully she'd get it—if she had even remembered to show up, of course. Gabby closed her eyes and sent out a cosmic plea that Daphne wasn't doing anything stupid during the interview, like smacking gum or texting her latest guy obsession. *Please don't let her start doing cheers when they ask about her experience,* she urged the forces of the universe.

Then again, knowing the way things were, probably all Daphne had to do was smile and bounce and she'd get the job.

Eventually Pinkwater finished messing with his files and looked up at Gabby. "Now then," he said, his chair letting out a crackling sound as he leaned forward. "What's so important that you are leaving the theater short-staffed for almost five minutes?"

Gabby bit the inside of her cheek to prevent herself from pointing out that *he* had kept *her* waiting.

"I was wondering . . . since I've worked here for a few years now . . . and I think I do a pretty good job . . . would it be possible for me to get . . ." She met his eyes—two glints of blue ice amid all that saggy flesh—and swallowed hard. ". . . a small raise?"

Mr. Pinkwater started shaking his head the second she stopped talking. "No, no. That's just not possible."

She'd been expecting this answer, but it still bothered her that he couldn't even pretend to think it over. "Why not?"

His brows rose, lifting mounds of skin so that his upper lashes were actually visible, and the craggy slits of his eyes regarded her for a long moment. Obviously no one had ever questioned him like this before. Gabby started to panic, worried that he might get angry enough to fire her. Then she'd really have failed her mom.

"It's my policy," he replied. "Yes, you've worked here a good while—longer than most. And yes, you do good work. But you'll be going off to college in less than a year, right?"

"Well . . . yes. I mean, I hope so."

"You see? I lose most of my teenaged employees after three years, tops. I've got to save raises for the people who stick around. People with families."

"But I'm trying to help my family."

"Yes, yes. I know cell phone bills can be big. But there's nothing I can do. Maybe if you young people spend less time texting, you'll find yourself with more money. You should learn that before you go off to college."

"But that's not . . . I don't . . ." Gabby pursed her lips and inhaled deeply through her nose, trying to cool the inferno raging inside her.

It was the stupidest of reasons. She was being denied a raise because she was smart and determined enough to go to college? Because Pinkwater thought all teens were irresponsible? She wanted to help with food and rent, not waste money on expensive clothes or the latest gaming system!

Only now it was too late. Mr. Pinkwater was already back on his feet and trundling toward the door. Judging by the steep curve of his frown, there would be no further explanation or second thoughts. She knew she'd already pushed things as far as she could with him.

"Thank you, sir. For . . . listening," she said as she stepped back into the glare of the lobby.

He waved away her words with a big mottled claw of a hand. "Yes, yes. Get back to work now," he said before shutting the door.

Gabby clenched her teeth and fists. Creepy old velociraptor! Normally she respected Mr. Pinkwater. He wasn't exactly likeable, but at least he wasn't calling her sugar and making chitchat about the football team like all the other shop-keepers in town. Right now, though, she wanted to string him up by his scaly hide and hang him next to the giant inflated hot dog above the snack bar.

She spun around angrily and nearly collided with Pren-tiss, who had walked up behind her for some stupid reason.

"Whoa!" he exclaimed, rearing back slightly. His right hand held a jumbo bucket overflowing with popcorn—obviously the work of Lila, who was known to short cups and cartons by a centimeter if she *didn't* like someone. "What's up? Bad day?"

He was still wearing a big doofus grin, as if everything around him were happening for his own amusement. As if nothing could ever go wrong. And even if something did—like a drunken joyride that caused a pesky car crash and ended someone's life—then Mommy and Daddy and all his fawning sycophants would step in to make it better.

This was a guy who would never have to work hard. A guy who had no idea what it was like to feel real frustration or disappointment or guilt.

Suddenly all the anger she felt toward Pinkwater shifted onto Prentiss, and if she hadn't been absolutely certain it would cost her her job, she would have punched him in his perfect-right-triangle nose.

"Excuse me," she muttered, and scurried past him to the box office before he could ask her which theater seat she rec-ommended he sit in.

Oh, it was a bad day, all right. One of the worst. As if

some archnemesis were sticking pins in her voodoo doll likeness. She had failed with apartment managers and she had failed with her boss. And the only person willing to talk to her was the most morally reprehensible guy in Barton.

Once she reached the snug safety and quiet of the ticket booth, Gabby rested her head on her hands and gazed out the partition glass, trying to clear her mind of Pinkwater's scowling face and Prentiss's idiotic grin.

Across the parking lot, a girl was strolling down the sidewalk of Bowie Street. Maybe it was the tilt of the head and the goofy half smile on her face. Or maybe it was the slow, twisted way she was walking with a gigantic plastic-wrapped garment slung over her shoulder. But something made Gabby fix on the girl and recognize her as Daphne.

And something else—perhaps the fact that she was two miles away from the Lucky Wishbone restaurant, ambling at the pace of a drunk snail—told Gabby that her sister, once again, had forgotten to apply for the hostess job.

The bad day had just gotten worse.

CHAPTER SIX
Narcis(sis)m

Daphne slowly turned the knob and eased the front door open a couple of inches. The living room was empty, and she could hear muffled voices coming from her mom's bedroom. If she was quick and quiet, she could make it.

· She widened the gap enough to slide inside, careful not to push it open to the angle where the hinges creaked and making sure her plastic-swathed dress didn't snag on the scuffed wood. Then she silently shut the door and tiptoed to her room. The plastic rustled a bit and the floor let out a faint moan when she stepped into the hallway, but otherwise she made no sound.

There, she thought as she opened her side of the closet and hung the dress on the far end of the rod. It gleamed slightly in the half-light like a gold nugget in a pan of pebbles, and she wondered if Gabby would notice. No, she decided. Gabby didn't even seem to take stock of her own clothes. Why would she go through Daphne's?

She slid the door shut, spun around, and instantly let out

a squeal of surprise. Gabby was standing in the doorway to their room.

"So you're home," she said. Her wavy hair hung down around her shoulders, free of its usual clips and elastics. She looked pretty but stony. Like a Roman statue. "*Please* tell me you applied for that job."

Daphne was prepared for this. Her mouth curved in a weak grin and she wrinkled her forehead apologetically. Now, what was it she was going to say? Something about after-school tutoring?

"I knew it!" Gabby exclaimed, before Daphne had a chance to launch into her rehearsed explanation. "So what's your excuse this time, huh? That you had to *buy a dress?*"

A prickly feeling spread over Daphne, like a sudden rash. "How did you . . . ?"

"It doesn't matter. What matters is that you let us down—again. Do you care that we're in dire straits and Mom needs all the help we can give?"

"Of course I care."

"Then why won't you go find a job? And why are you out spending money on stupid things? Please don't tell me you charged that dress."

"No! She let me put it on a tab or whatever. I'm supposed to go pay it tomorrow. And don't look at me that way. I'm going to use the money Grandma left me."

Gabby's eyes and mouth widened in a look of horror. "How could you do that at a time like this? What if we need that money for an emergency?"

"It's my money."

"It's *our* house. It's our well-being. God! It's like you don't care about anyone but yourself."

"Shut up!" Daphne pressed her hands over her ears. "Shut up! Shut up! *Shut up!*" It was so unfair. She'd had one of the best afternoons of her whole life and her sister was determined to ruin it.

"Girls! What on earth is going on here?" Great. Now Mom was swooping into the room, as usual. Like some wide-eyed, frowny superhero.

"More of the same," Gabby said. "Daffy is going daffy over some guy again. What else is new?"

"Leave me alone! You're just jealous because I found someone special."

Gabby rolled her eyes and made a huffing sound. "Please! You've just met the guy. How can you even know that he's *so special?*" She uttered the final two words in the breathy voice of a total ditz while waving her hands in the air.

"Because! I just do!" Daphne yelled. She quickly tried to think of some evidence to back up her claim. "He's . . . different. He's sweet. He reads Brontë and—"

Gabby started laughing. "Oh, my god. You are falling for a guy because you like the same *books?* If that's the best basis for a relationship, you should date Mrs. Shropshire down the street. She has stacks of paperback romances all over the floor of her living room."

"What do you know?" Daphne was really screaming now. Her throat felt warm and raw. "When did you ever even have a boyfriend? Real guys won't even come near you!"

"Girls, stop! I've had enough of this!"

Daphne pointed at her sister. "It's her fault! She jumped all over me for no reason! She thinks she's the one in charge but she's not—you are."

Mrs. Rivera studied her for a moment and then nodded. "You're right. Gabby, you really should let me handle things," she said. But before Daphne had a chance to look triumphant, her mom added, "Although she does have a point, sweetheart. You really do tend to lose your head over these boys."

"No! It's not like that. This time it's different. Why do you always have to take her side?"

"I'm not taking her side. I just don't want to see you get hurt."

"Now who's jumping to conclusions? You've never even seen him and already you think he's a jerk?"

"It's not that, honey. I've lived longer. I know more about men. . . . Boys . . ." Her mom seemed to be struggling to find the right word. ". . . Relationships."

She reached out and placed a hand on the back of Daphne's head, stroking her hair. It seemed more condescending than tender, the same gesture a preschool teacher would use with a sad four-year-old. Daphne's teeth clenched. It was more proof that they saw her as a baby.

"Real life, real *love*, isn't the way you see it in movies or read about in books," her mom went on. "I hate to see you risk yourself like this. I just wish you'd be more . . . sensible."

"Sensible." It was one of those words Daphne hated. Something she apparently wasn't—along with being "responsible" or "mature." "Sensible," she repeated, considering the term. The opposite would be "foolish," right? "Silly." "Idiotic." "Stupid."

"Do you mean sensible like Gabby, who's never even been on a real date? Or sensible like you, who couldn't make her marriage work?"

Gabby sucked in her breath. "Who the hell do you think you are? You can't say that to Mom! Say you're sorry! Say you're sorry *right now!*"

Daphne already felt bad. She knew she was hitting below the belt. But she couldn't help it. She wanted them to take her seriously. To realize that her feelings for Luke were real and special.

She glanced over at her mom, expecting to see her looking shocked or hurt. Instead, she just seemed really tired—as always. For some reason, this made Daphne feel even more angry and desperate. They weren't going to pull her down into their gloom. She wouldn't let it happen.

"I'm sick of you both telling me what to think and feel!" she said in a shaky voice. "Maybe I don't know anything, but you don't either! You're just . . . hypocrites!"

"You don't get to judge Mom!" Gabby's face had turned a deep red and her eyes flashed through thin slits. "Mom was just trying to *help* you! She was trying to stop you from embarrassing yourself over some redneck who thinks he can read!"

"Girls . . ."

Daphne shook her head. "Well, I don't want y'all's help! You guys are just sad and mean! I don't want to be like you!"

"Girls, *please!*"

"Fine! Keep on being you! Keep on being thoughtless and ungrateful!"

"You always think you know everything, but you don't!"

"And you think the world is just one big passionate drama and you're the star!"

"At least I'm not a cold bitch!"

"Stop it right now!" The tremor in her mother's voice made Daphne stop and stare at her. Now she looked sad as well as tired. Pink splotches had appeared on her nose and around her tear-filled eyes. "We can't treat each other this way," she said hoarsely. "I can't take it."

Daphne was used to the sighs and the pleading and the helpless glances at the ceiling. But sobbing? This was new— or rather, something she hadn't seen since the first few months after the divorce. It scared her, and she couldn't help feeling a rush of guilt.

"I'm sorry, Mommy. I didn't mean it."

Mrs. Rivera dabbed her eyes with the back of her right hand. "I know, sweetie. It's okay. Now please, apologize to each other." She set a hand on each of their shoulders and gently pushed them toward one another.

Gabby was the first to react. "Sorry," she said, stepping forward. "I shouldn't have been so bossy."

Maybe it was the flat tone of Gabby's voice, or the way she kept her chin raised at a snottier-than-thou angle, but Daphne was unmoved. She crossed her fingers and used them to push some hair out of her face as she mumbled, "Sorry too." All the while she kept her eyes on Gabby's, daring her to restart the fight by complaining.

She knew it was a babyish thing to do, but so what? They already thought of her as a baby. She had nothing to lose.

"Here's a proposition," Gabby said, pinning the phone against her shoulder with her chin as she pulled all the cereal bowls out of the dishwasher. "You always say it sucks to be an only child, so . . . I'll give you a sister at a low cost. No, make that free. Hell, *I'll* pay *you* to take her away from here. How about that?"

"Hmm. Does she know how to do an open C chord on a Stratocaster?"

She could hear some off-key strumming in the background. Lately Mule had been inspired to learn guitar but was upset to find that it wasn't as easy as it was on the virtual rock band video games.

"Can't say that she does," Gabby replied.

"Then no. Sorry. Not interested."

Gabby stacked all the bowls in the cupboard before speaking again. "So did you notice that technically I'm not complaining? That I'm not burdening you with the sordid tales of my evening here?"

"I did notice. Although I can tell you really want me to ask what happened."

"You don't have to," she lied. "This is a new goal of mine. I'm going to stop unloading on you all the time."

"Can I just ask if it's over? Has your sordid tale reached some sort of resolution?"

Gabby pushed herself onto the counter and held the phone with her hand again. "Well . . . kind of. We made up— in a way. But can you believe Daphne actually crossed her fingers when Mom asked her to apologize? Like a first grader! I swear, it's useless for us to even talk. It's like, no matter what, she just can't be grown-up about stuff."

"So . . . maybe *you* should?"

Gabby frowned. "Should what?"

"Be the grown-up."

"What are you talking about?"

"I'm just saying maybe you should keep on being the responsible one. Make peace—even if you're right and she's wrong. I mean . . . if you really want to help your mom and stuff. You said she's been stressed."

As much as she wanted sympathy, as much as she would have loved for him to join her in her outrage, Gabby had to admit he had a point.

Mule was always better at long algebraic equations. He could always spot solutions when she got hung up on the steps. In a similar way, he was good at sorting through the details of her life to get at the big picture.

And this skill—both of them, actually—was why she kept Mule around.

Gabby had been standing in the doorway of their bedroom for two whole minutes and still Daphne hadn't noticed her. She was sitting up against her headboard with her right thumbnail in her mouth, staring at some invisible point in the middle of the room. It was annoying, but also kind of amazing how Daphne could completely disappear into her thoughts. *Must be nice.*

Eventually Daphne became aware of her presence.

"What are you doing here?" she asked, narrowing her eyes.

"I was wondering . . ." Gabby took a breath and forced the words up out of her. "Could I see your dress?"

Daphne studied Gabby suspiciously. "Why?"

"I'm just curious. That's all."

She watched as Daphne's features slowly softened. "I guess." Her sister bounced up from the bed and over to the closet; then she reached into its depths and pulled out the plastic-sheathed garment. "Isn't it beautiful?" she said, holding the hanger up next to her collarbone.

Gabby stepped forward for a closer look and immediately froze. It was the dress in the window, the horrendous one she and Mule had made fun of. Sweetheart neckline. Layers and layers of skirt. The same shade of pink as a plastic flamingo lawn ornament.

But of course Daphne would love it. It was the kind of dress you'd see on the cover of a cheap romance novel. All she needed was to stand on a cliff with some muscleman's arms around her and the wind blowing her hair back into a billowy cloud.

"It's very . . ." Gabby fumbled for the right thing to say. ". . . romantic."

Daphne's face beamed so brightly and so fast, she practically made the same *ping!* noise as the computer when it sparked up. "Want to see it on?" she asked.

"Um . . ." Gabby wanted to say no and make a quick excuse about homework. But she knew it would sound lame. Besides, Daphne looked so wide-eyed and happy-hopeful— the exact same expression she woke Gabby up with on Christmas mornings when they were young. "Sure."

Daphne wriggled out of her school clothes at amazing speed. Then she carefully pulled off the plastic, unhooked the dress from the hanger, and stepped into it. "Could you zip me?" she asked, pointing to her back.

As soon as Gabby zipped her in, Daphne whirled about and struck a pose. "Well? What do you think?" she asked, grabbing hold of the skirt and swishing from side to side.

Gabby felt a tug of envy. Every day she told herself she wasn't jealous of her sister, but she was. Majorly. The girl was just so effortlessly adorable. All big brown eyes, broad smile, and dimples. And when she grinned really wide, her two dimples actually turned into four. *Four!* Even her dimples had dimples. Plus, she was just so cute and bouncy. Bouncy hair, a bouncy-sounding laugh, a bouncy frame—and two bouncy round globes that no guy could keep his eyes off of.

Gabby hated that this bothered her, but it did. She knew that in the Great Scheme of Things it was no big deal that she was a B-cup with room to spare while Daphne busted out of Ds. The logical side of her could fill a spiral notebook with reasons why her chest size wasn't important—and was even preferable in some situations (like distance running—which, unfortunately, she didn't do). But then they'd go someplace like the local pool and Gabby would feel like a drab twig next to her jiggly sister, and suddenly it all mattered. The inequality of their genetics. The way the lifeguard would lend Daphne money when she didn't have enough for the soda machine.

Just more proof that no matter how hard Gabby worked, Daphne would continue to have things easier in life.

"You look . . . amazing," Gabby replied truthfully.

"Thanks!" Daphne's eyes seemed to increase their wattage. "Oh, and look. I also bought this." She held up a small see-through jar full of silvery flecks.

"What is that?"

"Body glitter. Isn't it pretty? And don't give me that look. It was only a few dollars."

Gabby hadn't realized she was making a face. "What's it for?" she asked, trying to appear neutral.

"I'm going to put a little around my collarbone and maybe dab some on my temples. I just thought it would make it seem more . . . what's the word?"

"Las Vegas showgirl?"

"No!" Daphne laughed. "More *magical*. Doesn't this stuff remind you of pixie dust?"

"I guess." Gabby always thought Daphne had overdosed on fairy tales as a kid.

Daphne flounced to the mirror over the dresser and ran her fingers through her long, silky tresses. "Do you think I should wear my hair up? Or keep it down?"

"Up." Gabby was amazed to hear herself answer so quickly and decisively. But she always did think Daphne looked good with her hair pulled away from her face. It made her seem more sophisticated.

"Okay." Daphne flashed her a grateful smile. She lifted her mass of dark, shiny hair into a loose bun and studied her image in the mirror.

Gabby sat down on her bed and watched her sister. Strange that her opinion would mean so much to Daphne—especially since Gabby had never been to prom, or even been asked. No big tragedy, since she didn't want to go. Still, the fact that her thoughts mattered to her sister made her feel good for some reason. And she appreciated that Daphne wasn't holding a grudge from their fight. The girl was quick to cry over stuff, but she was also quick to forgive, something Gabby found incredibly hard to do.

She decided to continue being big about things and show some real interest. "So what about your shoes?" she asked.

"I've got those silver heels from when we went to Tía Olivia's wedding," Daphne replied, still staring dreamily at her reflection. "And I'm hoping Mom will let me wear some of Grandma's antique jewelry." She turned her head from side to side, as if imagining a pair of earrings dangling from her lobes.

"Do you think Luke will take you someplace fancy for dinner?" Gabby asked.

Daphne's shoulders hunched and her gaze drifted down to the top of the dresser, as if she were suddenly unable to look herself in the eye. "I don't really know. I hope so," she said. Her pitch was higher and the words took on a singsong quality, like someone *trying* to sound casual.

Gabby sensed deception. "So tell me," she went on, hoping to gather more clues. "How did Luke ask you to prom? Was he all romantic?"

Daphne let go of her hair and stuck the first two fingernails of her right hand between her teeth.

"Daphne?" Gabby repeated, adding a warning edge to her voice. She knew she was supposed to be acting supportive, but it was too strong an instinct. She had to trap Daphne, catch her, make her submit. It was the natural order. "What's wrong?"

"It's just . . . he hasn't exactly asked me yet."

"What?"

"But he will. I'm sure. He just needs...the right opportunity."

"Wait a minute. Let me get this straight," Gabby said. "You spent all that money on a dress—money we need to live on—*and you don't even have a date yet?*"

Daphne shrugged. "So?"

That did it. That one word, spoken with all the petulance of a bratty six-year-old, eradicated any residual warmth toward her little sister.

"God! I just don't get you. You know Mom needs that money, but you go spend it on some tacky dress you'll only wear once!"

Daphne looked as if she'd been slapped. "You said you liked it."

"Forget the stupid dress! We're in a real financial crisis here. Why can't you be more considerate?"

"You mean like you?" Daphne's skirt rustled as she stomped over to her bed and sat down, sounding as if she were tramping through a pile of leaves.

"Yes, like me! I work hard and give most of the money to Mom. And I still do more chores around here than you do. You don't seem to care about anyone but yourself."

"Neither do you! Here I thought you were being my friend. But you're never nice on purpose. You were just trying to trick me so you could yell some more. Why can't you just be a normal big sister? Why do you have to hate me?"

Gabby opened her mouth to say something...and let it hang there. The thing was, Daphne was right. Not about

Gabby deliberately tricking her, but about everything else. She was only pretending to be interested in the dress. She *had* lied. And she didn't exactly hate Daphne, but she did hate spending time with her. When they were together, they were either fighting or ignoring each other.

She was never purposely nice to Daphne. She never wanted her around.

"Fine!" Daphne yelled when it became clear that Gabby had no response. "Then I hate you, too! I wish you weren't my sister. I wish I could divorce you like Dad did Mom!"

Gabby stood motionless as Daphne swished out of the room. A second later she could hear the bathroom door slam.

Maybe it wasn't the fact that Daphne wanted to live in a fairy tale that bothered her. Maybe it was the fact that she kind of was living in one.

And Gabby was the evil villain.

CHAPTER SEVEN
Analy(sis)

Daphne sat cross-legged in the recliner with her green spiral notebook in her lap. She'd started out doing some overdue homework for Ms. Manbeck, which had turned into a big doodle session, which had then turned into a series of dress sketches. Wedding dresses, to be precise. For her wedding. To Luke.

Of course, she knew she wouldn't be walking down the aisle anytime soon. She and Luke would first have to finish high school and then college. Their love and the promise of a life together would spur them on through those long nights of studying and tough, penny-pinching times. Their dates would be economical yet romantic: Picnics in the park, where, while munching ramen noodle salad, they'd watch the children play and brainstorm what to name their own kids. Long walks during which they'd pick out houses they'd someday like to live in. Rented rom-coms or evenings when they simply read poetry to each other. Although they had years to go before their spring garden wedding with the string quartet and mermaid ice sculpture, there was no harm in being prepared with a good dress design, right?

For the past twenty-four hours, Daphne had been replaying their trip to the pharmacy like some mental high-def video clip. She was so happy that she had souvenirs of the fateful day. She'd carefully stowed her lucky penny in the hinged cut-glass box she'd gotten from Grandma on her sixth birthday. Now that her prom dress wasn't a secret anymore, she'd taken it out of the closet and hung it on the back of their bedroom door, where she could see it anytime she wanted. Even her forehead still prickled where he'd kissed her.

Whenever Daphne recalled the pressure of Luke's soft lips, a sizzling sensation rushed over her, like a sudden fever. This was true happiness. The kind that could only come from finding a lost part of you. From finally seeing things the way they were supposed to be. She'd spent the day at school smiling at everyone—including Ms. Manbeck. She'd helped creepy Buck Templeton when his notebook exploded, sending his science notes all over the 300 wing. She'd even forgiven her mean, nosy, know-it-all sister. Because when it came down to it, Daphne felt sorry for all those people who didn't have what she had.

Sadly, she'd only seen Luke once and in passing, but those pillowy lips had curled into such a wide, beautiful grin that the tingles had practically paralyzed her. It was all she could do to lift her left hand in a feeble wave. She'd been hoping he'd ask her to prom, but that was all they'd glimpsed of each other—especially since she'd finally gone by the diner after school to fill out an application and make her mom happy.

There was still time, though. In fact, he'd probably call her tonight.

"Girls, which do you think looks better on me? This blue blouse? Or the white one?"

Daphne stopped drawing her embroidered cap sleeves and glanced up. Her mother stood in the middle of the room looking like a statue of Justice. From each hand dangled a shirt on a hanger, and she took turns lifting one to look it over while simultaneously lowering the other.

Frankly, Daphne hated both options. One was dark blue and frumpy. The other was so ten years ago, with its wide collar and elbow-length sleeves.

"What's it for?" Gabby asked, leaning sideways from her seat in the dining room to get a better view.

"There's a job opening at the office. I wasn't going to apply for it since it means taking on some evenings and weekends, but now I think I should. It's a real step up moneywise. Probably not enough for us to stay here, but at least we could find someplace decent."

"Do you think you'll get the job?" Daphne asked. Maybe they could find a three-bedroom rental and she wouldn't have to share with Crabby Gabby anymore. Maybe they could get a better cell phone plan. Maybe she and Luke could rent a limo for prom.

Her mom's lips clamped together tightly, as if she was trying to prevent something from escaping her mouth. After a couple of seconds she shook her head. "No. I think Rick will get it."

"Who's Rick?"

"One of the other assistants. Young guy just a year or two

out of business school. You might have heard me talk about him."

"Wait." Gabby strode across the room toward them, her features bunched into a scowl. "If he's just out of business school, there's no way he's been working there longer than you."

"He hasn't. He's been there about two years."

"And you've been there four. You should have the advantage. You should get the job."

"That's not how it works, unfortunately."

"It's because he's a man, right?" Gabby went on, her hands resting in fists against her hips. "He's a man and your boss is a man and they all just look out for each other. Who cares about the women? If they need help, they should just get a man, right?"

Mom smiled and nodded. "Something like that."

"Is Rick a jerk?" Daphne asked.

"Well . . ." Mom tilted her head, her eyes swiveling up toward the water stain on the ceiling. "He's the type of man who's always pulling out your chair for you at lunch meetings, or rushing to hold open the door."

Gabby wrinkled her nose. "Ooh, I can't stand that stuff! Like we're too weak to do those things on our own." She pressed the back of a hand to her forehead and said in a thick Southern belle–type accent, "My, my! A glass door? How on earth will I ever manage it?"

Gabby and their mom hooted with laughter. Daphne felt embarrassed by them.

"God! You guys!" she exclaimed. "You sound like you hate men."

"We're just talking about Mom's job. You wouldn't understand." Gabby was using that bossy voice that Daphne despised. The one that implied that Gabby was the other parent now that Dad was gone, and Daphne was somehow four years old again.

"It sounds like you're blaming guys for everything that goes wrong," Daphne said. "You can't blame Dad for this one, so you're going off on some guy you haven't even met."

She tried to imagine this Rick person. For some reason, she pictured him as handsome. And likeable. He was probably the kind of guy who laughed a lot and gave people compliments and stopped at Mrs. Johnson's for a box of doughnuts to bring with him to meetings. Maybe that was why he'd probably get the job. If Daphne were a boss, she'd want to work alongside someone like that, not someone who never joked around and always looked as if they were sucking on an extrasour lemon drop.

Of course she was rooting for her mom, and she really hoped she got the promotion. But she kind of had to admit that she liked this Rick guy. Or at least, her version of him.

"Don't worry, Daphne. We're only being silly," Mom said. "I'm just hoping I do well in the interview."

"You should wear the navy blouse," Gabby said. Again, the certainty in her tone bothered Daphne. It was true Gabby was smarter about most things, but fashion was not one of them. She only wore jeans and T-shirts—or that hideous red polyester theater uniform. Nothing else.

"Really? This one?" Mrs. Rivera raised the navy shirt and studied it.

Daphne hung over the back of the couch. "Mom, do you still have that sort of wine-colored blouse? The one with the ruffles up and down the front?"

"I think I know the one you're talking about. Yes, it's still around. Why?"

"You should wear that. It goes good with your skin. Makes you look young and soft. It's pretty."

Gabby rolled her eyes. "This isn't a date. She doesn't want to look pretty. She wants to look professional."

Daphne glared back at her. "Why is pretty not professional? I mean, if she looks good and feels good, won't she do better in the interview?"

"I still say the blue."

"The wine one!"

"Girls, please don't fight. I appreciate the feedback, but I'll take it from here."

Daphne scowled. She'd probably wear the blue one and look all washed-out. No one ever listened to Daphne. Now Rick would get the job and get to take home more money to his perfect wife in their perfect house. Maybe they'd even trade up to a bigger place and have perfect kids and live happily ever after. Together forever. All because of a tacky blue top.

"Mom?" Daphne called out as her mother headed back to her room with the clothes.

She paused and looked back. "What, hon?"

"Next time you have a meeting at work . . . you should bring a box of Mrs. Johnson's doughnuts with you to share. It would be nice."

Gabby swirled the spoon inside the cast-iron skillet, making sure each piece of onion got equally coated by the oil. They were starting to get that perfect glassy look. Just another minute of sautéing and she could add the pork (already browned and waiting on a plate), some diced tomatoes, and the paste of crushed garlic and cumin seed she'd mashed in the big stone *molcajete*. Her mom had gone to see Sue Sandborne, a woman who ran a salon out of her home, in the hopes that a haircut and color touch-up might give her an edge over Rick the Wonder Guy at work. So it was up to Gabby to cover dinner.

Not that she minded. Cooking was more of an escape than a chore. All the chopping and stirring relaxed her, and the smells brought back fond memories.

Grandma Rivera had taught her this recipe for *carne guisada* the year before she died. Gabby was about eleven, and she and Daphne had gone to stay with her for most of the summer. Little did Gabby know at the time that her parents were already having huge problems, which was part of the reason why they'd shuttled the girls off to Grandma's old cottage in Victoria.

Gabby had loved those cooking sessions. The peppery smells permeating the tiny kitchen. The clouds of flour stirred up by Grandma's bony hands as she made tortillas. Even the sweat and calluses and burn blisters. It all made her feel important and empowered. And it made her feel closer to Grandma.

Of course, Grandma had tried to teach Daphne, too, but at age eight the girl had had the attention span of a caffeinated hummingbird, so she was quickly dismissed. Instead, Grandma lavished her with several home-sewn dresses made of bright pastels and covered with piping and bows. So while Gabby pounded meat, kneaded *masa*, and sliced vegetables until her hands were dotted with tiny stab wounds, Daphne spent the summer twirling about in her new clothes.

She still thought of Grandma whenever she cooked, and missed her terribly. She'd never really gotten to know her mom's mom, who had died when Gabby was three. Grandma Rivera, however, had been a strong, stable force in her life. When Gabby was little, she'd been scared of the short, round woman, who was always rushing around with various kitchen utensils, barking out orders in Spanish, hugging her too tightly, and poking her cheeks with her fingertips. But later she identified with her grandmother's bossy, methodical nature. It pleased her to know she came from hardy female stock.

The onions were now perfect, and she was just about to add the meat when the phone started ringing.

"Daphne, can you get that?"

"I'm busy," came her sister's muffled voice.

"I'm busy too! I'm cooking!"

"I'm in the bathroom! Besides, it's probably for you!"

Gabby let out an exasperated grunt, threw down the spoon, and headed for the nearby phone. Daphne was right: the caller ID display showed Mule's number. This only made her angrier.

In a huff, she picked up the receiver and said, "I'm quitting."

"Uhh . . ." came Mule's tenor voice. "What? Your job?"

"No. I'm quitting my life. I'm changing my name to Rosario and moving to Paraguay."

He let out a staticky sigh. "What's happened now?"

"The usual. My sister."

"Ah. You're still mad about the dress?"

"Among other things." Gabby returned to the stove and added the meat with her free hand, enjoying the angry hiss it made as it hit the heated pan. "Did I tell you she spent all that money on that dress and . . . get this . . . she hasn't even been asked to prom yet!"

"She will be. Probably by more than one guy."

Gabby stifled her annoyance by sucking in her cheeks. She didn't want logical, state-the-obvious Mule right now. She wanted loyal Mule. Devoted-sidekick Mule. Yes-to-whatever-you-say Mule. "Don't you get it?" she said, pouring in the tomatoes, which didn't sizzle nearly as much as the pork had. "I don't care if she gets asked or not. I care about her refusing to help out and getting away with it all the time."

"Mmm," Mule went. It was a halfhearted attempt at sounding sympathetic. That was all she was going to get? One lousy consonant? "Much as I'd love to hear you moan for the next half hour, I actually have to keep this short. I just called to let you know I can't come by and study today. Mom got called in to work a late shift, so I'm cooking and looking after Dad."

"How's he doing?" Gabby asked, remembering to be an understanding friend.

"All right. Still watching talk shows all day. Now he's convinced that he was a neglectful father who didn't say 'I love you' enough to me. So he's saying it, like, all the time. When I bring him food, or help him with his exercises, or even when I'm just walking past his room. Today I was in the living room and I sneezed and he yelled 'I love you' from the bedroom."

"Really? That's kinda . . ."

"High on the weird scale, I know."

"I was going to say sweet. But yeah. It's weird, too. He's still got my dad beat, though." She got a sudden image of her dad driving away with his leftover ribs while Mom dropped the bomb about moving. That reminded her of something she'd been meaning to ask. "Hey, Mule, is your neighbor still trying to rent out that garage apartment?"

"Uh-uh. Tiny Lewis is living there now."

"Mrs. Lewis?" Gabby exclaimed, remembering their fourth-grade teacher.

"Yeah, apparently she left Mr. Lewis. Caught him fooling around with some caterer from Elgin."

Come to think of it, Gabby hadn't been seeing the two of them at the cinema on their Friday date nights. That must be why. Poor Mrs. Lewis. She had been one of Gabby's better teachers. *Men!*

"Still no luck finding a new place?" Mule asked.

"Nope. It's turning out to be harder than we thought it would be. And unless you count trees, there isn't a whole lot of living space in Barton. We're running out of time."

"I'll keep an eye out for something, okay? There are lots of trees around here. Affordable ones, too. But the squirrels have an insane neighborhood watch program."

"Ha, ha."

There was some muffled talking on his end. Gabby could hear Mule's father saying something, followed by Mule making shushing sounds. "Hey, Gab. I really gotta go. Dad's hungry and he wants me to watch some game show with him."

"And he loves you."

"Shut up."

"Hi, Gabriella!" came Mr. Randolph's voice from afar.

"Tell your dad I said hi."

"Sure thing. Bye."

Daphne emerged from the bathroom just as Gabby was replacing the receiver on its base. Her hair was in a towel turban, and green gooey stuff was all over her face.

"Was that Mule?" she asked.

Gabby bit her tongue. It was such a stupid question, considering no other living creature with the ability to use a phone ever called her. "Yeah," she replied. "He's going to help us look for a place."

"That's nice." Daphne pushed herself onto the countertop and started swinging her legs in tiny circles. "He's really nice."

"Yes, he is," Gabby replied distractedly. The mixture was starting a slow simmer.

"And he's totally in love with you, you know."

Gabby let out a snorting sound. "Please! You see love everywhere. You think our oak trees are in love."

"They're growing toward each other," Daphne said, sounding defensive. "And stop changing the subject. Mule is in love with you. You have to know that. Right?"

"Whatever."

Gabby knew he probably was, in some muted, dawdling, totally Mule-like way. Except that Daphne meant the love of fairy tales and Kleenex-soaking romance movies. She didn't understand that two people could be completely committed and rational at the same time.

"You know, he's been cuter lately," Daphne said.

"I hadn't noticed," Gabby lied.

"Of course, he's still weird. But maybe he'll grow out of that, too. And at least he's smart, so he could end up rich."

"Your priorities are shallow and warped."

"So come on, tell me." Daphne nudged her with her left foot. "Don't you love *him*?"

"Give me a break. Not everyone is as hung up on stuff like that as you are."

"You're not answering the question. Do you love him?"

"Come off it. You're seriously obsessed, you know that? You're like a love addict."

"Still not an answer."

It was clear Daphne wasn't going to drop the topic. Gabby pretended the mixture on the stove was in dire need of more salt, buying her time to formulate a reply. She was used to people making assumptions about her and Mule. Everyone at school thought they were an item. Lila at work always referred to him as Gabby's husband.

Obviously, Gabby cared about the guy. And yeah, maybe

they would end up together. In a way it made sense. She could never see them getting schmaltzy and starry-eyed, though. Unlike other people their age, she and Mule were sane. Besides, as important as Mule was to her, he didn't exactly electrify her. Gabby was never going to tattoo his name into her skin or crawl across a desert in search of him. Plus, the thought of kissing the guy didn't so much excite her as it did confuse her—and weird her out a little. She knew it wouldn't be awful, but she wasn't sure it would feel entirely right.

At the same time, she couldn't imagine him not being in her life. After all, he could very well be the only male creature on the planet willing to put up with her. One day, far in the future, she would probably acknowledge this and the two of them would settle down. He was a great guy—loyal, smart, sweet—and he would make a great boyfriend/husband/ whatever. But right now, she couldn't take the chance. So-called love almost never turned out well, especially at their age. And if she lost Mule's friendship, she'd have no one.

"Mule is just a friend. That's all," Gabby said, looking Daphne straight in the eye. "If you think we're going to become one of those annoying supercouples who finish each other's sentences and use baby talk with each other, you're going to be majorly disappointed."

"You just won't let yourself love him."

Gabby let go of the spoon and it dropped against the pan with a loud clang. "Have you ever thought that maybe there's no such thing?" she said. "Has it ever occurred to you that love is a big myth? Just some excuse people use to go crazy?"

Daphne stared at her. A sad-looking crease appeared on her brow, cracking her partially dried masque. "You've really never felt it, have you?" she said. "Maybe you *can't* feel it. That's got to be . . . really sucky." She shook her head, pushed herself off the counter, and padded toward their room.

Gabby took a long, steadying breath. Then she picked up the spoon and lulled herself with some more stirring.

Daphne was wrong. Gabby had felt the hormonal maelstrom people called love—for Sonny. Those two days after kissing him, she'd been sure he was the One and had made up silly fantasies about him bringing her flowers, or asking her to prom, or even proposing marriage. But in the end, all that dreaming had just ended up hurting her. News of his death had left her completely debilitated. Since she hadn't told anyone about her meet-up with him, no one knew what she was going through. Her dad called her sudden sullen nature "mood swings," and her mom finally let her drop kickball, saying Gabby was just too busy and stressed. Even Mule gave her space, assuming it was a girl thing—a rare two-month-long bout of PMS.

After weeks of wandering about in a state of shock and countless nights of muffled crying into her pillow, Gabby eventually figured it out. She realized *she* was putting herself through all that misery, at least partly. She hardly knew the guy, so how could she mourn him? What she was really doing was grieving the loss of her imagined future with him.

It wasn't even two years later when her dad packed up his Honda and announced that he and Mom were splitting up.

That was all the evidence Gabby needed to know that "love" was a total sham, a chemical imbalance that makes its victims lose all rationality.

People want to believe it's magical and special and meant to be forever, but those giddy feelings go away. Mainly because they were never really there to begin with.

Love, one way or another, always dies.

CHAPTER EIGHT
Neme(sis)

"Did you hear about Tracy Regent's party?" Sheri Purnell asked as they sat in the school lobby selling prom tickets.

"What party?" Daphne asked. "When?"

"In a couple of weeks. Her parents are going to Dallas for some big getaway or whatever, so she's having everyone over. To celebrate our winning season and all."

"I didn't get an invitation."

"Don't be stupid. No one does that anymore."

Sheri was only a year older—actually, only ten months older—but because she was a junior and on the varsity cheer squad, she tended to treat Daphne as if she were still sucking on pacifiers. Sheri was also one of those girls who hardly ever smiled. She was quick with sneers and cutting remarks, and her cheers were like war cries. And yet she was probably Daphne's best friend in their group. She wasn't good with secrets and she ignored Daphne if the more powerful or popular girls came along to talk to her, but she did sit next to Daphne at lunch and often drove her home after practice.

Daphne didn't kid herself that Sheri would ever give her a kidney, but at least she saved her from always having to walk places—and the humiliation of the school bus.

"Think you'll go this time?" Sheri asked.

Daphne shrugged. "I don't know." The other kids always thought it was weird that she rarely went to parties and couldn't stay out till all hours. She had no idea how they finagled it with their parents, but living with her mom was like having secret service guards around her.

"You should go. You could hook up with that new guy."

"Luke," Daphne said, annoyed that so many people still called him "that new guy."

"Whatever. Anyway, you might want to show up and, you know, keep an eye on him."

"What are you talking about?"

"It's just that . . ." Sheri paused and glanced around. "Lately Lynette's really been flirting with him."

"What?" Daphne grabbed a corner of the table. It seemed as if the entire world had suddenly tilted to the right.

"It's probably nothing to worry about. I'm just telling you because you're my friend and all." Sheri was looking at her with an expression she probably intended to be sympathetic, but the way she was leaning forward, with her eyes all sparkling and superfocused, it seemed more . . . hungry.

"Yeah, well. She flirts with anyone," Daphne said, dismissing the comment with a wave of her hand. Not that it made her feel better. Lynette did practically *anything* with anyone.

"You're right." Sheri's watchful gaze lingered on Daphne. "I just thought you should know."

Daphne busied herself counting the money in the cash box. This could have looked weird, considering they hadn't sold a ticket since the last time they'd counted it, but if Sheri thought so, she didn't say anything. She simply pulled out her phone and started drafting her eighty-seventh text of the morning. Daphne took a quick peek and saw that she'd typed "THIS IS SO BORING!!!" to someone.

Sheri was right. It was boring. They'd been there for almost an hour and they'd only sold two tickets to a band nerd Daphne recognized from her biology class. It was that in-between time during the lead-up to prom. The super-couples had already snagged their tickets, coordinated their outfits, ordered matching flowers, and planned their other activities for the evening. And it was too early for those last-minute types. But it was still depressing to think that Jerry What's-His-Name, the sousaphone player, already had a date and she didn't.

Why was Luke taking so long? Surely a guy who read Brontë could see and comprehend all the Day-Glo prom posters around the school. And with Daphne manning the booth today it would be extra easy—he could get his date and tickets at the same time! That was why she'd volunteered in the first place.

She'd only spotted him once that morning, riding in a wave of jock guys, standing out in his impeccable dark jeans and crisp white polo. But he didn't even see her. And now Sheri had gotten her all confused with her gossiping.

No way would a guy like Luke be into Lynette. She would never sip a soda at the pharmacy with him or take in the view from the Chandler Creek Bridge or discuss epic English romance novels. She'd laugh at a lucky penny, and bowling was not her type of indoor sport.

And yet . . . Daphne couldn't help wondering: was Lynette the reason why Luke hadn't asked her to prom yet?

"Mom?" Daphne sprang up from the couch the second she saw her mother walk through the door. "Can I go to a party at Tracy's in a couple of weeks?"

She wiggled impatiently as her mother closed the door, set down her briefcase, took off her cardigan with the snag in the sleeve, and hung it on the accordion rack. Eventually she dropped into the armchair and sank down until her legs were straight out in front of her, her arms hanging over the sides. "What party? What's it for?" she asked, seemingly to the ceiling.

"It's just a party. Just for fun," Daphne said, then started chomping on her index fingernail. She knew it was a long shot, but she had to try her best to go to that party, if for no other reason than to make sure Luke didn't get cornered by Lynette.

"I suppose so," her mom said. But just as Daphne's heart started to leap up, she added, "Of course I'll need to talk to her parents and make sure you'll be supervised."

"What?" Daphne whined. That jittery, out-of-control feeling came back. How could she make her mom understand the importance of going to this party? She loved that Luke was old-fashioned, but she really wished her mother weren't. No one else's parents monitored their social life the way Daphne's mom did hers.

"Her parents won't even be there," Gabby said, striding into the room from the hallway. "I heard they're going out of town. That's probably the real reason Tracy's having a party."

Their mom leveled a look at Daphne that accused her of something sneaky. "In that case, the answer is no."

"But why? You don't get it! I *have* to go!" Daphne was so jumpy and stressed, she felt as if she might rupture something important. Like her spleen—whatever that was.

Her mom shook her head. "Not if there aren't any adults around," she said, to the ceiling again.

Daphne rounded on Gabby. "Why'd you have to butt in anyway? You're always trying to mess things up for me!"

"What?" Gabby looked innocent. "She would have found out eventually."

"God, I hate you!" Daphne hissed at Gabby. Why did she have to be stuck with such a know-it-all for a sister? A normal older sister would have figured out a way to help Daphne go to the party. She'd have volunteered to drive her there and even lent her a cool outfit. Instead, Daphne had to get some tattletale police-officer sibling who didn't even *have* cool clothes, let alone offer her any.

"Girls, stop. Please." Mom was sitting up now, resting her forehead in her hands. "There are some things I need to talk to you about right now. Important things."

Daphne and Gabby traded anxious looks. They recognized that defeated tone. It was the same one their mom had used when she and Dad had announced their divorce.

"What is it?" Gabby asked, rushing to sit on the end of the couch closest to Mom.

Daphne stayed put, frozen with worry and still reeling from her defeat.

"I have some bad news," Mom said, lifting her head enough to rest her chin on her hands. "We've looked all over Barton and there's no place we can move. And Mr. Tibbets has already rented out the house for next month. With only a week left, we're basically out of time."

"So where are we supposed to go?" Gabby asked.

"I found an apartment we can afford. But . . . it's in Sagebrush."

"Sagebrush!" Something seemed to crumple inside Daphne. Perhaps her spleen. "But it's so far away! Does that mean . . . ?" She couldn't finish. It was too horrible.

Her mom nodded. "Yes, sweetheart. I'm so sorry, truly I am, but we'll have to move you girls to a different school."

"No." Daphne staggered backward a step.

Her mom had on that pained, guarded look, as if she were bracing herself for something awful. "I'm afraid there's no other way."

"But . . . but . . . I'm getting a job! And we can sell stuff! We can't move away! We just can't!"

"Honey, the time for a job has passed. There was a message yesterday from the diner. They hired someone else."

"Then I'll get some other job! I can't leave, Mom! Don't do this to me! Please!" In her panic, she looked over at Gabby, pleading with her eyes for her sister to do something—anything—to help her.

Gabby's features twisted into an unreadable expression. Pain? Fear? Frustration? It was too fleeting to tell. A split second later her face was as blank as usual. "Whatever," she said with a shrug. "Sagebrush can't be as bad as Barton."

Daphne could feel a scream building inside her, and tears were jetting up behind her eyes. *This isn't happening,* she told herself. *This isn't supposed to happen.* Not now—not when she'd finally found Luke, her happily-ever-after.

Eventually the invisible clamps released her throat. "You guys are ruining my life!" she shouted. "And you don't even care!"

There was no reaction. Her mom was still slumped awkwardly in the armchair, looking as if someone had carelessly tossed her there. And Gabby wouldn't even meet her gaze.

It was proof—proof that no one understood her. No one really cared about her. Except Luke. And now they were taking her away from him.

With a cry of defeat, she turned and ran for her room.

Gabby sat at the kitchen table, trying to finish up a report on *King Lear,* but every time she stared down at her paper the words disappeared. In their place materialized her mother's tight expression as she announced the move.

Sagebrush? Gabby turned the thought over and over in her mind, breaking it in like a new pair of leather shoes. She didn't even want to call Mule yet. Not until she'd fully absorbed the information and figured out how it felt.

So far, Gabby had decided she was okay with the news. It wasn't the greatest of developments, but it could be worse. Besides, there wasn't anything she could do about it. She might as well accept it and help Mom.

Daphne was in their room, throwing a Richter-scale-seven hissy fit. Mom had trudged toward the back of the house, complaining that she could feel a headache coming on. Meanwhile, Gabby tried to ignore the sounds of banging and sobbing and her mom rummaging through the medicine cabinet in order to do her homework—or at least stare at it.

So of course someone would knock on the door.

"I'll get it!" she shouted. She knew no one else would come running; she just wanted to let them know she was being inconvenienced.

Gabby opened the door, and there, leaning against the frame, was Prentiss Applewhite.

What the . . . ? Gabby could not have been more surprised if the ghost of Abe Lincoln were standing on their porch wearing Daphne's tacky prom dress.

"Hi," he said. Just like that. No awkwardness at all. One clear, resonant syllable, as if he were making a proclamation. Then he seemed to do a double take, and he squinted slightly. "Well, what do you know? It's movie girl. What are you doing here?"

Gabby frowned. "I live here. What are *you* doing here?" She still couldn't fathom why Prentiss Applewhite would be standing at their front door.

"I . . . um . . ." He tilted his head, and his smile faltered slightly. "Are you Liz?" he asked.

Prentiss Applewhite was on her porch asking for her *mom?*

"No," she answered. "She's busy."

He waited a couple of seconds and then said. "Busy? So . . . I can't speak with her?"

"Afraid not," she replied.

"Okay, uh . . . then can I speak with you?"

"About what?" Gabby asked, folding her arms across her chest.

By now Prentiss's toothy grin had disappeared. His absurdly rugged jaw hung open, making him look stupid, as if he couldn't comprehend why she wasn't melting in his presence.

That was another reason to hate Prentiss. Good-looking guys knew they were good-looking. They strutted around acting as if they were superior beings who deserved to have other, lesser creatures—especially women—obey their every command. And Prentiss was probably the grand pooh-bah of them all. Even if Gabby hadn't known he was a spoiled sleazebag with no remorse for the pain he caused others, she still would have mistrusted him on sight.

Thank god Daphne was too busy bawling to answer the door. The girl would have been crawling into his arms at that point.

He cocked his head and shifted his weight onto his other foot. "So you really aren't expecting me? Um . . . I'm Prentiss?" he said, as if he weren't sure of his own identity.

"Prentiss!" Her mom's voice sounded behind her. "Oh, my lord, is it already that late? Come in! Gabby, sweetheart, let the boy in."

It was Gabby's turn to look confused. Why in hell would her mom be inviting Prentiss over?

She stepped sideways and yanked the door wide. "Mom? What's going on?" she asked.

"Honey, it's all right. Prentiss's mom is buying some stuff I posted on Craigslist."

Gabby was dismayed to see her mother smoothing her hair and discreetly checking her reflection in the nearby mirror for Prentiss's sake.

Prentiss, meanwhile, stood awkwardly in the corner of the living room. His smile was back, but it was tighter, more forced-looking. Gabby wondered if he'd ever been inside a poor person's home before. She was suddenly hyperaware of their grizzled carpet, the mildewy smell that permeated the place, and the old Jetta with the hail dings in the driveway. Her jaw clenched and her lips pursed into her tilde mouth. How dare he judge them.

"Please, have a seat," her mother said, gesturing to the sofa with the ripped armrest and saggy middle cushion. "I'll just be a second while I go get the things."

"Thank you, ma'am." Prentiss nodded in her direction and settled into the corner of the couch, next to the good armrest and close to Gabby. His eyes kept passing over her, as if he was checking to see where she was without overtly staring.

"Here we are!" her mom sang out as she breezed back into the room. Her hands were cupped together and held aloft. As soon as she reached the coffee table she set the contents down in front of Prentiss.

Gabby sucked in her breath. "Grandma's jewelry?" she asked, her voice screechy.

Mom's smile washed away, just like Prentiss's had a moment earlier, and her features drooped guiltily. "Honey, don't overreact."

"But those were Grandma's. They're heirlooms. Our family history!"

Her mother gave Prentiss an uncomfortable glance. "Gabby, honey, you know what the situation is. It's not like I *want* to sell them. But we have to move and—"

"I'll get another job!" Gabby could see Prentiss backing into the couch, his eyes as wide as the knit coasters on the table in front of him. She knew they were embarrassing themselves in front of town royalty, but she didn't care. Those items were the most precious things they owned—the *only* precious things they owned. It wasn't right that they should go to the richest family in the county, no matter how desperate things might seem. Besides, they'd belonged to Grandma. They held memories. If Prentiss didn't even value his cousin's life, how could he value the Rivera family's treasures?

"Be reasonable, honey. There's no way you can take on more work than you already have," her mom said.

"Then make Daphne work for a change. She'll get a job and I'll make Pinkwater give me a raise and Dad will—"

"Enough!" Mrs. Rivera shouted. She snuck another fleeting look at Prentiss and angled her body away from him. "Darling, please," she said, her voice lower and shakier. "We're overdue on bills and we need a place to live and we have no money for a deposit—not even for a cruddy apartment in Sagebrush. Just accept it. Don't make this harder than it already is for me."

Gabby was about to make another plea when she was interrupted again. This time by Prentiss.

"Excuse me," he said. "I hope you don't mind me asking, but did y'all say you needed a place to live?"

"Yes," her mother replied at the same time Gabby said "No."

"This is a private matter," Gabby said through her teeth. God, how dense could he be? Why didn't he just get a clue and leave already?

"It's just that . . . well . . . my parents are looking for some tenants to stay on our property . . . and I thought perhaps y'all might consider living there?" He met Gabby's eyes and grinned.

For a moment no one said anything. Gabby was too busy screaming inside the safety of her head. She couldn't believe Prentiss had the gall to butt in like that. Who did he think he was? And how delusional could he get? Anyone with a conscience would refuse to live on his property, knowing what he had done. Mansion or not.

She glanced over at her mother, ready to exchange a fleeting can-you-believe-this-guy? expression. To her horror, she found her mother smiling at him.

"You mean . . . you have a house available for rent?" she asked him.

"Yes, ma'am. It's not much. A two-bedroom guesthouse. But it's built well and has new paint. I've been fixing it up myself these past few weeks." He flashed Gabby another smirky grin and puffed up slightly, as if he expected applause.

Gabby could feel panic rising inside her. Surely her mother wasn't seriously considering this offer, especially knowing who it was coming from.

Thankfully, her mother's smile was gone and her usual

worry lines had reappeared on her forehead. "The thing is . . . I'm not sure we could afford it," her mom said. "I've been looking around and . . . well . . . rates have really gone up."

Prentiss leaned sideways and pulled something out of his back pocket, a folded piece of paper. He opened it up and handed it to Mrs. Rivera.

"This is the ad I wrote out. Only I haven't had a chance to post it yet. I don't know how much other people are charging, but ours might be more reasonable. And we could work something out as far as a deposit is concerned. We aren't looking to make money; we know times are tough. We just want good people."

"Oh, my. It's . . . You . . . I think we could actually manage this," her mother stammered, holding the paper tightly in both hands. She shook her head slightly, still staring down at the ad as if scared to take her eyes off of it. Eventually she looked up and proceeded to gaze at Prentiss as if he were some magical being. A young, strapping Santa Claus. "How could we apply for this?"

Prentiss smiled and held up a cell phone. "Just let me call my mom," he replied. "Excuse me," he said to Gabby as he stood and edged past her. Then he stepped out the front door to the concrete stoop.

"Mom, no!" Gabby said as soon as he'd shut the door behind him. "Shouldn't you ask me what I think? This does affect me, too, you know. And Daphne."

"But honey, it's not like there's a choice. There isn't anyplace else we can go. Not in this town."

"But . . . it's the Applewhites!" Gabby whisper-yelled.

"Surely you've heard about them. About Prentiss and all the trouble he caused!"

"Those things happened a long time ago. Besides, you know I don't pay any mind to town gossip."

Obviously the strain had gotten to her mother and she was in serious denial. Gabby decided to switch tactics. "But we'd be on their property. It'll be like living in slave quarters!"

"Don't be silly. It's just a rental agreement. Anyway, I've had the chance to speak with Rebecca Applewhite a few times. She's not the snob you might think she'd be."

"But we haven't even seen the place yet. What if it's . . . bad?" By now Gabby's voice had petered into a small whine. She hated losing debates, and it was clear she was going to lose this one.

Her mom gave her a knowing look. "Sweetie, like I said, there's nothing else available. Look . . ." She reached out and pushed a lock of hair off of Gabby's face. "I know where you are coming from. You are cautious, and you know I like that. And you are so proud. That's wonderful, too. But don't let your pride overtake your common sense. It's either this or I have to sell Grandma's jewelry so we can nab a cramped apartment in Sagebrush. What do you think we should do?"

Gabby let out a sigh and stared down at the spotted, smelly carpet. Carpet they would very soon leave behind. The whole thing was unfair. It was wrong that they endured constant stress while Prentiss got away with murder—literally. It was wrong that they had to make tough choices like this when people like Prentiss got everything. It was wrong that they had to work so hard when people like Prentiss got to cruise around town in expensive cars, pausing only occasionally to slap paint on a wall of their *extra* house.

Good god, what kind of shape must that place be in if *he* fixed it up? Gabby would probably end up missing this awful carpet.

"Fine," she said, meeting her mom's eye and trying to look calm. "Whatever."

Just then the door opened and Prentiss stepped in. He wore a phony-looking blank expression, but his eyes were practically dancing, giving him away.

"Well . . . ," he began, letting out a weary sigh, "you're in! Mom wants to know if you can move at the start of the month." He grinned gigantically, obviously pleased with himself.

"Oh! Oh, thank you!" Mrs. Rivera threw her arms around Prentiss. "Thank you so much!"

"You're welcome," Prentiss replied, grinning at Gabby over her mom's shoulder. "I just hope y'all are happy there."

Gabby didn't smile back. She was far too frustrated, not to mention a wee bit queasy.

Her mom let go of Prentiss and gazed up at him with tears in her eyes. "Oh, excuse me. I was just a little overcome. You have no idea what a burden this has been. You're saving us."

"Glad to help. Oh, and by the way . . . Mom's going to pass on the jewelry."

Mrs. Rivera cast him a grateful look. "I understand. Oh, my my my! I still can't believe it! Gabby, dear. Go tell your sister the good news."

"Fine." Gabby headed for the hallway, grateful for an excuse to get away.

She couldn't believe what had just happened. Had Prentiss Applewhite really shown up at their house and convinced her mom that they should basically live with him? Was she actually going to have to sleep only yards away from the person she hated most in the world?

She really had to call Mule for an emergency vent session before her head exploded, staining the stupid carpet even more.

Daphne lay in bed, listening to the mixed rhythms of crickets and frogs and Gabby's loud breathing. The digital alarm clock read 2:27, but still she couldn't sleep.

It wasn't the noise. She was used to all that. It was even worse during allergy season, since that was when Gabby did some serious snoring. Her sister used to deny it until five years ago when Daphne snuck their dad's old tape recorder under her bed one night. The next morning Daphne came out to breakfast and played the evidence. "Gabby snoring, part one," came Daphne's whispered voice, followed by Gabby's snorts and wheezes. Gabby had been furious, and of course Mom had taken her side and lectured for a full ten minutes on the importance of privacy. But Dad had laughed about it all day.

No, it wasn't all the night sounds keeping her awake. It was a feeling. A restlessness, as if her chest were packed tight with those trick snakes that spring out of fake peanut canisters. She couldn't help believing that something monumental had happened that day. Things had been going so well with

Luke, and then suddenly she'd heard about Lynette's flirting and had a close call with moving, all in the same day! It was as if the universe was testing her. As if Fate was letting her know that their love had to go through a few trials before everlasting happiness could set in—like with Jane Eyre and Rochester, Odysseus and Penelope, or . . . Spider-Man and Mary Jane.

She wondered where Luke was right now and what he was doing. Probably he was in bed. She pictured him lying shirtless among twisted sheets, and a warm, trembly sensation came over her.

Maybe he was awake and thinking of her, too. If only she could somehow connect with him, send him messages from afar.

She closed her eyes and concentrated on him. His shaggy brown locks . . . his dimples . . . his eyes like those aqua-colored rocks at the bottom of aquariums . . .

Luke! she called out silently. *Luke, can you hear me?*

She waited for a sound or a feeling, some sort of sign that he'd heard. But all that came back to her were crickets. And frogs. And her sister's steady breathing.

She tried again, this time squeezing her eyes closed so tightly that a roaring sound filled her head. The act seemed to tap into a dormant power within her. Surely this way she could hurtle her message across the miles and into his waiting mind. *Luke!* she cried telepathically along with the roar. *Luke, it's me!*

It seemed to Daphne that a vague warmth stole over her right after she transmitted the message. Could that be him?

Maybe he heard but didn't know how to answer. He probably didn't know about the eye-squeezing method.

Luke! Close your eyes tight and think of me!

She waited, but nothing came back to her. Maybe only she could transmit and only he could receive. Maybe he didn't even know Daphne was behind it—he just got the messages and assumed they were his own thoughts.

Ask Daphne to prom! she sent out. *Ask her next time you see her!*

A loud noise sounded nearby, and Daphne's eyes snapped open.

It was only Gabby letting out a snore, but it had sounded exactly like a scoff. She glanced over at her sister and studied the rhythmic rise and fall of her Astros T-shirt. The girl was definitely asleep, and yet Daphne still couldn't shake the feeling that she was being ridiculed. If not by Gabby, then perhaps by Fate, who had already toyed with her so much that day.

Suddenly she felt stupid. What was she doing, lying in bed trying to broadcast secret messages to Luke across town? It was silly and useless, and it was starting to bring on a headache. If Gabby knew, she'd hurt herself laughing.

Even the delicious jitters were completely gone, jolted right out of her. Now Daphne just felt chilly and ashamed. And very, very tired.

The important thing was that she'd get to stay in Barton, close to Luke. And she was willing to go through whatever trials she had to endure to get him. Just like she'd narrowly escaped the move, she would prevail against Lynette. Because if there was one thing Daphne had learned from all the fairy tales and romance novels, it was that true love could overcome absolutely anything.

Focusing on that thought, Daphne slipped her pillow out from underneath her head and curled around it, letting all the familiar noises shush her to sleep.

CHAPTER NINE
Ellip(sis)

Daphne peered over the shiny surface of her bowling ball, lining up her trajectory. Her first roll had resulted in a four-ten split, and she hoped to convert by knocking that four at just the right angle.

Just like on all her prior turns, she was more than a little aware that Luke had the perfect view of her backside. And just like on all her previous turns, she couldn't hold her concentration. Her hand released too quickly and she narrowly missed her mark, knocking over only the four pin.

"Nice," she heard Luke say. She spun around and grinned at him. "You almost got them all. That was close."

He looked so cute today. Instead of the usual nicely pressed polo he wore a simple green T-shirt with his jeans. It showed off his shoulders and arms and turned his eyes the color of weathered copper.

"Thanks," she said.

"I love that skip you do right before you release the ball."

A simmering sensation crept up Daphne's face. She loved

that he used the word "love." In so many ways, this was the perfect day. Her hair had behaved for a change. She'd found the perfect outfit to wear (a short-sleeved-sweater-and-skirt ensemble—to complement the oxford-style bowling shoes). She'd even managed to nab her favorite bowling ball, a sleek ten-pounder the same color as rose quartz.

And now he said he loved her form. Could it be code? Was he really saying he loved *her*?

"I love that you only picked up one point," said Walt Lively as he recorded her score.

That was the only bad part about the day. For some reason, Luke had assumed that their bowling excursion would be a team event and showed up with Walt and Todd in tow. Daphne had thought it was pretty much understood that this would be a date—a continuation of their soda counter meet-up—but perhaps that hadn't been made clear during their cell conversation. And being a guy, he no doubt believed that all sports-related outings involved a multitude of players.

Oh well. At least she got to spend the afternoon with him before things got crazy with the move. And at least he'd chosen her for his team.

"You're up, Carothers," Walt said to Todd.

Todd sauntered to the front of their lane, swung back his right arm, and sent his ball spiraling down the hardwood. Nine pins flew in different directions on impact. He easily picked up the tenth on his next try.

"Yesss!" he said, pumping his arm victoriously. "That's the game. Read it and weep." He gestured to the TV screen above their lane, where a cartoon rabbit was bouncing around in celebration of his score.

"Let's hit the road and find ourselves some burgers," Walt said. He turned and headed for the nearby shelf to replace his ball. Todd followed, still swaggering victoriously.

Daphne felt horribly let down, and not because they'd lost. It was the same panic she experienced at the end of one of her dad's visits—the feeling that she hadn't spent the time wisely enough and the fear that she might never get to see him again. She'd rehearsed all kinds of clever and charming things to say to Luke, many of them designed to steer the conversation toward the subject of prom. But with Walt and Todd there, most of the talk centered on basketball and the new tires Walt had put on his pickup truck.

"Can you come eat with us?" Luke asked.

"Um . . ." Daphne coiled a lock of hair around her index finger. She wanted so badly to say yes. So what if her mom had only let her come after Daphne had promised to be back in two hours ready to do more packing? This was more impor-tant. This was her future. But if she didn't get home on time, her mother would freak out and ground her. Then she'd never be able to meet Luke. In fact, she probably wouldn't be al-lowed to go to prom at all.

"I can't. Sorry," she said. "I'd love to, but my mom needs me to do stuff, 'cause we're moving and all." She bit her lip and studied his reaction.

Luke nodded solemnly. "I get it. Maybe next time?"

She smiled weakly. "Sure." For some reason the panic didn't

subside. She'd been expecting so much from the afternoon—a date to the prom, an invitation for a real date, something that would nudge their relationship into a higher gear. No matter how often she told herself that someone as gentlemanly and old-fashioned as Luke wouldn't want to rush things, she couldn't shake the feeling that time was running out. Prom was rapidly approaching. Lynette seemed extra-smirky toward her. And who knew what else Fate might throw in their path? How could they weather these storms if they were still at a polite, forehead-kissing stage?

For some reason she felt as if she might cry, just a little. She was that disappointed. Before he could notice the wetness in her eyes she said, "I better get my shoes," and headed for the check-in area, returning her pretty rose-colored ball along the way.

By the time she reclaimed her pink Converse sneakers, she'd managed to wipe away a couple of renegade tears and sniff until her normal breathing returned. Maybe she was being stupid. It wasn't as though Luke lived in another town—thank god. And even if Lynette was hovering about like some trampy bird of prey, at least he hadn't hooked up with her. So why couldn't Daphne have more faith?

Daphne filled her lungs with muggy, hot-dog-scented air and checked her eyes for any residual moisture. Then she headed back toward their lane. Since all the seats and benches were full of people, she sat down on the floor next to the ball shelf to put her shoes back on.

"You and Rivera, huh?" came Walt's voice.

At first she didn't know who he was talking to. Then she

realized he was standing with Luke on the other side of the shelf.

She paused midtie to listen. But if Luke said anything in reply, she couldn't hear it.

"So . . . are you guys . . . ?" Walt went on.

"No. She's cool," Luke said. His voice sounded different than it usually did—at least when he spoke to her. It was higher in pitch, and the words tumbled out on top of each other. "We're just . . . getting to know each other better, you know?"

"I hear you, man. But really, you shouldn't waste your time. That girl's a major prude. She never goes to parties and she never puts out. You'll see."

Daphne held her breath, waiting for Luke's response, but suddenly Todd's booming voice cut in.

"I am the Thunder Alley thunder cat. Next time, we play for money!" he said. "Now let's get out of these dork shoes."

His voice trailed off and she could hear the squeaks of their rubber-soled shoes as they walked away.

That girl's a major prude. A shaky feeling spread through Daphne's limbs. She knew—she had always known—that that was how the guys in Barton felt about her. And yet it still hurt to hear Walt say it aloud, as if he were some sort of expert on her. Which he wasn't.

Daphne yanked up on her shoelaces so hard, she wouldn't have been surprised if they'd snapped right off her sneakers. Walt didn't know her—not really. No one did . . . except Luke. He wasn't like all those other guys, who only cared about sex. Instead, he felt real love. He understood the magic of holding hands and staring at sunsets. He knew how to take things slowly, to savor every moment as it happened.

It suddenly occurred to her that *this* could be one of Fate's harsh trials: seeing whether she could withstand Luke's courting her at a nineteenth-century pace. Of course! That had to be it.

She glanced over at the front counter, where Luke was retrieving his green-and-white-striped basketball shoes, and smiled to herself. She could endure this. She'd always wanted her handsome prince, and she'd finally found him. Now she just needed to stop blaming him for acting princely.

She could wait, just like all those women whose lovers were sent off to war. She could be patient and strong and martyrlike. And then, when Luke finally took their relationship to the next level, it would be that much sweeter.

It would be epic.

Daphne had it so easy. She could whine and stomp and sniffle and get to do whatever she wanted, all the time.

It was only days until the dreaded move, and Gabby couldn't help thinking of this time as a long pause or an ellipsis—or a stay on death row before execution. And most of it was being spent packing, cleaning, and working at the theater. So here it was, one of the few hours Gabby had open, and what did she get to do? Deliver the signed rental agreement to the snooty Applewhites.

She understood that her mom couldn't do it. Gabby had already dropped her off at Anderson's Hardware so she could get a few necessary home repair items and maybe track down some more empty boxes. But since when had bowling become a priority? It was as though Daphne was taking advantage of their mother's distracted state to get her way.

Feeling that it would be presumptuous to take a spot in the carport, Gabby parked the Jetta on a worn grassy area and climbed out into the warm, rose-scented air. The estate was at least two acres, probably more, and she had to stand in the middle of the curved gravel driveway just to fully take in the surroundings.

Next to the covered parking area stood what was most likely the rental home, a tidy yellow cottage with white shutters and a railed-in front porch. It seemed nice enough, but Gabby refused to like it. Besides, who knew what it was like on the inside? It could be full of radon and termites and the ghosts of murdered tenants.

She abruptly turned away and headed for the main house, a beautifully maintained white Victorian with a wraparound front porch, transom windows, and so many staggered roofs, it reminded her of a tiered wedding cake. Gabby hated it on sight. She hated the way it sat so smugly on the hill, looking down on everything around it. She hated the way the scroll-ornamented eaves of the gables hung down over the windows, giving them a heavily lidded, haughty appearance. But mostly she hated it because Prentiss lived there, all safe and spoiled.

In fact, the house was just like him—striking, but in a way that made those who beheld it feel inferior.

Gabby blew out her breath and trudged up the drive, turning onto a paved walkway. Meanwhile, the majestic home loomed in the distance like the Death Star. It was so big, in fact, that it took longer to make it to the front door than she had anticipated. The place was much larger up close. Even the hedges were taller than she was. She felt like a trespassing bug.

She rang the doorbell and stepped back—either to allow a respectful distance or because she half expected a giant to step out. Several seconds passed and no one replied. So she rang again. Then a third time.

Finally the door opened and a woman stood on the threshold. She was tall and slender, with Prentiss's light blue eyes and blond hair cut in a sassy bob.

"Mrs. Applewhite?" Gabby guessed.

The woman nodded. "Are you Gabriella?"

"Yes."

"I'm sorry if you had to ring several times." She glanced down at a diamond-studded wristwatch. "You're a little late."

"Um, yes. Well, we only have one car and . . ." Gabby stopped. No reason to tell their life story. "Sorry about that."

Mrs. Applewhite smiled and genuine-looking warmth crept into her face. "No matter. Please come in." She stepped back, pulling the door with her, and Gabby crossed into the hardwood foyer. A wooden staircase sat at the rear and a chandelier hung over their heads. Double doors stood on either side, one pair hanging open.

"Prentiss was expecting you, but he had to go run an errand," she went on. "Typically he answers the door. Our quarters are in the back part of the house, and sometimes we can't hear the bell. But he's usually in the den"—she gestured to an elaborate living room off to her right, faintly visible through the open, curtained doors—"and his bedroom is close by"—she pointed above her—"so we've come to rely on him to greet visitors."

Quarters? A house so big you couldn't hear the doorbell from certain rooms? Gabby was suddenly all too aware of her clearance-rack clothes and worn tennis shoes.

"Please, won't you come sit down?" Mrs. Applewhite made a sweeping gesture toward the living room, and Gabby automatically obeyed.

The room was big—almost as large as their current two-bedroom bungalow—and although it wasn't exactly opulent, it was tastefully furnished with Asian rugs and antique furniture. Gabby headed for a linen-covered parlor chair and suddenly halted.

There, staring back at her from the mahogany sofa console, was an eight-by-ten photo of Sonny.

Something wedged in Gabby's throat, trapping her breath and sending wetness into the corners of her eyes. She'd forgotten the connection. It seemed strange, since that was why she'd opposed the rental agreement in the first place, but lately she'd been so consumed with tasks and family hassles. Besides, she hadn't expected to see Sonny's picture on display. One would think it would be especially hard for the Applewhites to see his face, considering their own son was responsible for his death—not to mention that they'd taken advantage of rumors in a desperate PR attempt to clear his name. Did these people have no shame? Or did they exist in constant denial?

She studied Sonny's smiling face, frozen in the polished

silver frame. He looked so young. Fifteen. She was older than him now.

"That's our Sonny," came Mrs. Applewhite's voice from behind her. "Poor dear. He was my brother's eldest child. Did you know him?"

Gabby hesitated. "No. But I . . . knew who he was."

"Such a beautiful boy." She stepped forward and lifted the photograph, shaking her head sadly.

For several seconds, neither of them spoke. The sudden somber mood seemed to thicken the air. Gabby tried to calculate whether the joy of screaming in the home of one of Barton's most powerful residents would be worth her mother's wrath, her sister's hysterics, and a move to a seedy apartment.

"Please," Mrs. Applewhite repeated, nodding toward the seating area. "Make yourself comfortable."

Gabby decided to continue playing the part of the appropriately awestruck townsperson. "Thanks," she said, and resumed her walk toward the parlor chair. The upholstery was so crisp and white, Gabby instinctively swiped the seat of her blue jeans before sitting down. "I brought the lease. It's signed," she said. She pulled an envelope out of her bag and tapped it against her knees.

"Yes. Thank you." Mrs. Applewhite replaced Sonny's photo and took the envelope from Gabby. "So," she said, settling onto the curvy patterned sofa, "Prentiss tells me you work at the theater."

Prentiss had been talking about her? "Um, yes. I do."

"You must be very responsible. And what about your sister? What does she do?"

Gabby pursed her lips. *Let's see, lie around daydreaming and chase brainless boys?* "She's into cheerleading and stuff," she said. "She's always been more . . . athletic than me."

Mrs. Applewhite nodded. "I was a cheerleader myself in high school. Seems like ages ago." She stared dreamily up at the ceiling. "Well then. I do appreciate your family's cooperation. The paper is such a silly formality, but our lawyer makes us do them."

"I understand." Knowing their son, it wasn't hard to imagine they had a team of lawyers available at all hours of the day.

"Really, I have no doubt that everything will be fine."

"Thanks. We"—Gabby swallowed—"we're glad to be here."

"I'm glad, too," Mrs. Applewhite said with a light laugh. "If you need anything, just talk to Prentiss. Henry and I are so busy with the library fund-raiser, we aren't home all that much. We've come to depend on him quite a bit. But not to worry. I'm sure you'll find he's very responsible and easy to deal with."

Gabby froze her smile to prevent a grimace.

"Well then . . ." Mrs. Applewhite rose to her feet and gestured back toward the foyer. "Welcome to the property. We hope you like your new home."

"Thanks," Gabby said, following her to the front door. She felt a little rushed but also relieved that her task was done. She tried to glance back at Sonny's picture, but Mrs. Applewhite had turned it to face the other direction when she'd set it down.

"I'm so happy we could make this happen," Mrs. Applewhite added with a smile. "I hope things work out well for you all and that you stay for a very long time. We'll be in touch."

Gabby nodded and stepped back out onto the porch.

She'd wanted to actively hate Prentiss's mom, but other than being a little erratic, she wasn't bad to deal with. Gabby had wanted to hate the rental house, too, but it also lacked any obvious exterior flaws. Even the grounds were lovely.

There was no escape route, no excuse she could find to back out of the deal. Like it or not, she would soon be living under the raised noses of the Applewhites.

CHAPTER TEN

As(sis)tance

The carpet in the Applewhites' rental house looked brand-new. It even smelled new, giving off faint chemical fumes that Gabby was fairly sure cooked their inner organs with every breath.

"Gab, look. Look how it springs back up." Daphne dug her sneaker into the carpet for a couple of seconds and then stepped back onto the shiny kitchen linoleum. The mushed fibers gradually straightened, like seedlings stretching toward the sun, until her footprint was barely visible.

"Whup-de-do," Gabby muttered. Only, Daphne didn't hear her. She was already skipping off to admire the high-end dishwasher.

Gabby had to admit the place was nice—for slave quarters. Even the paint job looked professional. When Prentiss said he'd done it himself, he probably meant that he had hired people and paid them all by himself with his mommy's credit card. She reached forward and brushed her fingers over the orange-peel texture of the dining room wall. The color made her hungry, reminding her of key lime pie. The trim was a milky white.

"Wow. I can walk into the pantry," came Daphne's muffled voice from the kitchen. "It's bigger than Mom's closet at the other place."

"Joy," Gabby grumbled.

She knew she should be happy about the house and the fact that it, amazingly, cost about the same per month as the rundown hovel they'd just vacated. But somehow she wasn't. For one thing, their furniture looked extrashabby in the Pottery-Barn-catalog setting. And it irked her how Daphne kept racing about, oohing and ahhing over every tiny detail. *The carpet stays standing! The cabinets close all the way! You don't have to wait ten minutes for hot water to come out of the faucet!* One would think they'd been holed up in a dirt-floor shack all these years, using an outhouse and bathing in the nearby creek.

"The top one goes in the bedroom, and the big one stays here in the living room." Mrs. Rivera stepped into the house right behind Prentiss, who was holding two large boxes in his arms. "Thank you again."

"Not a problem, Mrs. R," Prentiss said, carefully depositing the bottom box onto their stained, scratched coffee table. He flashed Gabby a smile before retreating into the nearby bedroom with the next box.

That was another thing—probably the worst part of all. Prentiss, for some reason, had decided to help them move in. He'd been there when they arrived that morning and made a big show of presenting each room. "This is the bathroom," he'd actually said at one point, gesturing to the white subway tiles, the periwinkle walls, and the (also brand-new-looking) toilet, as if they were prizes in a game show. Gabby almost bit her tongue off to keep from saying "Yeah, duh. Think we could have figured that out."

It also bothered her that he insisted on carrying in the large boxes from the car. Yes, it was helpful and polite and all that crap, but he was touching their stuff! He was pawing her books and her big outdated computer—and he even carried in a bulging bag full of her jeans!

Thank god the men they'd rented the truck from had already unloaded the heavy furnishings the day before. Gabby would have melted with humiliation if Prentiss Applewhite had helped bring in their stained, garage-sale-bought mattresses.

Speaking of which . . . where the hell were the bed linens?

Prentiss walked back into the room. "I don't think there's much left in the car. Y'all stay and take a breather. I can get it."

Gabby's mom let out a happy sigh and shook her head. "Thank you, Prentiss. I don't know what we'd do without you."

Prentiss just stood there, smiling dopily, as if he expected a pat on the head and a Scooby snack. Finally, he gave a nod and ducked out the door.

"I swear that boy is a savior," Mrs. Rivera said, staring at the air where Prentiss's athletic frame had just been.

Gabby rolled her eyes. Lately she couldn't understand her mom. Usually the two of them thought alike. They were the reasonable ones in the family. The ones who saw the world as it really was. And yet during the past few days she'd sounded more like Daphne with the way she regarded Prentiss as some knight in shining armor. If Gabby believed in storybook magic the way Daffy did, she'd seriously wonder whether her mother had fallen under a powerful spell.

She supposed she should be happy that Mom was happy. The perpetual line between her mother's brows had softened, and her eyes didn't have that sunken look. That was a good thing. And yet Gabby refused to let her guard down and give in to the Prentiss worship. Someone had to stay on alert around him. Someone had to remember his awful past. People didn't change—not really.

"Can you believe there are flowers out front?" Mrs. Rivera said as she stared out the living room window. "I sure hope we can keep them alive." She reached back and grabbed Gabby's hand, pulling her up beside her. "It's pretty here, isn't it?"

"Yeah," Gabby lied. Actually, one of the worst things about the new place was its view. If they ever got to feeling too hopeful, too cozy or prosperous, all they had to do was gaze out the front window at Applewhite Manor and their egos would automatically snap back down to their normal, scrawny size.

"Oh, my god! I love the pool!" Daphne appeared at Gabby's side, pointing to the glimmer of blue behind the mansion. "Can you imagine being able to swim anytime you want? They must have no stress at all."

The three of them stood there for a moment, gawking at all the opulence. Like rabble on the palace grounds.

"That reminds me," Mrs. Rivera said, letting go of Gabby. "I need to figure out which bag contains my medicine. I really don't want to get a migraine today."

She headed through a nearby door into her new room. They had already agreed that the girls would take the back bedroom since it had two closets and was large enough to accommodate their twin beds, dresser, and desk, while their mom would take the smaller bedroom since it was, as she put it, "closer to the coffeepot."

"This is the last of the big ones." Prentiss walked back through the front door cradling a massive cardboard box marked *Miscellaneous*. "Where do y'all want me to put it?"

Gabby bit her tongue again.

"Oh, just set it down wherever," Daphne replied.

Prentiss turned in a slow circle before carefully lowering the box onto the sofa. Gabby noticed how the muscles of his tanned arms actually rippled, just like those of heroes described in Daphne's romance novels. Gabby had always thought it was dumb, a way to imply that a man's power somehow matched that of running water. But there really was a wavy flow to the movement.

The rippling stopped and Gabby suddenly realized that Prentiss was looking right at her, smiling that idiotic grin of his.

"Gonna be a warm day," Daphne said, gazing through the window at the sky. "Think you might go for a swim later?"

Oh, no. Gabby knew exactly what her sister was up to. No way was she going to let Daphne bounce about in her bikini in front of Prentiss—invited or not. Prentiss plus deep water could equal a serious safety concern.

"Ooh, Daff, did you remember to get your prom dress out of the car?" Gabby asked in a worried voice. "It's going to get all wrinkled."

That did it. Daphne stretched up extratall to stare out at the Jetta, looking like a scared prairie dog. Then she pushed past Gabby and trotted out the front door.

"Y'all are welcome to come swim later," Prentiss said.

Ah, the feudal lord extends an invitation to the poor country peasants! How charitable. Gabby stared down at the springy carpet to keep from making a face. "That's okay," she said. "We have stuff to do."

"Right. Well then . . ." Prentiss stretched out his arms and Gabby couldn't help stealing a glance at his muscles. "You girls should keep this door locked. Y'all aren't all that far from the road. And some of these windows are kind of stuck from the paint. I'll come back and loosen them up for y'all."

"Don't bother. Really."

His eternal smile faltered. Gabby knew it sounded rude, but she had to say it. She had to limit his presence. The others might be gaga over his nice-guy act, but not her. Some things could never be forgiven.

"We're not *girls*," she added. "We're totally capable of moving into a place by ourselves."

"Sure. I was just saying—"

"We appreciate your help and all, but don't worry about us anymore. Spend the rest of your day swimming or doing whatever you do. We can take it from here."

Again he stood staring at her with a slackjawed expression, as if he were expending every ounce of mental energy trying to process her comment. Just when Gabby thought she was going to have to draw him a diagram, he broke off eye contact. "All right," he said, nodding and scratching his head. His gaze wandered from the wall to the floor to the rip in the sofa's armrest—anyplace but Gabby. "Guess I'll head on back if y'all are all set."

"We're set."

Suddenly his eyes were back on her. "You know, I really do hope y'all are happy here," he said.

His good-ol'-boy voice was surprisingly warm and earnest. Gabby had to turn away. Why didn't he just leave already? Did he expect a tip?

"I really don't mind helping. So if you girls—ladies—ever need anything . . ." He held something out toward her, and Gabby took it without really looking at it. "Just give us a holler."

She watched him head out the door. A second later he reappeared through the window, loping down the white gravel path to the main house.

Gabby glanced down at the object he'd given her: a thick, professionally produced business card that read *Prentiss R. Applewhite* in fancy embossed letters, followed by his cell number and email address.

"No, thank you," she muttered.

"Aw, man. He's gone." Daphne came back into the house holding her plastic-draped prom dress over her shoulder. "I was hoping he'd ask us to swim."

"I don't think they let tenants do that," Gabby said, quickly stashing the card in her purse before her sister noticed it and wanted it.

Daphne glanced out the window at Prentiss's retreating form. "He's cute."

"I'm sure you think so."

"Oh, come on! He's really cute. And I'm sure I'm not the only one who thinks so."

"You're right. I'm sure he thinks he's cute, too."

"And he's nice. Why do you not like him?"

"Because he's so . . . Paleolithic."

Daphne let out a frustrated grunt. "You're so negative."

"No, I'm smart. *I'm* the only one acting sensible around here!" Gabby exclaimed, pressing her hand to her collarbone. "Someone died because of that guy, and everyone seems to be forgetting that."

"What are you talking about?"

"I'm talking about Sonny Hutchins. Prentiss's cousin. Remember? Prentiss was driving."

"Oh, yeah. I do sort of remember," Daphne said, her eyes swiveling up toward the ceiling. "That was sad. But you're acting like he killed someone in cold blood. It was just an accident, right?"

"It was his fault. He was drunk, and he's obviously stupid to begin with, and he got them into a wreck."

"You make it sound like he's evil. You said it yourself—it was a big, stupid mistake. That's not the same thing as being evil. He probably feels awful about it."

"That's just it. I don't think he does," Gabby said, frowning at the mansion across the yard. "He got away with it, so now everyone—including him—is acting like it never happened. Like Sonny was never even here."

Daphne shook her head. "Only you could turn an awesome house on a rich cute guy's property into a big grumblefest." She spun around and headed for their new room, holding her dress high out in front of her.

Gabby looked around. The half-filled front room seemed to be smiling at her, with its cheery paint colors and rays of sunshine streaming through the freshly cleaned windows. Once again, she pressed her fingers to the nearby wall, sliding them over the rough texture. It felt almost tickly, like goose bumps. As if the house itself were excited to have them there. And Gabby was the only thing, living or not, who was less than thrilled with the situation.

Daphne lay on her back on her bare mattress, staring at the ceiling of their new room. It was so gleaming white and spotless—like a giant piece of printer paper. Their old room's ceiling had been covered in that bumpy acoustic spray—a popcorn ceiling, her mom had called it—and Daphne would search for pictures hidden in the texture. Throughout their years in the rental she'd managed to find a rose, a lion's head, a sailboat, a weeping willow tree, and a poodle on a skateboard. Then there were the fleeting images she discovered that stood out so clearly at the time, only to disappear the moment she looked away, never to be seen again. Her mom had hated those ceilings and the way they trapped dirt and rained down powder if you accidentally scraped them with something like a broom handle. But Daphne found herself missing them a bit. No hidden pictures here, just a broad white canvas. A big blank.

Bored with the vast stretch of nothing, Daphne rolled onto her side and watched Gabby as she sat cross-legged on the blue, yellow, and green braided oval rug, alphabetizing their books before she set them on the shelves. She wondered if Gabby had ever seen the pictures on their old ceiling. Probably not. Gabby wasn't the type to simply sit still and gaze about her, thinking and dreaming. She was always writing or doing complicated math or frowning down at the pages of some book thicker than a double burger. But she did seem kind of preoccupied right now, especially since she hadn't yelled at Daphne for stopping her unpacking.

She was probably still fretting over the whole Prentiss thing. She never could tolerate other people's imperfections, and his mistake was a huge one. Or perhaps she really was daydreaming. Maybe, like with everything else, she was more talented at it than Daphne. Maybe she didn't need to lie still and could actually daydream while doing other things.

"Hey, Gab?" Daphne propped her head in her right hand and let her left hand dangle, brushing the smooth hardwood with her fingertips. "Do you think you'll miss our old place?"

Gabby let out a snort. "No way. It was a pit." She squeezed Albert Camus's *The Stranger* in between Barrie's *Peter Pan* and *The Complete Illustrated Lewis Carroll;* then she glanced around the room and scowled. "Of course, this is probably just a different kind of pit."

"I love all the colors here," Daphne said, staring at the wall behind Gabby, a creamy taupe that subtly contrasted with the snowy trim and ceiling. "I wish Mr. Tibbets had let us paint at the old place. White walls are so blah."

"Colored walls are stupid. Everyone has different preferences, so if you want to rent or sell a place it's much smarter to keep the color scheme neutral."

"When I get married and have a house, I'm going to have my husband paint every room a different color. Pink, lilac, aqua blue . . ." Daphne flopped onto her back and began superimposing images of her multihued home—and Luke looking oh-so-cute in splattered overalls—on the empty ceiling above her.

"You really have to stop."

"What?" Daphne asked, annoyed that Gabby's tone had dissolved the vision of her colorful and Luke-filled future.

"Stop with all the marriage stuff," Gabby went on. "Why do you equate 'matrimony' with 'happily ever after' anyway? It's not always the same thing. In fact, it rarely is. Just look at Mom and Dad. Think about the parents of most of the kids we know. And did you hear about Mrs. Lewis? Even she's getting a divorce."

Daphne sat up and scowled at her. "So I should just give up all my dreams because *they* failed? What about your plans? I mean, if lots of kids drop out of college because it's hard, maybe you shouldn't waste your time going. Same difference."

Gabby just rolled her eyes, and Daphne couldn't help feeling triumphant. It wasn't like her sister to go quiet like that. The fact that she didn't have a snappy comeback meant Daphne really did have a point.

Feeling bolder, she decided to ask a question she'd been wondering about for a while. "Gab? Why are you so determined to not have a guy in your life?"

This time Gabby's eyes rolled the other direction. "Why are you so determined to *always* have a guy in your life?"

"I asked first."

Gabby made an impatient sound, as if she felt the answer was obvious. "Because it just seems . . . weak. Like you can't handle things on your own. Besides, guys our age are only slightly more mature than monkeys. All they care about is food and sex and goofing around." She frowned down at the cover of *A Little Princess*. "And lots of them probably get stuck that way, since there are so-called grown-up men who act like that, too."

"So . . . you're holding out for the perfect guy?" Daphne asked, trying to follow her logic.

"I'm not 'holding out' for anything," Gabby said, making quote marks in the air. "I'm just trying to earn the grades and money to get out of this crappy town. If you're smart, you'll do that, too."

Daphne shuddered. *If you're smart*. In other words, Gabby didn't think she was smart. Of course. She made that clear every time she talked to her.

"Well, I think you're just being snobby," Daphne said, slouching against the wall and crossing her arms. "You refuse to like anyone—or any place. Even this house. But Mom likes it here, and so do I."

"Of course you do. You like everything about this place. You refuse to see anything bad about *anything*. That's why you love every single guy you meet. That's why you even like Prentiss, no matter what sorts of crimes he's committed."

"So?" Daphne winced as soon as the word left her mouth. What made her think she could have a real talk with Gabby?

Her sister always had to turn everything around to Daphne and make her feel stupid. "You hate every guy. Except Mule, and I'm not sure he *is* a guy. Does he even have a penis?"

Even as she said it, she knew she was being unfair. And a total hypocrite. Just the other day she'd talked about how cute and manly Mule was looking—something Gabby could very well have pointed out to her. But she couldn't help herself. She was tired of living with boring, responsible robot people who never wanted to have a juicy conversation. She was fed up with being brushed off every time she made a comment.

And it was so worth it when she saw the look of horror on her sister's face.

"Uck! Stop!" Gabby exclaimed.

"Oh, come on. It was just a joke. I'm sure Mule has a penis." Daphne felt a surge of satisfaction when Gabby cringed again. "I mean, he does have a bulge in his pants."

"God, will you quit it!" Gabby's hands were out in front of her as if lamely attempting to shield herself from Daphne's words. "What is wrong with you?"

"Although . . . ," Daphne went on, tapping her index finger against her cheek. "Have you noticed it's typically on the left side instead of the right?"

"*Mom!*" Gabby shrieked, holding her hands over her ears. "Please do something about your sick, twisted daughter!"

Two seconds later Mrs. Rivera stood in the doorway with her usual weary expression. "What's going on here?" she asked.

"Oh, nothing," Daphne said casually. "I was just asking about Mule's penis."

Her mother's eyes grew wide. "What?"

"You see?" Gabby said, then went back to glowering at Daphne. "Quit acting like an idiot! I swear I always regret talking to you."

"Are you saying I should ask Mule about his penis, instead of you?"

"Daphne, please!" her mom said. "Enough with this nonsense!"

"Yeah, shut up!" Gabby's face was now almost the same color as the prom dress hanging on the closet door.

Daphne was thoroughly enjoying herself. "What? You guys act like 'penis' is a bad word or something."

"Well, it's certainly not a topic that I wish to discuss," her mom said, "nor do I want my fifteen-year-old daughter discussing it. So please just leave it alone. I want you girls to have this room unpacked before bedtime. Do you understand?"

"Yes," Daphne replied. Gabby nodded.

As soon as their mother trotted back down the hall, Gabby glared at Daphne fiercely. "You are such a weirdo," she mumbled.

"Penis!" Daphne hissed back. "Penis! Penis! Penis!"

Gabby heard the bell chime and hurried to open the front door before the others emerged from their rooms.

"Hey," Mule greeted her. He stood on the porch holding his calculus textbook in one arm and a three-liter Dr Pepper in the other.

Don't look at his bulge, Gabby told herself. *Don't look at his bulge.*

"Hi," she said, keeping her eyes firmly fixed on his. "Come inside." Eleven whole years she'd gone without ever considering Mule's private parts. Now, thanks to her warped little sister, she was trying her hardest to not think about them.

"This place is nice." He stepped into the living room and turned in a slow circle. "And it actually costs you guys less than the new rent at the other place?"

Gabby nodded. "That bit of information makes me suspicious," she said.

He set his soda and book on the dining table and stretched out his arms . . . and there it was. Mule's bulge. Gabby's eyes just locked onto it as if they'd been programmed to do so. Daphne was right; it did seem to be mainly on the left side. Was that a coincidence or had Daphne actually checked it out beforehand? And was going to the left normal? Or was it supposed to go right? Or was it like right- and left-handedness, with most people going one way and some going the other?

She was suddenly, vaguely aware of Mule's voice chattering away in the background. ". . . does it meet your expectations?" he asked.

"What?" Gabby's gaze snapped back up to Mule's eyes. She could feel her face warming over. *Damn it, Daphne!*

Mule chuckled. "Is this what it's going to be like now that you live at Applewhite Manor? You going to go all snot-nosed and ignore everything I say? Or did I not enunciate clearly enough for you rich, respectable folk?"

Gabby glared at him, but inwardly she felt better. The fact that he was being his typical annoying self meant he hadn't noticed her ogling his nether regions.

"I asked," he went on, "and let me go slower this time: What's . . . the . . . new . . . room . . . like? Does . . . it . . . meet . . . your . . . expectations?"

"Yeah." Her nod turned circular. "I mean no. I mean . . . The place might be nicer, but our room is actually a little smaller. I'd show you but Daffy's still unpacking."

"Seriously? Daphne's not done moving in?" Mule made an exaggerated look of surprise. "Shocker!" Gabby breathed a sigh of relief when he sat down at the kitchen table, moving his left-leaning lump out of sight.

She'd always known Mule was a boy, but that was just a technicality. A fact she'd filed away in the back of her mind—along with his eye color (hazel), shoe size (twelve and a half), and sandwich preferences (mayo, mustard—but not the kind with seeds—and extra pickle). It didn't matter, and it didn't affect how they interacted. She'd never let that little detail between his legs loom large.

Even after the crush of puberty and the disorientation brought on by brand-new feelings, brand-new body parts, and brand-new understandings, she refused to let herself think about her best friend that way. Sure, there had been fleeting curiosity once or twice, but she would always quickly dispatch it and then reprimand her insubordinate little mind. Perhaps someday she could freely entertain such thoughts, but not now. Not when there was too much history between them and too much to lose. Not after losing her first crush (or whatever Sonny had been) and getting dumped by the only other man in her life, her dad.

Happily, Mule never seemed to bring up the possibility

either. At least, not directly. Although lately all his talk of prom was freaking her out.

"And how are the landlords?" Mule asked.

"Oh, god!" Gabby exclaimed, dropping into the chair across from him. "Prentiss insisted on showing up to help—as if we're too fragile to handle boxes that *we* packed!"

"Really?"

"He even insisted on giving us a guided tour. 'This here's the sink. And this here's the door,'" Gabby spoke in an exaggerated East Texas drawl at half speed. "Lemme know if y'all need any help openin' this here door."

Mule lost it. She loved it when he really busted out with his big, loud honk of a laugh. It never failed to make her crack up, too.

"God, he's a moron," she said once she'd regained her breath. "And the sad part is, I think he really thought he was charming us. Like, just because he has muscles we're supposed to swoon at his very presence."

"Oh?" Mule's eyebrows disappeared beneath his curls. "The guy has muscles, huh?"

"Whatever. Muscles, yes, but brain? No. Empathy? No." She shut her eyes and shuddered slightly. "God, it makes me sick the way Mom and Daff think he's some guardian angel. As if he can lift a few boxes and suddenly all his past transgressions are forgiven."

"I heard he couldn't handle UT and left. That's why he's around this semester. In the fall he'll be going to community college."

Gabby's eyes widened. "Community college? Oh, my god,

how pathetic. He was probably out getting drunk every night and never studied. You just know his mom and dad are dying of embarrassment."

"Probably." Mule shrugged.

"Huh." Gabby nodded slowly, staring off into the distance. Now it all made sense, why Prentiss was always around. "What do you know? I'd just figured his parents were paying someone else to go to class for him."

"Anyway . . ." Mule looked sheepish. "Sorry I didn't show up to help. I'd planned to, but I didn't want you to think I was showing off my physique."

"Yeah, right." Gabby chuckled awkwardly, remembering that only seconds before she really had been checking out his physique—or sections of it.

"So . . . how often do you have to see Prentiss?" Mule asked, watching her strangely.

"What do you mean?"

"I mean, is he required to come by and check on you guys and stuff?"

Gabby wrinkled her nose. "Not if I can help it."

"You think he came by to help because his parents made him, or because he's just a great guy? Or do you think he maybe had . . . ulterior motives?"

Gabby took a moment to study Mule. His face was set in its usual easygoing expression. But there was something in his tone—a barb or jagged edge—that told her to be careful.

"I don't think Prentiss is smart enough to have ulterior motives," she said, with total conviction. "Frankly, I'm not sure he's evolved past the *Homo habilis* stage."

Mule seemed to relax into his chair a bit more. "Ah. Maybe he's studying spear making at community college."

"Maybe." Gabby laughed, but it felt forced and phony, powered more by nerves than delight.

She didn't like this. She didn't want to be uneasy around Mule. She didn't want to be scared of accidentally staring at his crotch or feel the need to protect his feelings by disparaging Prentiss. More to the point, she didn't want to be so very much aware that he was a guy.

Because guys couldn't be trusted.

CHAPTER ELEVEN

Progno(sis)

"How long has she been up there?" Daphne stood looking out the front window, biting her nails in loud, rhythmic chomps.

"I don't know. Maybe . . . forty minutes?"

"What could they be talking about?"

"Beats me." Gabby tried to look and sound uninterested, but in truth she couldn't stop wondering why her mom was meeting with the Applewhites in their showy chateau. They'd found her note on the kitchen table when they arrived home from school, but it didn't provide any details. Had she been summoned? Had she set it up? Maybe Prentiss had lost his license and they needed Gabby and her mom to become his private chauffeurs.

"I hope we're not in trouble," Daphne said. "Do you think they saw me accidentally step on those flowers the other day?"

"Not unless they have infrared vision. It was after dark."

"Maybe they want to invite us over to swim. Or maybe they want us to move into the big house!"

Gabby made a face. "Why the hell would they suggest something like that?"

"I don't know." Daphne shrugged. "Maybe they always wanted daughters or something."

"That would be creepy." Gabby went back to pretending to read her economics textbook.

"Here she comes!"

Gabby couldn't help tossing her book onto the coffee table and rushing to stand next to her sister.

Mrs. Rivera stopped in her tracks when she found her daughters standing just inside the front door. Gabby scrutinized her expression but couldn't glean anything from it. No smile, but no evidence of crying or a heated argument, either. Just the usual stress fissures. And a little extra powder and lipstick, as if she'd freshened up before meeting their landlord and landlady.

"Well?" Daphne asked, her whole body pitched forward with anticipation.

Gabby was torn between yelling at her sister to give their mom some space and bouncing along beside her demanding to know what was up.

Her mom slowly, infuriatingly, took off her sweater, hung it on a wooden peg next to the door, and then sank down into the nearest chair. "Well, I have good news and bad news."

"Bad news first," Daphne urged.

"No, let me start with the good news and continue from there."

"That means the bad news is really bad," Daphne whispered to Gabby.

"Be quiet," Gabby muttered, but secretly she agreed.

"Are we in trouble?" Daphne asked, chewing her left thumbnail.

"No, no. Now please listen. As it turns out"—Mrs. Rivera paused and a soft smile stole across her face—"I'm getting a promotion at work."

"Mom!" Daphne squealed. "That's awesome!"

"Does it mean more money?" Gabby asked.

"Thank you, dear," her mom said. "And yes, it's a little more money. Plus an office of my own. But . . ." She bit her lip and glanced at each of them.

"We have to move?" Gabby said. That would be so unfair. They'd only just settled in.

"No, we don't have to move," Mrs. Rivera replied. "But I have to go away for some training. This Wednesday, in fact. They're flying me out to Atlanta, and I'll have to stay there for three and a half weeks."

"But . . . what about us?" Daphne asked.

"You'll be on your own. Gabby is old enough to watch out for you guys, and the Applewhites said they would be glad to help if there are any problems. Of course, I'll be in touch by phone as often as I can. And it's only for a few weeks." Three faint grooves appeared in Mrs. Rivera's forehead and each hand took turns gripping the other.

"It'll be fine," Gabby said. She reached over and squeezed her mother's arm. "I'm so proud of you for getting that promotion. You deserve it."

Mrs. Rivera smiled and one of the worry lines disappeared. The grin also seemed to brighten her face and add sparkle to her wide green eyes. Gabby hadn't seen her look so young and pretty—and happy—in a long time. "Thanks," she said. "I knew I'd lost out on that one job to Rick, but then they told me I'd gotten this one. I didn't even know about the opening."

"Wait a minute." Daphne looked even more concerned than she had before she heard the news. "Does this mean Gabby gets to boss me around for almost a month?"

The crease reappeared in her mom's brow. "Not exactly . . . ," she began.

"What's wrong with you?" Gabby said to Daphne. "Why can't you be happy for Mom? You should be congratulating her, not complaining."

Daphne gestured toward her. "This is what I mean. She's going to do this the whole time. Can't Dad come stay with us?"

"That's not possible." Her mom's gaze lowered to her lap. "Not with his job, his situation."

"But—"

"Sweetie, try to understand. It's the only way." Mrs. Rivera reached out and grabbed Daphne's extended hand. "I'm going to be depending on you, too. Not just Gabby. She can't watch you all day and night, you know. So I'm going to need you to be a little more responsible and independent. Can you do that for me?"

Gabby watched her sister's expression ease into a smile. She knew exactly what Daphne was thinking: more time with her latest boy obsession, less nagging from Mom. Gabby wondered if she should say something, but her mom already had so much on her mind. Besides, she'd be the one in charge. She'd handle it.

"Don't worry. I can do that," Daphne said. She stepped forward and hugged her mom around the neck. "And I am really proud of you."

"Thanks, baby. Now what do you say we all go out to dinner and celebrate?"

"You mean . . . at a restaurant?" Daphne asked.

Mrs. Rivera laughed. "Yes."

"We've got that coupon for Whataburger," Gabby said, heading for the drawer in the kitchen where they kept loose papers.

"No. No coupons. No fast food. Let's go to the Rushing Water Inn."

Daphne sucked in her breath. "Really?"

"Sure, why not?" Mrs. Rivera said.

"Oh, thank you!" Daphne hugged their mom again and then trotted off toward the bedroom. "I'm going to change into something swanky!"

"Mom, are you sure?" Gabby asked once Daphne was out of earshot. "That place is so expensive."

Her mom held up both hands in a "stop" gesture. "I don't care. We have lots to celebrate. New house. New job. I think we deserve to spoil ourselves at least one night, right?"

"I guess," Gabby replied. She didn't like this shifting of positions. Daphne promising to be responsible. Mom offering to blow a ton of money on a fancy meal. It was disturbing.

"Well? Get to it," her mom said. "Like Daff said, go get swanky!"

Her mom looked so happy, so relaxed. Gabby knew she should be ecstatic for her. For all of them. So why was she so edgy? Why did all these good things feel . . . wrong?

"Oh, my god. I'm so full." Daphne patted her stomach as if Luke could somehow see her over the phone. "You won't believe where we ate dinner tonight. The Rushing Water Inn!"

"What's that?"

"The best restaurant in town."

Daphne lifted one of Gabby's T-shirts off the pile and checked it for stains as well as she could with one hand. She had offered to sort the laundry to prove to her mom that they'd be fine without her for a few weeks. It seemed like an easier chore than doing the dishes. Plus, the utility room in their new house was nice and secluded—a cramped little room off the kitchen with only one tiny window. When the dishwasher was running it muffled all noise, so there was little danger of her conversations being overheard.

"It's really awesome," she said, shoving the shirt into the washer. "I ordered something French-sounding. Chicken breast with this cheesy stuff inside it."

"Cordon bleu?"

"Yeah, that's it!" Daphne said. "It's nice. You should go there sometime." *Like, for prom,* she added mentally. *With me.*

"Yeah, I should."

She waited, hoping he would use this as a chance to finally ask her, but he said nothing further. Just made a little combination humming-sighing sound, as if he were stretching.

This was getting frustrating. Sure, prom was still three

weeks away, but so many people had already been asked. All they had left to do was brag and daydream. She at least had the dress, and was therefore slightly ahead of the game, and she was doing her best to be patient, but she still wished a fairy godmother would suddenly materialize atop the dryer and wave her magic wand, making Luke her official date.

In fairy tales, the heroine always had someone to help her, like a pixie or a band of dwarves or a flock of animated bluebirds. But who did Daphne have? Who was on her side? Definitely not Mom or Gabby or anyone on the cheer squad. This meant she had to figure things out herself. Only solving problems was more her sister's forte; Daphne was better at wishing them away.

"So what are you doing this weekend?" she asked as she reached into the hamper and pulled out another blouse. It was one of her mom's, beige with a light yellow floral design. Should it go with the lights or darks? It was medium in color and weight. And the label had faded so much she couldn't tell what the manufacturer recommended.

"I don't know. . . ." Luke's voice trailed off, as if he were considering something.

Daphne shoved the blouse into the washer and waited. Perhaps if he didn't want to take this chance to ask her to prom, he'd at least ask her out somewhere—this time excluding Walt and Todd.

"Oh, wait. There is something going on," Luke said. "I heard about a big party Saturday night."

Oh, no! So he knew about Tracy's party. Daphne's heart sped up so suddenly, the pile of clothes in front of her started to shimmer. She twisted her thumbnail between her teeth, envisioning Lynette in one of her slutty party dresses, targeting Luke like a blond heat-seeking missile.

"They said it was going to be pretty cool. Are you going?" he asked.

"Um, I'm not sure I can. Are you?"

"Yeah, I promised the guys I'd go. I hope you'll be there. I hardly get to see you. It would be nice to . . . hang out." His tone turned soft and rumbly. Almost like a purr.

Daphne leaned against the wall of the laundry room and closed her eyes, letting the warmth of his words ooze all over her. *Think, Daphne, think.* There had to be some way she could get out of the house without her sister knowing. But the front door squeaked, and Gabby was such a light sleeper, despite the snoring.

Opening her eyes, Daphne suddenly beheld the window . . . small but not too tiny to fit through, and perfectly situated above the sturdy dryer.

Could she?

No. She couldn't. Even with Mom gone, Gabby would be watching her like a hawk. No . . . a vulture. Yeah. A grumpy, killjoy vulture. And if she waited until Gabby went to sleep, the party would be almost over. Plus, even if she managed to sneak out of the house, what then? She couldn't exactly walk the ten miles to Tracy's house.

Her eyes clouded and her nose got that itchy feeling that always preceded a good cry. If only she had the freedom to come and go as she wanted—to attend keg parties and go on unchaperoned trips to the beach. Some kids had it so easy.

Meanwhile, she was stuck at home with a cruel older sister, doing drudge work, just like Cinderella.

It was Fate testing her again, seeing whether she could be the noble heroine. If she did something stupid, she could blow all her chances of going out with Luke. She had to remember that.

"I really want to see you, too," she said. "But we can be patient, right? And what about Sunday? Maybe, after you've slept late, we could meet up and bowl another game or two. You could tell me all about the party. And maybe this time it could just be you and me? You know . . . so I can give you pointers?" She bit her lip and shut her eyes again, wallowing in her longing for him, concentrating on each wrenching beat of her heart and the faint shushing sounds of the telephone connection.

"Sure. That sounds great," he said.

He sounded pleased, even excited. Daphne took comfort in it.

"Well, I gotta run. See you later, Daffodil."

"Bye."

Daffodil! Daphne shut off the phone, hugged it to her chest, and lay back against the dirty laundry. First he gave her a penny, and now a nickname? It was the best reassurance she could have asked for. (Well . . . second to an invitation to prom.) But still, it was a sign of closeness. Of love. It made her feel hopeful and strong enough to endure. Like a princess in a tower or a genie in a bottle.

Or a flower standing straight and tall in a storm.

CHAPTER TWELVE
Neuro(sis)

The springs in the old sofa let out their familiar squeaks as Gabby settled onto the cushion beside her mother and handed her a cup of coffee.

Her mom's flight left Houston at ten-thirty, which meant she had to leave Barton at six to check in at the airport two hours early. Luckily, the Sandbornes made occasional trips to Houston during the week for salon supplies and had offered to give her a lift. That way there was no need to pay for parking, and Gabby could use the car during her mother's absence.

Of course Daffy couldn't bother to get out of bed long enough to kiss her mother goodbye. Gabby wasn't surprised, and she was kind of glad to have her mom to herself, but it still irritated her that Daphne had, once again, gotten away with being totally selfish.

Gabby wondered why she'd bothered to brew up the Colombian Supremo, since her mom certainly didn't seem to need caffeine. Mrs. Rivera kept checking her watch, rummaging through her bag, and occasionally standing to gaze out the front window at the driveway.

"Do you have that list of phone numbers I gave you?"

"Yes, it's on the bulletin board," Gabby said, pointing to the wall in back of them.

"And you have the number for the Applewhites on your cell?"

"I have it," she said. She didn't, actually, but she did have Prentiss's pretentious business card in her purse. So it wasn't a total lie.

"And you put all that money in a safe place?"

"Yes. I told you. Part of it is in the empty tea tin and the rest is hidden in the bedroom—your bedroom. I figure I'll sleep in there while you're gone."

Her mom's nods slowed and stopped. Suddenly her fingers flew to her forehead. "Oh, honey, maybe I shouldn't go. I'm so worried that this is a mistake."

"Why? We're old enough to take care of ourselves for a little while."

"Yes, I know. But I can't help feeling . . . negligent."

Gabby gave her a shoulder bump. "Hey. Think of it as a vacation from us. You've never had that before, and you deserve it. Absence makes the heart grow fonder and all that."

"I'm already crazy about you girls." Her mom looked at her tenderly.

"Yeah, but we're not that fond of you." Gabby laughed as her mom's adoring smile disappeared, replaced by a look of indignation. "*Kidding!*"

Right at that moment, a car honked. Mrs. Rivera leaped to her feet.

"That's them," she said, her eyes wide and frantic.

"You remembered to pack your cell phone charger, right?" Gabby asked, handing her mother the tweedy blue garment bag.

"Yes."

"Good. And your neck pillow?"

Mrs. Rivera nodded.

Gabby grabbed the rolling suitcase and followed her to the door. "Did you get a refill on your headache medicine?"

"Right here." She patted her purse.

Gabby smiled. "Now, remember . . . if a handsome guy asks you for your room key . . ."

"I know, I know. Ask him for his bank statement, three references, and a clean bill of health from his doctor."

"Good girl."

Her mom's chuckles petered out. "You two really will be okay, right?"

"We really will be."

The horn sounded again. Mrs. Rivera threw her arms around Gabby and squeezed her tightly. "Wish me luck."

"You don't need it, but . . . good luck."

Gabby kissed her mom and passed her the handle to the suitcase. Then she followed her outside and stood on the porch waving and watching until the Sandbornes' minivan turned out of the drive and disappeared into the twilight.

She stepped to the edge of the porch and wrapped her arms around one of the posts, feeling suddenly small under the vast, colorless sky. There was something eerie about the predawn stillness. The world didn't seem to be sleeping so much as pointedly ignoring her. It reminded her of when she was really young and her parents would go out, leaving her and Daphne in the care of a babysitter—usually old Mrs. Palacky from next door, who, for some reason, would always bring over two bananas, one for each of the girls, and liked to teach them Czech drinking songs. Even at that age Gabby knew her mom and dad deserved to go out and have fun, but it still unsettled her. She couldn't help wondering what would happen if something went wrong and they never came back, and she couldn't fall asleep until she heard their car's tires crunching up the driveway.

Such fear made a lot of sense in an eight-year-old, but not in an eighteen-year-old. Gabby knew she should quit worrying and be excited for her mom. But then . . . in a way, that vague, childlike dread had come true. There really had come a day when her dad packed up his car and left, never returning—at least, not to stay.

Gabby let go the breath she'd been holding and headed back inside, locking the door as soon as her bare feet hit the spongy new carpet. The inside of the house felt just as ghostly. The dim light washed out the cheery paint colors, making the place feel drab and sad. No sunshine, no sound, no movements other than her own. It was as if time and everything in it had stopped—except her.

"If only," she muttered to herself. Having unchecked time would be wonderful. Maybe then she could finish the scholarship application and her extra-credit projects in physics and calc. But already the whooshy sound of traffic along Elmhurst was growing steadier. And according to the kitty-cat clock on the kitchen wall, she had only twenty-four minutes until her alarm went off.

Gabby trudged over to the window and glanced out, the same way her mother had kept doing before she left. Only there was nothing to see. Just darkness and the occasional glow from a passing car. Turning her head, she noticed that a light was on in an upstairs window of the main house. Prentiss's room, judging by the memory of her previous visit, when she'd dropped off the rental agreement. She wondered what he would be doing up at such an hour, especially with no classes to go to.

Did the quiet make him uneasy, like it did her? What did he think about? Gabby imagined him pacing around an incredibly messy room, shirtless and barefoot, his strong jaw flexing in sleepless anxiety. Maybe he was remembering the crash. Or maybe he was staring out the window and wondering about her light, the same way she was wondering about his. For some reason, that thought didn't upset her the way it should have. In fact, it made her feel a little better—less alone in the gloom.

"Oh, please!" she exclaimed suddenly, grabbing the curtains and pulling them shut. Her mom hadn't been gone five minutes and already Gabby was losing her grip.

She was tired and stressed and therefore unable to stop her mind from wandering into places she knew it shouldn't go. Her mom would return home safely—no need for concern. And for all she knew, Prentiss was only now coming home after a hard night of partying. That was probably why the light was on.

Not that it mattered to her. She didn't care what he did, as long as he stayed out of her way. And her thoughts.

Daphne couldn't keep still. She had begun pacing the living room as soon as Sheri had dropped her off a half hour before, and she was still at it. At this rate she'd be wearing a deep trench in the new carpet before dusk.

As jumpy as she felt physically, her mind was even more frenzied. She wanted to forget what she'd seen, but she couldn't. It was as if that horrible image she'd glimpsed after school had been scorched into her corneas.

She'd almost missed it. She'd been sitting in the passenger seat of Sheri's Outback, zonked from practice, and had just happened to glance out the window. That was when she spied Luke and some of the other guys heading into the parking lot from the basketball court. Lynette, who hadn't left yet, had run right up to Luke. Daphne could see her slinking around in his space, as if she were crooning a torch song right into his ear. Then Sheri had made the turn and she'd lost sight of them.

For a while Daphne just sat there, only half hearing Sheri try to sing along to some hip-hop tune, unable to accept what she'd seen. Then, when she'd recovered from the shock, she had wrestled with the impulse to grab the steering wheel and turn the car around herself.

Only she hadn't. And now she was stuck at home. And Luke was who knew where, possibly with Lynette, doing who knew what. Daphne told herself over and over that he'd never go for Lynette, but each time she found it more difficult to believe.

She sat down on the couch, grabbed the remote, and clicked on the TV. A cartoon came blaring on, all bright colors and silly sound effects. But her mind couldn't follow it. So she stood back up and resumed her laps around the room. Her limbs felt revved up and her eyes kept darting around as if searching for something. It was as if her own body were urging her to take some action. But what?

A knock sounded on the front door and Daphne's feet left the floor for a split second. Her brain was so focused on Luke that she felt sure it was him, with a bouquet of wildflowers and a rehearsed, ultraromantic speech asking her to prom.

She raced to the door and flung it open, and there, smiling over a big brown grocery sack, stood Mule.

"Oh," she said.

His grin faded as he registered the disappointment in her voice. "Expecting somebody?" he asked.

"No," she mumbled. "Come on in." She pressed herself against the doorjamb and made a halfhearted welcoming motion toward the living room. As he stepped past her, she glanced hopefully about the yard—but there was no one else around.

Mule went straight for the dining room table and started unpacking the bag, pulling out two two-liter bottles of Dr Pepper and a bag of Funyuns. "Is Gabby here?" he asked.

"She's not back from work yet," Daphne said. "But it shouldn't take her very long to get home since she's got Mom's car." She stuck her index finger in her mouth and started gnawing on what was left of the nail. Meanwhile, her right leg jiggled as if she were trying to dislodge an overly amorous Chihuahua.

"Is it okay if I just hang out and wait?" Mule asked, peering at her guardedly.

"Sure."

Daphne walked to the window and glanced out. There was still no sign of any other human being, so she did a complete about-face. She pulled her cell phone out of her pocket intending to call Luke, but then shoved it back in, unsure of what to do or say if he answered. Instead she started chomping on the nails of her index and middle fingers, and her right leg began quaking yet again.

"You okay?" Mule asked. Cradling the Funyuns in one arm, he slowly made his way to the couch, watching her the entire way.

"Yeah," she said. Only it came out all quick and high-pitched—more of a yip than an actual word.

Mule gave a tiny shrug and plunked himself on the sofa, slouching down so that his long legs slid under the coffee table instead of banging up against it.

Daphne turned her focus on Mule, studying him as he watched TV and crunched Funyuns. He really was getting cuter. His skin had cleared up and his face had new angles and planes. Funny how she'd known him for so long, but she'd never really thought of him as a guy. Oh sure, she'd considered him a guylike creature, the way koalas were bearlike without being official bears, the way Cheez Whiz wasn't actually cheese. But now she could see that he clearly was one.

Which probably meant he could decipher guy thoughts and actions. . . .

Daphne walked over to the couch and sat down beside him.

"Want some?" he asked, tilting the bag of Funyuns toward her.

She shook her head. "No thanks."

"Smart," Mule said. "These things are really bad for you. I once ate two big bags and almost OD'd. Woke up behind a Dumpster wearing roller skates and one of my auntie's nightgowns."

He paused, waiting for a reaction. She smiled politely but couldn't manage a laugh. Not even the Pepe Le Pew cartoon on TV could make her giggle. And she loved Pepe Le Pew.

"Hey, Mule," she said, waiting for his crunches to die down so he could hear her clearly. "If you really liked someone . . . I mean superliked . . . even loved . . . and you were pretty sure they felt the same way about you, but for some reason things weren't . . . progressing." She glanced up and met his eyes. "What would you do?"

Mule stopped chewing. His whole face seemed to lengthen. His eyebrows flew up and his mouth, sprinkled with yellow crumbs, hung down. "Seriously?" he said, after swallowing. "Are you pranking me or something?"

Daphne frowned. "No. Why?"

"It's just . . ." He broke off and shook his head. "Nothing. It's just weird that you would ask me advice on dating and stuff. You've had more success in that arena than I have."

"I'm just trying to understand a guy's point of view."

"A guy's view, huh?" He chuckled, only he didn't seem to be laughing at her. Instead, he stared right past her, out the front window. He looked almost sad. "You sure you want to know what I think?" he said, finding her gaze again.

Daphne nodded.

"Okay." He lowered the bag of Funyuns and sat up straight. "Here's the thing: guys are just as confused about what to do as girls are. They . . . We . . . are never really sure what's expected of us."

"So . . . if a guy isn't making a move, it could mean he's being polite and proper . . . or it could mean that he's afraid the girl doesn't feel the same way? That he's afraid of making a big mistake?"

"Bingo," he said, making a finger gun with his right hand. "That's it exactly."

"Huh." Daphne stared at the nearby wall. Luke was such a gentleman, she'd assumed he was waiting a respectable amount of time before revealing his true feelings. But maybe he was just scared? She'd never considered that before. It was kind of sweet to think so. And it made her feel a little better.

"So what, exactly, are girls supposed to do?" she asked Mule. "How can we let guys know that it's okay?"

"Any help is really appreciated. We like it when girls drop hints. You know, like neon signs, T-shirts with logos giving detailed instructions, heart-shaped tattoos with our names in them."

Daphne's eyes widened.

"Kidding," he said. Mule's lopsided grin faded and he stared thoughtfully into his bag of snacks. "Seriously, though, guys are so scared of doing the wrong thing they usually just do nothing. They can be pretty sure a girl likes them and then five seconds later talk themselves out of it. And being shot down is the worst feeling ever. They'd rather play it safe and wait until they're totally one-hundred-percent sure she won't run off screaming."

Daphne considered this. Mule was right. It was girls like Lynette—girls who made it undeniably clear that they were interested—who landed guys so effortlessly. Perhaps Luke just didn't want to offend Daphne by coming on too strong and was simply looking for a clear sign of what she wanted. She thought she'd already let him know with her hallway waves and phone calls and invitations to go bowling, but those might not have been obvious enough. And she'd been so swoony when he kissed her in the pharmacy that she hadn't visibly reacted to it. Poor guy! She'd even turned down his suggestion that she go to Tracy's party. She'd thought she was being patient and smart, that it was a test of Fate she had to endure to be with him. But what if *he'd* been the one testing her, to see if she liked him?

Walt's words at the bowling alley echoed in her head. *You shouldn't waste your time. . . . You'll see. . . .*

She shifted to face Mule again. "So how long will a guy wait for a girl? I mean, what if, through no fault of her own, it's sometimes hard for her to get away and see him?"

Mule scrunched up his nose. "You mean like Romeo and Juliet?"

Daphne laughed. "Yeah. Kind of like that. How long until the guy just gives up on her?"

"I don't know," he said with a shrug. "I guess most guys would think that if a girl was really into him, she'd find a way to be with him."

Daphne took a deep breath. She could feel herself filling with a shaky resolve. No more waiting patiently. She had to do something to let Luke know she wanted him. Something romantic, but not too bold. Something within her range of skills. Something that no guy their age could refuse—other than sex.

She glanced over at Mule, who was still digging into the bag of Funyuns as if his body depended on the stuff. That gave her an idea.

CHAPTER THIRTEEN
Parenthe(sis)

"Stupid, pea-brained, pampered cretin!" Gabby stalked across the dewy grass to the rhythm of the words. "Stupid, lazy, thoughtless caveman!"

A few more muttered syllables and she reached the Applewhite house. She hesitated for a couple of seconds before mounting the porch steps. At least Mr. Applewhite's Lexus and Mrs. Applewhite's Mercedes coupe were gone. Only the prodigal son was home. The stupid coddled Neanderthal.

Gabby strode up to the front door and pounded on it with her fist. Then she rang the doorbell. After fifteen seconds passed with no response, she rang it again. She also pounded again, mainly because it felt good.

Eventually she heard some muffled thuds and Prentiss opened the door. He stood in front of her looking sleepy and surprised. His hair was all flattened against his head, except for two or three layers in the back that stood straight out like a rooster's crest, and his face was puffy and inert. The only thing he had on was a pair of shorts—or maybe they were boxers. Gabby didn't want to keep glancing at them to find out.

"Hey," he said, blinking in the sunlight. He reached across his bare chest to scratch his left shoulder and Gabby forced her gaze back up to his eyes. "Sorry it took a while. I was sleeping."

"Yes, well, *I* have to go to school," she said. "Only I can't get my car out of the driveway."

Prentiss squinted in the direction of their house. "Really? It won't start?"

"It starts fine. But it appears that *someone* has blocked me in with their Mustang."

She patiently waited the two seconds for him to process this.

"Oh. Right. I'm sorry. I'm still not used to y'all living here."

"Yes, well . . . we do. Unfortunately."

She wasn't sure if he heard her. He stepped away from the doorway for a moment and returned wearing a brown leather jacket and flip-flops.

"Don't worry. I'll move it out of your way in a jiffy," he said, smiling at her. He tossed a wad of keys into the air and caught them with his right hand.

Gabby scowled. How dare he make it sound as if he were doing her a favor. If it weren't for him, she could have left six minutes ago.

He shut the door and headed down the same dewy path she'd traveled on the way up to the house.

"Gonna be a nice one," he said, grinning up at the sky. His pleasantness irked her. She'd expected him to be horrified and extra-apologetic at the way he'd inconvenienced her. Instead, he was acting as if they were on a friendly stroll, picking dandelions and looking for pictures in the clouds.

But of course he would act this way. Because he was do-no-wrong boy. Prince Prentiss of Barton had his own traffic rules and everything.

"So how are you guys liking the place?" he asked.

"It's fine."

"That new paint working out for you?"

Damn, that boy was proud of the paint. "Yes."

"I always knew there was potential for that little place," he said, nodding along in agreement with himself. "I always told my mom that—"

"Look," she interrupted. "I'm tired—as are you, I'm sure, considering you just woke up and all, no doubt after a hard night—and I'm really not in the mood for conversation. Plus, I have a hugely important physics test in exactly"—she paused to check her watch—"thirty-five minutes. So could you please just move the car?"

Prentiss gaped at her with that blank, openmouthed expression she'd come to know so well. Then he shook his head and chuckled slightly. "You know," he said, staring off toward the peach-colored haze in the eastern sky, "I don't understand it."

"Understand what?" she asked, unable to stop herself.

"How someone as pretty as you can be so darn grouchy all the time."

He met her eyes again. She expected to see irritation, but instead, there was still a warmth to his gaze, only sadder and more distant. It was a look of pity. Prentiss Applewhite had the nerve to pity her?

But that wasn't even the worst part.

What made it even more horrible was that up close, without his trademark dazzling smile and with his morning hair lying flat instead of in bristles, Prentiss looked like Sonny. Same blue eyes. Same worried wave in the eyebrows. Same indentation in his broad lower lip, like a tiny basin or fingerhold.

Gabby was so stunned by the realization that she came to a sudden halt, as if hit by a freeze ray. All she could do was stand there and gape after Prentiss as he climbed into his car and reparked it farther up the driveway. Once he was done he carefully shut the door, wiped some dirt off the front left fender, and headed into the house without looking back.

God, she loathed that guy! She disliked him so much, it made her stupid. She hated how clueless and cheerful he was all the time, as if he had nothing to hide. She hated the way he smiled as if he had no worries at all.

But most of all, right at that second, she hated the way his calling her pretty had set off a tiny jet of warmth inside her, like those sparks that spray up when you poke the dying coals of a fire. A familiar warmth. The same warmth stirred up years ago, by Sonny.

Prentiss R. Applewhite could be even more dangerous than Gabby had originally feared.

Daphne stood in the nook at the end of a row of lockers and watched the passing stream of students. It was strange looking out at the crowd without them seeing her—like being invisible. But then . . . it had always been a little bit like this. These were her friends and neighbors, people she'd known her whole life, and yet she had to admit, she sometimes didn't feel like she was one of them.

None of them truly saw her for who she was. Or if they did catch a glimpse, they sure didn't like it. The boys called her a tease when she wouldn't let them do more than kiss her. The girls called her a snob when she wouldn't use crude language or text topless pics of herself to the basketball team to celebrate a big win. And they'd all made fun of her when she cried at the end of *Romeo and Juliet* in freshman English. Even her own mom and sister didn't get her. Her dad did—he was an old-fashioned romantic, too—but he lived in San Antonio. That meant Luke was the only person in all of Barton who really understood and accepted the real Daphne. And this was why she was wedged up against the cinder-block wall waiting for him.

After talking with Mule, she'd realized she had to be more forward with Luke so he would know exactly how she felt about him. She wouldn't resort to Lynette-like tactics, but she could at least do her best to spend more time with him and drop little hints here and there. Then he would feel secure enough to ask her out. And then their fairy-tale romance could finally begin.

Daphne's left butt cheek was starting to go numb. She shifted her body as much as her narrow surroundings would allow and glanced at the clock on the opposite wall. Where was he? She would definitely end up being late for Ms. Manbeck's class, but this was the only place and time where she knew she'd run into him. She leaned forward slightly and scanned the nearby throng.

There was Walt Lively, the boy-king of the sophomore class, swaggering down the hallway as if he'd just inherited the place. There was Lee Bradley, who'd given her her first kiss at an eighth-grade dance—and then lied to everyone that she'd let him put his hands down her skirt. There was Todd Carothers, so pale and blond, as if he'd been faded along with his tight jeans. She'd always thought he was sweet until she heard him laughing about the time he ran over a stray dog with his pickup.

How could she have liked those guys? How could she have gotten it so wrong? Meeting Luke was like . . . waking up from a long sleep. All her life she'd been plodding along, thinking she was content, and then . . . *wham!* Suddenly her world was filled with color and music and all possibilities of magic. Like stepping out of Kansas and into Oz.

And there he was.

The second Daphne spied Luke's tidy haircut coming down the corridor, a tiny ember flared in her chest and spread through her limbs. By the time he approached her alcove, she felt cooked medium-rare.

"Luke!" she said, stepping forward to merge into the rush of students.

His upper body snapped sideways as if startled. But as soon as he spied her, his shoulders relaxed and his mouth boinged into a smile. "Oh, hey," he said. "What's up?"

"Nothing much. I was wondering if you wanted to come over tonight and have dinner with us?"

"Dinner?" For some reason he looked confused.

"Yeah. Say, around six-thirty or so?"

"Really? What about your parents? Is it okay with them?"

"Well, my dad . . ." She paused. "They're both out of town. But I'll cook us up something. Then we can take a walk and I can show you around our new place. It's really pretty." *And then you'll realize how I feel about you, and see that there's no reason to be afraid,* she added silently.

Eventually his features flattened into an easy grin. "Um . . . sure. Okay," he said.

"Great!"

They reached his classroom and stopped. "So . . . ," Luke said, glancing around at the thinning traffic. "Should I, you know, bring anything?"

"Nope. Just you! I'll text you the directions on how to get there."

"Okay. See ya, Daffodil." The bell rang as he backed into his room.

Daphne waited until he disappeared before turning around. Then she bounced up the stairs, breezed down the hall, and glided into her classroom.

"How very nice of you to join us, Miss Rivera" was Ms. Manbeck's drone of a greeting. "That makes three tardies. You owe me a detention."

"Okay," Daphne said, fluttering into her seat. She was vaguely aware of the other students' snickers and stares—and Ms. Manbeck's twitchy look of disapproval. But it didn't matter. The only thing that mattered was Luke, and that in eight hours' time he would be at her front door. And then everything would be perfect.

○ ○ ○

Gabby knew something was wrong the second she stepped through the front door of their rental home and a noxious odor hit her nostrils. This wasn't the new-paint or new-carpet fumes, which had (finally) subsided to a slight reek. Instead, this was the eye-watering stink of a recent mishap.

"Daff?" she called out.

No answer.

She sniffed her way through the house and finally tracked the smell to the kitchen trash can. Buried under the strata of old napkins, a plastic grocery sack, and several pages of that day's newspaper lay a blackened and slightly misshapen saucepan. She pulled it out and ran her fingers over the sullied surface. It was still warm.

"What the . . . ?"

Gabby gritted her teeth, her cheeks burning hotter than the pan's molten exterior. The saucepan had been a Christmas present to her mom—part of a six-piece cookware set Gabby had found at Target. Although it had been on sale, it hadn't been cheap. In fact, Gabby could calculate the precise number of hours she'd had to work and a very close approximation of annoying customers and Pinkwater grumblings she'd had to endure to purchase it.

"That little . . . !" There were no words bad enough. No names left to call Daphne. The day had sucked already once Prentiss made Gabby feel stupid with his "pretty" compliment— or put-down, actually. It had sucked even worse when she messed up a whole section on her physics test and scored only an 88—possibly because of Prentiss's mind trip. Then the suckiness had reached new heights when Ms. Coogan, her former history teacher, didn't have that letter of recommendation ready, like she'd said she would.

And now this.

Things would never change. Daphne would forever be undoing Gabby's hard work and Gabby would forever be swabbing up the messes.

How was it that they were related? It was as if they weren't even the same species. Daphne was one of those spoiled, fluffy cats that snoozed in a windowsill all day, able to preen and daydream through life. Meanwhile, Gabby was a work animal—an ox or a hunting dog, or maybe one of those sad-looking carriage horses—pushing herself day and night out of sheer instinct and loyalty.

Even as she thought this, she sprayed the glass cooktop with grease cutter and wiped it over and over with a cloth until the surface squeaked clean.

It isn't fair, the squeaks seemed to say. *It isn't fair. . . .*

She'd just finished tossing the rag into the garbage pail when the door burst open and Daphne strode in wearing her school backpack and a huge smile. The tops of her cheeks were flushed a deep coral, and wisps of hair had fallen from her ponytail, lightly framing her face. She looked so pretty and cheerful, it made Gabby boil even more.

"What is this?" Gabby demanded, holding up the ruined saucepan.

Daphne's face fell. "It was an accident. I was trying to make spaghetti and . . . it burned."

"Are you stupid? Or are you so selfish that you have absolutely no regard for other people or their property? Not only did you totally ruin the pan, you also could have caused a fire by hiding it in the trash when it was still smoldering! I mean . . . do you even think? Mom's gone—what?—*two days* and you almost burn down our new place?"

"I said it was an accident! God! Why can't you just accept it and move on with your life?"

"Because who knows when you'll strike next!" Gabby shouted, slamming the pan onto the countertop. "You could be keeping a rabid animal in the bathroom! Or maybe you left the window open and we got robbed!"

"Shut up. I'd never do that." Daphne crossed her arms and looked insulted, but there was a guilty chime in her voice. Gabby made a mental note to check all the windows later. "Why do you always do this?"

Gabby frowned. "Do what?"

"Try to make me feel stupid."

"Huh? I point out that you've totally destroyed this pan and *I'm* the one at fault?"

"You and Mom always just start freaking out. You never ask to hear my side of things. Besides, I took care of dinner. Don't I get credit for that?"

"You actually made dinner?" Gabby glanced around the messy kitchen.

"Yeah." Daphne unzipped her backpack and pulled out three bags with Golden Chick logos on them. "When the spaghetti sauce went bad I figured I'd buy us chicken baskets."

Gabby shut her eyes in some vain hope that she could make it all disappear. *When the spaghetti sauce went bad* was how Daphne had put it. Not *When I burned the spaghetti sauce and the expensive Christmas gift it was in*. She'd removed herself entirely from the sentence and the action. As usual, she was taking no responsibility. In Daphne's warped little mind, the sauce had spontaneously combusted and taken the pan down with it.

She opened her eyes again and there was Daphne, laying out the table, all swingy ponytail and perky momentum. Gabby counted the place settings.

"Daff, don't forget that Mom's not here," she said.

"I know. The extra place is for Luke. I invited him over."

"What? Oh, no. No way."

"Why not? I'm the one who made dinner. Well, okay . . . *bought* dinner. But still! Shouldn't I have the right to ask over a friend?"

"No! For one thing, it's a school night. And for another, I promised Mom."

Daphne's eyes narrowed. "You promised Mom what?"

"To watch over you."

"What does that mean?"

"It means no having boys over while she's gone."

"That's not fair!" Daphne screeched. "You have Mule over all the time!"

"But he's just Mule. Mom loves him. She's known him and his family forever."

"So? It's not Luke's fault that he's new. That Mom hasn't met him yet."

"He can't come over. I promised." Gabby turned toward the kitchen counter to signal the end of the discussion and to clean up the final bit of greasy residue.

"Oh, really?" Daphne's voice was an angry sizzle. "What if I have him over anyway?"

Gabby rounded on her. "Don't make me call Mom on you! You think I'm freaking about the stupid pan, if you ruin Mom's chances at getting this job she deserves, I will make your life hell!"

"God, I hate you! You love this, don't you? You love it that Mom's out of town so you can boss me around and ruin my life!" Daphne's face was as red as the congealed spaghetti sauce. Her features were twisted with rage, but her eyes looked wide and helpless. She stared at Gabby for a few seconds, as if waiting for something. Then, with a little cry of defeat, she spun around and ran down the hall toward their bedroom.

Wrong again, Daff, Gabby thought as she scrubbed the last smear of burnt sauce off the stove. *It's my life that's getting ruined.*

Daphne slammed the door of their room and took a running dive for her bed, knocking the headboard into the wall as she landed. She grabbed a fistful of blanket in each hand and let loose with several angry screams into her pillow, followed by a series of sobs.

God, she hated her sister. She'd yelled it before in the heat of anger, but this time she truly meant it. She loathed Gabby, totally and irrevocably. She could even feel the hatred inside her, like a disease chewing away at her insides, a toxin simmering through her bloodstream.

It was clear to her now that Gabby didn't want her to be happy. The girl was miserable, and she wanted everyone else to be, too. So she went around spreading her gloom the way

Ruth Collett and her mom, in their floor-sweeping cotton dresses, knocked on doors every weekend spreading their religion.

Luke made Daphne happy, but Gabby couldn't have that. No-o. And it wasn't as if Daphne were asking for anything major. All she'd wanted was to have Luke over for supper to try to show him how much he meant to her so he wouldn't be nervous about asking her out. Now everything was ruined!

It was another trial, just like their almost-move to Sagebrush, just like Lynette's flirting and Luke's cautiousness, only now it came in the form of her cruel and overly bossy sister. And there was nothing she could do but endure it. She needed to be the forlorn but strong heroine, like Jane Eyre. Steadfast. Ever hopeful. Beautiful and courageous in her suffering.

Her limbs heavy with despair, Daphne slowly pushed herself upright. Then she grabbed the phone off the nearby dresser and punched in Luke's cell number.

"Hey. What's up?" he answered.

"Um, hey." She took a deep, shuddery breath and forced the words out. "I'm sorry, but . . . I'm afraid we can't do supper after all. Some stuff came up and, well, it's not going to work out."

"Aw, no. I hope everything's okay."

No. Everything is horrible. "It's fine. And I'll have you over for dinner soon. Just . . . not today."

"No worries. I'll eat. I appreciate the invite."

His voice was so melodic and sweet. Daphne once again

fell back on her mattress, caught up in swirls of self-pity. After a few tortured heartbeats, she eventually regained control of her voice.

"I—I really need to go," she squeaked. "I'll see you."

"Okay. Bye."

After she clicked off the phone, she lay back on her bed and let the tears flow. She was tired of everyone treating her as if she were a silly toddler. She loved Luke—really, deeply loved him—and all anybody did was belittle her or make fun of her or nag at her to grow up. Even her own family! She wasn't an orphan like Jane Eyre, but she might as well have been, for all the support she got.

Suddenly she felt a familiar yearning. She remembered the last time she'd felt this abandoned: the day her dad had loaded up the Honda and given her a long hug goodbye, a hug so tight it actually hurt a bit in the ribs, and the whole time she could hear tiny noises inside his throat, as if he was trying to prevent himself from crying. The day he'd left. The worst day of her life. Worse even than today.

Her dad didn't live with her anymore, but he still understood her. He would sympathize.

Feeling reinvigorated, she seized the phone and selected his number. A few rings later she heard his voice say, "¿Hola?"

"Daddy?" she said, her voice raspy from crying.

"Hey, *mijita*! How are things going?"

"Terrible! I hate Gabby! She thinks just because Mom's gone she gets to take over everything—including my life."

"Ah, *chiquita*. I'm sure that's not true."

"It is! She gets to drive the car and sleep in Mom's room

and tell me what to do all the time. And she's so mean. She won't let me have any fun. She does things just to make me upset—on purpose!"

He let out a long sigh. "Do you want me to talk to her?"

"That won't help. I want . . ." A lump of emotion rose in her throat, but she swallowed it. "I want you to come live with us. That's the only way to make things better. To put her back in her place."

There was a long pause. "I can't do that, *mija*."

"Maybe not for good, but for a little while? Just while Mom's gone? Please, Daddy. I need someone on my side."

"I know. I wish I could, but I can't go back and forth from Barton to my work. And I can't take time off right now."

"Then can I come stay with you? Just for a few days next week? I can't stand it here. If I have to get bossed by Gabby one more day, I'll . . . I'll go crazy!"

"*Mija*, I'm sorry you're so sad. I wish you could come, but it's not possible. You won't make it to school on time, and school is important. Besides, there's no room here anyway."

"I'll sleep on the couch! I don't care!"

"The thing is . . ." He blew out his breath and a sharp crackling sound came over the receiver. "I was going to tell you soon, but . . . well, I might as well let you know now. There's someone else living with me."

"Huh? Who?"

"Her name is Sheila. She's . . . my girlfriend."

The world around Daphne seemed to wriggle and warp, even though she was lying completely still. Dad was . . . with someone else? That couldn't be right. She'd always pictured him sitting at home, alone, eating food he'd microwaved and watching reruns on TV. She'd imagined he was often lonely and felt sorry for him.

But he wasn't alone. He had a woman living with him. A woman who wasn't Mom. A . . . lover?

The woman even had a name: Sheila. Daphne tried to picture her but could only see a shadowy female outline. She tried to envision her father with his arm around this Sheila person, but she couldn't. It was too tough. Too weird. Too wrong. Wrong, wrong, wrong, wrong, wrong.

Daphne shut her eyes and shook her head. "I don't understand," she said. "How long have you two . . . ?" She couldn't finish. She wasn't even sure what verb to use.

"For seven months now."

"*Seven months?* But . . . but you never said anything."

"I know. I should have told you sooner. I just couldn't. I didn't want you girls to think I was leaving you."

"You already left us!" She was surprised to find herself on her feet. Tears were once again dripping down her face, but they were hot, angry tears that sizzled against her cheeks. "How can you do this? Why are you doing this to us?"

"I'm not doing anything to you guys. This is about me. Me and her."

"But it's wrong! You aren't supposed to be with her. You're supposed to be with Mom. With *us*."

"*Mijita* . . ."

"Stop it! Don't *mijita* me! I'm not a baby! Why does everyone think I'm a baby?"

Daphne was vaguely aware of him saying something else,

but she couldn't make out the words. She was holding the phone out in front of her, squeezing it and shaking it, as if it were a snake she had to slay with her bare hands. She'd been counting on him to understand. She'd needed him to come to her rescue, but he wouldn't. Because of something named Sheila.

With an angry grunt, Daphne drew back her arm and hurled the phone across the room. The white receiver ricocheted off the far wall and landed on Gabby's bed. It looked dead lying there, facedown, like a shellfish that had curled inward in its final throes. A faint crack was visible along its backside.

Great. She'd killed it.

Some back compartment of her brain warned her of new doom: Gabby's horrified shriek when she discovered the broken phone . . . her whiny blabbing to Mom . . . Mom's weary sigh and demand for restitution. But it so didn't matter. Not now.

Daphne dropped to the floor and slouched against the side of her bed. Everything seemed weird and unnatural, as if she'd tumbled into someone else's nightmare.

Dad has a girlfriend? No. The very thought was heavy and slippery and difficult to grasp. It just couldn't be right. If it was, it would change everything. It would mean he and Mom could never get back together. It would mean that some other girl meant more to him than Daphne did. And it would mean that he'd been lying to them for months. That his smiles were lies. His hugs lies. His declarations of love—all lies.

"No!" The word shoved its way past Daphne's lips. No

way could this Sheila person love him as much as they did. She was probably just a stand-in because he missed them so much. Maybe she was superpoor and he felt sorry for her, so he had let her move in. That was the sort of thing he would do.

Yes, that had to be it. He was trying to help someone out. And it was probably nice having someone—*anyone*—around, considering he was so far away from the people he really loved. She shouldn't even be mad at this Sheila person, since he would end up breaking her heart anyway, once he realized the mistake he was making.

Then again, this Sheila could be tricking him, too—using him for his house and money. Well, maybe not money, since he didn't have much. And his house was a one-bedroom apartment. But still . . . what if she was trying to keep him all to herself? Perhaps she'd been trying to turn him against his family and convince him that he didn't need them anymore. Maybe that was the real reason he wouldn't come save Daphne.

Gradually a hazy image of this Sheila person came into her head—an older and less stylish version of Lynette—and a jittery panic spread through her. She considered heading back out to the living room to tell Gabby but decided against it. She was still mad at her, too. Besides, it wouldn't change anything. Gabby already hated Dad. In fact, it would probably make her more annoying. She was always so down on guys, saying they couldn't be trusted. Accusing Daphne of bingeing on fairy tales. Telling her there was no such thing as love . . .

Could she be right? After all, how could love just come

and go like that? How could Dad say he loved them and then let some stranger into his house? Into his life?

All of a sudden, a loud noise split the air, startling her. The phone on Gabby's bed had started beeping the disconnected signal. Obviously the thing still had some life in it. Daphne snatched it up and silenced it, then shuffled over to the dresser to replace it in its base.

Her cut-glass keepsake box sat nearby, glinting in the waning light that squeezed around the drapes. She lifted the lid and peered down at its contents: her old charm bracelet with the broken clasp, ticket stubs from the ice-skating show her dad had taken her to see, and the penny Luke had found during their walk to Quick's Pharmacy. Daphne picked up the coin and closed her hand tightly around it, trying to draw some power from it, to relive that magical moment when he'd given it to her. After a while, a fizzy heat stole over her and her mouth curled into a smile.

No. Gabby couldn't be right. Love was real. It was strong. Maybe Dad and Mom had misplaced theirs, and maybe Daddy was playing pretend love with someone else right now, but she still had the real thing with Luke. He was sweet and romantic and loyal. And he was hers—or he would be soon.

All she had to do was go to that party on Saturday.

CHAPTER FOURTEEN
Telekine(sis)

"Thanks for picking me up," Daphne said. She settled back against the passenger seat of Sheri's Outback and exhaled loudly—apparently she'd been holding her breath without realizing it. Her hands shook slightly as she fastened her seat belt, her pulse still twanging in her ears. She was not cut out for a life of crime.

Sneaking out had not been easy. Mule and Gabby had been parked on the couch for the longest time, and Daphne couldn't make it to the laundry room without passing them. She'd toyed with the idea of going out the bedroom window, but it would have been loud. Plus, the new paint on the frame and sill had glommed together, sealing it shut. She knew the window in the utility room wasn't stuck, since she'd opened it to let out the smell of burnt spaghetti sauce the day before. But she hadn't anticipated her dictator sister's having her best friend stay late. Could Gabby have suspected her plan? Had she done it on purpose?

Eventually Mule and Gabby had gone into Mom's

bedroom to find something—a book or a movie—bickering about some sci-fi factoid the whole way. Daphne hadn't wasted a second. She'd grabbed her purse, taken one last glance back to make sure the pillows under her blankets made a convincing human form, and tiptoed all the way to the laundry room. Once she'd climbed outside and made it safely to the street corner, she called Sheri to pick her up.

"You look really good," Sheri said, giving Daphne's swingy-dress-and-boots combo an up-and-down appraisal. She always gave compliments as if she were complaining, with a wrinkled brow and an irritated tone. But Daphne didn't mind. It seemed more honest, in a way. She wasn't just saying things to be polite.

"Thanks. So do you."

Daphne hoped her flattery sounded sincere, even though she really thought Sheri had overdone the makeup and that her low-cut blouse only accentuated her lack of cleavage. But perhaps some guys thought rib cages were sexy.

By the time Sheri was parking along Deerfield Road, Daphne had become, if anything, even more jumpy. The party was already going strong. People were standing in knots all over the front lawn, and dozens of heads and torsos were visible through the windows. A low rumble of voices merged with the thumping bass of a sound system, punctuated every so often by laughter or a high-pitched shriek.

"All right then," Sheri said. "Don't expect me to stick with you all night." She stepped out of the car and strode toward the house, Daphne following close behind.

Daphne wondered if Sheri felt as nervous as she did. Probably not. Sheri always acted as if her presence was not only expected, but strongly desired. Meanwhile, Daphne, because of her superstrict mother, had only managed to attend three high school parties—the ones like this, at least, with lots of alcohol and no adult supervision. Each time, she'd felt overwhelmed by the crowds, the noise, the general chaos. And Jarrett Ellerbee getting drunk and streaking around outdoors. It was a wonder he kept up the habit—especially since it didn't help him get girls—but he seemed to think that it was his forsworn duty and that he would seriously disappoint people if he stopped.

This night, though, she was on a mission. She had to find Luke. She would surprise him with her presence and tell him that she had come after all, just to see him. She'd drop little hints to let him know exactly how much he meant to her. Then he wouldn't be scared anymore and they would finally start their love story. Or at least plan a prom date.

So now that she'd arrived at her intended destination, it really didn't matter if Sheri blew her off.

They pushed their way through the clot of people hovering around the door.

"Hey, lookee here." Todd Carothers stood near the entrance. He held a big Longhorns cup full of foamy beer and was teetering to the left as if gravity were cranked up stronger on that end of the room. Even his features seemed to have slid sideways. "Welcome, ladies," he said with a leering, lopsided grin. "Can I get y'all a drink?"

Daphne shook her head, but Sheri lifted her nonexistent chest and said, "Hell yeah. I could definitely use a cold one."

As Todd steered Sheri off toward the back patio, Daphne scanned the living room for Luke but didn't see him anywhere. She took a few more steps through the foyer and ran into Walt Lively. He, too, was at a slant, looking like an abandoned broom, with his left shoulder pressed against the wall.

"Hey," she said. "Is Luke here?"

"Oh, I know he's somewhere," he said, with a smirk. Now Daphne could tell that his inclined position wasn't so much from drinking as it was a premeditated pose, designed to make him seem ultracool. "Been here awhile, in fact. Is he . . . expecting you?"

"Yeah," she said, sounding a little offended. "I mean . . . sort of. I tried to get here earlier, but . . ." She wasn't sure how to explain, so instead, she let the sentence just hang open, lamely.

Walt continued to grin smugly at her. After a few beats he stared down into his plastic cup, as if suddenly bored with her. "I think I saw him headed toward the kitchen a minute ago," he said.

"Thanks," she mumbled, and headed toward the bright yellow lights beyond the dining room.

Her heart rate had sped up again, thrashing in double time to the indie rock song coming through the speakers. She squeezed through a group of senior guys and entered the kitchen area. The crush of people was intimidating. There seemed to be three times as many warm, tipsy bodies in here as in the front room. Apparently the party had been going strong for a while; so many people were already acting drunk. Maybe Luke was drunk. Or maybe he'd already left. She really hoped she wasn't too late.

Then again, Jarrett Ellerbee still had his clothes on. That was a good sign.

A familiar laugh reached her ears, high and wheezy like a seagull's call. Tracy's laugh. She pointed herself in the direction of the sound and eventually spotted Tracy sitting on the countertop, holding an enormous Sonic Drive-In tumbler of beer. Daphne pushed through another mass of upperclassmen and found herself near the sink area, where Tracy's head hung above those of a half dozen others, including Luke, who stood nearby with his back against the counter.

To his left was Lynette. She stood sideways, facing Luke, her body practically molded around him, her hips nestled close to his thighs, her breasts almost grazing his elbow, and her head cocked forward toward his neck. She appeared to be mumbling something.

Daphne felt a squirming sensation in her chest, as if her organs were all swarming upward to protect her heart.

Eventually Luke saw her. "Hey," he said. He straightened up, breaking away from Lynette. Was he glad to see Daphne? She couldn't tell. His smile was kind of glossy-looking in the weird amber light of the kitchen.

Lynette leaned back against the counter, facing Daphne. She seemed amused at the interruption, rather than disappointed. "Well, hey," she said. "You actually came."

Daphne wasn't sure whether Lynette meant to that party in particular or to a party in general. "I came," she repeated lamely. "Finally." She was still too stunned to move. So she remained in place, grinning stupidly, trying to figure out how to get Luke away from Lynette—or put herself in Lynette's place. She wanted to tell him that she was there to see him, but it was hard with so many people around.

Just then, the back door opened and Todd Carothers came in holding his Longhorns tumbler aloft. "Hey, Trace! This cup is leaking. Can I have another?"

"Quit dripping all over the floor!" Tracy leaned forward and opened a cupboard. "We're out of glasses, but you can use this," she said, handing him a baby bottle.

Todd blinked at it for a few seconds. Then he set it on the counter, unscrewed the top, poured in the beer from the tumbler, and replaced the cap. Glancing around to make sure everyone was watching, he brought the nipple to his lips and began slurping noisily.

The room erupted with laughter.

"Crap, Tracy. I didn't realize this was bring your own bottle," said Lynette.

Again people cracked up. Luke's head tilted forward and he laughed that silent laugh of his. Lynette seemed to take this as some sort of cue and started cozying up to him again.

Daphne felt panicked.

"Hey, Luke?" she said, stepping forward. "Can I talk to you for a second?"

He stopped chuckling and met her gaze. "Uh . . . sure. I guess."

Everyone around them exchanged knowing stares, a few even made high-pitched "whoo's." Daphne didn't even have to look directly at Lynette to notice the smirk on her face.

Daphne looked up at Tracy. "Is there somewhere we can speak in private?"

Tracy peered at her for a moment. It was clear she found Daphne's actions highly entertaining. "You can use my sister's room, if you promise not to make a mess."

"I promise. Where is it?"

"Upstairs. First door on the right."

"Thanks."

Daphne glanced over at Luke. He pushed off from the counter and loped up beside her. She couldn't tell if he was hesitant or surprised. Then again, maybe he was just scared. Even she was too nervous to smile.

Somehow they made their way through the masses of partygoers and up the stairs. Daphne opened the door on the right and flicked on the light.

"Oh!" she exclaimed.

Inside was the room of her dreams—or the room she would have wanted when she was little. It was all done up in a colorful fairy-tale theme. The walls were a lavender ombré and tiny pixies with glowing wands had been painted at various spots, all of them flying through a swirling current of sparkling silver. There was also a fluffy white flokati rug, lace curtains, bedding with eyelet trim, and a beautiful sheer canopy draped high over the crib. Both the crib and dresser were made of white antiqued wood with curlicue legs.

It was the perfect romantic setting—except for the pungent aroma of dirty diapers.

Luke shut the door and walked over to where she stood beside the dresser. "So, what was it you wanted to talk about?" he asked. A grin wriggled across his face and then he slipped his arms around her, pulled her close, and pressed his lips against hers.

Daphne felt a rush of sensations: joy, heat, astonishment, excitement—*everything* all at once, times ten. She was so overwhelmed it was hard to pay attention. Instead, she found herself focusing on the pink crystal drawer pulls of the dresser, and the frayed ends of a lavender ribbon used to tie back the curtains, and a smudge on the side of the diaper pail. . . .

Wait. She didn't want to think about a gross smudge. She was with Luke. She was kissing him. He was kissing her!

She closed her eyes and concentrated on the slight taste of beer on his mouth, and the feel of his hands as they slid down from her shoulder blades to the small of her back. *This is the magic I've always dreamed about,* she told herself. *This is what a real True Love's kiss feels like.*

Obviously he could feel it, too. He sure didn't seem scared anymore. Had he been expecting this? How could he if he'd had no idea she was coming? It had all happened so fast. Of course she'd wanted this—eventually. But she'd wanted to make her intentions clear first. To see the look in his eyes when he realized how she felt about him.

"Wait," she said, but her voice was lost amid all the breathing and kissing. She pulled back and said it again, more clearly. "Wait!"

"I'm sorry." Luke looked worried. "Did I hurt you?"

Daphne shook her head. "It's fine. It's . . . wonderful. It's just . . . I have something I need to tell you."

They had to confess their feelings first. This wasn't just a party hook-up like everyone else thought it was. This was

True Love. They should acknowledge that and make it official; then they could go back to kissing.

Taking a deep, steadying breath, Daphne stared into Luke's sea-green eyes and began. "Luke, I want you to know that . . . I get you. I see you. I understand you like no one else ever will."

She paused, checking his reaction. But other than a slight widening of his stare, there was no change in his expression. So she pressed on, her words picking up volume and speed.

"We're so much alike. We're old-fashioned and romantic and . . . and . . . we like the same books." She grimaced slightly. This was not the way she'd imagined it. It was time to get to the point. "What I'm trying to say is that . . . I knew the first time I saw you, when we ran into each other, that we were meant to be together. And now I'm even more sure. There's no reason to be frightened. I . . . I love you, Luke. And I always will."

Daphne blew out her breath and grinned. It felt good to say everything aloud—to free the thoughts that had been trapped inside her for so long.

She could tell he was moved. His eyes glistened and a light pink shade had spread over the tops of his cheeks. His mouth hung open, moving slightly, as if he was drinking in her words . . . or, more likely, as if he was getting ready to make an announcement of his own.

Which, of course, he would. Any second now.

"Well?" Daphne said, signaling that she was done.

She braced herself, waiting for his confession.

The man let out a whimper and backed up against the wall. Unfortunately, the mysterious shadow advanced faster, darkening the man's face. At the last second the man crossed his arms in front of him, desperately trying to shield himself, but to no avail. He let out a horrified shriek just as the music crescendoed, and the TV screen went black. The next shot showed the guy's corpse facedown on the hardwood floor.

"He could have run," Gabby remarked. "All those people—the bald dude, the blond lady, the old man with the eye patch—they could have been out the door before Shadow Thing even grazed their feet."

Mule shook his head. "You can't outrun evil."

"Oh really? And you're an expert?"

"Hey, I hang out with you, don't I?"

Gabby raised an eyebrow at him.

"Sorry," he said, lifting his hands in a surrender gesture. "Please don't sic your minions on me."

Gabby gritted her teeth. She already had Daffy calling her cruel and sadistic; she didn't need to hear it from Mule, too.

Mule grabbed the plastic bowl he'd brought over, which held some sort of chunky gold substance in it, and started dipping in tortilla chips he'd pulled out of the kitchen. Meanwhile, on TV, the strange dark matter oozed down a sleeping street, stirring up fallen leaves and making stray cats puff up and hiss.

"You know," Mule said, between crunches, "this kumquat salsa isn't that bad."

"Is that what that is?" Gabby asked, wrinkling her upper lip. "*Kumquat* salsa?"

"It was Dad's idea. The past few days he's really gotten into cooking shows. They showed this recipe and he got all excited and asked Mom to make it. Hey, did you know the kumquat comes from China? I always thought the word sounded Germanish. And not in a good way, either."

"It also doesn't sound very appetizing—or look it. I'm sorry, but salsa should not be yellow. It should be red. And spicy."

"Snob," Mule said, rolling his eyes.

Gabby launched a pillow at him, but it only grazed his curls. "Are you just going to insult me all evening or what?"

"Hey. I was just kidding." Mule's dopey grin was gone. Now he was looking at her as if she were the Shadow Thing from Hell.

Great. She was tired of being referred to as mean. So what did she do? Went all mean on him.

"Sorry," she mumbled. "I'm just in a bad mood. And this movie is lame. Why are we watching it, anyway?"

"Because nothing better was on. At least at the time."

Mule picked up the remote and started flipping through the channels. After a few clicks he let it rest on a black-and-white sitcom. A mother stood in the center of a spotless 1950s living room. She wore a starched dress, heels, and pearl earrings, and her blond hair was in an immaculate bob. The only clues pointing to the fact that she was a mother—and not, say, a model in a furniture store showroom—were the crisp white apron and the sullen-looking boy sitting across from her on the couch. Judging by his guilty expression, the boy must have done something wrong. But since the laugh track was cranked up and the mom looked more bemused than angry, it couldn't have been too bad.

"Hey, Gab," Mule said, turning around to face her. His shoulders were hunched and his mouth was set in a grim line. He seemed worried all of a sudden, not unlike the boy on the television. It made Gabby uneasy.

He scratched his head and cleared his throat. "I've been doing some thinking."

Ho boy. Again Gabby's anxiety level increased. The Randolphs were not idea people. Mule could crunch numbers and analyze algorithms like a six-foot-tall computer. But any jolts of inspiration tended to produce things like . . . kumquat salsa. She bit the inside of her cheek, steeling herself for his latest crazy notion.

"Just listen," he began. "I know you don't want to go to prom and all, but . . . what if we did something else? We could drive into Austin and see a show. Or just plan some adventure around here. Whatever. It's our last year of school, and I think it would be cool if we did something up big for a change."

Oh no oh no ohno! For the past several days things had been getting steadily weirder between her and Mule—and now this? His jokes about prom . . . his nervousness about Prentiss . . . Daffy's teasing about his boy parts and her insistence that Gabby secretly loved him . . . they all seemed to gather, building on one another, taking on weight and mass and consciousness until finally, they could rise up and engulf her like . . . well, like an amorphous evil Shadow Thing.

For years he had been good ol' reliable Mule. And even though lately Gabby had seen signs that he wanted to be more than just friends—a lingering gaze or a quick eye-avert—he'd never actually made a move. Which was exactly how she wanted it to be. How she needed it to be. How the universe stayed in balance.

And now he had . . . thoughts?

"Do you mean . . . ?" She paused, wondering whether she should say the words—the words that could alter absolutely everything. "Do you mean like a date?"

She hoped he would laugh. Looking at his tight expression, she found herself trying to force it, telekinetically. She willed his mop-topped head to fall backward, his crumb-streaked mouth to open wide, and the room to fill with his loud, crazy, car-horn cackles.

But just as Mule's lips started to part, the doorbell rang.

Gabby sprang up from the sofa as if a small explosive had gone off underneath her and quick-stepped to the door. She opened it without even thinking, already smiling at the individual who'd interrupted the tension.

It was Prentiss, holding a large paper sack. "Hi there. I saw that the lights were on and thought it would be okay to knock." He nodded as if affirming that he'd done the right thing, no doubt encouraged by the preset look of joy and relief on Gabby's face.

Her grin faded, and she resisted pointing out the fact that he'd actually rung, not knocked. "Um . . . hi," she said. "What's up?"

"I've got something for y'all," he said, patting the bag in his arms. "Mind if I come in?"

Gabby considered saying no but decided against it. The night was already strange—why fight it? It would be like trying to outrun evil.

"Sure." She opened the door and stepped out of the way.

"Oh, hey." Prentiss nodded at Mule as he loped into the living room.

Mule rose to his feet, smiling awkwardly. "Hi."

There followed a brief, queasy moment when Prentiss looked from Mule to Gabby and back again. "I'm sorry. I didn't mean to interrupt."

Mule glanced at Gabby, as if volleying the statement to her. Prentiss followed his gaze.

"Uh . . . no. We were just . . ." She faltered. "We weren't really doing anything." Out of the corner of her eye she could see Mule droop slightly, like a blow-up toy with a slow leak.

She could feel the annoyance building inside her. Suddenly she was mad at Prentiss and Mule and anybody who'd gotten her to that point in time. Why did absolutely everything in her life have to be complicated? Why couldn't one thing—one lousy little detail—be nice and simple and always make perfect sense?

Prentiss headed over to the dining room table and set down his bag. "I won't take long. I was just up at the rodeo and went a little nutty buying corn dogs. Thought maybe you and your sister would like some. And you, too," he added, looking at Mule.

"I wish you hadn't done that," Gabby said. She was telling the truth. She didn't want his charity. She didn't want Prentiss thinking he needed to help take care of them.

But Prentiss seemed to think she was just being humble.

"Aw, it's no big deal," he said, grinning. "I know your mom is gone and I figured y'all could use some good food."

Gabby clenched her teeth. The guy didn't even realize how sexist he sounded. Did he actually think they were starving just because their mom was out of town?

He pulled a grease-stained paper box out of the bag and held it up. "Y'all help yourselves. They're homemade, you know."

Almost instantly the smell of corn-fried wieners hit her nose. "You say that like it's health food," she said, making a face. "Do you know what they put in those things?"

Prentiss's smile washed away. He shrugged lamely and set the box on the table. "Well, feel free to give them to your friends or something," he said. "Sorry I butted in."

He headed for the door, avoiding all eye contact with Gabby.

"Y'all have a good night." He gave Mule a little head bob, smiled dimly at Gabby, and disappeared into the purple glow of the porch light.

"Jesus, Gab," Mule said. "Couldn't you at least say thanks?"

She opened her mouth to fuss at him, then quickly closed it. He was right. She'd been a bit harsh with the guy. Plus, she'd been snappish all evening. She'd complained about Mule's choice of words, TV programming, and snacks. And she hadn't even thanked him for bringing the lousy salsa.

Mule didn't seem nervous anymore, just appalled. But somehow that was worse. She wanted to tell him that she wasn't mean—not really. Even more than that, she wanted to prove it to him.

"You know, Daffy really likes these," she said, looking at the abandoned bag of corn dogs. "I should let her know."

She headed into the hallway and knocked on the bedroom door.

It was a risky move, considering Daphne still wasn't speaking to her. The girl had pouted all day, avoiding Gabby and holing up in her room with her cell phone. Chances were this kind gesture would be met with angry screams and an object being hurled at her. But she wanted to do something to demonstrate her thoughtful side.

After several seconds she knocked again and opened the door. The light was off and Daphne lay in bed, completely cocooned in the covers. It was unlikely that she was asleep—especially at this hour. Obviously she was just pretending so Gabby would leave her alone, and to keep punishing her with the silent treatment.

"I know you're awake," Gabby said in a loud whisper. "You might as well come out and have some corn dogs. Prentiss brought them. From the rodeo."

Still no answer. A vague feeling of dread settled over Gabby. Something wasn't right.

She flicked on the light switch. "Daff?" she said. "Daffy, get up."

Somehow she knew it before she crossed the room and threw back the covers, revealing the carefully molded pillow shape. She knew by the absence of sound and tiny movements—by the absence of *presence*. She knew because of the feeling of disquiet she'd had all evening long, as if some invisible force had been trying to warn her.

Her sister was gone.

"Damn it!" she shouted. "Damn it, damn it, damn it!"

She paced the room, gripping the sides of her head, as if she could somehow squeeze a plan of action out of her own skull.

"What's wrong?" Mule raced into the room, wide-eyed with fright.

"Daphne's not here!" she yelled, annoyed that she had to say something so obvious, annoyed that she was in the predicament in the first place.

"But . . . why?" Mule asked. "Where would she go?"

A fragment of memory broke loose from Gabby's mind, like a leaf detaching from a branch, and slowly zigzagged into view.

"That little bitch," she grumbled. "She went to the party after all."

Luke didn't talk for a long time. He simply stared at Daphne, blinking fast as if her image were too vivid to behold.

Finally he opened his mouth. Only he didn't utter an actual word. It was more of a long braying sound. "Errrryuuuugh." Then he shook his head and chuckled.

Daphne laughed, too. "What? What's so funny?"

"Nothing," he said. He was moving now, grabbing his hands in front of him and shifting his weight from foot to foot. "Look, um . . . I can't . . . I don't . . . Wow."

It was cute how blown away he was. How shy. "It's okay. You can say it," she said, reaching for his hand.

He jerked out of reach.

Daphne's fingers went numb as blood escaped them, rushing up to her face. "Oh, my god," she said. "You think I'm being too forward, don't you?" Her words started calmly enough, but midway through, her voice seemed to catch on something, making the rest come out ragged and hoarse.

"No, no. It was sweet. Really. It was just kinda . . . heavy. You know?"

Daphne felt a giant sucking sensation behind her sternum, as if her body were collapsing in on itself. Surrendering. Failing. She crossed her arms over her chest and held on tight.

Oh, god. She blew it! She should have been more patient. She'd panicked over the whole Lynette thing and tried to rush it all. Fate had tricked her, and she'd failed the test. How could she have been so stupid?

"You okay?" Luke asked.

She couldn't reply. She couldn't even look at him. Instead, she glanced around the storybook room, but somehow it had lost its magic. The purple walls appeared darker. The air felt colder. Even the fairies on the wall seemed malicious, with their pinched little faces and grotesque smiles.

"Maybe we should go back downstairs?" he suggested.

She nodded lamely.

He turned and walked back out onto the landing. Daphne fell into step behind him, focusing on the back of his navy sweater. She wasn't sure what else to do. All she could do was stay close, watch, and wait.

The living room was relatively empty when they reached the bottom floor. Just three random couples making out on the couch and in the corners. Seeing them produced a sort of backdraft inside her, fanning the flames of embarrassment and remorse.

She followed Luke's crew neck toward the kitchen, then almost plowed into his back when he stopped suddenly. Veering around to his side, she saw that the room was filled with even more people than before. All wore matching smirks as they stood there silently watching her and Luke.

For a while, no one said anything. Then Todd Carothers broke from the crowd and fell to his knees in front of Luke. "Oh, Luke! I missed you, man! Because I love you so much! I love you, and I want to marry you, and I want to have your babies!"

The place erupted with laughter.

"What the . . . ?" Luke said.

Before he could finish, Tracy—still perched atop the counter—held something up and waggled it around in a sort of triumphant dance. The object was white and rectangular, with an antenna sticking up from one side and a power cord coming out the bottom: a baby monitor.

Daphne let out a gasp as the horrifying realization came over her.

"We heard everything," Tracy said, stating the obvious. "Oh, my god, it was so hilarious!"

Again, they all laughed. Daphne scanned their taunting faces. Lynette. Todd. Walt. Tracy. Rachelle. Cody. Tricia. Jarrett. Even Sheri stood in the back, snickering along with the others.

Lynette broke out of the group and sauntered toward Daphne. The fluorescent light made her heavily painted face look scary and slightly yellow, as if she'd been manufactured from cheap plastic. "You know, if you were checking to see if he was gay or not, you shouldn't have bothered," she said, smiling smugly. "I already tested him earlier tonight and he passed. With flying colors."

"What?" Everything around Daphne seemed to tilt and wobble, and she put a hand on the doorframe to steady herself.

She glanced over at Luke. It wasn't true. It couldn't be true.

He quickly avoided her stare and hunched guiltily, telling her all she needed to know.

"Whoa! *Damn*, dude!" Todd stepped forward and punched Luke in the shoulder. "You need to turn down the charm or something. Two in one night? Girls saying they love you? That's some intense stuff."

Luke put his hand on the spot Todd had hit. A strange look darkened his face for a split second; then he let his hand drop and broke into a grin. "No kidding, man," he said. "What a trip." He laughed his quiet laugh as Todd steered him into the kitchen, patting his back in the same section of sweater Daphne had let guide her downstairs. A second later Luke was folded into the crowd, grinning and jostling along with the rest of them. And Lynette reattached herself to his side.

No.

Tears filled Daphne's eyes, rippling the scene in front of her. She stumbled backward, half blind, barely able to form a coherent thought. Pressing her hands over her ears to muffle the hooting laughter and shrill cries of "I love you," she turned and fled through the living room, colliding with a few hazy shapes until she somehow made it outside.

No! her mind kept screaming. She leaned against a pecan tree and took deep, shuddery breaths. *No . . . No . . . No!*

This was not the way it was supposed to happen. Somehow it had all gone very wrong. Luke loved her. He had to love her. But then why would he . . .

No! Please, no!

Her limbs trembled and her head wouldn't stop shaking. She pressed her hands against her temples, trying to stop the thoughts. To somehow force the horrific images from her memory.

Never before had she felt so solitary. So trapped in her body, cut off from anything big and powerful. How could he do this to her? How could Fate do this to her? How could Love?

After a long, loopy ride of time, her brain finally hushed and she felt capable of walking again. She crossed the yard and headed down the street, past the line of cars and out of range of the party commotion. At the corner, she pulled out her cell phone and pressed a set of numbers.

"Gabby?" Her voice sounded as weak as she felt. It seemed to blend with the night wind and fly away. She tried again. "Gabby, it's Daff. I . . . I need you."

Gabby coasted down Deerfield at five miles an hour, craning her neck to search the side of the road for her sister. The darkness felt extragloomy for some reason, and she wondered if it was because of her sour mood, or if that lame horror flick had some residual hold over her.

Eventually she spotted Daphne at the corner of Travis Street, leaning against the stop sign. Perhaps it was due to her dismal state of mind, but Gabby couldn't help thinking that Daphne resembled some sort of specter. Her pallor looked ghostly gray under the sickly glow of the streetlamp, and the skirt of her sundress undulated in the invisible breeze. Her head was downcast, curtained by her hair. She could be the Faceless Witch of Deerfield Lane, who snuck in and out of bedrooms and kept older sisters up late. Or the Spoiled Spook of Barton, who wailed incessantly when she didn't get her way.

Gabby coasted to a stop and lowered the passenger-door window. "You're lucky I came. I'd already discovered your little stunt and was all set to go drag you out of that party in front of your friends. Then you had the nerve to call and ask me for a ride?" She shook her head. "Amazing! I should have blown you off."

Daphne pushed away from the sign and trudged toward the car. Without a word, she opened the door and climbed inside.

Still with the silent treatment, Gabby thought as she accelerated back onto the street. *Not even a thank-you.*

"You know, because of you I had to call off my plans tonight." She glanced at Daphne, checking to see whether she might be rolling her eyes, but she was staring out the window.

Gabby pursed her lips. All right, so the part about her evening being ruined wasn't exactly true. If there was one upside to this latest Daphne mess, it was that it had given her a reason to send Mule home early. At first he'd insisted on helping find her sister, but after Daphne's phone call he complied, leaving her with the leftover kumquat salsa but still no answer to her question. She had no idea what he'd meant by wanting a "big night out" with her. Hopefully he wouldn't mention it again and the whole thing would blow over.

Despite her relief over the reprieve from Mule, she was still furious with Daphne. The girl would have never tried such a stunt if Mom had been in town—which meant she didn't respect Gabby. All she cared about was getting to do what she wanted.

"You know I'm going to have to tell Mom about this, right?" Gabby grumbled, tightening her grip on the steering wheel. "She told you not to go to the party and she made me promise to keep an eye on you. It's like she knew you might try to pull something. She knew how low you would go."

Daphne tilted her head against the seat and closed her eyes. Gabby suddenly noticed how awful she looked. It hadn't just been the street light; her complexion really was pale and waxy. And it was weird how quiet she was. Silent treatment or not, she'd usually pitch a screechy fit over Gabby's tattling to Mom about her transgressions. Come to think of it, she'd sounded really out of it on the phone, too.

"Oh, my god!" Gabby exclaimed as a sudden realization came over her. "You're drunk, aren't you? Dámn it, Daff! How can you do this to me? Mom's really going to freak now."

By now they were pulling down the long drive of the Applewhite property. Gabby threw the gearshift in park, switched off the lights and engine, and spun around in her seat to better direct her anger at its source. Meanwhile

Daphne remained slouched and unmoving, barely aware of her surroundings.

"God, it's like you don't think—ever!" Gabby shouted, making tiny flailing motions with her hands. "Do you even know how stupid that was? Do you realize all the awful things that could have happened to you?"

Daphne stirred suddenly. Her chest heaved as if she were rearing up for a hearty scream. Then she pushed open the passenger door and started vomiting on the crushed granite drive below.

"Lovely. Just lovely," Gabby said as the stench of puke hit her nostrils. She grabbed a fistful of hair on top of Daphne's head and held on tight. Of course this would happen. It was the poetic cap to an epically bad night.

After a while the retching stopped. For a moment Daphne remained doubled over, panting heavily. Then, like a zombie crawling out of the ground, she jerked and lurched until she was standing outside the car.

"You're going to have to clean that up!" Gabby called out. "I'm not doing it!"

But Daphne was already staggering off toward the house, her cowboy boots making a sickening scraping noise against the gravel.

Gabby let out a moan and fell forward against the steering wheel. "God, I hate my life."

CHAPTER FIFTEEN
Paraly(sis)

Daphne opened her eyes. She couldn't tell from the light in her room whether it was day or night. Through the tiny gap in the curtains she could see putty-colored clouds and a sprinkling of drops on the window. She shuddered with cold and ran her hand up her bare arm. Looking down, she saw that she was lying on top of her covers, still wearing the floral-patterned dress from the night before.

All at once it came back to her. The party. The cruel, distorted faces of her classmates laughing at her. Luke . . .

Her gut felt crumpled and her heart seemed to be writhing in agony instead of simply beating. It had really happened. It hadn't been a bad dream. And now everything was just . . . over.

A sob rose, straining inside her, building in intensity until it burst from her throat with a high-pitched wail. Daphne rolled over onto her stomach, pulling her arms and legs underneath her. Then, with only her back exposed to the world, she cried into the muffled darkness of her mattress.

She cried until her throat felt raw and her head throbbed. She cried until her pillowcase felt warm and slick.

Eventually her thoughts took on a hazy, garbled quality, and she spiraled off into another fitful sleep.

Gabby sat at the dining room table swirling a stale tortilla chip in the kumquat salsa. Remnants of conversation from the night before kept popping in and out of her mind without her even trying to think about them. It was like that time Mule had dragged her to see some guitarist in Austin and a sharp tone had echoed in her ears the whole day after. This time, though, images appeared with the sounds. Mule looking so disappointed after she'd been rude to Prentiss . . . Prentiss's dopey grin . . . Daphne all doubled over in the driveway . . .

She glanced at the yellow kitty-cat clock on the wall. It was a quarter to noon and Daphne still wasn't up. Figured. The girl almost certainly had a hangover. Her body was probably so poisoned and depleted of nutrients that she couldn't face sunlight or food.

Good. She deserved to have the world's worst headache after what she'd pulled. If this was what it was like being a mom, Gabby figured she should have her uterus removed.

"Oh, no. Mom." Gabby suddenly realized she was supposed to call her that morning and report in. What the hell was she going to say? *Oh, hey, Mom. Daphne snuck out to a kegger and got drunk, and Mule has suddenly started making fruity salsa and hinting that we should be more than friends. What's up with you?*

Again she glanced at the clock. She couldn't put it off any longer. Making Mom wait would only cause more anguish.

Gabby reached for the phone and punched in the programmed number of her mom's cell. The rings sounded distant, for some reason. And their peal seemed cheerful and trusting. Gabby wasn't the one who had broken the rules, yet she couldn't help feeling she was letting her mom down.

Soon she heard a click, followed by a barrage of noise. "Honey!" her mom sang out. "I was just about to call you, but we went to this incredible place for a late brunch and just got carried away." Muffled voices sounded in the background, followed by her mom's shrieking laughter.

Her mom seemed so . . . giddy—almost Daphne-like. It was unnerving.

"Sounds like someone has had a mimosa. Or three," Gabby said.

"No, no," her mom said. "Well . . . perhaps I did have a bit of Bailey's in my coffee." She giggled and the background voices soon joined in.

Mom was giggling? Now things were getting scary.

"I'm just having a great time," her mom said. "The people here are very nice. And I'm learning a lot."

Gabby smiled weakly. "Good."

"So how are things going?" her mom asked. "Has the car been holding up for you?"

"Yeah."

"What about Daphne? Has she been keeping up with school without me nagging her?"

"I think so."

"Put her on. I want to speak with her."

Gabby's stomach tightened. "Um, Mom? You're not going to believe this, but . . ." She stopped. How could she do this? Her mom sounded so relaxed, so happy. Telling her would only push her back into panic mode. And it wasn't like she could do anything about it all the way in Atlanta.

"What? What's going on?" her mom asked. "You're cutting out."

She could already hear the worry creeping back in to Mom's tone. No. Forget it. Gabby would handle things herself.

"I said, you're not going to believe this but"—Gabby glanced around, searching for something quick, something unbelievably believable, and her eyes rested on the discarded Golden Chick bag that Daphne had left on the counter a couple of days ago—"Daphne bicycled over to Golden Chick to pick us up some food."

"She did? That's thoughtful."

"I know, right?"

"Hmm. Is she trying to apologize for something she did wrong?"

"No! Nothing like that." Gabby laughed nervously. "But maybe she's buttering me up for some big favor she's going to ask."

"Could be. Keep your guard up."

"I will. Well . . . I should let you go. Bye, Mom. Keep on having fun."

She laughed. "I hope I will. Take care, sweetie. Love you! Love to Daphne!"

Gabby shut off the phone. Damn Daphne! The girl better appreciate all Gabby had been doing for her. Fetching her in the middle of the night and now lying to Mom. Maybe it wasn't sickness that was keeping her in their room, but fear—fear of what her older sister might do to her. *Should* do to her.

She stirred the chunky yellow salsa with the point of a fresh chip and then suddenly pushed it away. She wanted to like the stuff, but she didn't. As much as she hated to see it go to waste, she'd most likely end up feeding it to the garbage disposal.

As she opened the door to the refrigerator to put it back, she immediately spied the squat, stained paper boxes filled with corn dogs. With a resigned sigh she pulled a dog out of the nearest container, set it on a plate, and warmed it in the microwave for several seconds. Then she added a squeeze of mustard and took a bite.

"Oh, my god!" she exclaimed. It was so much better than she had expected. Better than she remembered. So what if it was bad for her? She deserved some delicious deep-fried contaminants after the weekend she'd had.

She could go wild, too.

"Quit pouting and get in the car," Gabby said.

"I can't." Daphne hung back on the porch, shaking her head. The motion made her a little dizzy, and she steadied her skull with her right hand. This also smarted, since her face was swollen from crying off and on for the past thirty hours. The mirror that morning had shown how puffy and bulged-out her eyes were, making her seem more iguana than human. Yet another reason to stay home.

"You have to go to school."

"But I don't feel good."

"Don't give me that!" Gabby pounded her hand on the roof of the Jetta. "I let you sleep all day yesterday. I cleaned up your stink from the damn driveway. Don't make me call Mom and tell her what you've done."

Daphne felt a tiny swell of hope. "You haven't told her?"

"No," Gabby heaved a sigh. "I just don't want to bother her with it yet. She'll be so upset, and right now she needs to concentrate on her training."

Daphne twirled the end of her ponytail and pondered this. Gabby was right. Her mom didn't deserve to be pulled down into her mess. But school? Just thinking about it made the few sips of milk she'd had for breakfast turn lumpy and sour in her stomach.

Would throwing up in front of Gabby again make her change her mind? Probably not. It might make her madder, since she assumed Daphne had drunk herself sick at the party. And Daphne wasn't about to tell her what had really happened. Saying it aloud would only destroy that last flimsy filament keeping her upright.

Maybe she could go to school and avoid anybody who was at the party. She could hide in the bathroom or volunteer to sort the equipment room for Coach Harding. She could even show up for one of Ms. Manbeck's tutoring sessions.

"Well? Are you coming? Or do I have to call Mom on the cell right now?"

Daphne glanced down and was astonished to see her legs walking toward the Jetta. She felt like a ghost. Her body was doing what it had always done, and yet everything felt different, unreal. Eventually she climbed into the car and clicked the safety belt around her.

She settled against the seat as Gabby backed out of the driveway and headed down the road—all just as usual, and yet it felt weird. Even the passing scenery seemed unfamiliar. It was as if she'd somehow slipped into a stranger's body.

Maybe she wasn't really there. Maybe she was still in bed, asleep, having one of her bizarre dreams. It was a comforting thought.

"I have to be at work by five, so meet me at the car as soon as school lets out," Gabby said. "Otherwise you'll need to get a ride from one of your friends. Or just walk."

"I'll be there," Daphne said emphatically. No way was she getting in Sheri's Outback ever again.

By the time Gabby had pulled the Jetta into the student parking lot, Daphne's hands were trembling and the numb, dreamlike feeling had left.

She really was here. This was her body. Her own sucky life.

"Well?" Gabby was already out of the car and was jerking her head impatiently toward the building. "Get a move on."

Daphne rose unsteadily from her seat, shut the door, and pulled her backpack over her right shoulder. By the time she started walking after Gabby, her sister was several steps away. Up ahead, the school loomed menacingly. The brown bricks of its exterior reminded her of dark scales, and its big front windows glinted in the sunlight on either side of the entrance, making the facade look like two flashing eyes and a wide-open mouth.

And standing in front of the gaping maw were her former friends—the backstabbing party crowd.

Her throat squeezed shut and her legs started to quiver. "Please, Gabby. Don't make me go through with this." Only Gabby didn't hear. Because Gabby didn't care. But also because Gabby was now several yards ahead of her and Daphne's voice had been a tiny croak.

You can do this, she told herself. *Don't even look at those people. Forget about them. Forget about Luke.*

Luke . . . A fresh misting of tears veiled her vision. Would a time ever come when she could think of that name and not feel blasted away on the inside?

Daphne cleared her throat and blinked repeatedly until she'd bullied the moisture back into her ducts. Then she headed for the main entrance while focusing on the concrete walkway, still shiny from all the drizzle.

"Look," she heard someone say.

From the corner of her eye she could see people clustering together; then came the steady drone of their murmurs.

"Daphne!"

She glanced up on instinct, too startled to stop herself, and saw Lynette staring straight at her.

"Oh, my god. You must feel like the biggest ditz ever," Lynette said, her eyes flashing inside thick borders of eyeliner. "I can't believe you said all that dorky stuff to Luke, right after he'd hooked up with me. And then he totally shot you down!"

A tremor shook Daphne. She felt an urge to buckle, to burrow into the earth or curl back up into her protective ball. A few of the others were laughing—some wickedly, others nervously. And the nearby murmurs had strengthened in volume and number. Daphne did not want to be here. She didn't want to get swallowed up by the school and laughed at by all her classmates. She did not want to be reminded that the love of her life had messed around with Lynette Harkrider. Most of all, she didn't want to see Luke.

So she wouldn't.

Just as the shudders started and the stinging wetness flooded into her eyes, Daphne spun around and ran down the sidewalk, past the parking lot, and down the road toward her neighborhood . . . her home . . . her dark room . . . her bed . . . and the safety of sleep.

Where the hell is she?

Gabby stood in front of the Jetta, scanning the vicinity for Daphne's ponytailed head. School had let out fifteen minutes ago—plenty of time for Daphne to make it to the car. She'd tried Daphne's cell phone, but it had gone straight to voice mail. She'd even circled the building in case Daphne couldn't remember where they'd agreed to meet. But there'd been no sign of her.

She should just abandon Daphne's butt at school. That might teach her to be more considerate.

Gabby marched over to the driver's side and opened the door, ready to leave. Then she quickly shut it. *Fine. One last chance.* She walked to the front of the car, shielding her eyes from the sun as she again checked the surroundings.

A familiar figure strode past, tall and skinny, her bushy hairstyle almost as wide as her shoulders.

"Sheri!" Gabby called.

The hair stopped and swished around as the head it sat on searched for the voice.

"Over here," Gabby said, waving to get her attention. "Are you taking Daphne home today?"

"Ah, no. No, I'm not. Definitely not." Sheri shook her hair, her expression a mixture of shock, amusement, and annoyance.

Gabby put her hands on her hips. "Then do you know where she is?"

"She isn't here."

"Where is she?"

She shrugged. "She left, like, a long time ago. She didn't go to school."

"What?"

But Sheri didn't elaborate. Just gave an enigmatic little smirk and drifted toward the edge of the lot, where five different versions of the same twenty-first-century cowboy stood around someone's pickup.

What the hell did she mean Daphne didn't come to school? Gabby had brought her pouting the whole way. Was Sheri so high on hair-product fumes that she didn't know what she was saying?

It didn't matter anyway. Daffy could walk.

"Gabby! Gabby, wait!"

Mule was running across the courtyard, his frothy curls bounding along a half step behind his feet.

Great. Was everyone determined to get her fired today?

He slowed to a stop right beside her. "Hold up," he said, panting. "I just heard some stuff you ought to know."

Gabby shook her head. "Sorry, I really don't have time to chat. My stupid sister just stood me up and I'm going to be late for work."

"But it's about Daphne. And what happened at the party. I really think you need to hear this."

Daphne lay curled on her bed like a pill bug. She couldn't move or think. She couldn't even cry anymore. Her eyes had gone dry, and the tightness in her throat had subsided.

She'd probably just run out of tears. Maybe that was why she felt empty inside. It was like she'd already squeezed every bit of emotion out of her and was left feeling limp and used up. A discarded dishrag.

The crying might have stopped, but not the constant ache. Deep and scorching, yet oddly hollow, as if something vital had been torn out of her. "Shot down" was the phrase Lynette had used. And that was exactly how it felt. As if something had ripped a big hole through her, causing her to plummet to the ground, flightless and wounded.

If only she could go back in time and stop herself from saying those things to Luke. If only she'd stayed home that night. If only Lynette were ugly and shy. If only Luke had never moved to Barton . . .

But she didn't want to think about the "if onlies."

For as long as she could remember, she'd used daydreams as a way to cope with sadness or boredom. Not anymore. Her fantasies were what had let her down this time. All those stories of love and hope, they were just lies. And she'd been stupid to buy into them. God, she was pathetic. A silly little kid, just like everyone thought.

She turned toward the window and the intense rays of the afternoon sun seared her irises, making her head ache even more. She so preferred the dreariness of yesterday's rain. Sunshine was too cheerful, too warm. It made it harder to sleep and, therefore, forget.

As she turned back toward the center of the room, a new brightness hit her eyes. A stream of sunlight had angled onto her dresser, making something flash and sparkle. It seemed to be beckoning her.

Daphne slid out of bed and plodded toward it. When she reached the dresser, she could see that two items had been infused with light: her cut-glass box with the penny inside, and the tiny jar of silver body glitter she'd been planning to use for prom.

Anger seized hold of her—spiked heavily with shame. She grabbed the jar of glitter, then flung open the lid of the box and plucked out the penny. Clenching the items in her fists, she stalked down the hall to the bathroom.

"Screw you," she said, dropping the penny into the trash.

"Screw you," she said, dumping the glitter into the toilet. She tossed the empty jar into the waste can and clapped some glistening fragments from her hands.

Turning to go, she caught sight of her reflection in the mirror.

"Screw you, too."

"Daphne? Why is our toilet all sparkly?"

Daphne opened her eyes to see her sister looming over her. She must have just woken up. Her hair was a mess of tangles and her face looked extrasnarly. Probably hadn't had any caffeine yet.

"I dumped my glitter makeup," Daphne mumbled.

Gabby rolled her eyes. "Great. That'll probably gum up the plumbing."

Daphne pulled the blanket over her head. She really wished her crabby sister would go away and leave her alone. And turn off the light again and close the door. She even wished the sun would slide back down below the horizon. She wished the whole world would simply shut itself off.

"Are you going to school today?" Gabby asked. There was a tentative challenge in her voice. Daphne could almost hear the arguments lining up inside her.

"No."

She heard Gabby let out an enormous sigh. Sure enough, she commenced making her case. "I know it's hard, but you can't stay home forever. You'll get behind and we'll get in big trouble. Do you want to be hauled in front of a judge?"

Daphne didn't bother to reply. She honestly didn't care. What could happen to her that would be so bad?

"Look . . ." Her sister's voice was soft but tight, as if she were forcing herself to sound gentle. "I know I told you that I wouldn't call Mom. But maybe I should call Dad and—"

"No!"

Daphne sat upright so quickly, her head throbbed. Gabby looked shocked.

"But why?" she asked. "You guys are so close."

How could Daphne explain? She'd always basked in the fact that her dad adored her. She knew she was his favorite, and she appreciated his loving her the way she was, never telling her to stop daydreaming and be responsible. But after the party and the whole Sheila thing, she wasn't sure if he still loved her best. She wasn't sure of anything anymore.

She couldn't face him right now. The same way she couldn't face Luke and the others.

"Just . . . don't. Please?" she said. "I don't want him to know. I don't want him coming here, calling me *mijita* and acting so understanding."

Now Gabby really looked confused. "Why not?"

"I just don't! Okay? I don't want to talk about it! Not with anyone! Even Daddy!" She gripped her head in her hands, but it kept on pounding. All that shouting had left her panting and weak.

The bed shimmied as Gabby sat down next to her. "Fine. I won't call him. Don't freak out." She was still scowling, but her eyes looked more worried than anything.

"Thanks," Daphne said. She lay back against her pillows, waiting for her breathing to steady and her head to stop aching and for sleep to come steal her away again.

Gabby bit her lip. "I guess . . . I guess you can stay home another day," she said. "But you have to promise me you won't go anywhere. Stay here."

"I promise."

"And you'll have to keep up with your homework. I'll tell your teachers you're sick."

For some reason, this made Daphne's throat swell up with a sob. "Thanks."

Gabby sat there a moment longer, rocking slightly and tugging the fingers of her right hand one by one. Daphne braced herself for more lecturing, but after a while Gabby simply blew out her breath and rose to her feet. "Bye," she said. Then she switched off the light and headed out of the room, quietly closing the door behind her.

CHAPTER SIXTEEN
Sta(sis)

![decorative band]

"Come on, come on," Gabby muttered as she turned the key in the Jetta's ignition. There followed a lackluster electronic whir and then . . . nothing. "Stupid car!" She wriggled the steering wheel, popped the gearshift into neutral and then back into park, and tried the key once again. The engine let out a high-pitched whinny, as if startled, and eventually turned over. "Finally!" she exclaimed.

The clock on the dashboard read 4:43. She was running late for work—again. Another day, another pile of stress. And another twenty-four-hour nap for Daphne. This made day three of her hibernation.

As much as it bothered her, Gabby could sort of understand that instinct. When Sonny died, she'd had the same urge to hide from the world. To power herself down in order to escape the pain and confusion. She hadn't missed any school; she'd just wallowed miserably in the privacy of her head and cried beneath her covers at night. But Daphne was probably more sensitive and therefore needed more time and space to deal. Also, her ordeal with that Luke guy was not the same as an impromptu fifty-minute kissfest.

Still, Gabby wondered if it was smart to let the girl stay home alone so much. Only what else could she do? Gabby had already missed her Monday shift, calling in sick since she couldn't use the real reason. "My sister is comatose with a massive attack of self-pity" probably wouldn't have cracked Pinkwater's titanium-shelled heart. And it didn't make sense for her to also miss school.

So she left Daphne at home, calling her periodically from a girls' room toilet stall to check on her. (The gossip in the Barton High teachers' lounge that day probably centered on whether Gabriella Rivera had a bladder infection or some gastric disorder.) Each time Daphne answered she sounded half asleep.

"Must be nice," Gabby grumbled as she pulled the car onto the road and headed for the center of town.

She felt shaky with stress. Her scholarship application deadline was next Monday. Meanwhile, school was really piling it on: all kinds of projects and exams were due right now. Plus everyone was still going on about prom as if it were the very point of their existence. Work was the usual pressure cooker of annoying people and her grouchy boss. And now with Mom gone, Gabby had even more chores to do: paying bills, doing grocery shopping, overseeing meals.

So of course Daphne would choose this point in time to have a major freak-out.

"I should just call Mom," she said to the windshield as she stopped for the light at Central and Buxton. "I should call her right now." But she knew she wouldn't. Mom's leaving her training to deal with a drama-queen daughter would only make things worse.

It was horrible what those stupid snots had done to Daphne. The girl was a dreamy, idiotic, frustrating ditz most of the time, but she meant well. Now she just seemed broken. A loud, annoying toy without its power source. Daphne didn't deserve to be treated that way. But then, Gabby didn't deserve to have to clean up the mess, either.

Catching sight of the neon-framed cinema marquee, Gabby steered the Jetta into one of the remote, dimly lit parking spaces on the side of the theater that Pinkwater insisted the employees use (never mind safety issues) and cut the engine. Then she settled back in the seat and shut her eyes. Sure, she was late, but she really didn't want to go inside yet. Instead, she just sat, enjoying the stillness and silence. It was nice out there, in the mugging zone. No one needed her. No one expected her to do things or feel things.

A thought entered her mind—slowly at first, just a trickle, then gradually building up until it saturated everything in its path: she really should call Daphne one last time. Before the half-price-night crowds kept her too busy.

With a dismal sigh, she lifted her phone and called home. After several rings her mother's recorded announcement came over the line. "You have reached the Rivera residence. No one can take your call right now. Please leave a—"

"Damn it, Daphne." She tried again. Again she got the machine. She let out a frustrated moan and tried a third time. And for a third time, her mother's businesslike tone met her ear.

Why wasn't Daphne picking up? She always picked up.

She could be in the bath—but that was unlikely, since she seemed to have given up bathing along with school. And the last time Gabby had spoken with her, it sure hadn't sounded as if there'd been a miracle turnaround in her mood. So had she gone somewhere in her pajamas? Was she ignoring Gabby? Playing loud music? Trapped under something heavy? If that girl had gone and gotten herself hurt, Gabby would wring her neck.

But . . . that seemed all too possible. Daphne was distracted, and she could barely operate the stove when she was normal. Any number of things could have gone wrong.

"Where is it? Where is it?" Gabby pulled out her wallet and rummaged through the cards and pieces of paper she'd stored in its many pockets. Eventually she hit upon the stone-gray business card with raised navy lettering and punched Prentiss's number into her phone.

"Hello?" he answered.

"Prentiss? It's Gabby. Gabby Rivera. Your tenant?"

"My what?"

She sighed. "Your tenant. *Ten-ant.*"

"My aunt? Sorry. I can't hardly hear you."

Just great. She got a lousy connection with a total imbecile. "It's Gabby!" she shouted. "I'm renting the yellow house on your property!"

"Oh, hi. How are you?"

"Listen, could you do me a favor? Are you at home?"

"Sure am. What can I do for you?"

"My sister is . . . well, she's sick. And I can't seem to get through to her. Would you mind walking over there and checking on her? Then maybe calling me back at this number?"

"You bet. Hold tight and I'll phone you as soon as I can."

As soon as he hung up, Gabby felt foolish. Why had she called Prentiss? The guy would dawdle on his way over there, maybe stop to wax his fancy car, and then chat with Daphne about the weather while she bled all over the kitchen floor. Gabby could have driven over there herself and been faster.

She drummed her hands on the steering wheel, trying to ignore the awful visions that kept rearing up. Their rental house in flames . . . Daphne sleepwalking into traffic . . . Daphne's face turning a bright shade of cerulean as she choked on a piece of corn dog.

Lila, late as usual, pulled her Dodge Viper into a nearby space and started touching up her lipstick while some country song blared from her speakers. After a couple of seconds of admiring herself she noticed Gabby and let out a tiny shriek. Then she turned down the music and lowered her window, motioning for Gabby to do the same.

"What are you doing?" she asked, her freshly painted lips curled in annoyance.

Gabby held up her phone. "I'm waiting on a call. It's . . . personal."

"Uh-huh," Lila said, climbing out of her car. "You do know you'll be late?"

Gabby simmered at the irony of that statement. "Yeah, I know," she said, forcing a smile. "Please tell Pinkwater I'll be there right away. Okay?"

Lila flashed her a look that said *Fine, but it's your ass in the deep roaster, not mine* before she shouldered her purse and headed around the corner.

"Come on, come on," Gabby grumbled to her phone. It remained dark and silent. She could see her face frowning back at her in the view screen. Her forehead was bunched and her eyebrows had scrolled together, making her look haggard—the same stressed-out expression her mom often wore. Was everyone who looked after Daphne doomed to have premature wrinkles?

All at once the cell started ringing, erasing her reflection as it lit up.

"Yeah?" she said, answering.

"She's all right," came Prentiss's voice. "I think I woke her up. Poor thing looks really bad. When's the last time she ate something, you think? You girls doing all right with food and all?"

Gabby paused. She hadn't really noted her sister's eating habits. She'd just been so busy. Come to think of it, she really hadn't seen her eat much lately. Guilt welled up inside her— and quickly boiled over into anger.

All she'd needed was for Prentiss to check on Daphne. She hadn't asked for a damn commentary on their standard of living.

"How about I have my mom make some soup?" Prentiss went on. "I could bring it over later and—"

"No!" Gabby shut her eyes and pinched the bridge of her nose with her thumb and forefinger. "Look. I appreciate your help, but we're fine. Really. We don't need any pity and we don't need any handouts."

"I didn't mean it that way. I was just thinking it must be tough without your mom and all."

"I said I can handle this! God! Why won't anybody give me a break?" Gabby shut off her phone, tossed it into her bag, and headed into the theater, ready to disappoint her irate boss, her lazy coworker, hordes of annoying moviegoers, and anyone else who might depend on her.

Daphne lay stomach-down across the couch. Only her left thumb revealed signs of life, moving occasionally to click the Channel Up button on the TV remote.

Prentiss had woken her from a deep sleep. And even though she felt worn out, she couldn't seem to drift off again.

God, she was bored. Not restless-bored, just . . . tired of absolutely everything. It was hard to escape her thoughts while awake. Everything her mind hit on seemed to twist and deform until she found herself thinking about Luke. Thoughts of school warped into thoughts of him. But thoughts of family also led to thoughts of him—or of Dad, which only amped up her anger and pain. Even seemingly safe thoughts could distort themselves into Luke-centered ones. Musing about clothes would lead to picturing dresses, which would cause her to think about prom. The sight of a book would remind her of that awful *Jane Eyre* that used to mean so much to her. Even the simple act of watching dust swirl in the sunlight from the window would remind her of that ridiculous glitter makeup.

She'd hoped watching TV would be a nice diversion, but so far it hadn't been. It was all sad and horrible, and it only made her feel more wretched. Talk shows featuring shouting guests, soap operas featuring Lynette-like women in jewels and fancy clothes, medical-drama reruns, a science program discussing the possibility that gamma rays could end all life on earth.

Her thumb clicked the remote again, and she found herself looking at a newscast. A wandering deer had caused a six-car pileup on Highway 77. The camera kept zooming in on crushed metal, flashing emergency lights, and debris littering the roadway.

Obviously there was nothing she could watch that would ease her sad, sore little brain. Everywhere there was suffering, destruction, fury. What a naïve baby she'd been to have never noticed it before.

The doorbell chimed its overly cheerful *ding-dong*. Daphne closed her eyes and made a small whimpering noise in her throat. Gabby had probably schooled Prentiss on the art of lecturing little sisters and sent him back over to holler at her. She thought about ignoring it but feared that that might make things worse. Their concerned neighbor might very well have the Barton police break down the door.

She muted the television and slowly pulled herself to a standing position. Her limbs felt as if they'd been cast from iron, and her joints seemed rusty from lack of use. Eventually she made it to the door and opened it a crack. But instead of Prentiss, Mule was grinning awkwardly down at her.

"Hi," he said. "Is Gabby here?"

Daphne shook her head. "She's . . ." But she couldn't remember where her sister was. Work? The store? The bank? Someplace important. What time was it, anyway?

Mule cocked his head and studied her. She could almost see him taking note of her blank expression, her gravity-defying hair, and her rumpled pajamas with the cartoon monkeys all over them. No doubt by now he could catch a whiff of that sharp scent, like overly ripe fruit, that her body was giving off after three straight days of no bathing.

"Are you okay?" he asked.

His voice was so full of worry that her eyes automatically misted up and her throat got that just-strangled feeling. She wanted to say yes, but that would be such an obvious lie. On the other hand, saying no would just invite more questions. And saying anything right now would squeeze the tears out of her. So she just stood there, feeling helpless and pitiful. And stinky.

"Hey, uh . . ." Mule shifted his weight and raked his fingers through his curls. "How about I hang around until Gabby gets back. Would that be okay?"

Daphne nodded. She left the door hanging open and flopped down on one end of the couch, propping her bare feet on the coffee table.

Mule walked inside and set down his backpack, keeping his eyes on Daphne the whole way. "Sure is nice out today," he said, slipping off his jacket and draping it on the nearby chair. His movements and voice were extrasteady, as if he were an expert negotiator and Daphne were some crazy person with explosives strapped to her chest.

Slowly and gently, as if trying not to spook her, he settled himself on the opposite end of the sofa. Out of the corner of her eye she could see him watching her as she focused on the muted television. Reporters were now interviewing one of the drivers of the pileup. The guy appeared dazed, but not too freaked to ramble into a microphone. The camera then panned to a dead deer lying on the shoulder of the road. Its mouth was open and bloody, and its glassy eyes seemed to be staring right into Daphne. Once again she could feel that downward-tugging sensation inside her. It felt as if she were teetering on a ribbon-thin brink, in danger of plummeting into a dark, cold abyss.

Then Mule loudly cleared his throat.

"So I'll just say it. I . . . heard about what happened," he said, turning his torso enough to face her. "I'm really sorry about what those guys did to you."

Water filled her eyes, blurring the scene until it was just blotches of color, like a bad Impressionist painting. She wanted to put her hands over her ears and scurry off to her room, but she couldn't move. She could only sit there, hugging her knees to her chest and staring at the fuzzy glowing blob of the TV set.

"Don't let those lowlives get to you," he went on. "They're emotionally stunted and totally inhuman—believe me, I should know. And you have nothing to be ashamed of."

Daphne felt a rush of anger. "Yes, I do! I was stupid! Just like everyone says." Her shouting dislodged tears, which were now streaking down her face, dotting the legs of her pajamas. Meanwhile, her hands balled into fists, the nails digging into her palms. It hurt, but she didn't care. It was kind of nice to feel it—to feel *something*—after the dullness of the past few days.

Mule just sat there, watching her as she swiped her wet cheeks with her fists. "I don't think you were stupid," he said. "I think you were brave."

"Brave . . . ha!" Daphne let out a snort. "I totally embarrassed myself. I said all kinds of crazy stuff to a guy because I thought he . . ." Her voice trailed off. She swallowed hard, stuffing the unsaid words back down inside.

"I know." Mule stretched his arm across the back of the couch and let his fingertips graze her left shoulder. "It hurts when you realize you don't mean as much to someone as they mean to you. Makes you feel like an idiot."

Daphne nodded. She crossed her arms in a self-embrace and stared at the TV without really seeing it. He was right. Luke's not wanting her was way more of a blow than what those jerks did.

She'd thought he was different—sweet and wonderful and heaven-sent. She'd thought they shared an almost magical connection. And then he went and . . . *connected* with Lynette. *Lynette!* Yes, she was pretty, but there was nothing at all old-fashioned or romantic about her. Like Gabby, she probably didn't even believe in true love. She was the anti-Daphne. The polar opposite of Daphne. So . . . how could he even be with someone like that? More importantly, how could he be with Lynette and then move on to Daphne *on the same night*? She wasn't even sure what had happened between Luke and Lynette, and she didn't want to imagine. Whatever it was, she was certain it hadn't been special. But then, he obviously didn't think what he had with Daphne was special, either.

How could she have been so wrong? She'd been so sure Luke was meant to be with her. She'd literally felt it, like a flu. Now that he was gone, she was left weak and unsteady. Lost.

The world seemed harsher now, outside the fever dream. Even the colors looked washed-out. And the worst part was, this was reality. This was where she had to remain. She could never return to that fantasy realm.

She glanced over at Mule, astonished that he could understand this, at least partly. Suddenly it hit her: he'd been through it, too—sort of. He was in love with Gabby. Only Gabby was too stubborn and hard-hearted to let herself love him back.

A newer, stronger affection for Mule came over her. She smiled at him, but her face was still rigid from so much sleep, and she couldn't be sure it looked friendly.

His mouth crooked into a semigrin and he hunched forward, fumbling with his hands. He seemed embarrassed to have revealed so much. "So anyway," he said. "What are you going to do about school?"

Daphne frowned. "What do you mean?"

"Well, not to sound like a parent or anything, but you have been missing a lot. And it's really tough to get caught up after you get way behind on stuff."

"So?" Daphne slouched down on her cushions. "It doesn't matter. I was probably going to fail anyway. At least in geometry."

"Really? Is it hard?"

"Ms. Manbeck always explains things like it's so obvious, but I can never follow her. Plus, she hates me."

Mule chuckled. "Yeah, she's a dried-up relic. It's amazing she hasn't retired yet. How come you don't ask Gabby to help you?"

"Are you kidding? She's way too busy. So's Mom. I went to tutoring once, but Ms. Manbeck just got me more confused. And she kept yelling at me about not sitting like a lady—even though I was in jeans."

"Hmm." Mule tapped his fuzz-covered chin with his index finger. "I might have an idea. What if I came over Saturday afternoon and tutored you myself?"

"Really? You'd do that?"

"Sure. Maybe in exchange for those cookies you sometimes make? What do you call them?"

"Camp cookies." They were basically oatmeal cookies with chocolate chips—the only thing she knew how to make that didn't involve the microwave.

"Ah yes. Camp cookies. Snack food of the gods. You make me some of them, and I'll guarantee you at least a C in Manbeck's class. Deal?"

Daphne felt her mouth stretch into her first real grin in days. "Deal."

There was nothing grosser than movie theater hot dogs. Those raspberry-colored oblong shapes gleaming in brown bubbly grease as they rolled on the warmer certainly didn't look edible. Their smell was more reminiscent of bathroom cleaner than any sort of food. And their taste, going by a half-buried memory from Gabby's childhood, could only be summed up as garden-hose-meets-expired-baloney.

Who on earth would think up such a recipe, anyway? Who decided it would be a great idea to take all the unmentionable parts of an animal, grind them up, pump the mixture full of dye and chemicals, and then squeeze everything into a protective casing, as if it were some sort of explosive? Her grandma's tamales, which probably shared some of the same meat components, had been far less offensive. Or at least more sincere.

And yet every Wednesday evening, with their half-price admission special, the cinema sold gobs of hot dogs. It was amazing half the residents of Barton weren't red and glistening.

Nothing made Gabby more glum than having to serve an overweight townsperson one of their "Date Night Dawgs" with a bucket of extrabuttered popcorn and a thirty-two-ounce soda—usually a Diet Coke, ironically enough.

"I'm a murderer," she said to Lila after serving Letty Pension, who was four feet tall and almost as wide. "I'm poisoning our neighbors."

"Please!" Lila tossed away the comment with a flick of her long-nailed hand. "It isn't like you're forcing them to eat it."

"I'm still an accomplice."

"Oh, give them a break. They're here to have fun. Anyway, you can't stay away from all bad stuff all the time."

Perhaps Lila was right. Maybe they ate nothing but salad, tofu, and flaxseed bread the rest of the week. Besides, Gabby had eaten a few corn dogs recently and she'd survived.

Gabby stared back down at the rotating hot dog rack and thought about her call with Prentiss earlier. He was bad stuff, and yet he'd done her a favor. She'd really gone off on him, too. She supposed it had been unfair of her—not to mention unwise, since he was technically their landlord. She didn't have to like the guy, but she should probably be a little more civil, if only for the sake of her family.

"Hey, girl. The next movie rush isn't for a while. Mind if I go outside and take a smoke break?" Lila asked, patting the rectangular-shaped bulge in the pocket of her uniform.

Gabby nodded. "Go ahead."

"Thanks, sweetie. Cover for me if Old Raisin-Face comes out of his office."

She watched as Lila sashayed out of the theater and disappeared around the side of the building. The lobby was quiet, except for the steady hum of the fountain machine and the intermittent buzzing of the tube lights. Looking around to make sure no patrons were headed her way for popcorn refills, she slipped her cell phone out of her pocket and redialed Prentiss's number.

"Hello?" he answered.

Gabby took a breath. "It's me again. Gabby. Listen, um . . . I think before when we were talking, we might have gotten cut off. Sorry about that."

"No big deal," he said. He didn't sound mad at all.

"Okay then." Gabby kept nodding, as if he could somehow see her. "Well, I better—"

"Are you having a good day?"

"What?"

"I said, are you having a good day?"

Gabby frowned. "I . . . uh . . . It's okay."

"Good."

"Are you having a good day?" she asked, only because she felt like she should.

"I am," he said, his voice a low murmur. "Especially now."

A weird sensation came over her, as if a pitcher of molasses had been poured onto her head and was slowly oozing down her body. "Yeah, so . . . I gotta go. Bye."

"Bye."

Gabby hung up the phone and rested her head on the counter. God, what was she thinking calling him? What did it matter if he thought she was rude? It was preferable to his thinking she was hot for his tan, muscular body. Which she so was not—ever. Never, never, never.

Ugh. Suddenly the day didn't feel so okay anymore.

The front door banged open, making Daphne and Mule jump, and suddenly Gabby was there.

"Pinkwater kept me after closing so he could ream me out for being late. I guess the trick is to make it a habit, like Lila does; then you can get away with it. But if you're usually responsible and prompt, you better not come in fifteen minutes after your start time or you'll get a major chewing-out."

Daphne was amazed at how her sister's presence changed everything. Her voice drowned out all other sound; her rapid motions distracted from the cartoon on the TV; even the temperature seemed to fall. It was as if all the energy in the room had been diverted to Gabby's end.

Daphne was disappointed to see her. She'd actually enjoyed being there with just Mule, watching TV and occasionally talking. It was shocking how nice he was being to her—especially considering how awful she must look. And she appreciated the way he took her seriously. He didn't shy away from mentioning the craziness at school, and instead of lecturing her about her grades, he'd actually offered to tutor her.

She still felt miserable, but not quite as helpless. As if she'd been thrown a thin tether of a lifeline.

"Well, I guess we should get started," Gabby said, standing over Mule. She turned to Daphne. "You didn't have any supper, did you?"

"Yes, I did."

"Really? What did you eat?"

"I don't know."

"What do you mean you don't know?"

"I mean, I don't know what it's called. There was this yellow stuff in a plastic thing in the fridge. It was like . . . spicy fruit salad."

Gabby and Mule exchanged looks. Mule started laughing.

Daphne frowned. "What? There really was. It was pretty good, too."

"Just . . . never mind," Gabby said, waving her off. "Why don't you go take a shower or something? We have to do homework."

Being so near her gorgeous sister, Daphne suddenly felt self-conscious about her tangled hair and half-marinated sleepwear. The urge to run and hide returned. "Fine," she mumbled, and stood to head off toward her room.

Mule reached up and touched her elbow as she passed. "Hey," he said. "So I'm still coming by Saturday to help you, right?"

Daphne smiled. "Right," she said. "See you then."

"And I'll expect cookies!" he yelled after her as she rounded the corner of the hallway.

"What are you talking about? What's going on Saturday?" came Gabby's whispered voice. Daphne paused outside her door to listen to them.

"She's having a hard time in Manbeck's class, so I told her I'd help her out," Mule said.

"Really?" Gabby exclaimed. "You don't have to do that."

"It's no problem."

"Well . . . thanks. And thanks for sitting with her tonight, too."

Mule made a scoffing sound. "You make it sound like she's seven or something. It was no big deal. We talked. It was kinda cool."

"You talked? What did you talk about?"

There came a pause. "Nothing, really. So tell me, when Pinkwater gets mad, does he unzip his skin and reveal his true form? Does he have tentacles?"

Their voices became muffled as they pulled out books and papers and drinks from the fridge. Daphne stopped eavesdropping and continued to her darkened room.

She was glad Mule hadn't shared any of the stuff they'd discussed. And she wouldn't say anything, either—even though he'd practically confessed to being in love with Gabby. She owed him that.

If only her sister would wise up and go for him. After all, at least one Rivera girl deserved to be happy.

CHAPTER SEVENTEEN
Hypno(sis)

Sunlight streamed through the dining room window, casting a bright square on the table and making the salt on the rim of the shaker glisten like microscopic gems.

Gabby yawned over her cup of coffee. It was one of those gigantic yawns—the kind that brings tears to the eyes and nearly unhinges the jawbone. It was one in the afternoon on a Saturday and she still had a crapload of stuff to do. But even after a second brewing of Colombian Supremo her brain was like a dawdling child who was always five steps behind.

For the first time since she was three years old, she had a room to herself. It should have been wonderful. Mom's bed was cozy, and there was no fidgety sister a few steps away. And yet, for some reason, sleep was eluding her. Every night since Daphne's sneaking out to the party, she had found it difficult to drift off. She'd stew over the events of the day. She'd worry that she'd been too tough with Daphne, then worry that she hadn't been strict enough. She'd toy with the idea of calling her mother and asking her how to handle a despondent, hooky-playing little sis, then scold herself for even thinking about ruining things for Mom. And she thought about Mule, and whether the slight weirdness that had crept between them was there to stay, and what, if anything, she should do about it. Thus, deep, uninterrupted sleep had become a tantalizing lover to Gabby (or so she imagined, never having actually been tantalized, or with a lover).

Daphne, on the other hand, still did nothing but sleep. And while this made Gabby somewhat jealous, it also worried the hell out of her. She never thought she'd wish her sister would be more talkative, more energetic, or more cheerful. But lately there was just so little life emanating from Daphne. Even when she was awake, she plodded around the house as if she were dragging an IV pole behind her, her features slack and her eyes dull and half-closed. It made Gabby feel powerless. And scared.

Just as she was slurping down the last sip of coffee in her cup, the doorbell rang. Gabby leaned back and squinted through the gleaming window. "No way. No freaking way," she muttered. There on the porch, fidgeting like a little kid, stood her father.

She ran to the door and threw it open. "What are you doing here?" she demanded.

"Hi, *mija*."

"It's not your day to visit."

"I know," he said, chuckling. "Do I need a reason to come see my beautiful daughters?"

"Yes. We have stuff to do, you know. We can't just drop everything because you've shown up." Her eyes were wide with panic and her voice had risen to screech level. This was so not what she needed. She was dead tired and overloaded with chores and deadlines—not to mention busy dealing with a catatonic sister. It was the absolute worst time for a family reunion.

His smile faded. "You're right," he said, nodding. "But I do have a reason. I . . . feel bad. The last time I talked to your sister, well . . . it didn't go so well. She took it pretty hard."

"What are you talking about? Took what hard?"

He looked at her searchingly, as if checking to see whether she was teasing him. "You mean she didn't tell you?"

"Tell me what?"

Her dad moved his eyes from hers, staring instead at the freshly painted red door flung open beside them. "I told Daphne about Sheila, my new girlfriend, who's living with me now. She was pretty upset."

"Y-you have . . . ?" A strange unfastening sensation swept through Gabby, as if a key fragment of herself had disengaged from the rest of her. "How long has this been going on?"

"Seven months."

"Jesus Christ."

"Don't talk that way, *mija*. It's offensive."

"Don't tell me how to talk!" she shouted. "Since when do you care? You're the one shacking up with some *chica* you hardly even know!"

Her dad's gaze sharpened and his nostrils flared. "You want to be rude to your own father? Fine. I just came to check on Daphne and apologize to her."

"No," Gabby said, shaking her head. No way was she going to let him in. Daphne was wounded enough.

"What do you mean 'no'?"

"I mean you can't see her! She's sleeping."

"Still?" He glanced at his watch. "Don't you think it's time she got up?"

"She hasn't been feeling good and she needs her sleep. You can't go in there. This is our property, not yours."

"She's my daughter."

"She's *my* sister. And you're here, unannounced, on the *wrong day*!" Gabby was really losing it now. Pumping her fist and screaming like a banshee. She had a sudden urge to hurt her father. To push him backward or toss a rock at him. Why wouldn't he just leave?

Her dad's eyes reddened and filled with tears. "Gabriella, *mija*," he said, "what have I done to make you hate me so much?"

She stayed silent, averting her gaze so that she was squinting at the nearby bushes instead.

"You're becoming so cold. So hard," he said. "What happened to my happy little girl?"

Gabby gritted her teeth. She wanted to ask what had happened to her loyal, reliable father, but she didn't. She wanted to ask how *he* had turned cold, how he could have stopped loving his wife and abandoned his family. But she couldn't. Plus, she didn't need to—she already knew the answer. Love was just a flash flame. It burned bright and then disappeared. Unless people stayed strong and committed, they left, too. Most people, it seemed, went away.

"You want to push me away? Okay. I understand," he went on, his voice shaky. "But don't push me away from my baby, too. Please let me see my little girl."

She stared right at him. "Daphne isn't a baby anymore," she said. "We're growing up. Maybe you should, too."

Her dad looked as if she'd given in to her impulse and slapped him across the face. His skin reddened and his mouth trembled slightly. For a while he just stood there, blinking rapidly. Then, with a barely perceptible nod, he turned and walked down the steps toward his car.

Gabby waited until the Honda had disappeared down the road before heading back inside. Her knees felt quaky and her breath was coming in quick gasps. She turned in a circle, feeling disoriented, not knowing what to do. She could tell she was about to break down, but she didn't want to. She needed to make it go away.

Only she couldn't stop it. A fierce sob was already rising, and she clamped her hand over her mouth, trying to hold it back. The sound died in her throat but the force made her lurch forward. Tears began streaming down her face.

Gabby raced through the kitchen, heading for the most remote place in the house, the laundry room, and shut the door. There, in the stuffy seclusion, she sank to her knees, doubling over onto a pile of towels she hadn't gotten around to washing, and let the emotions come.

The intensity of her crying surprised her. Deep, violent sobs, each one in a loud descending scale that sent tremors through her body. She'd forgotten what it was like to weep like this. How startling it was to lose control, and how helpless she was to stop it. Meanwhile, her mind rolled a little slide show of her past: She and Daphne playing in the waves at Mustang Island . . . The time Daphne tore her knee open at the park and Gabby somehow managed to pedal her home, balanced on the end of her bicycle seat . . . Grandma singing *"De Colores"* as she plaited Gabby's unruly waves into a long braid . . . Daddy laughing and chasing them through the yard that time it snowed . . . Daddy's sad eyes as he looked at her on the porch just now . . . Each vision seemed to rip through her, eroding layers of protection and bringing forth a fresh set of pains.

Suddenly, a loud thump cut through the sounds of her crying and snapped her back to the present. Gabby sat up and glanced in the direction of the noise.

Prentiss was peering at her through the high window.

The sobs subsided. Instead, a fiery rage swept through her, clearing her mind and repowering her limbs. She scrambled to her feet and ran out of the house to the porch.

"What the hell do you think you're doing?" she screamed.

Prentiss just stared at her. His jaw was hanging open wide enough for her to stuff something inside and choke him. "I . . . ," he began.

"I saw you! I saw you looking at me, you . . . you sick pervert!"

His eyes widened. "N-no," he said. "I wasn't . . . I was just . . ." He held up something in his right hand: a large, swirly lightbulb. "I came to put this in y'all's porch lamp. It's . . . energy efficient."

"And what do you call staring into windows? Energy-efficient entertainment?" Gabby was so angry, she felt as if she might spontaneously combust right there in front of him. She'd almost love for it to happen, if only to see the stupefied look on his face. But knowing Prentiss, he'd probably just go get a broom and clean up her ashes before they marred the wax job on his Mustang.

"I'm sorry," he said. "I heard something strange and . . . looked in. It was just a reaction. I didn't mean to spy or anything." He took a small step forward and tilted his head, his brow furrowing into neat little folds. "Are you all right?"

A renegade sob crept into Gabby's throat. How dare he act all concerned. He had no right. After what he'd done. After everything he'd taken from her. "God, I hate you," she whispered. "I wish you'd just leave us alone. I wish you'd go away and never come back!"

Prentiss looked down at the porch planks. "Why are you like this? What did I do? You know, I think . . ." He glanced up again, his mouth moving soundlessly, as if he were trying to pronounce something foreign. Then he pursed his lips, shook his head, and walked away from her— just like her dad had several minutes earlier. Just like she wanted him to.

Only, for some reason, it didn't make her feel better.

What was that noise?

Daphne sat up, shielding herself behind her bedcovers, and listened intently. Eventually, she recognized it as the bathroom fan. Gabby must have left it on after her shower, and the muffled noise always penetrated their wall as a low, ominous growl.

It sounded so sinister. But then, lately, most things seemed that way.

She slid out of bed onto her feet and then immediately sat back down. Just the thought of leaving her room made her feel tired. Her sister was already up and showered and had probably completed several tasks with her typically amazing efficiency and resourcefulness. But Daphne had nothing to do. And there was nothing she wanted to do. There was no point.

Daphne used to pretend she was a character in a film. It wasn't the kind of fake behavior meant to impress other people, because she usually did it while she was alone—like when she was stewing in her room over something Gabby had done, or walking to the corner store feeling sorry for herself for having to do such a menial chore, or even just gazing dreamily out a window. She would move and stand and contort her features as if a camera were zooming in on her, often accompanied by appropriate background music on her iPod. It helped her deal with her emotions and made them feel more . . . poetic.

Not anymore. There would be no more pretending. She was stuck in the real world now, and that meant being stuck with her regular, stupid self.

She scanned her room, noticing how messy it had gotten without Gabby's tidying skills—yet another way Daphne was defective. Her eyes landed on her geometry book, the gloomy chocolate-brown cover triggering an automatic stress response.

Suddenly she remembered something. She really did have a reason to get out of bed that day: Mule was coming over to tutor her.

It wasn't the most fun thing that could happen—in fact, it probably wouldn't be fun at all—but it was something.

She slipped on her fuzzy pink slippers and headed out into the living room.

Sure enough, Gabby was already stomping around the kitchen, slamming cupboards and muttering to herself. It looked as if she'd deep-cleaned the whole room. And she must have been doing laundry, too, because a fuzzy piece of dryer lint was stuck to her shoulder.

As Daphne entered the dining area, Gabby looked right at her and then quickly turned away.

"What's wrong?" Daphne asked.

"Nothing," Gabby muttered. She grabbed a wet cloth and started wiping the nearby counter with quick, angry strokes.

No doubt she was mad at Daphne. She was sick of having a good-for-nothing blob of a sister, and Daphne couldn't really blame her. She was useless.

Gabby suddenly blew out her breath and stared up at the ceiling. "Actually . . . I guess you should know. Dad came by earlier."

"Daddy?"

"Don't worry," Gabby said, twisting the dishrag between her hands. "I told him he had to leave. I knew you wouldn't want to see him right now since you're still . . . you know. It just made me mad that he would show up like that, all apologetic and stuff. He told me about that new woman."

"He was apologetic?" Daphne felt a tiny plucking sensation, as if a little plant were sprouting inside her.

Gabby scoffed. "Yeah. Can you believe it? He thinks he can just hook up with some stranger and bring her into our lives like it's no big deal. That's probably why he always has to run off so fast after his visits. That's probably why he's always so broke."

Daphne's mind went awhirl. She'd thought the exact same thing before, but now . . . "You should have woken me up," she said hoarsely.

Gabby's eyes widened. "What?"

"Why didn't you come get me?"

"Because you said you didn't want him to know what happened."

"That's different," Daphne said, shaking her head. "I wouldn't have told him."

"What are you talking about? He would have taken one look at your sorry-ass state and known something was up. Besides, you made me promise."

Daphne pushed a tangled knot of hair out of her face. Gabby was right—she had made her promise. She'd been so mad at him at the time. But there was another part of her that really did want to see him. To have him hug her tight and tell her everything would be okay.

"You could have at least asked me," she said to Gabby. "You didn't give me a chance. He wanted to say he was sorry, and maybe I would have wanted to hear it."

"Why would you want that?"

"Because!" Daphne's voice grew loud and shaky. "We hardly ever see him. And now the one time he shows up to help out you chase him away!"

"That's it! I give up!" Gabby screamed. "I was looking out for you and now you're angry at me? Well, screw you! Do you even know how messed up things have been for me lately? I'm sick of taking care of you! I'm sick of this stupid life! God, I can't wait to leave this hellhole town!"

Throwing the rag to the floor, Gabby pushed past her and stalked out the door. Daphne felt the porch quake from the force of her stomps, and then . . . silence. Only it wasn't a good silence. It was more like the eerie quiet of a battlefield after a particularly bloody skirmish. It made Daphne feel shaken and vulnerable, with nothing to focus on but her muddled thoughts.

She'd been wrong to yell at Gabby. She really didn't want to be mad at her—or at her dad. In fact, she wished she didn't feel mad at anyone anymore. All that anger felt poisonous inside her. And she didn't like the sensations that came with it. She needed to feel good about something for a change.

"Hey," a voice called out.

Daphne glanced up and saw Mule stepping into the living room.

"The door was open," he explained.

"Gabby must have slammed it too hard," she said. "She got mad at me and . . ." She motioned out the window to where Gabby was stomping off toward the Applewhites' rose garden.

Mule's gaze followed her hand. "Ah, yes. There she is. I'd recognize that high-speed pissed-off walk anywhere."

"It's okay. You don't have to stay with me. You can go after her."

Daphne felt suddenly self-conscious in her pajamas and slippers. At least she'd finally changed out of the rancid monkey-face ones. Now she had on her Christmas-themed ones with the peppermints all over—the only clean pair she could find since they were so behind on laundry. She must resemble an oversized toddler.

Mule shook his head. "Oh, no," he said with a wry laugh. "Gabby always needs to be by herself to cool down. Other people are just cannon fodder, not comfort." He nudged Daphne with his elbow. "Don't worry. She'll eventually come back and be nice—or at least . . . not as grouchy."

Daphne managed a feeble smile. It was strange how he seemed to know her sister better than she did.

"Come on," he said, nodding toward the dining room table. "Let's get started on that geometry. Normally I charge hundreds of dollars an hour for tutoring, but for you I'll do it for cookies."

"Crap!" Daphne exclaimed, clamping a hand to her forehead. "I totally forgot!"

Mule chuckled. "That's okay," he said, peering out the window at Gabby's retreating form. "Something tells me you've had a rough time of it lately."

Gabby veered around a crepe myrtle tree that had been planted—somewhat spitefully, it seemed—right in the middle of the worn grass path, and immediately stepped in something squishy.

"Crap!"

And that was what it was. Literally. A dog had left a little land mine right there for her to step in. Just more evidence that the whole world was conspiring against her.

She continued toward the rental house, muttering curse words and dragging her soiled shoe against the grass as if her right leg had suddenly gone lame. Twenty minutes of walking around the perimeter of the Applewhite estate and she felt no better than when she'd left. If anything, she was madder.

She was tired of people making her feel like a horrible person. Was she so awful for shying away from Mule's clumsy advances? For coming in late to work because she was busy playing mom to her sister? For shielding Daphne from their self-centered father? For trying to keep a spoiled, reckless, manslayer from butting into their lives? No. But everyone seemed to think she was.

God, she hated being the older sis. The example setter. The one who should know better. It was so unfair. Daphne got to live in a dream state, but Gabby had to live in the real world—the one of schedules and chores and never-ending responsibilities. And no one ever said thank you.

She could see the back of the rental house now, all freshly painted and tidy, like one of those storybook cottages in those mall paintings Lila went nuts for. And there, parked along the western side, was Mule's dad's Range Rover.

Right. The tutoring lesson. She was glad someone with a brain would be helping Daphne with her math homework— the girl needed to get her act together fast if she wanted to pass. But she also couldn't help wondering if this was a ruse on Mule's part to spend even more time with Gabby. Not that she hated spending time with him. It was just that lately he'd been so unpredictable. Even his expressions were different— his eyes all big and soulful and extra-alert. As if he was expecting something. Something from her.

Now there were two people in the house she was leery about seeing.

"No," she said to the house and the Range Rover. Not yet. She was sick of trudging around the grounds, dodging animal poop and looking like an idiot, but she also wasn't ready to return and face New Mule and her broken sister. Thank god she had the car keys in her back pocket. She could make a clean getaway and clear her head with a long drive.

Gabby corrected her trajectory, heading instead toward the carport. But as soon as she rounded the nearby trees, she could see that Prentiss's Mustang was parked cockeyed in the driveway, blocking her in.

Of course.

That pea-brain! That waste of vital planetary resources! She was so sick of him and his obnoxious sports car showing up at the worst possible times. Maybe he wasn't a complete idiot like he seemed. Maybe he was doing this on purpose, to punish her for yelling at him earlier. That or his inner evil was finally showing.

Gabby marched up to the main house and rang the bell. Soon the door opened to reveal Prentiss's blond spikes and toothy grin—which immediately disappeared once he saw her.

"Were you hoping to make me more energy-efficient by trapping me here? By making me walk everywhere?" she asked before he had a chance to say anything.

His Ken-doll features contorted in confusion.

"Your car!" She waved her thumb in the direction of the carport. "You've blocked me in—*again!*"

"Aw, man," he mumbled, clapping his hand to his forehead. "I'm sorry."

He leaned to the left and returned with a cluster of keys in his hands. Then he shut the door and strode across the lawn toward his Mustang.

Gabby wasn't about to let his lame apology be the last word on the subject. "I know our car isn't as expensive as yours," she said as she trotted along beside him. "But we are paying rent, and we were told that included a spot in the carport. I assumed that meant a spot we could actually get in and out of."

"I just forgot, okay?" he said. "I waxed it earlier and was hoping the sun might help it dry faster. No big deal."

Gabby's nails dug into the palms of her clenched hands. It pissed her off that he had it so easy. That the finish on his car was his biggest worry in life. It didn't matter if he inconvenienced anyone. Or caused them pain. Or death.

No big deal.

A fierce rattling sensation came over her. It was as if Prentiss—all his stupid words and careless actions—had been slowly drilling into her these past couple of weeks, boring through the tough shell until, finally, right at this moment, he struck the highly pressurized center, releasing a white-hot anger.

"Waxed it, huh?" she said, with the emphasis and diction of a maniacal newscaster. "That's great! Because that shine is *soooo* important. More important than safety, even. Or cautious driving. Who cares if you crash as long as that crushed metal has a beautiful gleam, right?"

A little bit of glow seeped out of Prentiss's expression. "What are you going on about?" he asked in a hollow voice.

"You!" she shouted, whirling so that she was standing right in front of him. "I mean, why bother waxing that thing? No one's going to want to get near enough to see that shine— not after what you did to your cousin."

Prentiss's face crumpled. "What?"

"You know it's your fault. Why won't you admit it? You think because your parents made the whole duck-pond incident go away, and who knows what else, that they made this one go away, too. But they didn't. They can't. Sonny's still dead!"

"You think I—" He broke off, letting his mouth hang open. He looked shocked, unable to believe that someone was actually pointing out his imperfections.

"How can you stand it?" Gabby said, shaking her head. "How can you stand yourself?"

Prentiss stared at her intently "So that's why you hate me, huh?" His eyes broke off from hers, focusing instead on an invisible scene in the yard behind her. "You think I got away with murder. You think I crashed the car and killed Sonny."

"Yes." Gabby was surprised at how loud and clear her answer was. It felt good to say it. Maybe it would strain relations with their landlords, but so what? She was glad the truth was out there. Now he'd know that at least one person was going to hold him accountable.

"You've got it all wrong," he said. "I wasn't the one driving that night. Sonny was."

"Yeah, right. That's the story your family put out there to keep you out of trouble. Well, guess what? You don't have everyone fooled. I know you killed him."

Prentiss rounded on her suddenly. His eyes blazed and his cheeks and neck were as red as his Mustang. She'd never seen him so emotional.

"How dare you," he said through his teeth. "You know, someone smart like you really should check her facts. We skidded off the road and hit a bank of trees on the left side of the car. How could I still be standing here if I'd been the one driving?"

Gabby felt her face go slack. She had no answer for this.

"See? You really *don't* know anything," he went on. "You don't know what it's like to see your best friend bleed to death. You don't know what I think and feel and relive every single goddamn day. You don't know. You weren't there. *So shut the hell up!*"

Gabby stayed frozen in place, unable to move or talk or even breathe. All she could do was watch as Prentiss stormed over to his car, climbed inside, and raced it onto the road, stirring up tiny eddies of dust.

He's lying, she thought, not bothering to step out of the way as a cloud of grime washed over her. *It can't be true. Please. Don't let it be true.*

Because if he was right, she'd have no reason to hate him. And for some reason, she really needed to hate Prentiss Applewhite.

◦ ◦ ◦

"*Uuugghhh!*" Daphne set her head down on the table. "This is so hard! I don't understand why we have to learn math anyway. I mean, we have calculators and stuff now that do it for us."

"It's not just for cashiers," Mule said. She could hear him digging in the bag for another Dorito. "All these theorems and algorithms are like . . . secret codes. A way to make sense of the world."

"Really?" Daphne sat up straight. "That would be nice, all right."

"I actually find math kind of comforting. Much more straightforward than art and literature, with all those feelings and interpretations and blah, blah, blah. That's the kind of stuff I find tough." He stared off toward the living room, his eyes all droopy. Daphne had a sudden urge to pat him on the head or scratch him under his whiskered chin.

"Yeah, well, I *used to* think I was good at the feelings part," she said, absently running her finger along the edge of the table. "Now I realize I suck at everything."

"Don't say that." Mule was frowning at her.

"Why not?" she said with a shrug. "It's true."

"No, it's not. Come on, I've known you a long time now. You're good at lots of things."

Daphne scoffed. "Oh yeah? Name one."

"Well . . ." Mule's khaki-green eyes swiveled up to the ceiling. "You're good at making people feel good."

"Are you talking about cheerleading?"

"No," he said with a grin. "What I mean is . . . you smile

and laugh. You put people at ease. You're easy to talk to." He said that last part as if he himself were surprised to discover it. "Not a lot of people can do that."

Daphne had never really thought about it before. She supposed he could be right.

"So . . . you're saying I'd make a good stewardess?"

Mule laughed. "No. I mean, yes, you would—and I hear they make excellent benefits. Besides, I think they like to be called flight attendants these days," he added. "But seriously, I don't just mean jobwise. Wherever you go, you'll always have people around you. People who like you."

"Where have you been lately?" Daphne asked, feeling annoyed. "I'm the *least* popular person in Barton right now. My friends totally turned on me. I have *no one* around."

"Yeah, right," Mule mumbled. "Just someone like me."

Daphne's face grew hot. "That's not what I meant."

"I know." Mule put his hand on her shoulder and smiled slightly. "Look, this thing at school . . . it's temporary. And you probably won't even be in Barton forever. But wherever you end up, you'll pull folks in. You'll have tons of friends— easily. Meanwhile, people like me and Gabby . . ." He broke off, letting his hand drop, and sighed down at the floor.

"I think you and Gabby should be together," Daphne said. "Like a couple."

He looked right at her, startled. "You do?"

"Yeah. You're good for her. You're great. She'd be stupid not to go for you."

Mule peered at her for a long moment. Then a grin slowly spread across his face. "See? This is what I mean. You always know what to say to people."

Daphne couldn't help smiling. "Yeah, well . . . it's probably the only thing I'm good at."

"Not true. You make excellent cookies. Which you still owe me, I must add."

"I overslept." Daphne wrinkled her nose apologetically.

He grinned. "I know. But you gotta count cookie baking as one of your talents. They are seriously addictive."

"You're just being nice. That's like saying my animal noises count as a major skill."

Mule perked up in his chair. "You do animal noises? Cool! How did I not know this? Well?" He moved his hand in a circular motion. "Go on, then. Demonstrate."

"No." Daphne ducked her head. "I'd feel stupid."

"Aw, come on! I'll do my air trumpet for you." He stooped over to meet her eye. "Pleeeeease?"

She laughed. "Okay, okay. But really, they're not that great." She sat up straight and opened her mouth . . . then chewed her bottom lip. It wasn't that easy. She'd done her animal sounds for the family many times—usually when they *didn't* want to hear them. But for a guy?

It's just Mule, she told herself. *No big deal.*

Daphne took a breath and did her horse, a long whinny followed by a shake of the head and a raspberrylike snort. Then she immediately clasped her hands over her face in embarrassment.

"Oh. My. God. That was awesome!" Mule exclaimed.

She peeked at him through her fingers. His face was all lit up like those million-dollar-grand-prize winners on TV commercials.

"Do more! Do more!" he urged.

"Uh-uh." She shook her head. "Your turn."

"Okay. Deal's a deal." He held up his hands as if quieting an invisible audience and then pantomimed playing trumpet while blowing through his pursed lips. It did sound somewhat convincing.

"Very good," Daphne said, applauding. "You know, that's actually pretty similar to my elephant. Want to see?"

"Bring it! And we'll see who the better trumpeter is."

Daphne bent over and let her right arm dangle by her ear. Then she suddenly rose, lifting her arm and making a loud bugling noise through her lips.

Mule threw back his head, guffawing. "Aw, man!" he said, between laughs. "Okay, I give up. You win. It takes a big man to admit defeat, but you totally stomped me. Like a good elephant should."

"Why, thank you," Daphne said, taking a small bow. It felt good to laugh—like a warm bath after a particularly grubby day.

For some reason, Mule was easy to laugh with. Maybe because he had such a great smile. It made his eyes twinkle and pushed his cheeks into perfect oval shapes.

"You know, it's weird," she said. "I never noticed how cool you are before."

His smile crooked sideways. "Um . . . thanks?"

"No, I mean . . . I didn't hate you or anything. You were just always with Gabby. So I felt like I wasn't supposed to hang around you. It would have been like befriending the opposition or something."

"Really?" he said, giving her a strange look.

She suddenly realized how silly she sounded. *"Ugh!"* she exclaimed, slapping her hands to her forehead. "I don't know what I'm trying to say. Just . . . thanks. I haven't had this much fun since . . . you know."

Mule smiled. "Glad to hear it. So how about we look at this next set of problems? If you make a good score, I'll do my Elvis voice for you."

Again Daphne laughed, and again it was as if her insides were being scrubbed clean. "Deal," she said.

Gabby slowly rolled the car down the gravel drive and into their spot in the carport. Two spaces down, Prentiss's Mustang sat gleaming in the waning light. So he was back.

She turned off the engine and rested her forehead on the top of the steering wheel, trying to purge the stresses of her day with a few deep breaths. While she was out she'd stopped at the local library and looked up a news report on the accident. It confirmed that Sonny, even though he only had his learner's permit, had been the one behind the wheel, just as Prentiss had told her, and just as she'd remembered reading, and rejecting, at the time of the accident. She didn't want to accept it now, either, except for one thing: the accompanying photo. Gabby hadn't been able to truly look at it when it originally ran, so she'd failed to notice something important: the driver's side was torn and mangled, while the passenger side barely had a dent.

There was no denying it now. It really hadn't been Prentiss's fault. And that only confirmed something else: she was a mean person. Everyone was right about her.

She'd been unfair. She realized that now. At the time of the accident, all that had mattered to her was that Sonny was gone for no good reason. She hadn't cared about the truth. She cared only about punishing someone for Sonny's death— and it was all too easy to focus her anger on Prentiss. And while Prentiss still might not be the finest individual ever to roam the planet, he probably didn't deserve to be judged so harshly.

He was right that Gabby didn't know anything. She'd never thought about his side. It never occurred to her that he'd seen Sonny die—actually witnessed it happening, right in front of him. She couldn't imagine how horrible that must have been. Prentiss never seemed to be all that torn up about the accident, something she'd always found appalling. But maybe he was and just didn't show it. Gabby, of all people, should know that was possible. And earlier that day, when he'd been yelling at her, she'd seen something in his eyes that she recognized: pain mixed with helplessness. It seemed real, which made him seem more real, too.

Perhaps things weren't always so easy for him, like she'd thought. If that was the case, well . . . then she really did feel ashamed about how she'd treated him. Moreover, there was a part of her that wanted to hear the whole awful truth from Prentiss about the car crash. To find out exactly what he'd gone through—or, more precisely, what Sonny had gone through. But then . . . part of her *didn't* want to know. Not that it mattered. Prentiss probably never wanted to see her again in his life.

No matter what, Gabby knew she should apologize. It was

the right thing to do. Anyway, Prentiss was their landlord, and like it or not, she had to accept that her family was dependent on his. So she made up her mind to say she was sorry, but *not* in person. Every time she got around the guy, her brain—and sometimes her mouth—went rogue. He was just too linked with her crazy past. He reminded her too much of Sonny.

After leaving the library, she had driven over to Hawthorne's for some sweet tea and written him a letter. It was the perfect solution. She'd labored over it for close to an hour, making sure it was repentant enough without sounding phony. *Sorry if I offended you. I was wrong to jump to conclusions. It won't happen again. Best regards . . .*

It would have to do.

Gabby picked up the paper lying on the passenger seat and looked it over. Then she shoved it into a bank deposit envelope she found in the glove compartment and carefully wrote Prentiss's name across the front. Taking another deep breath, she climbed out of the Jetta and headed up the sloping lawn to the main house.

Darkness had fallen quickly, and none of the front lights were on at the Applewhites'. The porch was a muddle of foreign, blocky shapes and various shades of black. Creepiness aside, Gabby was relieved to see the house look so sleepy. It gave excellent cover for her to slip the note into the mailbox and sneak away.

She tiptoed onto the front terrace, squinting to make out the mailbox. Eventually her eyes found the whitewashed iron bin on the wall. But just when she was about to approach it, a movement startled her. A quick shifting of the shadows just to her right.

Gabby gasped and spun around, staring at the place where the darkness had fluttered. Then she watched in horror as one of the shadows rose in front of her.

It was Prentiss. Apparently he'd been sitting in the wicker rocking chair.

"Oh, my god! You scared me," she exclaimed, pressing her free hand to her chest.

He didn't reply. Just moved over to the porch railing and leaned against it, crossing his arms over his broad chest.

"I—I was just going to drop this off," she went on. "It's . . . for you. An apology."

Again he said nothing. By now her eyes had adjusted, and she could see him in the half-light watching her, his expression completely blank. She held out the letter, but he made no move to take it.

Now she wasn't sure what to do. Should she just leave? She had to at least try to explain.

Gabby cleared her throat and stared down at her ragged sneakers. "I'm sorry about what I said," she began. "I was out of line. I assumed . . . well . . . I assumed a lot of stuff, without knowing the facts. And I guess I was sort of . . . mean."

Still no reply. No movement at all.

She lifted her gaze to him. He was so like a marble statue—cold, still, perfectly formed. And just as imposing as the bronze cast of St. Joseph in her grandmother's church. She felt small and ashamed. She ached for forgiveness.

"I'm not a bad person. Really," she said in a whisper. "I

just . . . I don't know. I just say stuff—not only today, but all the time. I lose my temper too easily. I'm not sure why."

Okay, now she sounded stupid. And she felt utterly foolish babbling on in front of him. Obviously Prentiss was never going to forgive her, and she really shouldn't be surprised. She'd just wanted to make things right. For her family's sake. And maybe for the sake of Sonny's memory, too.

"Anyway . . . here." Gabby set the envelope down on the chair he'd been sitting in and turned to go. But before she could walk down the steps, he put his arm up against the opposite post, blocking her escape.

Gabby glanced at him, confused. Was he going to yell at her? If so, she would stand there and take it. She deserved it. Her family shouldn't have to lose the house because of her bitchiness.

Only he didn't yell. Instead, Prentiss just stood there, gazing down at her—or *into* her. His eyes were intense, and there was something behind his stare. Something that held her in place like a tractor beam. Suddenly he swooped forward and pressed his mouth against hers.

A thousand thoughts swarmed through Gabby's mind. She wondered what was going on. . . . She wondered why she wasn't ducking and running away. . . . And she marveled at the softness of his lips, the feel of his hand on the small of her back, and the giddy aroma of woodsy deodorant mixed with spearmint gum.

Then all at once, her brain gave in—just overloaded and shut down. It was liberating. Hundreds of nagging worries seemed to rise out of her and dissipate in the evening air.

No more gridlock of thoughts. No more time and place, or her and him. There was only softness and warmth and a rushing current of . . . something. Something familiar. Something she hadn't felt in years . . .

After an immeasurable amount of time, the kiss ended—not abruptly, more like the gradual, gliding stop of an amusement park ride—and she was left wobbly, her heart palpitating.

Prentiss pulled away and stepped back into the shadows. Meanwhile, Gabby turned in a slow half circle, blinking hard and trying to get her bearings. Everything had gone murky again. She could only see a dim, Prentiss-shaped outline and the glow of the new energy-efficient porch lamp bulb from across the yard. The whole front of the rental house seemed to be in soft focus.

It was just like it had been four and a half years before on Make-Out Ridge. She didn't say goodbye. She left no glass slipper. She simply stumbled down the front steps and, like a woozy moth, followed the light toward home.

"No, the critical value is right, but that's not the answer," Mule said. "It's not enough to just work out the problem, you also need to pinpoint the item they're asking for."

"Ohh!" Daphne exclaimed. It all made sense now; it just clicked into place, like a new app for her brain. Amazing.

It was so good of Mule to help her. She'd never thought doing schoolwork could be fun, but it actually had been. And Mule didn't even seem to mind her messy hair and peppermint pajamas.

Daphne had never felt so relaxed around a guy before. She didn't worry about how she looked or acted. She just . . . *was*. It was easier than she'd thought it would be—just like geometry.

Right at that moment the door opened and Gabby strolled into the house.

"Hey, there you are," Mule said, leaning back in his chair.

She looked startled, as if she were surprised to find them there. "Here I am," she said.

"Where have you been?" Daphne asked.

"Around," Gabby replied. She stretched out along the couch and folded her arms behind her head.

Mule and Daphne exchanged puzzled stares. This didn't seem to be Gabby. This person moved too slowly and spoke too quietly. Even her face looked weird. It was looser and pinker.

Daphne got up from the table and walked to the couch for a closer look. "Hey, Gab . . . I'm sorry about before," she said. For hours she'd been stewing about it in the back of her mind. She really had been unfair to Gabby. Things had been hard on her, too, these past few days—especially with Mom gone.

Gabby seemed confused. "Huh?"

Daphne frowned. "The fight," she reminded her. "About Dad."

"Right." Gabby nodded slowly. "No big deal."

No big deal? Okay. Something was definitely up. In fifteen years she'd never known Gabby to voluntarily back down from an argument.

She looked at Mule again. He was hanging over the back

of his chair, scowling hard in Gabby's direction. He also seemed thrown by her behavior. Or even downright alarmed.

Daphne decided to give them some alone time. If anyone could get to the bottom of this, Mule could.

"Oh, man. This studying has really worn me out," Daphne said, stretching her arms. "I think I'll go on to my room now." She headed to the table for her books, giving Mule a tap on the shoulder. "Thanks for everything."

"No problem," Mule said. "You did great."

"Because of you. You're so good at this."

"Hey," he said, gently grabbing her elbow as she walked past. "You're good at a lot of stuff, too. Don't forget."

For some reason, Daphne felt a lump in her throat. "Thanks," she whispered, and continued on to her room.

"So where'd you go?" Mule asked.

"Oh, just . . . out," Gabby replied. She didn't want to talk to him. In fact, it felt funny just moving around. Her limbs felt floppy and everything looked fuzzy around the edges, as if the entire world were wearing an angora sweater.

It was hard to concentrate on the here and now when most of her gray matter was busy pondering what had just happened on the Applewhites' dark porch.

"What is up with you?" Mule asked.

Gabby tried to tear her mind from her thoughts and focus on him. Even he seemed outlined in wool. "What do you mean?"

"You're acting kind of strange."

"I am?"

"Yeah. You're all distracted. And you keep touching your mouth."

"I do?" But even as she asked this she realized that the tips of the first two fingers of her right hand were perched on her lower lip. It felt numb and tingly, like the time it snowed and her face had half frozen—only this time it was warm to the touch.

She'd only been kissed three times before this. The first time was in fourth grade when she'd kissed Sammy Farnsworth on a dare. It had been the quickest, wettest smooch in history, made worse by the stink of pepper sausage on his breath. Then, during the sixth-grade Fall Ball, she'd accepted Lane Brinkley's offer of a slow dance. Basically they'd just clutched each other and swayed in a rhythmic circle until she was in a dizzy stupor, but during the song's final, schmaltzy crescendo, he'd stopped and leaned in for a kiss. Unfortunately, he didn't seem to have the basic principles down, and he'd sucked her lips between his, making a loud smacking sound when he finally let go. Afterward, he'd ducked into the crowd and disappeared, leaving Gabby with a dark pink ring around her mouth for the next two hours. They avoided each other's glances in the hall for the next month. Soon after, his family moved to the Dallas area. And, of course, the last time she'd shared a kiss had been with Sonny during their secret encounter in the woods. That, too, had ended badly.

Those three sad anecdotes made up her entire romantic history—if one didn't count Mule's attentions, which she didn't. And now this.

But what, exactly, was *this*? What did it mean? She hadn't

been sure with Sonny and she wasn't sure about now. Typically kissing meant you shared feelings with someone. Her feelings for Prentiss had been strong and plentiful—mainly hate, anger, frustration, annoyance, and, more recently, remorse. Not anything romantic.

And yet . . . she hadn't pulled away from him. It hadn't seemed weird. Surprising, yes, but not weird. It was only now, as she pondered the whole scene, that she thought it odd.

Gabby rolled onto her side and propped her head in her hand. What did other girls do in this situation—normal girls with normal love lives? From what she understood of the world, they talked things out with their friends. Of which she only had one.

She glanced over at Mule, who was now sitting on the chair opposite the couch, studying her with his most analytical, heavy-browed, scientific stare. Could she talk to him about it? He was her pal, after all. And he was smart and logical and able to find answers to the most impossible-looking problems—in math and physics, anyway.

"What is going on with you?" he asked again. "You really seem out of it."

He was concerned about her, too. That was a friend thing. Maybe she should just come out with it and see how he viewed the whole situation. Maybe he would see something she didn't.

"I'm just weirded out over something that happened," she said, sitting up and facing him.

"What?"

"I went over to the Applewhites' to"—she paused—"to

drop something off, and I ran into Prentiss. While I was talking to him he just . . . kissed me."

Mule seemed to shrink about a centimeter. "Oh, really? Just like that?"

"I certainly wasn't asking for it."

"So . . . what did you do?"

Gabby absently pressed her fingers to her mouth. They still throbbed slightly, as if the lips themselves were also replaying the kiss. "I just left," she said, lowering her hand. "I guess I was in shock. Maybe I still am."

"Right."

By now the jealousy was evident in Mule's sad, droopy eyes. Oh, god. It had been a mistake to tell him. She hadn't been thinking straight. Things between them were icky enough already, and here she was adding more excrement to the mix.

"Look. He was probably just drunk or high or something," Gabby said. "It was stupid of me to wander over there in the dark. He's just a clueless ape who misreads social cues."

Mule nodded. And yet he still wouldn't stop staring at Gabby as if she were some cafeteria bully who'd stolen his Twinkie.

"It was nothing. Really," she went on. "The guy was just messing with my mind."

It suddenly dawned on her that this could be the truth. Kissing her could have been some sort of mind game— revenge for her yelling at him all the time and accusing him of things he didn't do. A way to shut her up, throw her for a loop, and turn her into the distracted, babbling idiot she was being this very minute.

The tingles stopped and her hazy vision corrected itself. Now she just felt embarrassed, and more than a little pissed off. Mainly at herself for being so overwhelmed by it all. Sure, she'd treated him unfairly. Prentiss might not be a cold-blooded killer, but that didn't mean he was a great guy. There were plenty of other blotches on his record.

"Anyway, enough about me," she said, eager to change the subject. "Let's do something. Want to watch TV?"

Mule shook his head. "I've gotta go." He stood and started shoving his things into his backpack.

Gabby felt disappointed. Mule's leaving had an unsettling déjà vu quality to it after both her dad's and Prentiss's angry departures earlier that day. "Are you mad at me?" she asked.

He frowned out the window, as if he were giving Apple-white Manor a dirty look. "No," he said, turning toward her with a blank expression. "I just need to check on Dad."

She stared at him, trying to gauge his mood. But it was as though she couldn't read him anymore. Had she forgotten how? Had Mule suddenly been converted into a jumble of wingdings?

No. It was more like . . . static. As if there were some nebulous interference between them, preventing clear speech. "Um . . . okay," she said. "Guess I'll see you later."

"Later." Mule slipped his pack over his shoulder and headed outside.

Gabby locked the door and slumped against it. The day had been so full of highs and lows and whirly maneuvers that she felt woozy and jet-lagged. She closed her eyes and put her hand to her mouth. For a second, she was back on the shadowy porch, being kissed by Prentiss. Feeling the crush of his arms and the soft pressure of his lips. She hadn't felt that way since . . .

No. She opened her eyes and shook her head, dislodging the memory. What was wrong with her? Prentiss was not Sonny. Sonny was gone. Besides, she wasn't a stupid thirteen-year-old. She was older and wiser now. She knew better. Even though she could sort of understand how addictive it was, and how someone like Daffy could get hooked on such emotions, she also knew it would be a mistake. Those hormonal surges never lasted, and people only ended up getting hurt down the road. Like poor Daffy. And Mom.

She pressed her forehead against the window, wishing Mule would come back inside so they could do something like study or watch bad TV—something that would make her feel normal. But his car was already rolling down the driveway.

Gabby waited until she saw the lights of the Range Rover fade into the distance. Then she closed the drapes and turned off the nearby lamp. Because those were the kinds of things she did.

Because she was responsible. And safe.

CHAPTER EIGHTEEN
Cease and De(sis)t

"You're going!"

"No I'm not!"

"You are!"

"No!"

"Get in the damn car!"

Daphne threw down her hairbrush. "No! You can't make me!" She knew she sounded like she was four, and the truth was, it did feel as if she'd time-traveled back to the days of pigtails and Hello Kitty. She felt ganged up on and defenseless, too small to be heard. All she could do was scream and stomp.

"You've missed way too much school already," Gabby continued. "If you stay home another day, they'll probably send the truant officer over. Then we'll have all kinds of explaining to do, and Mom will have to fly home to prevent us from being sent to juvenile hall. Do you want that?"

Daphne pouted as furiously as possible. No, of course she didn't want that. But she also didn't want to walk back into Barton High with all its surly teachers and traitorous friends.

"You don't understand," she said. "Those people ruined my life."

"So what?" Gabby said.

"God! You're such a cold bitch sometimes."

"Yep. That's me. Now quit whining and let's go."

"You don't even care, do you? Everyone's going to be picking on me!"

"You have to face them sometime. Just deal with it!"

Daphne stared at her sister's crimped features. Gabby was so unfeeling, so by-the-book. She didn't care about anything or anyone, just the rules. "I won't *just deal with it*. I don't have to!"

The sound of crunching gravel distracted them. For some reason, Mule's Range Rover was rolling down the drive. As he reached them, he lowered the driver's-side window.

"I think I left my calculator here the other day," he said. "Mind if I run in and look?"

"No," Gabby said, flicking her hand toward the door.

Leaving the truck running, Mule jumped out and bounded into the house. As soon as he disappeared from view, Gabby rounded on Daphne again.

"Get in the car! I swear, I will call Mom if you don't. I'll call Dad. I'll call the freaking truant officer myself!"

"But you don't get it!" Daphne said, panic making her voice high and whimpery. "I can't. I can't take any more. I don't want to see those people. I don't want to see . . . *him*."

"Damn it, Daphne!" Gabby looked at her watch. "I don't

have time for this. I'm supposed to be in the counselor's office in fifteen minutes. Ms. Kephart needs my scholarship application today. I've got to go *right now!*"

"Go ahead. I'll take her." Mule emerged from the house, holding his futuristic-looking calculator in his right hand.

Gabby shook her head. "She's my problem. You go on. Save yourself."

Daphne felt a little stabby at being referred to as a problem.

"Really, it's no big deal," he said. "I don't have to be there for a while."

Gabby looked at Mule, then at her sister. Her lower lip disappeared beneath her front teeth. "Fine," she said finally. "But if she's not there, she's in the biggest trouble of her whole life." She hesitated another few seconds before huffing away to the car. Mule and Daphne watched silently as she drove away.

"She's right, you know. Staying home isn't going to help," Mule said. "You really do have to go to school now."

"But I don't think I can take it. Not the school part. The . . . being there."

"Don't worry about those jerks. They're not worth stressing yourself out over."

Daphne let out a sigh and slumped against a porch post. "You say that like it's so easy. You guys don't know what it's like."

"Maybe not exactly, but I've been their target before. They've shoved me in the halls and called me all kinds of bad things. They even gave me my nickname. Because of them

I've had to go through life being called a sterile hybrid farm animal."

Daphne tried not to laugh, but she couldn't stop her mouth from curving upward.

"Yeah, okay. It's kind of funny—I know. But seriously, Daff. Those people don't matter." He walked over and placed his big hand on her shoulder. "You're better than all of them."

"You're just saying that."

"I'm not. You're strong. You were willing to take a risk with someone. It didn't work out, but so what? You were brave enough to go for it. Lots of us . . . lots of people never do that. You should be proud."

Daphne met his gaze. He really did seem to believe what he was saying. Once again, he was calling her bold and brave. But was she?

Mule pushed a lock of hair out of her face. "Come on. Go back there and hold your head high. They can't hurt you if you don't let them."

This made sense. She didn't exactly feel strong, but maybe she could act it. Maybe she could pretend to be Gabby and raise invisible ice sheets around herself to stay safe from their teasing.

"Okay," she said in a shaky voice.

"Atta girl," he said. He started to steer her toward the Range Rover, but Daphne stayed put, gripping the post tightly.

"I'll go. And it'll be okay. Because . . . I'll just avoid them," she said, to herself more than to Mule. "I'll ignore what they say and just stay by myself. That's what I should do . . . right?" she asked him. "No one can hurt me if I'm alone."

Mule smiled at her. "You won't be alone," he said, grabbing her hand. "I'll be there if you need me."

The car was doing that weird racing thing again. Gabby popped it into neutral at the stoplight, to prevent it from bucking up and down like a two-dollar mechanical bull ride. She just needed to get to Mule's house. Maybe before they started studying he could check to see what was wrong. Maybe for some free pizza and Dr Pepper.

Good old Mule. She'd buy him a whole pizzeria if she could, just to make up for hurting his feelings Saturday night when she'd stupidly told him about Prentiss's kiss—and for all his help that morning. She had no idea how he'd talked Daphne into going to school, but she was so glad he had.

She'd nearly done a happy dance when she saw her sister in the hallway before first period. Daphne seemed fine, too. Her eyes were rather wide and cautious-looking, but she'd smiled. She'd even given Gabby the smallest of waves.

Thankfully, the gossip mill had mostly turned its focus off of Daphne, which they should have expected. Lynette Harkrider had been caught messing around with the new assistant football coach, and the whole school was buzzing about it as if it were their very own daytime TV drama. Daphne's antics were boring in comparison, barely worth a mild nudge and whisper.

So Daphne was sane again—or at least not as batty as she had been these past several days. Now it was Gabby who was acting loopy.

All day at school she'd been distracted and weird. Her

disobedient brain kept reliving her kiss with Prentiss, complete with cricket sounds, that strange shivery warmth, and a vague taste of spearmint. Because of these invasive daydreams, her notes were spotty and her planner was incomplete. She'd even stopped in the middle of the annex hallway at one point, unsure whether she was headed to AP English or physics.

It was scary. The only other time she'd lost control of her own thoughts was in the aftermath of Sonny's death. But how could this cause the same reaction? Had kissing Prentiss triggered the muscle memory of her zombielike stupor four years ago? Or was it more like a pathogen? Maybe Prentiss passed along some sort of pernicious germ that was toying with her body temperature and causing sense-surround hallucinations.

She didn't like feeling so powerless. The more she made herself examine the situation logically, the more she was convinced that what had happened on the porch was in no way significant. So what if Prentiss wasn't as bad as she'd originally thought; that didn't mean he was good . . . right? Besides, she was way too smart to fall for a handsome face. And they had nothing in common—absolutely zilch. She knew all this. So why wouldn't her mind just accept it and move on?

"Stop being so stupid," Gabby told herself. "Just get a grip."

Great, now she was talking to herself. She really was sick. But it wasn't as if there were a surefire cure. She couldn't exactly kick him out of her mind.

Suddenly she had an idea.

The light changed. Gabby shifted back into drive and hit the gas before the Jetta could decide that it would rather sputter and die. At the next break in the median, she made a quick U-turn, ignoring the groaning sounds in the steering wheel, and headed in the opposite direction, toward Elmhurst. Soon she was pulling down the Applewhites' long crushed-granite driveway.

Prentiss was outside watering the rosebushes. He lifted his left hand in greeting as she drove past, then waited patiently for her to park the car and join him. For some reason, this irked her—even though she really was coming to see him. It was as if he was expecting her. As if he assumed everything was hunky-dory between them, which it so wasn't. In fact, things couldn't be weirder.

"Hi," he said as she strode toward him.

"Hi," she said back. Her voice came out all breathy and in the high soprano range; it seemed to belong to someone else entirely. This was going to be harder than she'd thought.

Gabby studied his face. His eyes were shielded by sunglasses, which made him tougher to decipher. His smile appeared warm, but was it genuine? He could be glad to see her. Or he could be congratulating himself on his little mind game of the night before.

"Have you had a nice day?" he asked, setting down the hose. Water bubbled up in the grass and began spreading out along the driveway. This seriously bugged her.

Prentiss walked over and stood beside her. Too close. She could now catch whiffs of his sweaty scent—which, surprisingly, wasn't all that awful. His perfect teeth seemed extra-gleamy in the sunshine. Maybe too dazzling, too reminiscent of a game show host. Yep, he was probably mocking her.

"I came to tell you something," she said. Again she winced at her airy, Marilyn Monroe–like tone. Clearing her throat, she tried again. "I think it would be better if . . . if you stay away from me. From us."

She paused, but he said nothing. She could see her own big-eyed, fearful expression reflected in the sunglasses. It only made her more irritated.

"Look, I know I haven't been the best . . . um . . . tenant you've ever had," she added. "I'm sorry for that. I've already apologized in the letter, and I hope you've forgiven me. I also hope you'll let us stay here. I just think we should . . . stay out of each other's way. Keep things professional."

Again she stopped for breath—which she suddenly seemed to need a lot of. Still Prentiss didn't move. He hadn't even flinched. His lips were set in a squiggled line that could convey dismay or amusement, she couldn't tell.

Gabby pulled her eyes away. Staring at his mouth reminded her of the kiss.

"Okay then. I just thought you should know," she said, feeling as though her speech needed a closing statement.

When he still didn't say anything, she spun around and headed toward the Jetta, careful to step over the small rivulet of water that was now coursing down the driveway.

"Wait," he said.

Like a brainless automaton, she stopped and turned back.

"You still don't trust me, do you?" he asked. He stepped forward, closing the gap between them so that they were back to a body heat–sensing distance.

Gabby stared down at her navy blue Chuck Taylors. What could she say? He was right; she didn't trust him. But she didn't want to make things worse by admitting it.

Besides, it was more than that. She also didn't trust

herself. Her own feelings went completely haywire when it came to Prentiss. She liked him, yet she didn't like him. She felt drawn to him—but she wasn't sure if she was attracted to him or to some half-buried memory of Sonny. She thought he liked her, maybe even hoped that he did, but she also couldn't buy it. Someone like him would never fall for her. The kiss had just been an anomaly—either a takedown ploy on his part or a glitch in his behavior brought on by stress and rage. The same way mugging victims sometimes laugh as they stare down the barrel of a loaded gun.

And even on the off chance that he did like her and she liked him, that could very well be the worst possible situation. Because such feelings never lasted. They just hung around long enough to create chaos.

The water was now pooling in a small hole along the side of the driveway, taking on a sickly, chalky color from the crushed gravel.

"You can't stop blaming me for the crash," he said, answering his own question since she'd gone mute. He shook his head. "I don't get it. Are you always so hard on people? I mean, it's not like you knew Sonny. Did you?"

She hadn't meant to react. She just . . . did. Her body, for some reason, flinched in response. Her head jerked up and her torso shuddered. Gabby wrapped her arms around herself to stop the sudden flow of emotion. But just like the water racing down the lane, it kept on surging. The ache of loss. The confusion. The anger and unanswered questions.

"*Did* you?" Prentiss repeated. His softened tone revealed he'd noticed her spontaneous reflex.

Gabby's hands flew to the sides of her head. She didn't want these thoughts. She didn't want to be here, with him, talking about this. "No," she said to herself and the universe, but also to Prentiss. Because it was true. She hadn't known Sonny—not really. She had no right to mourn him. No right to miss him or punish anyone for his death. "No," she said again.

She had to get out of there. At some point she'd lost control of the conversation. It was more proof that she couldn't rely on her own wits when it came to Prentiss.

"Just remember what I said earlier," she said, backing toward her car, not caring if her shoes sank into the murky water. "We should try to avoid each other. It's just better that way. Simpler."

Her hand hit the Jetta, sweeping over the familiar hail dents on the trunk. She quickly spun around and climbed inside, trying to ignore Prentiss's sunglassed stare.

Thank god the car restarted. It shuddered and coughed and finally snarled to life. Gabby backed out of the space, careful not to mow down Prentiss. Meanwhile, he kept on watching her through his shades, thumbs hooked in his front pockets, as if he were posing for some gardening calendar. As if he had nothing else to do but marvel at her stupidity. It annoyed her to no end.

Gabby rolled down the window. "And one more thing," she yelled as she drove past. "Quit wasting water!"

Daphne skipped down the road, her ponytail swinging, sneakers pounding out an iambic rhythm on the sidewalk. All her sweat from cheerleading practice cooled in the breeze.

It hadn't been a great day. In fact, parts of it had really sucked. Tracy and Sheri had yakked about her all through fourth period. Todd Carothers had pointed at her in the annex corridor and laughed. And while the other cheerleaders hadn't wasted too much time slamming her during workouts, they also hadn't included her in their gossip sessions about Lynette—who'd been absent, unsurprisingly.

Daphne had only seen Luke once, in the hall after science class, but thankfully he hadn't spotted her . . . or at least he acted as if he hadn't. Her knees had almost buckled at the sight of him, and slightly lesser amounts of the familiar pain and confusion had shot though her like an earthquake aftershock. But somehow she had remained upright. She wasn't sure if this newfound strength had been implanted inside her—by Gabby or Mule or a week of fitful hibernation—or if the whole, awful ordeal had uncovered forgotten reserves deep within her.

Whatever. It didn't matter. She was proud of herself for making it through the day without running away, throwing up, or weeping uncontrollably. And for approaching her teachers to see about make-up work. All in all, she felt triumphant, and she wanted to celebrate her victory in some way. How, she wasn't sure. But she knew who with.

Mule's house was looming into view. A blue, turn-of-the-century bungalow on a cul-de-sac near downtown, it had been a great source of pride when his dad had been healthy. Mr. Randolph had always been out on the roof replacing shingles or trimming the hedges that bordered the yard. Now the place looked kind of neglected and sad. The yard was mowed, but not carefully edged, as it always used to be. A piece of plywood had been nailed up over a missing windowpane, and the paint job had been streaked by grimy rainwater seeping from the overstuffed gutters. Gabby said that Mule always did what he could, but he was too swamped with watching his dad and trying to make the grades for a scholarship.

A familiar figure was sitting on the porch swing, flipping through a textbook the size of a small suitcase.

"Mule!" she shouted, and broke into a run.

Mule got to his feet and squinted through the sunshine toward her.

"Daphne? What's wrong?"

"Nothing's wrong," she said, coming to a halt on the top step. "Why?"

"Just . . . you never come here. I thought . . ." He shook his head. "Never mind. What's up? How'd it go today?"

"It went great! That's why I'm here. I wanted to thank you for your help."

"Thank me? I didn't do anything."

"You did! If it wasn't for you, I would have spent the whole day at home crying into a bowl of ice cream. You were so awesome."

Mule made a face and then smiled down at his shoes. Bands of red spread over his neck and across his nose and cheeks, making him look like a curly-haired peppermint stick.

"I faced down those creeps, just like you told me to," she said. "I can't believe I got through it."

"Of course you did. I knew you could," he said.

"And guess what else? Ms. Manbeck gave one of her surprise quizzes today . . . and I passed with an eighty-three!" She pressed her hands together and hopped up and down on the toes of her tennis shoes.

"Really?" A wide, open-mouthed smile lifted his features. "That's so great!"

Daphne threw her arms around him in a tight hug. "Thank you! Thank you so much!"

She hadn't meant to hug him; it had just happened. Even Mule seemed surprised. He stiffened at first and then relaxed into it, wrapping his long arms around her back. It was nice, actually. His left pectoral made the perfect pillow, and she could feel him resting his chin on her head. Good old Mule.

Eventually they pulled apart. He grinned awkwardly and tamed the strands of hair his whiskers had pulled loose from her ponytail.

"I'm happy for you," he said, nodding. "Glad to hear things are set back to right."

Daphne laughed. "Yeah, now all I need is for Luke to move to Siberia and for Shelly's Boutique to take back that stupid prom dress I'll never use. Then everything will be perfect."

"I could take you to prom."

Daphne's eyes popped wide. She cocked her head, unsure whether she had actually heard right. "What?" she asked.

"I mean . . . if you don't want to waste the dress and all . . . I could take you."

"You'd do that?"

"Sure, why not? It'd help show everyone that you aren't

giving in. Besides, it'd be fun. I mean"—he bit his lip, looking unsure—"don't you think so?"

Trickles of warmth were shooting all over her. It was so sweet! Once again Mule was coming to her rescue. She'd get to dance under the streamers and be seen in her princess gown. Why couldn't more guys be like him? Why couldn't Luke?

The sound of a car door slamming startled them. Daphne glanced up to see her sister coming up the sidewalk toward them.

"What are you doing here?" Gabby asked her. "I thought you were at cheer practice."

"It's over," she replied. "I came by to say thanks and . . . guess what?" Her feet started bouncing all over again. "I get to go to prom after all! Mule's going to take me!"

Gabby's mouth fell open and her brow lost its trademark furrow. She looked so stunned, Daphne almost started giggling.

"Can you believe it?" Daphne said.

"Ah . . . no." Gabby glanced over at Mule, who gave her a thin smile. "I can't."

"What a wild day," Daphne went on. "I thought it would be the worst one ever, and it's ended up being one of the best." She slung her right arm around Mule in a sideways hug.

"So . . . I guess this means you say yes?" Mule asked.

Daphne laughed. "Yes. The answer is yes."

"You know what?" Gabby lightly thumped the side of her head. "I totally forgot my calc stuff. What an idiot. Could be at home. Or work. Maybe school . . ." She backed down the steps to the sidewalk. "I'll go look for it, but it'll probably take a while. Luckily homework isn't that bad today."

Mule peered at her strangely, as if studying her face for signs of rational thought. Could he tell she was lying? Probably. He knew her too well. Plus, her book bag was clearly sagging with the backbreaking weight of her calculus textbook. Meanwhile Daphne kept on grinning, her pretty, baby-deer eyes glistening with fresh daydream material. She hadn't looked this happy in days. And yet all Gabby wanted to do was shake her till she stopped smiling.

"So I'll just go," Gabby called out as she turned toward the car. "You guys carry on!"

For the second time in fifteen minutes she prayed to an almighty being for her car to start. Thankfully, her wish was granted. The Jetta roared to life immediately, its entire frame shuddering as if it, too, wanted to get away from that place as soon as possible.

She had to steer into the driveway in order to go the other direction. The polite thing to do would be to give one final wave, but she didn't. She couldn't bear to see Mule's baffled expression. Or Daphne bouncing on her toes as if the floor had suddenly become burning hot. Or the lack of physical space between the two of them.

As soon as she accelerated out of sight, she let herself think about what had just happened.

This was too weird. Daphne and . . . Mule? But he was Gabby's. Sure, they weren't a couple. It was totally platonic and chummy and even boring at times. But they were still exclusive. They'd never said so out loud, but it was understood. Other people weren't allowed. Especially siblings! And especially now.

She hadn't driven over there just to do homework. She'd also needed Mule—the faithfulness and simplicity of him. She'd wanted to tell him about confronting Prentiss, hoping to make Mule feel less threatened, hoping that a good vent session on Prentiss's water wasting would make things feel normal between them again. It even occurred to her on the drive over that maybe she and Mule actually *could* do something special for prom night—a yay!-we've-almost-made-it-through-high-school sort of thing. Only now . . .

Damn it, Daphne! Gabby was surprised to feel tears running down her cheeks. All the numbness and confusion were slowly hardening into anger. The more Gabby thought about it, the more unjust it seemed. Daphne always got everything. Looks, popularity, the freedom to screw up over and over again. Now she got Mule, too? The one guy on earth Gabby trusted? The only person who could help her feel sane again?

Gabby found herself puttering down Main Street, unsure where she should go. She didn't want to head home and risk seeing Prentiss, and she really didn't want to go back to Mule's. She'd give anything for Pinkwater to call her on her cell and beg her to work a shift at the theater, but that would only happen if she were having a particularly good day.

So instead, she just . . . drove. Past Quick's Pharmacy and the boutiques of downtown, their display windows all done up in a prom theme. Past Hawthorne's Barbecue and Duke's Burgers and Thunder Alley, the sites of so many awkward dates with Dad. Past Chandler Creek, which flowed southeast, toward Make-Out Ridge, the site of her dreamy afternoon with Sonny. Every place brimmed over with memories, most of them bad or sad. Every site seemed to be thumbing its nose at her and going "nyah nyah nyah." There was no safe zone, no sanctuary.

Stupid town! Thank god she had turned in her scholarship application that morning. Hopefully it would seal the deal on her escape. She couldn't wait to get the hell out of there, away from her family and her so-called best friend. Away from Prentiss and Dad Saturdays and Sonny's ghost.

There wasn't anything here for her in Barton. Not anymore. The whole town, it seemed, was done with her.

CHAPTER NINETEEN
Incon(sis)tent

Daphne frowned at the display case in Galvan's Floral and Gifts. Apparently she had a lot to learn about flowers. She'd thought picking out a boutonniere would be easy, but it wasn't. There were all different types of blooms, greeneries, ribbons, and colors to consider, as well as overall price.

At least she knew which ones she didn't want. Not the ugly tropical one that looked like it snared flying insects with its long, spotted petals. Not the puny single chrysanthemum that would probably disintegrate before the first dance. And not the superlarge, superexpensive one that dwarfed most of Mom's houseplants.

"Could I see number eight again?" she asked as sweetly as possible.

"Of course," said Nicholas, the clerk. By now his polite smile had fallen at the corners.

He pulled out the well-worn sample and a laminated photo. This one was nice and simple. It had very little greenery, no ribbon, and a large rosebud the color of a ripe strawberry—not exactly her dress's shade of pink, but close enough. Plus, it was in her price range.

"I think I'll take that one," she said.

Nicholas sighed through his nose, making his nostrils flare. "You *think* you will?"

"I will take it," Daphne said more decisively.

He rang up her order, moving at the pace of a NASCAR pit crew member, and soon she found herself stepping out into the afternoon sunshine.

Daphne paused beside the front window, feeling a tug of doubt. She was pretty sure Mule would like the simple rose boutonniere, but she really didn't know his likes and dislikes that well. Maybe she should just ask him? If nothing else, she knew he was easy to talk to.

Checking the time on her cell phone, she saw that it was earlier than she'd thought. She wished Gabby had come with her, but her sis had refused, saying she had too many weekend chores. Daphne had then offered to pick up some food while she was out running prom errands, but Gabby hadn't seemed all that grateful. Of course, she probably didn't believe Daphne would actually remember. Lately her older sis had been extra cranky and standoffish.

She'd show Gabby. Daphne shouldered her purse and headed toward the grocery store. Not only would she provide the meal, she'd cook it herself. That ought to prove she could be responsible.

The Minimax was surprisingly packed. Daphne grabbed a basket and headed for the instant foods section. She might be more dependable lately, but she hadn't magically learned to cook.

She scanned the shelves, looking for something easy yet nutritious enough to stand up to Gabby's standards.

"Pardon me," she said to someone standing in the middle of the aisle. Just as she started to veer around him, she paused and did a double take. It was Luke.

"Hi," he said.

Daphne didn't respond. She was caught off guard. For days she'd managed to avoid his gaze at school, and now here they were, face to face. A million conflicting thoughts and feelings jammed inside her, rendering her motionless. She suddenly understood why deer don't run out of the path of an approaching semi.

"You shopping?" he asked, then he shook his head and chuckled somewhat lamely. "Course you are. That was a stupid question." He seemed nervous. That was weird.

By now her emotional logjam was sorting itself out. Mainly the old familiar hurt had welled back up, like a puddle of water returning after a dry spell.

"I guess you're not speaking to me," he said. "I don't blame you. We were—I was—pretty awful, huh?"

Daphne focused on a nearby box of Rice-A-Roni. Luke's question seemed too obvious to answer. She wouldn't give him the pleasure.

"I just . . . *Damn!* I don't know how to put this. I don't even know how to act around you. . . ." He raked his hand through his hair and scowled down at the can of chili in his basket.

Daphne was amazed to see such misery in his face. She found herself wondering what he must be going through, what it must have been like for him. "Look," she said, gazing at him neutrally. "You don't have to be freaked out around me. I got carried away at the party and said some pretty heavy stuff. I didn't know that you . . ." She paused and took a breath. "Anyway, I promise I'm not a stalker or anything. I'm just getting dinner."

A smile stole across his face. "I know. I don't think that. I mean, yeah, I was kind of blown away by what you said, but I know you aren't weird." He swallowed hard and looked past her. "I'm sorry, Daphne. You were, like, the nicest person to me when I moved here, and then I treated you like a jerk."

Daphne's vision clouded. This was exactly what she'd wanted to hear from him. It almost felt unreal.

"I just . . . I was new and I wanted to be part of an in crowd. I never have been before. And here were guys like Walt and Todd wanting to hang with me. And here were girls like Lynette—" He broke off, eyeing her guiltily. "Anyway . . . I was stupid. I did stuff I don't normally do."

"Stuff like what?" she asked. She couldn't help it. She had to know. For over a week she'd been tormenting herself, wondering how she could have been so wrong about him.

"Like messing around with Lynette," Luke said to his shoes. "I don't even like her. I mean, she's cute and all, but she just came on to me and I didn't know what to do. It was weird, but flattering. And I felt like it would be . . . I don't know . . . *impolite* to turn her down."

Something gripped Daphne on the inside, in the space between her heart and stomach. She instinctively raised the plastic shopping basket to her chest and cradled it in her arms.

"And you weren't coming, or so I thought. And I wasn't even sure if we were friends or . . . something more." He closed his mouth and sighed heavily through his nose.

"But then I did show up," she said. "And you went with me. Upstairs. After you'd already—"

"I know," he said quickly, to cut her off. Even though she wasn't going to say it aloud anyway. "I know," he said again, more softly. "Like I said, I was stupid. I was just doing what I thought I was supposed to do. I was trying to act like them."

"What do you mean 'them'? You *are* them. You stood there with them, making fun of me!" Daphne's voice cracked, just slightly, but she held on to her anger and managed to keep herself steady. No matter what, she was not going to cry.

Luke's shoulders hunched guiltily. "I know. I just . . . chickened out. I was all mixed up because of what you said, and then there they were making fun of you. If I'd stood up to them they would have totally written me off. . . ." He paused as a lady came down the aisle, picked up a can of French-fried onions, and made her way around the corner. "Anyway, I'm sorry. Really. I'm all mixed up. It's like I want to be part of that crowd and I don't want to. It can be really fun, but sometimes . . . sometimes I don't feel like I'm really one of them. Like I'm just too different."

Daphne peered at him, measuring his expression and replaying his last few sentences in her mind. How strange that he should say all that—things she herself had felt for years. It was as if all this time she'd been looking at him from the bottom of a swimming pool, beholding him through the distorting effects of water. Only now she'd suddenly resurfaced. And she realized he wasn't a perfect soul mate sent down from heaven to complete her. Nor was he an evil poser playboy. He was a real person, just like her. And maybe just as lost on the inside.

"You still hang out with them, though, right?" she asked. But of course he did. After all, that was what she'd done all through school—until recently. It was the safer choice. Once you'd been pulled into the orbit of the power group, it took too much effort to break out of it.

Luke nodded. "Yeah, I guess. But I don't feel great about it. It's not like any of them are my real friends. Or girlfriends."

Again Daphne felt a clawing sensation in her midsection. What did he mean by that? Surely he'd realized that Lynette was done with him immediately after the party was over—if not sooner.

"Are you taking anyone to prom?" she asked. She couldn't help herself. She was just too curious.

Luke's features slackened. "You know," he said, "that's a great idea. We should go together. That would show the gang that we're better than them."

"Huh?" It took Daphne a moment to realize he'd misunderstood her. He'd assumed she was *asking* him to prom.

But of course he would. After all, she'd already professed her undying love to him.

"That would totally show those guys!" he went on, his eyes shining brighter than the nearby Gatorade sign. "If we show up arm in arm, all smiles, it would be like saying we don't care what they say about us. Like all the stuff at the party never even happened."

Never happened . . .

Daphne liked the sound of that. Maybe he was right. Maybe it could be a total do-over—a way to get her old care-free life back, a way to purge all the leftover hurt and embarrassment. She already had plans with Mule, but he would understand. In fact, he'd probably be relieved. The only reason he'd asked her was because he felt sorry for her.

Daphne gazed up at Luke's smiling face. Her heart seemed to be teetering precariously, like a tipped vase. She had loved him so much, but then he'd hurt her so damn much. Now he wanted to get together. He'd even said he was sorry! Everything was working itself out, like a happy ending.

She was getting her fairy tale after all.

The phone rang and Gabby woke with a start, gasping and sweating.

She was lying on her mom's bed, her open math book roofed heavily across her chest. Daylight streamed through the windows. She couldn't remember when she'd gone from studying to sleeping, but she did remember the dream she had. In it, she had somehow shrunk to two or three inches tall. She was standing on the dining room table, waving her arms to get Mule's attention, but he was too busy with Daphne to notice. The last thing she remembered was Mule carelessly tossing his calculus text onto the tabletop—the heavy blue-black cover crashing down on her head. . . .

Again the phone rang. Gabby sat up and rubbed her eyes, trying to remove all traces of the nightmare. Then she grabbed the extension off the nightstand. "Hello?" she said, yawning slightly.

"Gabby, honey? Is that you?"

"Hi, Mom." Just hearing her mother's voice made Gabby's eyes water. Or maybe it was a residual effect of the dream. Whatever the reason, she suddenly wanted to be caught up in one of her mom's tight hugs.

"How are things going?"

"Okay."

"Did you hand in the scholarship application?"

"Yes. First thing Monday."

"Good! And how's Daphne?"

Gabby paused. "She's fine."

"You say that like you aren't so sure. Is something wrong?" she asked, sounding worried. "The last couple of times I talked to her she sounded very distracted and sleepy. And now you do. Are you guys staying up really late?"

"No. It's just . . . you know. She drives me crazy sometimes. Lately we've been kind of avoiding each other. But we're dealing."

"Can I talk to her?"

"She's out. She's busy running errands for prom."

"Oh, that." Her mom chuckled. "Please make sure she focuses on other things, too, will you? Like school and chores?"

"I'll try."

"So are you going?"

"Where to?"

"Prom!"

"No way," Gabby said, laughing sharply. "What a waste of

time and money. Besides, who would I go with? All the guys around here are lying lunkheads."

"Don't say that. What about Mule?"

Gabby swallowed. "Mule especially."

"Did something happen between you two?"

Again a watery haze covered Gabby's eyes. "I don't want to talk about it."

"Sweetheart . . ."

The soft lilt in her mother's voice increased the tears to a steady trickle. Mom hadn't used that gentle inflection with her in years. Part of Gabby wished her mom could be right there, holding her and rocking her and smoothing her hair with her hands, the way she used to. But another part of her was angry—angry at her mom for bringing up the latest in a whole string of subjects she couldn't bear to think about, and angry at herself for transforming into a weepy toddler who wanted her mommy.

"You were right all along," Gabby managed to say as her throat constricted with emotion. "Guys suck! They all end up betraying you in some way."

For a long moment, Gabby couldn't hear anything, and she wondered if she'd somehow lost the phone connection. Then her mother let out a long breath that ended in a small moan. "Oh, dear, I've really been unfair, haven't I?" she said. "I should never have said those things."

"What are you talking about? You've told me the truth. You warned me about men, and you were right."

"No. I wasn't," her mom said. "I was angry and scared. I needed a buddy and I used you. But that was a mistake."

"What do you mean?" Gabby rose to her feet, her calculus textbook crashing to the floor with a huge thud. "It sounds like you're saying it was wrong to be my friend."

"It was." Her mom's voice broke. "Oh, sweetheart, I hate discussing this over the phone, but I'm worried about you. I'm worried that I've made you bitter. I messed up."

"No! *You* didn't do anything wrong. It was Dad. He's the one who screwed things up. And he still is! I hate to tell you this, but he's got a girlfriend, Mom. They're living together."

"Yes, I know. They're pretty serious."

"You . . . knew?" Gabby was now pacing the room, clutching the top of her head with her free hand. "How? How did you know?"

"He told me. Why do you think I've been such a mess? Why do you think the ice cream kept disappearing in the middle of the night? But it's okay now. I'm dealing with it. And I feel so much better about myself now. Stronger. Men aren't the problem, Gabby. You have to forgive them. You have to forgive your dad."

"No! I *don't* have to! How can you say that after what he did to you?"

"Do you think that would have been fair, your dad sticking around when he only halfway loved me? When I only halfway loved him?"

"Frankly, yes!" Gabby yelled, pumping her free arm in the air. "Yes, he should have stayed here. With us."

"He deserves better. *I* deserve better. I don't want that for you, sweetheart. I don't want you to find someone who only halfway loves you."

"Who says I need to find anyone?"

"We all need people. We need friends, family . . . but one day I want you to have someone special, too."

Gabby dropped onto the edge of the bed. "What's going on with you?" she mumbled. "Why are you talking like Daphne?"

"I'm talking like Daphne?" She chuckled slightly. "Oh, I don't know. These past couple of weeks have made me understand some things better. It's like I've reintroduced myself to myself. Does that even make sense?"

"No," Gabby said.

Her mom laughed again, and Gabby refrained from slamming the phone against the floor until it burst into its component parts. "Look, I'll be back soon. We can talk about this more then. In the meantime . . . please don't be so hard on people—especially yourself. You can't dwell on the past, Gabriella. I realize that more than ever now. You have to look forward. Live your life."

Gabby didn't say anything.

"See you in a few days, okay?" her mom said.

A *few days*. She could hold on. She owed it to her mom. "Okay," Gabby mumbled, drying her cheeks with the back of her hand. "Bye."

"Bye, sweetie."

Gabby hung up the phone and flopped back against the mattress. Nothing made sense anymore. No one was acting the way they were supposed to.

Somehow her life had become the world's hardest calculus problem. It made her feel small and lost and very much alone, like the two-inch-high Gabby in the dream . . . just waiting to get mashed.

"Gabby! Gabby, guess what?" Daphne ran into the house and set her grocery bags on the dining room table. The place looked empty, but she knew her sister had to be around somewhere. The car was outside.

She looked at the closed door of her mom's bedroom, a big slab of oak with a fresh white paint job. It was so silent and immobile it seemed to be snubbing her. Of course it wasn't, but the sister behind it could be.

Daphne crossed the room and rapped on it a few times. "Gab? Can I come in? I have some good news."

She thought she heard a moan but she couldn't be sure. "Just wait," came Gabby's muffled voice. "I'm busy."

"Okay, okay." Fine. Let Crabby be crabby. She had to call Mule anyway. Daphne pulled out her cell phone and selected his number.

"Hey, you," he said, answering on the second ring. "Just in time. Listen to this." She heard him set down the phone, followed by a distant jangle of guitar chords. "It's the Beatles' 'Nowhere Man,'" he said when he got back on. "Or it will be, eventually."

"That's really great. So you'll never guess what happened to me today!" She knew she was changing the subject too fast, but she couldn't help it. She was too excited.

"What?"

"I ran into Luke at the store."

"Really? Are you okay?"

She laughed. "I'm fine. Great, in fact. He actually said he was sorry for what he did to me."

"That's . . . Wow."

"I know, right? And then—and this is even crazier—he asked me to prom!"

"You're kidding me."

"No! Well, it was a little more complicated than that, but he said he wanted to take me. Isn't that wild?" Daphne twirled past the coffee table, letting her long hair fan out. "It's like . . . magic or something. Now we can go back to where we were before this whole mess. It'll almost be like nothing ever happened!"

There came a pause. "Wait a minute . . . you didn't actually say yes, did you? Because that would be stupid."

"What?" Daphne stopped whirling. "Don't call me stupid."

"I'm sorry but, how can you trust that guy?"

"He knows what he did was wrong and I forgive him. Because I love him."

"You don't love him. You just want him to love *you*."

Daphne frowned down at the carpet, shaking her head over and over. She couldn't believe this was happening. Why was Mule treating her like this? "Look, it was really nice of you to offer to help me out. Really. But you don't need to worry about me anymore. Everything's better now."

"Is that what you think? That I just felt sorry for you?" Mule's voice was angry-sounding—not exactly yelling, but sharp. "And what about you? Did you just think of me as some sort of guidance counselor? A long-lost brother?"

Daphne wasn't sure what to say. Apparently she'd done something wrong, but she wasn't sure what.

This was so unfair. All she'd wanted to do was spread her

joy and thank Mule for being so nice. He should be happy for her. He should be proud of her for working things out, just like he'd been proud of her for going to school and doing well on the geometry quiz.

Forget it. Obviously Mule wasn't as supportive as she'd thought he was. He might be smart about math, but not about love. And she was not going to let him ruin this amazing thing that happened.

"I've got to go," she mumbled. "Bye."

She hung up the phone and tossed it onto the couch just as Gabby emerged from the bedroom.

"What was that all about?" she asked. "Who were you just talking to?"

"Mule," Daphne replied, dropping into the armchair.

Gabby raised her eyebrows. "What did he do?"

"He's treating me like a baby, just like you and everyone else. I told him I was going to prom with Luke after all and he told me I was stupid."

"You're . . . what?" Gabby's eyes grew wide. "You're going to prom with *Luke*? Since when?"

"Since this afternoon." Daphne grinned and bounced on the seat cushions. "Can you believe it? He said he was sorry and he wants to be with me!"

"Oh, my god."

"I know! I almost can't believe it myself. It's so . . . dreamlike."

"You are such a spoiled, stupid brat!"

Daphne gaped at her sister. "Screw you!" she yelled, jumping to her feet. "Screw Mule! Screw everybody!" She pivoted around in one last, hair-lifting twirl and ran to her room, slamming the door behind her.

What was going on? Why was everyone dumping on her good mood? It was as if it were against the law to be happy around here. As if an evil sorceress had cursed the entire Rivera household, dooming them to everlasting misery.

Well, not Daphne. She didn't care if the whole town, the whole world even, came and yelled at her. Her mom might have turned to stone and her dad might have been ensnared by a siren from San Antonio and her sister might be a wicked witch-in-training, but Daphne would escape. Somehow she would break the spell.

Gabby threw the Jetta into park and raced up the walkway to Mule's house. Crossing the porch, she could see him through the window sitting on the couch, bent over the guitar he'd scored off of Craigslist last summer.

She knocked three times and then let herself in—just as she usually did.

"I heard what Daphne did to you," she said.

Mule shrugged. "Yeah, well . . . whatcha gonna do?" he said in his lousy mobster voice. He looked down at his unplugged Stratocaster and plucked out a random series of notes.

Gabby stood in front of him, shaking her head. "I can't believe you even asked her in the first place. I knew it was a bad idea the minute I heard it."

"And why was it such a bad idea?"

"Aw, come on! It's Daffy. I would have thought you had

enough sense to see through her cutesy-poo charm. The girl is spoiled and selfish and stoned on her own daydreams."

Mule held up his hand. "You know . . . you can stop. That's enough from you."

"What?" Gabby's face felt hot and prickly. "Why are you talking to me like that? I'm on your side. I'm pissed off at her."

"So you're mad. Whatever. That's your reaction to everything."

"Of course I'm mad! She's always pulling stuff like this. Welcome to my life."

"Have you ever thought that maybe one of the reasons you get so angry with her is because she's willing to take risks that you aren't? She's not too scared to feel things—to feel for *people*, and even tell them about it."

"And I am?"

Mule's silence was answer enough.

"This is ridiculous! You're actually defending her, after what she did to you? The girl wouldn't even give you the time of day a few weeks ago. Do you know what she used to call you behind your back? Nerd King. Isn't that sweet?"

Mule reached over and slammed his fist down on the coffee table, causing papers and pencils and empty fountain-drink cups to jump. "Stop it!"

Gabby stared at him in mute disbelief. Over the years she'd seen a whole variety pack of expressions on Mule's face, but this was by far the worst. Rutted and streaked with red, his eyes like tiny coin slots. He looked so . . . non-Mule-like.

"What I need right now," he growled through his teeth, "is an understanding friend. And since you obviously don't know how to be one, I think you should just leave."

Gabby shook her head. "You don't mean that."

Tossing his guitar aside, Mule sprang up from the sofa and stalked to the door, opening it wide. "Awfully nice of you to come by and cheer me up, Gab," he said. "Time for you to move your ass on out of here."

She wavered in place for a second, blinking hard. "Fine!" she said, and marched past him into the annoyingly bright sunshine. The door shut with a loud *wham* behind her, like an exclamation point.

Gabby stood there on the creaky porch, replaying the previous two minutes in her head and trying to pinpoint the precise second it all went wrong. But she couldn't figure it out. What had she done, exactly? Why was he so mad at her?

Maybe she shouldn't be so surprised. After all, her mom was happier without her. Her dad was happier without her. And now Mule had literally tossed her out of his house—and maybe his life.

Gabby often said she didn't need people, and she really hoped that was true. Because right now, she had no one.

CHAPTER TWENTY

Cathar(sis)

Daphne studied her right hand. Ten minutes into her prom date and she'd already messed up her manicure by repeatedly chomping down on her nails. But she couldn't help it. It was the most important night of her life—the night that would undo the worst night of her life—so she was understandably nervous.

As happy as she was with the dress, Daphne felt awkward sitting down in it. The skirt poufed up several inches from her lap and made rustling noises every time Luke drove over a bump. Meanwhile, her overuse of hair spray was filling the car's interior with fumes, and the safety belt threatened to crush her corsage. (Not that she minded too much, since it was made out of the same scary-looking flower she'd rejected for the boutonniere—the tropical monster with the little spiky things sticking out from the center.)

Neither of them talked. Over the past couple of days they'd spoken on the phone a lot, mainly discussing all the last-minute prom preparations. But now there didn't seem to be much to say, and the topics Daphne came up with were too tied to excruciating past events.

Meanwhile, Luke seemed to be concentrating on driving. He was ultracareful with stops and checked the mirrors every few seconds, and he never got his parents' green SUV up past thirty miles an hour. Daphne felt as if some dotty fairy godmother had converted their coach out of a turtle instead of a pumpkin.

She wondered where Luke could be taking her for dinner. The whole time he'd been very secretive about it, saying it was a surprise. Maybe the Rushing Water Inn? Of course. That was probably it. And he'd remember to order two chicken cordon bleus. She couldn't wait to see him in the candlelight.

Just then, Luke pulled off the road into an empty gravel lot.

"What's wrong? Car trouble?" she asked.

"Nope. We're here," he said, smiling sneakily as he cut the engine.

"But . . . where are we?"

"It's time for dinner." He reached into the backseat and lifted up a cooler. "I thought we would have a picnic."

Daphne looked out the window. Sure enough, they were across the street from Monroe Park. There was hardly anyone there. Just a couple of middle schoolers in the far corner kicking around a soccer ball. "Oh," she said, trying to sound pleased. "Great."

She probably shouldn't feel so let down. After all, she'd daydreamed about their having romantic picnics in the park.

But it was prom; it was the night they would face up to all the teasing and show everyone they were together. For something this big she wanted to feel more like Cinderella the princess instead of Cinderella the scullery maid.

She followed him to the park and across the grounds to one of the picnic tables. Her heels sank into the dirt, and gusts of wind kept lifting the back of her dress, revealing the netted slip underneath. But Daphne stuffed down her disappointment. Instead, she focused on how beautiful the evening was. The sun was low on the horizon, streaming through the nearby trees and throwing streaks of orange and pink across a deep turquoise sky. Except for the clouds of mosquitoes newly hatched from the nearby creek, it really was a dreamy setting.

They sat down at the table and Luke immediately began pulling wrapped sandwiches and sodas out of the cooler.

"We have tuna, turkey and Swiss, and PB and J. Whatever you like." He grinned awkwardly as he lined them up on the tabletop. "Pick your poison."

Daphne selected what appeared to be a turkey sandwich, figuring it was the least messy option, and a can of Sprite. She smiled back at him and took a bite.

Luke looked so handsome in his tux. He hadn't bothered to match the cummerbund and tie to her dress, explaining that he'd borrowed the suit from his dad. But at least the silvery gray color was nice and sleek and didn't clash with the boutonniere she'd pinned on him. She really loved how the flower brought out the rosy tint in his soft curvy mouth, and the way his eyes stood out even more on his face since he'd combed back his wavy hair with a bit of gel.

"This is nice, isn't it?" Luke gestured about the park. "No crowds. No waiting. Lots of fresh air."

"Yeah," Daphne said, waving a bug out of her face.

By now the middle schoolers had stopped their game and were pointing at them and snickering. It reminded Daphne too much of Tracy's party, so she leaned sideways, letting Luke's neatly coiffed head block her view of them.

Everything was quiet, except for the sounds of their chewing and the drone of the cicadas in the trees above. She searched her mind for something to say before the silence felt too long or squirmy. But once again, she couldn't think of a good subject.

Just then, a rustling came from the nearby weeds and a duck waddled out, appraising them with a tilt of its head.

"Well, hello," Daphne said to the duck. That gave her an idea—a great way to break the tension. "You know, I do an awesome duck," she said to Luke. "Want to hear?"

"Um . . . sure."

Daphne slouched down, folded her arms into wings, and retracted her head slightly. Then she let loose with a whole series of nasal-sounding quacks, ending with her bursting out laughing.

She couldn't tell who looked more startled, Luke or the duck.

"That's funny," Luke said, even though it was clear he thought the opposite.

Daphne felt foolish. "It's just something I do," she said with a shrug. "Not all the time or anything, just . . . for fun."

Luke nodded and gazed off toward the sunset. He swallowed hard, making his neck bulge out like a bullfrog. Daphne had a fleeting urge to do her best frog noises but decided not to. Luke just wasn't loosened up enough for joking around like that.

She chomped on her left thumbnail and again tried to come up with a nonstressful conversation starter, something besides school or parties or his move. Or anything animal-related.

"So . . . where do you think you'll go to college?" she asked.

"I don't know," Luke said, lifting his shoulders. "There's still time for me to figure that out."

"You'll probably want to go to a small college, right? I mean, you like small towns and all, so I'm guessing you won't want one of those superhuge universities, huh?"

"I guess."

They lapsed into another silence. This time even the cicadas went quiet.

"So what do you think you'll study?"

He shook his head. "Beats me. What about you?"

"I don't know, either." She thought about what Mule said. "But it will probably have something to do with people. I think . . . I think maybe I'm good with people. Do you?"

Luke looked right at her, and his lips slowly curved into a smile. "Yeah," he said. "I mean, you sure made me feel welcome."

Daphne grinned. Finally, she was making progress.

"You know, I was thinking . . ." Luke leaned across the table and lowered his voice. "What if we just blew off prom? We could do something else—just the two of us. Without all those other jerks."

"But . . . didn't you already buy the tickets?"

"Nah. I was going to get them at the door."

A sudden realization swept through her, tightening her gut. "You can't go through with it, can you?" she said. "That's why we're here. You don't want to risk being seen with me."

Luke opened his mouth as if he was going to protest, then quickly closed it. Guilt weighed down his features.

"It was your idea for us to go together. Remember?" Daphne said, her voice rising. "You wanted to show them all."

"I know. I thought I could do it, but . . . Look, the guys really teased me about your little speech at the party. If they see us together, they'll probably start up all over again. You have no idea what it's like." He stopped, noticing the glare on Daphne's face. "Okay. I guess you do know. But it's not the same. I'm new. Everything I do counts big-time. If I'm going to spend another year here, I need friends. Right?"

"I thought you said you didn't really think they were your friends. That you didn't feel like one of them."

He shrugged. "Sometimes I don't like them all that much. But it beats not having anyone. And it's not like there's a lot of people in this town. I don't have a lot of friend options."

"But you have me, right?" she asked, her voice shaky. "What about me?"

"Um . . . sure," he said, seeming confused. "I like you. Really. I just can't risk everything for you. If you're my friend, you'll understand."

Daphne glanced around. Everything felt suddenly unreal, as if she'd fallen down a rabbit hole into a bizarre, parallel world. The sky seemed full of cartoon colors. Even the duck looked as if it were shaking its head in pity.

"Can't we just be a secret for a while?" he said, placing his hand on hers. "At least until things get better? Until everyone has totally forgotten the whole thing? We could still hang out, you know, away from everyone."

So he did want to be with her. But only if no one saw.

She stared hard at him, studying his face in the psychedelic sunset. She'd thought he was a gentleman. She'd thought he was sweet and loyal and old-fashioned. But he wasn't. He was just lonely and whiny—and kind of boring. He wasn't even Luke. Sure, he looked the same, but he wasn't the ultrasensitive, superromantic guy she'd been daydreaming about. In fact, he didn't even seem all that cute anymore. He wasn't ugly, just . . . okay. Although his eyes were too wide and scared-looking. And he had that annoying silent laugh, a mere smile and shoulder jiggle.

Mule was right. She didn't love him. She just wanted love. She wanted to be adored by the Luke of her dreams.

Luke let out a groan and pressed his fingers to his temples, the same way Daphne's mom did whenever one of her migraines started. "You know, you're right. I'm being dumb," he said. "Let's just go. I asked you, so I should take you."

"Oh, well . . . how can I refuse?" Daphne said, placing a fluttering hand over her heart.

"Look, I'm sorry. I'm just mixed up."

"Forget it. You already chickened out. It's obvious you don't want to go with me."

"But I do like you. I do want to be with you—just not there."

Daphne shook her head. "Not good enough. Besides, I

don't want to be with you. Not anymore." As she heard the sentences come out of her mouth, Daphne realized she meant every word. She wasn't just saying them to hurt Luke. She was really, truly over him.

She got to her feet, packed up her sandwich wrappings, and tossed them into a nearby trash can.

"What are you doing?" he asked.

"We're done here," she said. "I'm leaving."

"Wait. I'm sorry. We could still—"

"Don't be sorry. I made a mistake. I thought going out with you tonight would totally erase what happened at the party. That things could go back to the way they were before. But that won't happen. Things *are* different. *I'm* different." She picked up her purse and tucked it under her arm. "So you're off the hook. No more me. No more teasing. You don't even have to drive me home."

Daphne headed across the park, wobbling a bit in her heels. As she reached the road she glanced back, wondering whether Luke might come after her. But he was still sitting there, gazing down at his half-eaten tuna melt, looking kind of forlorn. The soccer kids had already gone home. Even the duck had wandered off.

She supposed she should feel sad or angry, only she didn't. It was like . . . finishing a story. There'd been thrills and surprises and some not-so-great turns of events, but now it was over. If anything, she felt sorry for the guy. She really hoped he would find his place here. Just like she had.

∘ ∘ ∘

"Stupid!" Gabby yelled. "Stupid! Stupid! Stupid!"

She was so stupid.

She gazed through the window of the Jetta yet again, hoping she wouldn't see what she'd seen earlier, hoping it had all been a bad hallucination brought on by her rushed dinner of Dr Pepper and movie theater hot dogs. But no such luck. There they were: her keys, hanging from the car ignition. And every single door was locked tight.

Why, Universe? Why? She'd already worked a double shift at the cinema since so many of the usual Saturday staffers had taken the day off for prom. She'd even stayed late to help with the broken popcorn machine, making certain she'd avoid seeing Daphne get dolled up for her date with that twit. Now all she wanted was to change into her pajamas and watch some mindless crap on TV, preferably some reality show featuring dim-witted egomaniacs whose lives were even more screwed up than hers.

Only she was the dimwit. She hadn't even realized what she'd done until she'd tried to unlock the front door with her cell phone.

Now what?

She wandered around the house, trying every window, including the one above the dryer, Daphne's favorite escape hatch. But they were all locked tight, thanks to her own recent safety check. Yay, Gabby! Such a responsible girl!

She tried the front door one last time, jiggling the handle every which way and trying to pick the lock with a spring she'd pulled out of one of her pens. But all she managed to do was spill the contents of her purse all over the porch and get splotches of blue ink on her hands.

"Damn it!" Gabby threw down her makeshift pick and plunked down on the front step.

There was no one she could call. Not her parents. Not Daphne. Not Mule—definitely not Mule. She'd rather sleep on the porch than call him up. It wasn't that she was mad at him so much as . . . guarded. Too scared of doing even more damage to the friendship or relationship or whatever-ship she had with him.

Why did she even bother having a cell phone if there was no one she could call? It was kind of pathetic.

Lately Gabby had felt haunted by her aloneness, as if it were a shadowy entity. She had Nobody. Nobody was part of her life, stalking her from place to place, peering over her shoulder, sitting with her during meals, and—quite possibly—making her lock her stupid keys in her stupid car.

"Now what?" she asked Nobody.

As if guided by an unseen force, her gaze wandered across the grounds toward Applewhite Manor.

"Right. Okay," she said.

She pulled herself to her feet and lumbered across the lawn.

"This could be a bad idea," she said to Nobody. Raising her fist, she gave a tentative knock.

A vague sense of déjà vu came over her as she stood there in the hazy evening light. Glancing around the porch, she found herself reliving Prentiss's kiss and wishing there were some photos or footage of the incident, something she could study so she could more accurately view those moments and figure out what they meant.

The door opened and Prentiss appeared on the threshold, silhouetted by the soft peachy light of the foyer.

For some reason, Gabby smiled. "Hi," she said. "I did something stupid, and . . . I need help."

"I was stupid," Daphne said. "I'm sorry."

Mule stood in the doorway to his house, frowning and scratching his messy curls. "What the heck . . . ?" He stepped out onto the porch, pulling the door closed behind him. "What are you doing here? What happened to you?"

Daphne teetered on the porch planks. One of her heels had come off on the walk over, and her perfectly upswept hairdo had come undone yet still defied gravity due to the sheer power of hair spray. Making things worse, she'd also tripped and fallen—probably because of her differing shoe elevations—and ended up muddying the bottom of her dress. She must look like a zombie homecoming queen.

"I'm fine," she said, scratching a mosquito bite on her arm.

"What do you mean you're fine? You look awful." Mule's face was all crimped with concern. It was nice to see. "Did that guy . . . Did he . . . ?" His hands balled into fists.

"No! Luke didn't do anything," Daphne said. "I just . . . called off our date and walked over here. It was farther than I thought."

"Samuel? Who is that?" came a man's voice from inside the house.

"It's okay, Dad!" Mule shouted back. "It's . . . a friend of mine! Go back to sleep." He waited a few beats and then turned back toward Daphne. "Come here," he said, grasping her hands and pulling her toward the porch swing. "You should get off your feet."

They sat down, side by side. Daphne kicked off her shoes—or what was left of them—and tucked her legs beneath the many layers of skirt.

"So what happened?" Mule asked. "Why'd you call off your date?"

"Because it was a big mistake." She looked over at him. "You were right."

"Right about what?"

"I don't love him," she said, smoothing the wrinkles out of her skirt. "It was just me. Like . . . I have all this love inside me, and I can't wait to give it to someone. So I made up someone perfect and pretended Luke was him. I went out with him for all the wrong reasons."

Mule stared out at the darkening sky. His big Converse sneakers pointed and flexed against the wooden planks, rocking the swing back and forth . . . back and forth. . . . Daphne was struck by how easy it was to just sit with Mule and say nothing. She felt comfy and protected, free of all worries.

Except one.

"Mule?"

"Yeah?"

"Did you ask me to prom because you felt sorry for me?"

He looked at her, one side of his face in shadow, the other lit up by the glow from the nearby window. "No," he said.

"Was it because I'm Gabby's sister?"

He shook his head, and the soft light danced across his features. "It was because you're you, and because I like being with you."

She smiled. Gradually, Mule's mouth stretched and curved until he was grinning back at her.

He reached over and gently pushed a wing-shaped clump of hair away from her face. "You know, we could still go to prom," he said. "I still have a suit."

Daphne laughed. "I'm a mess!"

"You look great," he said, sliding his finger down her cheek. "Nothing a box of wet wipes won't fix."

"No," she said, still chuckling. "I think I'd rather just . . . stay here. If you don't mind." She leaned sideways and rested her head on his shoulder.

"That's fine, too," he said, circling his arm around her.

Once again his shoes moved them back and forth . . . back and forth. . . . And once again a snug sense of belonging settled over Daphne.

"Mule?" she murmured.

"Hmm?"

"Have I ever shown you my duck impression?"

"There you go," Prentiss said, opening the door wide. "You got a spare car key somewhere so you can get back in there?"

Gabby nodded. "Yeah. Thanks."

"No biggie," he said to the door, instead of her. He examined the jamb. "You know, y'all really should have a kick plate on here. I'll talk to my parents about it."

"Okay."

"All right then," he said with a nod. "I'll be on my way."

"Prentiss?"

He spun back around, looking wary.

Gabby stood there, not knowing what to say. She'd just felt as if she needed to stop him. He'd done her a favor—yet again. But the whole time he was stooped and mumbling and averting his eyes. It made her feel radioactive, and she wanted to make things okay between them. Somehow.

"Hey, look," he said, before she could come up with any words herself. "I'm sorry about the other night on my porch. I was out of line."

Again he was talking to the doormat instead of to her. His jaw muscles flexed as if he were gritting his teeth, and a neat little groove divided the space between his brows.

"I just thought . . . I thought there was something between us," he went on. "It won't happen again." He turned to go.

"Wait," Gabby said. Again she had the unsettling feeling that the entire world had been reinvented without her knowledge. Nothing made sense, and she needed to get some answers. "I don't get it. What made you think there was something between us? Especially after the way I treated you."

"It was just . . ." His mouth curved into a small smile. "It was something in your eyes. You frown an awful lot, but your eyes don't. They're all big and round and shy, like you're always asking a question. And that night, when you looked at me, they'd gone all soft. It was like they were asking me to kiss you. Like you needed it. Know what I mean?"

"No."

Prentiss's face fell. "My mistake." For a third time, he turned to leave.

"Tell me about Sonny," she cried out. The words seemed to burst from her mouth of their own accord, surprising even herself.

Prentiss stopped in midstride. His back bowed slightly, and then . . . nothing. He simply remained rooted there, slightly hunched, as if the wind had been knocked out of him.

"Why do you want to know?" he asked. His tone was low and scratchy. And because he remained motionless with his back to her, it didn't even seem to emanate from him. A dismal, disembodied voice.

"I just . . . do," she said.

He slowly pivoted to face her. "You knew him, didn't you?"

"No. Yes. What does it matter?" For some reason, tears were running down her cheeks. She hadn't planned that, either. Now even her own body wasn't acting the way it was supposed to.

"You think I'm the one at fault." Prentiss took a step toward her. His face was twisted in a look of utter despair. "Go ahead and say it."

"No, I don't. Not anymore. You weren't driving."

"That doesn't mean it wasn't my fault!" he shouted, his words echoing throughout the house. A deep cranberry-colored flush spread over his neck and cheeks.

All of a sudden, his eyes switched from angry to startled, and his hands balled into fists. One he raised to his mouth, his thumb knuckle pressed hard against his lips; the other he banged repeatedly against his left thigh. Each time he shuddered, she could hear a tiny sound, like a moan trapped inside his throat.

Seeing him like that, seeing someone in more distress than she was in, somehow made Gabby feel strong again.

She grabbed hold of his clenched left hand and pulled him over to the couch. "Sit down," she said. He dropped onto the end cushion—the same one he'd sat on when he'd visited them at their old place—and bent forward, rocking slightly as he battled to control his emotions.

Gabby sat down on the middle cushion and laid a hand on his shoulder. It pained her to see him so agitated. "It's okay," she whispered. "Let it out." At the same time, she realized how strange it was to hear herself say this. She, who pretended most of her emotions had been surgically removed. She, who only days before had screamed at Prentiss for having seen her in a similar vulnerable state.

Eventually, he quieted down but remained slumped over, head in hands. She couldn't tell if he was embarrassed or just spent.

"It really was my fault," he said into his lap. "The accident."

"So . . . you *were* driving?" she asked, feeling a slight wrenching sensation, as if she were preparing herself for imminent fury.

He shook his head and sat up. His face was streaked with tears, and his inflamed eyes focused on a spot of nothingness in front of him. "I was drunk," he said. "I'm talking real drunk. And I talked Sonny into driving. He was only fifteen and hadn't ever driven at night before, but I talked him into it. I said it would be okay." Prentiss's voice quavered and he swallowed hard. "So stupid. I could have just called home, but I didn't want to get in trouble."

Gabby sat perfectly still, afraid that any movement on her part might break the spell he seemed to be under and send him scurrying from the house. She needed to hear this, even though it hurt. It was like getting stitches, only this was mending an old wound hidden deep inside her.

"He was scared, but he didn't want to let me down. He always looked up to me, and I guess I took advantage of that." Prentiss shut his eyes and cursed under his breath. When he opened them back up, he looked right at Gabby. "Did you know he saved my life?"

She shook her head.

"I wanted to stretch out in the backseat, but he made me sit up and put on my seat belt. Wouldn't start the car until I did." He smiled weakly, his bottom lip quivering. Gabby smiled, too. It seemed like the kind of thing Sonny would do—at least, the person she assumed he was. "Anyway," he continued, taking a long, shaky breath, "I guess I sort of passed out a bit. I don't know what happened. I heard screeching sounds and a big bump and then . . . then . . . the whole world exploded."

Prentiss once again focused hard on that invisible point in front of him. His chest heaved and his hands gripped his knees tightly. Gabby wanted to reach over and rescue him, to pull him out of the intangible wreckage and guide him back to the present. But she stayed put, waiting and watching.